To Denys (with a
                Welcome.
and thank you for your company

THE BREAKING STORM

over the years.

Derek H. Skinner

(Author)

THE NETHERGATE TRILOGY
BOOK ONE – GATHERING CLOUDS
BOOK TWO – THE BREAKING STORM

THE BREAKING STORM is the second book in the Nethergate Trilogy. Each book stands on its own, but it will add to your enjoyment if you have read the previous book(s) in the Trilogy. You will thus have a deeper understanding of the characters, the nuances of their motivation, the setting and the plot.

THE BREAKING STORM

BOOK TWO OF THE NETHERGATE TRILOGY

A SAGA OF THE AMERICAN CIVIL WAR

DEREK H SKINNER

The Book Guild Ltd

First published in Great Britain in 2020 by
The Book Guild Ltd
9 Priory Business Park
Wistow Road, Kibworth
Leicestershire, LE8 0RX
Freephone: 0800 999 2982
www.bookguild.co.uk
Email: info@bookguild.co.uk
Twitter: @bookguild

This work is entirely fictitious and bears no resemblance to any persons living or dead.

Typeset in Aldine401 BT

Printed and bound in Great Britain by CPI Group (UK) Ltd, Croydon, CR0 4YY

ISBN 978 1913208 097

British Library Cataloguing in Publication Data.
A catalogue record for this book is available from the British Library.

With true gratitude to
the late
JOHN RICHARD TANNER
for friendship forged
in spartan schooldays at Christ's Hospital
and enjoyed for a lifetime.

NETHERGATE FAMILY TREE

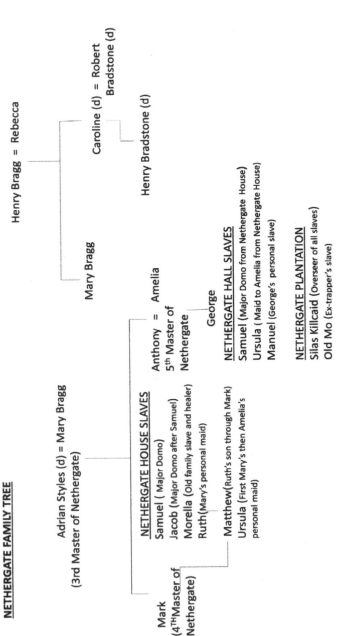

Henry Bragg = Rebecca

Adrian Styles (d) = Mary Bragg
(3rd Master of Nethergate)

Mary Bragg

Caroline (d) = Robert Bradstone (d)

Henry Bradstone (d)

Mark
(4TH Master of
Nethergate)

Anthony = Amelia
5th Master of
Nethergate

George

NETHERGATE HOUSE SLAVES
Samuel (Major Domo)
Jacob (Major Domo after Samuel)
Morella (Old family slave and healer)
Ruth (Mary's personal maid)
Matthew (Ruth's son through Mark)
Ursula (First Mary's then Amelia's personal maid)

NETHERGATE HALL SLAVES
Samuel (Major Domo from Nethergate House)
Ursula (Maid to Amelia from Nethergate House)
Manuel (George's personal slave)

NETHERGATE PLANTATION
Silas Killcaid (Overseer of all slaves)
Old Mo (Ex-trapper's slave)

See page 331 for the list of characters thus far.

1

Amelia Lays a Trap

Ursula was now no stranger to George's room or to his bed. She frequently crept up the silent corridors of Nethergate Hall in the still, early hours, to seek the comfort of his arms and the warmth of his embraces. Though she knew it to be an illusion it was the only place where she felt truly secure and safe, for she placed herself utterly under his care and protection. There had been no further talk from her mistress of the public whipping with which she had been threatened. The moratorium on all further floggings issued by George's father, the Master of the Nethergate Tobacco Plantation, had come into effect. Ursula knew that this was as a direct result of George's new influence with his father. Whenever she thought of George, which was a great deal, she felt that her heart must surely burst with the strength of her feelings. As personal maid to the Mistress, it sustained her during the endless working hours when she endured the spite and bile of George's mother, Amelia, the waspish Mistress of Nethergate. It allowed her to smile and be civil to the woman who so cruelly mistreated her. It brought back the sunshine into her life and a return of her happy disposition so that all the world smiled with her. And all the world wondered how she could be so happy with such a tyrant for a Mistress who had tried to take from her even her own name, given to her by her long-lost mammy, before the Lord Himself. Her name had been perhaps the only thing that was truly her own.

George too was lost in the blissful world of his love for Ursula but eating at his heart now was the thought of his commitment to the Confederate cause and the summons he must soon receive to serve the flag. It had been a rash act to declare to his parents his intention to join the armed struggle. He heartily regretted that moment whereby he had sought to bring his parents to heel with such a dramatic pronouncement. But it was done now and there could be no going back. What would happen to Ursula then, he dared not think. So far, he had only shared his fears with Samuel, the head slave. He had not yet told Ursula of his volunteering for fear of the anxiety it would cause. That at least was what he told himself.

They were lying together in each other's arms after their lovemaking. George was half asleep. Ursula was listening to the pattern of his breathing as his passion subsided, savouring the peace of the moment; secure now from the fear of further beatings, for some few weeks had now passed since George's father's declaration. Suddenly she went rigid. She was sure she had heard the floorboards creak outside the room. She listened, hardly daring to breathe. Unmistakeably, the sound came again. George was immediately alert to the change in her. She placed a finger over his lips in case he should speak out loud.

"There's someone outside," she whispered into his ear. Her immediate thought was that it was his mother, such was the fear that that lady generated within her. Both lay still listening. The sounds of the night crept into the room; a distant owl's forlorn call, and the old oak scratching at the window pane in the gentle night breeze. The house itself seemed to settle into the stillness. Then it came again; someone shifting their weight outside the door to George's room.

George eased himself out of his bed frantically seeking for his night shirt. He crept on bare feet to the door. There was a soft knocking, repeated twice more after a pause. Then the door handle began to turn. The door opened, and a dark shape entered the room. George was about to launch himself on the intruder when he recognised the outline of Samuel.

"Samuel!" he hissed. "What on earth are you doing here?"

Samuel, the urbane major domo of Nethergate Hall, whose effortless efficiency was rewarded only by the smouldering resentment of his Mistress because she could never fault him, was clearly agitated. "Thank the Lord you is awake Massa George," replied Samuel. "It's Ursula. I cannot find her."

George for a moment debated whether to try and deceive Samuel but decided against it. "She is here," he said.

"That's good," said Samuel, not seeming in the least bit surprised. "We must get her away, soon as possible."

"What on earth are you talking about?"

"It's the Mistress. I've had word that she has ordered the whippin' cart to call here this very mornin' to take Ursula for a public whippin' in New Haven. I knew nothing about it. She must have done it all through Mister Killcaid."

George's heart sank at Samuel's news. He looked to his bed where Ursula sat up with the sheets pulled up about her neck. The thought of the coffee-cream smoothness of her back and the gentle curve of her shoulders being scarred and torn by the lash made him feel physically sick. How could his mother be this cruel? She had recently been surprisingly considerate, so much so that Ursula had thought that things might be getting better between them. But all the time she had been biding her time like a cat with a mouse, waiting to defy her husband and to vent her spleen on Ursula. Anthony, the Master, was absent in Louisville arranging for the tobacco crop to be re-routed down the Mississippi. With him away, she had struck. She would simply present her husband with a fait accompli, knowing he

3

could do nothing after the event. A feeling of burning hatred and resentment swept over him. He felt nothing but loathing for the bitter, vengeful woman that his own mother had now become.

"We must get her away from here straight 'way," announced Samuel. "Since we spoke, I has tried to find a safe place for her to go, but dese tings takes time and we can't afford no risks. This has come 'bout afore I was ready." Samuel and George's previous conversation had concerned possible plans that would allow Ursula to flee by the Underground Railroad, to the Canadian border and freedom, should his mother's treatment become unbearable. It was this conspiracy which formed the basis of the mutual trust and friendship between them. But George was always aware that the consequences of discovery would be infinitely worse for Samuel than they would be for him. Samuel had already endured a public flogging at the hand of the Mistress for giving a fugitive shelter. It was a measure of the upright nature of the man that he had not tried to hide from George the connections he now had with such a clandestine movement since his own ordeal. He could have pressed George to secrecy, but he had simply assumed that the trust was there. George felt humbled before this simple man of such natural nobility of spirit.

"What can we do?" he asked turning to look at Ursula, who had not moved. She could not hear their whispered conversation and was still looking apprehensive at the obvious discovery of their secret.

"The first thing we must do is to get her away from this house and out of reach of any search for her that will surely follow the discovery of her absence."

George thought frantically, but there was nowhere on the estate that would be safe, but Samuel was ahead of him. "The only safe place is to hide down in the bayou, but someone would have to go with her so that we can find her again when we have secured somewhere else."

Then a thought occurred to George. He knew he could trust Samuel with his own special secret. "Listen Samuel," he said, "Matthew from Nethergate House, is down in the bayou now. He is lying up there until the hue and cry from his escape dies down. There is a safe place there, a cabin known to no-one. It was built in secret by Old Mo, before he was so unexpectedly sold. She could stay secure there, at least until you could arrange for her to move on. I can take her there."

"If you say so, Massa George," but he sounded doubtful, then he paused. "But I don't think you personally should take her there. If you are not in the house as usual, it will link you with her when she does not wake your mother and her disappearance is discovered. Is there anyone else who could meet up with Matthew?"

Manuel, his personal slave, was the only choice left, but Manuel had already betrayed him twice and George doubted that he could be trusted again. "Manuel," he said slowly, "But he is weak, and I am not sure he can be relied upon not to talk, particularly if Killcaid gets hold of him."

Silas Killcaid was the chief overseer of slaves. Now in his early fifties he had served Nethergate's Masters for some thirty years. His black beard was now flecked with grey, but he had lost none of the venom and cruelty that marked his rule over all who lived at Nethergate. His sharp, weasel eyes missed nothing, his network of black overseers and informers, ever anxious for his favour, ensured that nothing escaped his notice. He and the Rattler, his beloved whip, whose bite was as sharp and vicious as the hand that wielded it, were feared by all at Nethergate. Even Anthony Styles, the Master of Nethergate, secretly dreaded his disapproval.

Then yet another thought occurred to George. Manuel would never find the second dugout that lay concealed in the swamp. He would have to reveal to Manuel the signal to summon Matthew, with all the dangers that that might bring, particularly to Matthew whom Killcaid still believed to have perished in the bayou. It seemed he had no option. He would just have to trust Manuel a third time. He wondered whether Manuel's new determination would be proof against the withering interrogation of Killcaid. But Samuel was already turning to go, and the die was cast.

"If he is the only one, we must trust him Massa George. He is a good man at heart," he whispered as he moved away. "I'll wake him when I gets downstairs. In the meantime, we must ready Ursula to leave." With that he passed through the door and softly closed it behind him, never once glancing over to the bed where Ursula was still sitting up.

George returned to Ursula, now full of anxiety. At the news of her mistress's intensions she gave a low moan and began to shake uncontrollably.

"You said the Master was going to stop floggings after what happened with Matthew," she said accusingly.

"It's true," said George, "But you know my mother. She is a law unto herself. I'll bet she has done this just to spite my father. She will present him with the deed done on his return. After that there is little he can do. Sometimes I hate my mother. I'll wager Silas Killcaid has a hand in all this too. I cannot believe my own blood could do this."

George hastily got dressed and then cautiously escorted Ursula back through the sleeping house to the slave quarters where Samuel was waiting with Manuel who was shivering with more than just the early morning chill. Ursula soon joined them carrying the canvas bag Morella had given her with the brooch and rings from Mary Styles and her mother, the coloured stones that were so special to her and two Sunday dresses. There was little else for her to show for her seventeen years of servitude.

Ursula was trembling too. Her whole life was about to change. Everything she had known, good and bad, was being ripped from under her feet. She was about to become a fugitive, fleeing from slavery and the law. Everyone's hand would be turned against her. What little protection she had enjoyed from the flimsy arms of justice for the slave, would apply no longer. She was angry and full of resentment. No-one had asked her. The two men in her life who meant most to her, the one she loved, the other she trusted and respected had assumed that she would want to make this momentous choice. Strangely her bitterness was directed towards these two who were now risking everything to help her rather than to the woman whose spite was the cause of her misery. But what choice did she have? She knew she would die rather than endure the shame and humiliation of being flogged in public with her nakedness displayed to all.

George hastily scribbled a note for Manuel to give to Matthew explaining the situation and asking for his protection for Ursula saying that he would join them as soon as he could safely do so. Matthew and George were like brothers, for both shared the same grandmother in Mary Styles. George was the legitimate son of Anthony, Mary's youngest child and Matthew the illegitimate progeny as a result of the brutal rape of Ruth, Mary's personal maid when she was barely a teenager, by Mark her now-deceased elder son. Matthew was now a fugitive from justice having been unjustly accused of the murder of a black preacher, killed by Killcaid in a fit of temper. The two young men, with no-one else their age on the estate, had formed a very close bond of friendship and trust. George now was Matthew's only link with life outside the bayou.

But it was time to go. Ursula cast one last look about all the old familiar sights that had become so much a part of her life. Suddenly they seemed the most precious things in all the world, the very walls seemed to cry out for her not to leave.

"Oh George! I don't want to go. Isn't there some other way?" she cried in sudden desolation.

George realised for the first time how desperate a decision this was for Ursula. He had been so preoccupied with the ways and means that he had neglected to consider how she must be feeling. His heart went out to her in a sudden surge of emotion and he drew her to him, not caring in the intensity of the moment who might witness this declaration of his love for his beautiful mulatto slave girl.

George and Ursula embraced once again with a feverish desperation, made the more intense by the uncertainty of what lay ahead.

2

Into the Bayou

It was only on their final embrace that George realised the enormity of the step that he was taking and the abyss into which he was asking his beloved Ursula to plunge. She was leaving all that was familiar to her. The Hall was her home, her life, everything. No longer would she be able to steal along the corridor to his room. No longer would he lie awake, wondering if she would come to him. She would now be a fugitive, an escaped slave with every hand turned against her and no-one to protect her. For a moment he hesitated, but then he thought of the alternative that awaited her when day dawned, and the whipping cart came trundling into the courtyard of Nethergate Hall, bearing its tremulous and fearful cargo.

George turned to Manuel and gave him his revolver. Manuel took it as if it were red hot, for it was against the law for a slave to carry weapons. The gesture told Manuel that his master was once again placing his trust in him. This time he told himself, he would not fail, he would be worthy of this trust. But then he thought of Killcaid and felt his bowels tighten.

George told him to fire it three times when they reached the spot where they had last met up with Matthew. That would bring Matthew to them. After that his job was done.

"Don't let me down this time, Manuel," he counselled, staring hard into Manuel's eyes. "Your charge is worth more to me than life itself."

"Not this time, Master George, nor never agin'." In his simple way, Manuel really meant it. He even believed that because of the trust his young master had once more placed in him he could withstand the fear of the Devil himself as well as that of Killcaid. Truly he did not know which of the two was worse.

With that they were both gone. As the sky began to lighten in the east, two lonely fearful figures wended their way down the path that led to the bayou and the swamplands. Furtively they kept to the shadows as they went. Only after they had gone a good mile did they dare to relax and walk more in the open. They made good time after that.

At last Manuel called a halt when he reckoned that they were far enough into the heart of the bayou and near enough to the place he remembered. He took George's pistol and fired three times. Each time Ursula winced, fearful that the noise would reveal their presence, but they were deep enough into the canopy of the bayou to drown the report of the pistol from any at Nethergate. After that they moved on at a slower pace until Manuel was certain they were at the right spot. Then they waited.

"Who are we waiting for?" asked Ursula. In the gathering light, he caught the glisten of tears in her eyes and his heart went out to her. He could understand how his young master must feel for her and how lonely and uncertain she must be at this sudden turn of events. Only then did Manuel feel it safe to tell her who would soon be emerging from the undergrowth. George, for her own protection, had not told Ursula how he was sheltering Matthew in the bayou. Ursula felt a little reassured, for she knew Matthew briefly from when she had been lady's maid to the old Mrs Styles. She remembered her sadness when Ruth had returned with her son to take over her old position as maid to Mary Styles, the old Mistress, leaving her without a job. She had been so grateful when Mrs Styles had got her the new job as maid to Amelia at Nethergate Hall. Neither though were to know what an ordeal that would turn out to be. Now she was intrigued to meet up with him again, particularly after all she had heard about his mystical escape from the clutches of Killcaid and the feared Nethergate coonhounds. She knew too that he was no killer. All the same it added a certain lustre to his name.

After what seemed like an age, Matthew appeared as if by magic. He had been closely observing them both to ensure that they were not being followed. Curiously, he approached the unlikely pair. Manuel explained the situation and gave Matthew George's letter which it was still too dark fully to read, but he understood enough to know what was being asked of him. He remembered Ursula from when he had first arrived at Nethergate House. She looked a lot different now from the young girl he had met then.

Turning to Manuel he said, "Tell Massa George that I will look after her well till next I see him and you… You take good care you don' get take by dat Killcaid. He'll winkle your secrets from you faster'n quicksilver."

Manuel wasn't sure what quicksilver was, but it sounded mighty quick and he nodded his head vigorously. "Not anymore I won't. Not anymore." In his fervour, he even believed himself. As he set off back to Nethergate Hall he racked his brains for some likely tale he might spin if he were to be questioned.

Matthew was acutely conscious of how dishevelled he must look beside this scrubbed and clean-looking maid from Nethergate Hall still dressed in her smart Nethergate maid's attire. It was the first time he had ever thought about his appearance. He didn't stop to wonder why.

"Here, let me take that," he said, taking the meagre bundle of her possessions. "Best lift your skirts. The way to the boat's a mite muddy." She obediently did as she was told and together they made their way to where Matthew had left the dugout, each acutely aware of the other's presence and the change that this would mean for them both. She stopped when she saw the dugout, clearly apprehensive at travelling in such a precarious-looking craft, but after a moment gamely gathered up her skirts and gingerly settled down. Large patches of damp were already spreading over her clothes where they had met the swampy waters.

Matthew paddled in silence along the bayou to the hut. He watched his passenger. She had long delicate hands, fingers that would be strangers to the rough life she must now endure until George could arrange for her departure. He could understand how she must be feeling, but all the same he felt a growing resentment at how he must now adjust his own life to having a companion whom he suspected would be nothing but a burden. Living and surviving in the bayou was a far cry from laying out the clothes and jewellery and arranging the coiffure of a pampered white lady. He had no intention of acting as nursemaid to this spoilt product of a system he detested. Hopefully, it would not be for too long.

George had told him about Ursula and of his feelings for her. He could understand how he must view the prospect of her being exposed bare-breasted to the coarse flotsam of New Haven whilst she endured a public flogging. He remembered only too vividly how he himself had felt at the prospect of all that pain and humiliation. All the same, he could not but be irritated at this intrusion into the even tenor of his life in Old Mo's cabin.

Manuel made good progress back to the big house. It was the first time he had ever been out alone at night, for slaves were all subject to curfew during the hours of darkness without a permit from their owners. He was too, acutely conscious of the illegal bulge of George's pistol in his pocket and the consequences of bearing arms.

The dawn was touching the eastern sky with fingers of red and gold and the birds were beginning to stir like an orchestra tuning up, with sudden bursts of completed melody erupting through. It was the first time he had ever been alone to experience the freshness of the birth of a new day. Manuel felt proud of what he had done for his young master. In his own mind too, he was preparing an account of his breaking bounds and venturing out at night which might just bear scrutiny. The ingenuity of their excuses was perhaps the only real creativity allowed to a slave.

As he neared Nethergate Hall he heard sounds of raised voices and the general hubbub of people moving about. There were yellowy lights showing in the courtyard, casting pale shadows against the gathering brightness of the day. It served his purpose well. He could slip into the scene without attracting attention and then go up to his master's room to resume his general duties as if nothing had happened.

He edged into the courtyard. The first thing that caught his eye was the whipping cart. Two terrified young girls, crestfallen and defeated were shackled to its sides, together with one white-eyed young lad, surely not yet in his teens. The yard was all commotion. Mrs Styles, with a coat thrown over her night clothes was in a high passion. She was berating both Samuel and Killcaid, in equal measure.

Killcaid's cruel eyes sparkled with anger and resentment at this public dressing down. He, who virtually ran Nethergate, was accustomed to the respect of those whom he served. Even the Master, particularly the Master, would never have dared to have spoken to him in this manner, but Amelia Styles was a law unto herself. He glared about him, challenging any to smirk at his discomfort. No-one did.

The slaves scurried about their duties trying to look busy, but covertly relishing Killcaid's discomfort. Killcaid's usual gang was ranged about him, but noticeably drew away as the mistress's fury fed upon itself. Even the horse between the shafts of the whipping cart grew restless at the riot of raised voices.

Ursula's absence had of course been the subject of the initial hiatus. Then Manuel's absence had been noted too and conjecture began. George had been sent for, but he had been deliberately slow in appearing. He hoped that by the time he did so, much of his mother's passion might be spent.

It was at this point that one of Killcaid's overseers spotted Manuel.

"There's one of them!" he shouted as Manuel tried to sink into the shadows. "Were she worth it?" A chorus of coarse guffaws greeted this remark.

Glad of the chance of breaking away from the strident voice of the Mistress and turning the attention elsewhere, Killcaid strode purposefully to where Manuel cowered. At last he had a target on which to vent his fury.

All eyes fell upon the unfortunate Manuel. All fell silent. There was pure venom in Killcaid's eye.

"Well now," he said in a voice heavy with menace, "here comes little old Manuel all muddied and dirty like. Now perhaps he will explain to us all how we find a lady's maid who should be here but ain't, and the only other one as has gone missing as well, is this here Manuel. Has yo' been misbehavin' yoself I wonder?"

A titter of nervous laughter rippled round the group at this second insinuation. Manuel felt the bottom drop from his world. His terror of this man crowded in upon him. Then he remembered his promise to his young master and the failures of the past. His hand stole into his pocket to hide the bulge of George's pistol. He was thankful for the shadows cast by the lights in the yard.

Killcaid was now standing over him hefting the new Rattler which had replaced his beloved old whip burnt in the cabin fire, which had near cost him his life when the son of the preacher Killcaid had murdered had sought his revenge. Killcaid's threat was unmistakeable; his menace boundless in Manuel's mind.

"Now boy, per'aps you'll be telling us where you bin. Eh! An' where Ursu... Angela's gone?" He corrected himself just in time to use the new name Amelia Styles had given to Ursula. No-one noticed the slip. Killcaid then pulled up Manuel's shirt as if looking to see whether Ursula lay hidden there. Again, the crowd laughed.

Manuel's thoughts now were only of the pistol. He kept his hand thrust firmly in his pocket. Killcaid smiled at this, thinking that the terrified slave was holding himself to stop his bladder revealing his fear. He had him just exactly where he wanted him.

Manuel's mouth was dry, and he tried to speak. All that came out was a hoarse croak. Out of the corner of his eye he saw George come down the steps into the courtyard. Manuel, his voice breaking with the fear that was so clearly mirrored in his face, mumbled, "Ah's bin wid dat Angela."

George shut his eyes and lent his face against the cool of the stonework. He knew all too well what would now come spilling out.

3

Mary in New York

In New York, Mary the dowager Mistress of Nethergate and
Ruth her personal slave, were settling down to their new life in
the city. It had been a long-delayed visit for Mary, made more
difficult because of the war. Rebecca, Mary's mother, was now
clearly suffering from dementia and Mary had wanted for a
long time to see how she truly was and also to visit her father,
whom she had not seen since her husband's death.

For Mary, the visit brought back tragic memories of the
last time she had stayed in her father's house when she had
rushed back to New York to be at her husband's bedside, to
be with her dear Adrian before he had died. There were too,
hosts of childhood memories over which her father had always
loomed like a colossus. As a child she had loved her father, but
she feared him too and for preference always sought the gentler
comfort of her mother. She had been a dutiful daughter, unlike
feisty Caroline, her younger sister who had openly defied her
father in a way she would never have dared. Caroline would
face up to Henry Bragg's roaring and rampaging and endure the
inevitable punishment with a carefree stoicism. But in the quiet
of the night she would creep into Mary's bed, her face damp

with tears and mourn the loss of her father's love. Mary could still feel her chill, bony frame and her icy feet.

"No Cari dear," she remembered once saying, "Papa loves you and I both. It's just that you make him so cross, but he doesn't love you any the less because of that. You still loved Candy even after she tore Lucy to shreds," she added, remembering how their new puppy had once destroyed her favourite doll. But she could tell by Caroline's silent shaking form that her words had failed to convince.

What a change to the confident young woman she last remembered who gave solace to her in her turn on the death of Adrian. Poor Caroline to have had such a sad end to her young life and still to be at loggerheads with her beloved father. For the father would never see his own nature that was mirrored in his child.

This visit was the first time she had had the opportunity to get to know her father as a person rather than a parent, since she had left home as the teenage bride of a great southern plantation owner. Her mother she knew was lost to her in some twilight world, but she loved her no less for that. Now at least she could repay her for her care in the past. She spent a lot of time with her father whenever he was home. Invariably one of the maids would come to find her and announce, "The Master will see you now Mrs Styles." She knew she was expected to stop whatever she was doing and come at once.

It made her laugh. It was as if her father imagined that her entire day was spent in waiting for a summons from him. But increasingly she looked forward to their private meetings. For them both it was a time of shared memories and family concerns and the forging of new bonds of understanding between them. Mary, in her talks with her father, had impressed him with just how sure a grasp she had of the precarious situation at Nethergate and how many of her thoughts resonated with his own. It had provided him with much food for thought. Against the wealth of his own prejudices about women and business he was beginning

17

to formulate fresh ideas for the future of Nethergate in which he saw Mary playing a pivotal role. But the main vehicle for his anxieties remained concentrated upon Rebecca.

"How do you find your mother?," he would often ask as if hoping that Mary might, with her new perspective, have detected some improvement that remained hidden to him.

"I think she knows who I am now," she would reply, "and she doesn't call me Caroline any more. But you know Father, inside she is still the dear, sweet Mama we always knew and loved."

"I know she is. Sometimes, you know, she comes back to me. It is as if the blinds are suddenly drawn and for a moment, she is suddenly there, smiling with me. Then she is gone again. I cannot tell you Mary how much I live for those few brief moments." The tears would spring to Mary's eyes at these confessions. And she wondered, wondered how a man who wielded such power and influence, who in his eighties was as thrusting and energetic as a man forty years younger, could at the same time show such compassion and devotion to one helpless now of returning it.

On one such occasion he turned to her and placed his hand with a gentle urgency upon her arm. "You know, my dear, you are the only person with whom I can share such thoughts… and I am grateful." It was the first time her father had ever reached out to touch her or shown any true affection and her heart warmed towards him at the tenderness of its cause. The daughter he had once disowned was now often in his thoughts. "Caroline…" he said, and it was as if he still found it difficult to actually say her name. "Caroline. I drove her away didn't I? She must have hated her father; not without good reason, I guess," and his eyes pleaded with her to deny it.

"No Papa. That's not true. Caroline was born a rebel. She was always going to go her own way. The young man you chose for her would doubtless have made her a perfect husband and she would have been very happy with him, but only if she had chosen him of her own free will. As it was, she made her choice and for the year and a bit that she had, she and Robert Bradstone were supremely happy. As to caring for you, Father, she named her child after you. She would not have done that if she did not love you still."

Both were silent for a moment, Mary reliving again her memories of Caroline's tragic death and that of the child she bore who had lived for barely a week. The loss was more than her young husband, a jobbing journalist, had been able to bear and he had taken his own life shortly afterwards.

Their life together had been beset by poverty. Caroline in her letters, confessed that her husband's career seemed to have faltered after their marriage. Robert had been so full of hopes and aspirations as to how things would be, but once they were married, he found it increasingly difficult to get his writing published. Perhaps he was trying too hard to produce the right sort of material. Yet to Caroline his work seemed just as inspired as ever it was. He began to suffer from lack of confidence in his abilities and Caroline was forever fighting hard to boost his failing spirits. For a time, they maintained their standard of living by selling off many of Caroline's items of jewellery, but then cruelly they were burgled, and all the rest of her valuables were taken.

They had to move to a tenement block in the Lower East Side in conditions of the utmost poverty and there were no private washing facilities or lavatories. Yet Caroline's letters were still full of the love that she and Robert shared and of the kindness and compassion of the mostly immigrant families who were her neighbours. Robert was now working as a kitchen hand, but at least he was able to bring home some left-over food. By this time Caroline was expecting their child. Far from destroying their relationship, their poverty and hardship seemed to have cemented their love for each other.

As Caroline's time drew near her letters became fewer. Mary had asked Adrian to send money to her sister and he assured her he had done so. Caroline though never mentioned it. Abruptly her letters ceased altogether. Eventually Mary wrote to her father, who after Caroline's elopement, had declared that he had only ever had one daughter. His reply saddened her, that he still could not find it in his heart to be reconciled with his rebellious daughter. He said he had no idea where Caroline might be: "Caroline had chosen to go her own way. She had made her own bed and must lie on it."

Mary's letters continued to be returned. Finally, someone had written on the envelope that Mrs Bradstone and her son, called Henry, had both died a week after the child was born. Robert Bradstone had been found in New York harbour. It was thought that he had been robbed since no money was found on his person.

As Mary emerged from the sadness those memories had rekindled, she found her father staring at her in a strange way.

"What is it Papa?" she asked, full of sudden concern.

"I never knew," he said.

"What?"

"I never knew that she had named her child after me. I was so angry with her, that I never even knew the name of the child she bore."

Mary reached out and touched his arm.

"If only she had not been so damned opinionated – never listening – always doing what she thought was best. She made me so cross at times, but God knows I rue her passing now. If only things could have been different between us."

Mary gave his arm a gentle squeeze. "She was perhaps a little like the father she loved so much?"

He looked at her as if he were seeing her for the first time. "Maybe," he said at last. "Maybe there's some truth in what you say," and he gave a rueful smile. She knew it was the closest he would ever get to owning his own failings in his treatment of his daughter.

4

Henry Bragg

Despite his wealth and influence, Henry Bragg could never quite escape from his secret envy of those who possessed "old money" and the lese-majeste that went with it. He could never quite rid himself of the envy with which he regarded the possessor of an ancient name, with their quiet certainty as of the divine right of kings. In a strange way he now held Mary in that same esteem, since she too was now the possessor of just such a name.

Mary's son Anthony was now the only second generation of his line still living. Anthony was not half the man his father had been, despite his pedigree. He was presiding over a crumbling empire, in which the profligacy of Mark, his older brother, who had succeeded their father as Master until killed in a riding accident, had drained the estate of reserves. The war had now deprived Nethergate of the bulk of its export income. Henry's hopes now rested upon the young shoulders of George, his only grandson. On the few occasions they had met he had seemed a polite and orderly child, who he hoped might yet develop more of his grandfather's talents.

But if the war had created difficulties for Nethergate, in contrast Henry's fortunes had soared. Despite his age, he still hungered to make money with all the frenetic energy of one who thinks he can buy eternity. He had seized the opportunities the war gave and had prospered. He had turned over many of his factories from producing farm machinery to the manufacture of wagons and gun carriages for the Northern Armies. Without a qualm of conscience or a tremor of doubt as to the possibility of a conflict with his firmly held Christian beliefs, he had been turning ploughshares into swords for the past two years and was fast becoming an extremely wealthy and powerful man. He could afford to make considerable donations to charitable causes and basked in the plaudits of his peers, public acclaim and a sense of virtuous satisfaction.

Regardless of his success though, Henry Bragg was still a driven man. The more he accrued, the more he had to lose, and the more he acquired the less value he placed upon what he owned. There was always someone with yet greater wealth. Henry was now secretly engaged in a far more dangerous game, for much of the produce of his factories found its way by clandestine channels to the other side in the conflict. It was as if money could somehow assuage the disappointment of having no sons of his own and being compelled to rely upon the flawed issue of the Styles family, despite their undoubted pedigree.

He had regretted the untimely death of Mary's husband, Adrian Styles, but he had seen in his successor Mark Styles, Adrian's oldest son, a strong hand at the helm. He recognised in Mark a man who knew his own mind and had the confidence and assurance to plough his own furrow. He had been appalled at just what a self-indulgent and hedonistic channel that had proved to be. Even worse was the way the estate had suffered. It offended against his every instinct as a businessman to have to witness Mark's squandering of the very assets that lent substance to his ancient name.

It was pride that had led him to lend Mark money to keep the estate afloat for fear that his daughter should bear the stigma of being tied to a failed enterprise. The crash of such a prestigious establishment as Nethergate would have been a crushing blow to a man who prided himself on his ability always to pick winners. In his fiercely competitive world it would have shown his rivals that in the matter of investing in his daughter's future, he had revealed a fatal flaw of judgement. His competitors he imagined would laugh behind his back at such a monumental failure.

When he had heard Mark had died in a riding accident, to his shame, he had felt profoundly relieved. He had continued to pump money into Nethergate when Mark's younger brother, Anthony took over. He had never been impressed by Anthony and looked forward to the end of hostilities when he would, with his now considerable investment in the estate, influence its running in ways which he had no doubt would bring it back to prosperity. Just how he might exercise the close control that would be necessary, had until now escaped him. However, despite his prejudices about women's abilities in the men's world of business and commerce he had been more than impressed by Mary's deep understanding of the situation at Nethergate and how it dovetailed into his own vision for the future. He was beginning to toy with the idea that he might yet be able to exercise control over Nethergate through the hands of his daughter.

Yet Henry Bragg remained a troubled man, for he dreaded what would happen should Mary discover the full part he had played in the circumstances about the untimely death of her younger sister. It had of course never been his intention that things should turn out as they had. He wasn't used to being defied in the way that Caroline practised. He intended no more than to bring her to heel and with her the young man she had married. It had been simplicity itself to put it about that the publication of material from young Robert Bradstone would not be looked upon with favour by Henry Bragg.

That had been enough to deny the new Bradstone family of earnings through Robert's writing. A few months of privation would he felt be sure to bring them both under his control. It hadn't worked. He discovered that they were simply living off Caroline's jewellery and other assets. To speed things up, he had arranged for their house to be burgled. He would return all her treasured possessions when she came back to him. It would be easy enough to invent some tale of the newly formed NYPD pulling out all the stops once they realised whose daughter had been robbed. He imagined the delight on her face when her belongings were miraculously restored to her.

Events had simply not followed Henry's intentions. The new Bradstone family had simply vanished, swallowed up into the dark interior of the New York slums. He waited daily for Caroline to make contact. He would make her wait a little time in uncertainty and then magnanimously forgive her, hoping thereby that she might have learnt her lesson. But Caroline's pride was every bit as strong as his own. She would never come crawling back. It simply wasn't in the nature she had inherited from her father. He could still never bring himself to think that the tragic consequences could have ever been anything other than a cruel turn of fate. However, he suspected that Mary might not see things quite in the same light. It was important to keep Mary on side to further his plans for the future of Nethergate.

5

Ruth

Ruth's experience of New York was like nothing she had ever imagined. In almost every way she was no longer a slave, for slavery had been abolished in the Union States. She was free! Almost, but not quite. At the back of her mind was always the thought that Nethergate was her home and if she wished to see her home and more importantly Matthew, her son, again then inexorably she must return once more to Nethergate and to the savage embrace of slavery.

At first the idea of her mistress that she should masquerade as her lady's companion instead of being introduced as a freed-slave in New York had filled her with alarm. The consequences for her would be severe. She could understand her Mistress not wishing her father to visualise Matthew's mother as a slave. She understood how the taint of slavery fed the prejudices of whites whether they came from north or south of the Mason–Dixon Line. Gradually though her doubts had evaporated. The idea had grown on her. It appealed to her sense of adventure, but the possible advantages for her son soon outweighed all her other fears. She had benefited from the education she had received over the years from her mistress and had experienced years of observing how the whites of education and culture worked and played. She had no fears of being unmasked through ignorance or behaviour. Now that the reality was upon her, she seized it with gusto.

There was another and deeper reason why she wished to follow her mistress' wishes. She had regarded Mary almost as another mother ever since she had taken her into her household after she had been run down as a small child by Killcaid in his buggy. She had become her personal servant and over the years the affection and intimacy between them had grown. All that had changed dramatically when she had been cornered by Mark, Mary's oldest son and brutally assaulted and raped. Ruth tried to hide the resulting pregnancy, but by the time Mary had discovered the truth her dear Adrian had died, and Mark had become the Master of Nethergate.

With Mark as Master events had spiralled out of control. Mark had indulged every hedonistic whim and fancy and with his equally wayward friends had pursued a course of profligacy and debauchery. Even the great resources of the Nethergate Estate were eventually unequal to the strain and Mark began to sell off his slaves, thus breaking up families who had served the Styles family for generations. It was a time of great bitterness and recrimination.

Mark would not hear of Ruth continuing to work in Nethergate House and she returned to work once more in the tobacco fields with Matthew at her side. Mark took every opportunity to humiliate Ruth mainly because it rankled with him that she had fought and struggled against him and even struck him when he had taken her by force. It never occurred to him that a mere slave would find his advances to be anything other than acceptable. He had never acknowledged Matthew as his own, but simply used him as a tool to torment Ruth in revenge for trying to refuse him. When, however, he had threatened to sell Matthew to a team of slave traders for the sexual gratification of a client with such tastes, it had proved too much for Ruth. Once Mark and the traders' attentions were drawn elsewhere, Ruth strode to where Mark's horse was tethered. She had picked up a sharp stone and edged it under the horse's saddle. Then quietening the restless beast, she returned to where Matthew stood and waited. She had made no attempt to hide what she did. All those who witnessed her action said nothing, thus becoming conspirators in whatever might ensue. Every one of them remembered some act of casual cruelty or some family member or friend whom they saw no more and remained silent.

They remained silent and watched in silence as one by one the traders had mounted. Eventually Mark too gathered in his horse. He paused for a moment, perhaps aware of the unusual intensity in the eyes of the watching slaves. He too mounted. Instantly the horse reared. The more Mark brought down his crop to beat the animal into submission, the more violently it bucked. No man could have stayed in that saddle. Eventually he was thrown clear. His body spiralled high into the air and thudded to the ground with an awful finality. He did not move.

A few of the crowd ran forward. They stared curiously at their master as the life ebbed from his staring eyes. Amongst them was Matthew, who too stared into those eyes so curiously like his own. A slave quietly walked across to where Mark's horse was standing trembling with agitation. He quietened the animal. Removing the stone from under the saddle, he passed it to his neighbour. Conspiratorially it was passed from hand to hand until sharp and warm it came to rest with Ruth. She opened her fingers and let it fall to the ground.

It had never been Ruth's intention that Mark should die, but at least Matthew was still safe and with her. Many years had passed, but still the guilt of that secret lingered on. She dared not confess to the Mistress whom she loved like a mother that it was she who bore the responsibility for the death of her oldest son. She feared that the knowledge would shatter the bonds that held them both. What mother could ever love the murderer of her son, however wayward and wanton that son might have been?

Despite her guilt, the experience for Ruth of her new-found freedom in New York was like ambrosia and nectar combined. She lived for each moment and savoured every second of the present. As time passed, she began to relax from the inevitable tension of living a lie and felt daily more secure and confident in her new role. Above all she began to savour the unexpected light in which this place seemed to bask. It was as if she had suddenly become a different person in a different world. People listened to what she had to say. Her opinions mattered. Even strangers she met on the streets would smile and look her in the eye and politely allow her to pass, instead of expecting her to move aside for them. Gentlemen would raise their hats when they met her in company. People tried to please her with a thousand little acts of kindness and consideration; and she found herself responding. She was discovering within herself a new, yet sunnier disposition. She felt for the first time in her life that she was truly alive. She sparkled; she became aware of herself as a woman in her own right, not just as a potential artefact for the gratification of men's desires, or simply as an object to be used, discarded or sold. She came to realise too how attractive she was to men. She felt empowered with the age-old wiles of her sex and it excited her. At times she felt almost giddy with the delight of it all.

The Yankee North she found was so different from the sunny laissez-faire of the South. It was full of foreign-born Americans. Their language was different. They radiated energy and purpose. She could sense the huge, moving mass of the population of New York. It was a monolith that was somehow stirring and coalescing into a living shape; a force that would be irresistible once it had found its true purpose and direction. It was brutal and powerful and overwhelming. She had no doubt which side would emerge the victor in this great struggle.

By comparison the gay, indolent and charming folk of the South lived a pampered, surreal existence. They danced like children on the deck of a galley, delighting and laughing in the foam and the spray, unaware of the black, whip-scarred backs bending to the beat of the drum below, whose pain and power alone propelled their craft. Yet there was a carefree innocence and enchantment about the slave-owning community in the South and the life they led. Even as a slave she could understand it, though she revolted against the brutality which so often sustained it.

For both Mary and Ruth, though, there was but one cloud in this otherwise sunny sky. That cloud was in the sinister shape of one Colonel Thomas Gladstone. He was an officer from the Southern Confederate Army. Wounded and captured at Mill Springs early in the war, he was on parole awaiting exchange with a Yankee prisoner of equal status. Since they had been good friends well before the war, Henry Bragg had offered to house the Colonel until such an exchange could take place.

Colonel Gladstone was an enigma to both women. Tall and distinguished, he was every inch the Southern gentleman. Yet there was something mysterious about him. They were certain that he had some private agenda that he was working towards, but so far, he had not revealed his hand. Though he seemed to spend a lot of time away from the house for someone who was nominally a prisoner of war, it was his base and he would turn up unannounced, but for ever welcomed by Henry Bragg. He always seemed to seek out Ruth for his special attention and reawakened in her all her old feelings of insecurity. She was sure somehow that he sensed that she was not all she seemed to be.

Colonel Gladstone had early on in their acquaintanceship revealed another facet of his nature that somehow seemed

29

at odds with the suspicion and fear which he engendered in the two women. He had a prodigious musical talent. He both played and sung at the piano as most gentlemen did but put a violin in his hands and he was a man transformed. With him the instrument simply sang. Heavenly tones and chords arrested his audience and held them spellbound awaiting the next caress of his bow. The instrument and the man were as one. No-one engaged even in whispered conversations or whimsical asides when he was playing. He carried his audience with him down musical corridors to every last exquisitely strung note. But even then, it seemed to Ruth, that he was always watching her whilst he played; following her if she moved, like a portrait where the eyes track the viewer wherever they might go. It was as if he was saying, "I may seem to be totally absorbed in what I am doing, but I haven't relaxed, and I will ferret your little secret out."

6

Manuel's Story

Back at Nethergate, another drama was unfolding. George, his face pressed against the cool of the stone walled steps into the yard, was waiting for Manuel to break, as he had broken before under the withering scrutiny of the villainous Killcaid. All eyes were now upon Manuel as he stood trembling in front of his tormentor. George, watching from the stairs, was thinking rapidly as to what he should do when Manuel's story came pouring forth.

"So," said Killcaid, his voice heavy with menace, mainly for the benefit of the watching Mistress of Nethergate, "You bin goin' with Angela and helping her escape her jus' punishment, has you? You know what the penalty for that is!"

Fear lent Manuel conviction.

"Escape, Massa? Ah don' know nothin' 'bout no 'scape Massa, but there ain't no 'scape for dat poor chile."

Killcaid was puzzled. It was not the response he had expected. "What d'you mean – no escape?" he barked.

"No 'scape for dat poor soul. She a goner, God rest her spirit." And he shook his head so vigorously that his cheeks rattled, and he crossed himself several times as he'd seen the Catholics do.

Killcaid clasped Manuel by his shirt front. "What the blazes you blathering about, you stupid coon?" he growled.

"Like I said, she a goner. One moment she was dere and de next dere was jus' her basket and de flowers a'floatin' on de water."

Killcaid was about to grasp Manuel again to shake some sense into him when George intervened from the stable steps.

"Can't you see he's too terrified to string two sentences together? He doesn't know what he's saying." Then turning to Manuel, he said quietly, "Now what is it you're trying to say Manuel?" hoping against hope that his new-found faith in Manuel was not to be misplaced.

Manuel drew breath. "Angela, she wanted to pick some of dem marsh marigolds, and some other plant Morella tell her of. It for de Mistress's headaches. Morella say dat de best time to pick dem is when de dawn is breakin'. But de poor chile, she too damn fright to go on her own an' she ask me to go wid her. An' now she gone, took by dem spirits of de swamp jus' when ma back was turn." A low moan of fear escaped from the lips of his listeners, for all knew of the demons that protected the secrets of the bayou. "One moment she was dere, de next she was gone. She not even cry out." Manuel's shaking head and palpable fear lent him conviction. It was clear that his audience believed him even if Killcaid may have had his doubts. He had their sympathy now as all contemplated the fearful manner of Ursula's death. Everyone was wary of the bayou that could swallow the incautious in a moment and of the evil spirits that sucked them down and fed on their victim's souls.

Manuel's demeanour spoke of the awful event he had just witnessed. His terror of Killcaid, and his awareness of the pistol bulge in his pocket, added conviction to his word. With a supreme effort he mastered his fear once more to shake his head and mutter, "De dreadful spirit of the waters got dat poor chile, sure as I stand here." His audience shuddered, and another low groan escaped their lips.

George could only marvel at the ingenuity that Manuel had revealed in this explanation. Indeed, he was so convinced, that half of him began to fear that Ursula might indeed have perished. As for Manuel, he had been racking his brains on the way back for some plausible reason for visiting the bayou at such a time. The idea of collecting medicinal plants had suddenly occurred to him, for Morella always insisted that there was a right and a wrong time to pick plants when their gifts for healing were at their best. It was his very dread of Killcaid that had truly lent conviction to his words. He wondered at the back of his mind if indeed there might be a lesson there somewhere.

Those in the yard were now breaking into small groups, the drama over and acted out. There were many low murmurings of sympathy and shaking of heads at the awful fate to which Ursula had succumbed. Midst cries of "Lord have mercy" and "God bless dat poor chile", the crowd slowly dispersed about their business. Even Mrs Styles was taken aback by the news. She did indeed suffer from migraines but could not recall confessing such weakness to Ursula. The fact that the child had ventured into the dark on her behalf gave her a small pang of guilt. The presence of the whipping cart perhaps more readily bore witness to the true nature of her compassion.

"Silly girl," she muttered as she left to face the inconvenience of preparing herself unaided for the day.

The whipping cart, deprived of another victim, rattled and lurched out of the yard, bringing down the curtain on the drama of the morning.

Samuel watched Manuel collect his master's boots and clothes as he did every day, behaving as if nothing had happened and wondered at the depth and ingenuity that seemed to exist in every man and at their infinite capacity to surprise. As they passed their eyes met and Samuel briefly grasped Manuel's shoulders in a mute gesture of respect. As he did so, he felt the tension in Manuel's body and a wave of even greater regard washed over him as to how this man had mastered his fear, or at least if not entirely mastered it, had used it to his own ends.

In the privacy of his master's room Manuel's first action was to rid himself of the Smith and Wesson pistol which had been the cause of so much anxiety. Then he set to his duties as he did each morning. George strode over to him and took his hand, in both of his. "God bless you Manuel," he said. "I'll never doubt you again." Two such accolades were finally too much for poor Manuel. No longer able to contain himself, he gave way to a fit of uncontrollable shaking and trembling. George put his arms about him and held him until the reaction passed. Thus, were master and slave united in a bond of affection, loyalty and mutual respect. He also realised that Manuel had hoodwinked Killcaid and that the latter would never let rest even the suggestion of such a thought. He must get Manuel away before his courage crumbled. Suddenly the answer came to him.

"Manuel," he said, "I am soon to join the Confederate cause. How'd you like to come to the wars with me as my personal servant same as here? That way we'll keep you out of the grips of Killcaid."

Manuel's eyes filled with tears. Now at last he felt he had the trust and respect of his young master and had made up for his past failings. The thought of a life far away from Killcaid was like walking suddenly into the sunshine. "Ah sure would like that, Massa. Ah sure would. Pretty damn good."

With that settled George began to wonder how soon he could get down to the bayou to visit Ursula and Matthew. He thought of the two of them, now both truly free from the chains of slavery. They would be living the true natural life at one and in harmony with nature, the very essence of the life espoused by Rousseau, whom all three had avidly read and absorbed from the old Mrs Styles's library. It was a book that Matthew first had found and seemed to him so much in tune with the new spirit of the times. With that thought a sudden wave of jealousy swept over him. Why could it not have been him and Ursula and not Matthew now living that life of true emancipation? Then, insidiously, the thought crept into his mind, like a worm in the bud, could he trust his friend? If the boot were on the other foot would he have trusted himself? The urgency of getting Ursula set on the Underground Railroad loomed ever larger in his mind.

7

Two's a Crowd

Ursula had brought nothing of any use with her, just two dresses fit for Sundays, and a packet full of mementos in the same canvas bag that Morella had given her when she had moved to Nethergate Hall. Morella was a huge, stately and motherly figure who had been a pillar of comfort to her when she had been torn from her own mother's arms at the slave market at the behest of Killcaid and brought in chains to Nethergate. Now it was Morella whom she missed most.

Morella's canvas bag contained all she had in the world that she could truly call her own. Matthew had to admit that she was a pretty girl, but she was George's girl. Here, attired as she was in the blue dress and white starched collar and cuffs of a maid at Nethergate Hall, she was a pathetic parody of her previous life. Her dress was already splashed with mud and sodden at the hem. She was about as much use, he reflected, as a Bess with no ball. She was a passenger, an intruder on his new-found freedom, and would make his life now doubly difficult.

He could understand why George had asked this of him. He knew only too well what it was like to face a public whipping. It was his escape from just such a punishment that had led to his present

36

exile and to the price now on his head as a "wanted man"; wanted for the murder of the black preacher who had allegedly tried to apprehend him. At least that was the story put about by Killcaid. It was the giant preacher who had bravely carried his exhausted form for some way and had laid a false scent using Matthew's shirt for the hounds to follow. It was Killcaid himself who had struck the fatal blow. When his huntsman had shown him how the preacher had fooled the hounds and when that same preacher railed at him for what he was doing, with all the authority of the Holy Gospel behind him, his temper had snapped. Matthew knew full well whose story would be believed if ever he were apprehended and appeared before a white man's court. The word of a white man, supported no doubt by those who dared not gainsay him, would hold sway. Some knew the truth though, as witnessed by the attempt, led by the preacher's son to kill Killcaid by burning down his cabin. It had very nearly succeeded.

A flogging, Matthew reflected, would be worse for a girl. Stripped to the waist, it would be doubly humiliating. Nevertheless, she was a complication he could have done without and he found it hard to hide his resentment. Perhaps, in a few months' time, he might have been glad of company, but now he was enjoying the freedom of being his own master. Her presence would stifle his sense of freedom with new obligations. There would have to be changes in Old Mo's hut which wasn't designed for two. There was also the realisation that those discussions and arguments with George and the music they made together with their shared passion for the flute, their forays into the wildness of the bayou, would all now be a thing of the past. George would want to spend time alone with Ursula. He would be shut out. That special relationship that they had enjoyed would be but a memory.

Ursula had said nothing as they journeyed in the dugout to Old Mo's jetty. She scrambled ashore, desperately trying to keep her clothes away from the mud and damp.

"Not much point you doin' that," he observed laconically. "It's pretty well wet anywhere here."

She said nothing, but Matthew noticed she continued to lift her skirts. He continued to lead her up to the bushes which screened Old Mo's homestead. He drew them aside to reveal, with pride, Old Mo's cabin where she would be living whilst she stayed in the shelter of the bayou.

When they reached the hut, he opened the door and showed her his little domain. Her reaction was instinctively to draw back as she stared aghast at the primitive conditions in which she was now expected to live, at least until George could arrange for her escape. Her instinctive response was not lost on Matthew, to whom Old Mo's construction was a palace indeed, and he felt another surge of resentment. In a way she was mocking of Old Mo's memory and all he stood for.

"Ain't as grand as the Hall," he muttered sullenly, "but it's all you got now. So best get used to it."

Again, she did not respond, this time because she feared any utterance would bring forth a flood of tears.

To Matthew it seemed she was simply putting on a show of petulance. Old Mo had been almost a father figure to Matthew. He had discovered Old Mo through his wanderings about the estate. Matthew had been nominally employed at Nethergate House where Mary resided, in what had once been the main residence, before Adrian had built the much grander Nethergate Hall. Mrs Styles had allowed Matthew to do much as he pleased. She did not wish to see him working as a slave, for in her eyes he was her grandson. She had encouraged his desire to educate himself and had made the Nethergate library freely available to him and had helped and directed his learning in every way she could, even though she knew it to be against the law. Matthew had grasped the opportunity with both hands. He had no assigned work to do, but to appease the comments of Killcaid that he should be properly employed she had made him responsible for exercising the Nethergate horses, still stabled at Nethergate House. This had allowed Matthew to roam where he pleased. His wanderings had led him to explore the bayou, and it was here that he had met up with Old Mo.

Old Mo's job was trapping game in the bayou for Killcaid and his other overseers. He took an interest in Matthew who was full of admiration for his skill in trapping and his knowledge of animals and the bayou. Old Mo was not good to look at. He had been slave to a fur trapper out West. Both he and his master had been scalped by the Indians. Only he had survived. Morella had been able to relieve Old Mo's sufferings. He now passed on much of his backwoodsman skills to Matthew who was an avid pupil. Soon Matthew was helping him in secret, so much so that the output from the bayou shot up, even when Old Mo would vanish sometimes for half a day at a time on some secret business of his own. Soon they were feeding the cabins as well with the largesse of the bayou.

This though, had unforeseen consequences, for when Matthew fell ill, the output from the bayou fell too. Killcaid was convinced that this was either deliberate on the part of Old Mo or that his vigour was failing. When a slave trader happened to be passing through, he took the opportunity to sell off Old Mo, convinced that he would soon become a liability to the estate.

Only when Matthew had recovered did he learn how Old Mo had carefully planned for his "retirement" and his own personal freedom from slavery, to be taken at a moment of his own choosing. In secret even from Matthew, over the years he had gradually been building a cabin in the depths of the bayou on some naturally rising ground. He had established a garden there with all he needed to feed himself, augmented by the game from the bayou. Matthew's help had allowed him to complete his plans. When he was ready, he would tell Matthew of his plans, but not before. Matthew would be his link with the outside world should he be needed. Old Mo's intention was to go to work as usual, but never to come out again. It would be assumed that he had simply perished from the many hazards in the bayou. No-one would come looking for him lest they too fall victim. Thus did Old Mo intend to see out his days, having taken his own freedom when he was ready. Had he but known it, it was Matthew's enthusiasm to please the old man that had led to such an increased output that now Old Mo, left on his own, could not match what was now expected of him.

Old Mo knew in his heart that it was time to go, but he had grown very fond of Matthew and was deeply concerned when he fell ill. He had confided part of his escape plans to Morella, who was nursing Matthew. But when she could not assure him of Matthew's survival, he had delayed his move. That delay had been fatal. Matthew, when he learnt how things stood, could only mourn the passing of such an indomitable spirit, robbed at the eleventh hour of the fruits of all that labour.

Old Mo had left a message for Matthew that only he would understand as to how to find his cabin. Now seeing how Ursula seemed to be scorning all Old Mo's efforts had made him unreasonably cross. "Here," he said, relenting somewhat at Ursula's crestfallen look, "you'd better have something to eat. It's all there is, so you'd best get used to it."

He offered her some bread he had baked himself in the oven Old Mo had constructed outside the cabin. He had not yet perfected the art of baking and noticed with irritation how Ursula picked out the bits of twig and extraneous vegetation that had somehow got into the dough and left the rather soggy middle bit, all of which he usually ate with indifference. She did however more readily consume the gruel and some of the meat left over from his evening meal, but some of the mixture was to her eyes unidentifiable and she pushed the plate away unfinished. Although hungry after her ordeal, the thought of how her life must now be ordered had robbed her of her appetite. Apart from the nightmare events when she had been torn from her mother at the slave market and betrayed by Killcaid, she had never experienced physical discomforts and had always enjoyed much the same diet as those whom she served. She instinctively recoiled from the way she would now be expected to live.

Ursula remembered Matthew from when he had first come to Nethergate House as the awkward and shy son of Ruth, the slave who had replaced her as lady's maid to the old Mrs Styles, when she had been reinstated in her old job. He hadn't said much then and was clearly in awe of the new world into which he had so suddenly been thrust, so different from the smoky warmth and clamour of the slave cabins he had always known.

Now here she was pitched into the care of that same boy, but now a young man unrecognisable, with a growing beard, ragged clothes and carrying the pungent aroma of the wild and primitive life he undoubtedly lived. Would she soon sink to this level, she wondered, and what would George think of her then? There wasn't even a mirror in which she could see herself. So preoccupied was she with her thoughts that she was unaware of Matthew's contemptuous scrutiny.

8

Growing Resentment

Matthew continued to watch Ursula as she ate. At last, unable to endure her fastidious picking over the food he had provided, he pointed to the bed in the corner. "You'd best take over that and put your bag there. There's one clean blanket you can use. It won't take long for me to make another bed. Now, I'd best go and look to my traps. Food don' jus' appear by magic, you know."

With that he strode out of the cabin and down to the boat, still smouldering with resentment. His new world had suddenly lost its charm. He didn't know what Old Mo would have made of his cabin's new occupant. Dismissed her, no doubt, with the same contemptuous snort he would give at a badly tied knot or a poorly set trap.

Once out in the bayou, the familiar noises and birdsong began to exert their magic and his resentment started to ebb away. He knew he was behaving badly. At least he should give her a chance. One of his traps held a racoon spitting and hissing defiance. He let it go, making sure it had an obvious route of departure, for racoons can give a nasty bite. It lolloped off, rumbling and growling its outrage. For the first time that day Matthew smiled, enjoying its obvious indignation.

"Ah knows jus' how you feels, boy," he muttered to its retreating rump. These things he understood as Old Mo had understood them too. He would have chuckled as well at the racoon's affront and ruffled loss of dignity.

One of his traps held a young deer which he quickly despatched. He was in no hurry to get back to the cabin but gutted and skinned the deer in situ taking his time over the process. Then he cut some vines and the wood he would need to make himself a new bed. Securing the carcass, he carried the wood back to the cabin. He could see Ursula moving about inside, but didn't go in. Instead he turned to the construction of the new bed for himself. As he tugged and jerked each vine strand into place his anger returned and with it his resentment of its innocent cause. His bitterness began to feed on itself. She was nothing but a halter about the neck of his new-found freedom. Just at the time when he was savouring a sense of real emancipation, he would now have to consider the needs of someone else and someone who would be a complete passenger, whose only talent was the ability to sculpt the coiffure and lay out the clothes of a sour-faced white lady whom everyone hated. He could not even consider his own plans for escaping whilst he had Ursula to care for. George was like any other white master the way he had assumed that Matthew would do as he asked. He had always considered George and himself as somehow friends and equals when in the bayou, never as Master and slave, but now the thought came unbidden. Then he remembered the wording of George's note to him, "I beg you, dear brother, to take good care of Ursula, for she is more to me than life itself", and he felt unworthy of the notion.

Without a word to Ursula, he returned to collect the meat for their evening meal. When he came back, he found that the bed had been moved into the cabin. Ursula had watched Matthew's return. She had seen him constructing his new bed. The lack of any attempt to greet her on his return was not lost on her. As she watched, she found herself admiring the skill and dexterity he displayed in the task of construction. She saw too the angry way in which he tugged the vines into place and guessed it was a message for her. She knew that he resented her coming for the way it would disrupt his life and the fellowship he shared with George. She saw that her presence was an added burden to him. The thought of enduring his anger for the next few weeks, or however long it took for her to be on her way, filled her with dismay. Considering the awful nature of the existence she now faced, had there been some way in which she could have returned to Nethergate Hall, she would have gladly taken it.

Perhaps if she waited until the Master returned and claimed she had become lost in the bayou. Perhaps Amelia would not carry out her threat to have her publicly humiliated if the Master were in residence. Yet it seemed that every avenue was closed to her and that she was rejected wherever she looked. She yearned for her mother, who was so cruelly torn away from her by the hand of Killcaid, and wondered again what would happen to her now.

It was true that life at Nethergate Hall had been unmitigated misery at the hands of a vindictive mistress, but there had been compensations. There was a warm sense of community among the remaining slaves under the avuncular and kindly regime of Samuel. There was the routine of life, which lent a pattern and security to her days and of course there were the creature comforts of living in the great house, for the slaves inevitably shared in the luxuries of their betters. But most of all there had been the snatched meetings with George when both could get away and the supreme moments of joy in his arms at night.

Now all was uncertainty. Her future rested in the hands of those who sought to send her down the secret corridors of the Underground Railroad to an unknown destination and away from everyone she knew and most of all, away from George. She would be a fugitive, an escaped slave. Her flight to Canada was full of uncertainty. She would be a pawn in the hands of each person into whose care she would be entrusted. She would know no-one. What would she do even if she got to Canada? How would she live? Would she ever see George again? It seemed to her as if the whole world had suddenly turned against her. She was certain too, that there would be little comfort or understanding to be had from her new companion in exile.

When Matthew returned with the meat and began to prepare their supper, she emerged tentatively from the cabin, anxious to be given some task to play her part in their new life together. Matthew seemed unaware of her presence. The silence grew between them. Matthew at last looked up to acknowledge her presence. The incongruity of her standing in the bayou in the muddied mockery of her maid's attire struck him afresh. He felt he had to say something. "Ain't you got anythin' better to wear than that get-up?" he asked, his voice sounding harsh even to his ears. "It hardly suits fo' how you's got to live now."

Ursula looked mortified. She had no mirror to see how she looked, but she was acutely aware of the mud stains and splashes on her dress and of her shoes spoilt and damp with mud. She didn't say anything for fear that the tears that were but a heartbeat away would come unbidden to her eyes and that would never do. Instead she hastened back to the cabin with a mumbled excuse to hide the hurt of his rebuke. But in truth, amongst her meagre possessions, she had no sort of practical attire that would in any way suit her new life in the swamplands. Once inside the cabin the tears she had fought against so bravely suddenly overwhelmed her. Alone at last, she fell onto her new bed and silently wept.

9

The Song of the Bayou

Whilst Ursula struggled with her tears, Matthew busied himself with their evening meal. He planned a hearty supper for them both, determined as far as possible that there would be no excuse for Ursula's fastidious picking. He mostly cooked outside on an open fire the way Old Mo had shown him and he soon had a fine meal simmering and spitting away. With the prospect of food and the smell of the roasting meat, his mood began to mellow. He began to regret the roughness of his remarks to Ursula.

His thoughts turned to the idea of the war, the part he might yet play and the prospect of gaining his freedom by military service. The notion had always been there in the background, a possibility that he might take up when the moment was right. He began to feel anxious that the war might yet pass him by or that the trumped-up charges against him might follow him into the Yankee Army. For the moment though he was marooned here, looking after George's little fish out of water when he could be doing heroic deeds for the freedom of his people.

He was brought abruptly from his reverie by a voice beside him. "Will this do?" What he now saw made him gape like a gawking schoolboy. Ursula had effected a transformation of her maid's uniform. She had turned the cuffs inward, showing the slenderness of her arms, and opened the buttons to the front and split the skirt to give greater freedom of movement. Gone was the silly mob cap and instead she had let her hair flow down in its natural black tresses. She looked every inch the child of nature envisaged by Rousseau about which they had all read with such empathy in old Mrs Styles's library. The sight of her long locks had the same effect upon Matthew as they had had upon George when he had first seen her with her hair flowing free. There was a wildness about her now that he had never suspected in one so outwardly demure and submissive.

"Better," he grunted, but now he understood why George had been so captivated by his Ursula. "Want some?" he muttered, trying to hide his sudden admiration and to avoid looking at her too directly.

Ursula replied with enthusiasm. "It smells real good." He glanced up at her and found himself smiling.

"Here," he said, with the first warmth he had shown, "come and sit down." She sat down eagerly beside him on the log where he and George had so often sat. He was aware of the subtle female scent of her and the new bareness of her arms and legs. The two settled down to their first meal together in the watery world of the bayou in a somewhat more amiable atmosphere.

After the meal Matthew cleaned the bowls and stowed the remnants of the carcass out of reach of animals. Ursula watched and noted and helped where she could. The work was soon done. Then Matthew went to fetch his flute, for it was his habit and pleasure to reserve this time of day for such an activity and the presence of a stranger was not going to stop him. Without a word of explanation, he left and was swallowed into the greenery.

As he made his way to a favourite spot where he would often come just to think, his thoughts turned to his mother and the old Mrs Styles. They might be able to do something about Ursula, they might even be able to do something about his situation in general, but they were lost to him in the North. As a branded murderer and an escaped slave, all the forces of the law of the warring states, both North and South, would be united against him. Some of the same harsh laws would apply to Ursula too as an escaped slave.

He pulled out his flute and began to play. Soon the old familiar tunes he and George had learnt together began to exert their magic and he became lost in the world of the music he created.

Ursula was alone again. It was a rare experience; mostly it had been when she was waiting for George at any of their meeting places. She was aware of the hum of the insects and the feel of life burgeoning about her, of things moving and growing. Slowly the bird-song came back again, disturbed momentarily by the alarm created by Matthew's departure. The whole harmony of nature seemed to enfold her. Then softly, far away, came the distant sound of Matthew's flute rising and falling. Its melody seemed to be part of the wilderness itself, now briefly her home too. She listened spellbound, then there came an air she instantly recognised. It was a favourite song of her mother's. It was as if her "Mamma" was sending her a message. Softly her mouth formed the words and whisperingly she sang them so that she could still hear the distant melody too. She felt strongly the nearness of her mother, almost as if she had but to turn around and she would be there. She could feel the love that her presence always brought with her.

For the first time in that stressful day she felt suddenly at peace.

So elusive and intangible was Matthew's playing and so much a part of the sounds of the bayou itself that Ursula seemed to go on hearing it, even when the melodies had ceased. She knew that Matthew would now be on his way back. The greenery parted, and he strode up towards the cabin. His face was more serene than she had ever seen it as if the music had washed the tension away. He smiled a greeting, a smile that was all warmth.

"I was listening," she said. "That was lovely. You play very well. I loved that last tune. My mother used to sing it to me."

Matthew was pleased despite himself. In truth the music had calmed him down. "You mean this one?" he said taking up the flute once again and beginning to play. After a moment or two Ursula joined in, singing the words in a rich contralto which in its turn entranced Matthew. They discovered other tunes they both knew and soon the bayou was echoing to their music. Finally, when the insects drove them indoors, a sort of empathy was born between them.

"It'll be dark soon," said Matthew, "I have to conserve as much as I can our supply of coal oil for the lamp otherwise it's jus' candles and there's none too many of them. Usually with me, when it gets dark it jus' stays that way till sun-up."

"I've got all I need," she replied. "Give me a moment an' I'll settle down."

He busied himself in setting the fire so it would smoulder through the night and he could blow it alive next morning. He did a final round to check that all was clear from curious animals during the night and entered the cabin. As he struggled out of his day clothes he was acutely aware of the other occupant of his cabin. He had erected a screen behind which Ursula could have some privacy and had explained about the toiletry arrangements that Old Mo had instigated. He wondered if like him he slept naked.

"Goodnight, Ursula," he whispered as he settled into his new bed in the darkness.

"Goodnight, Matthew," she murmured. "And thank you for taking me in. I'll try not to get in the way. Hopefully I'll soon be gone."

He felt guilty at her words. He knew he had been churlish. He knew too that all this must be an awful ordeal for her, but still he resented her uninvited presence in his new-found home. At the same time, he could not deny the feelings which the sight of her long hair trailing free and the sight of her bare arms had aroused in him, but it only added to his resentment, for he knew she was denied to him by the trust that George had placed in him.

He could see the darkened sky through the slats about the window. Slowly the night sounds of the bayou crept into his consciousness. They held no fears for him, only the assurance that all was well with his world and that he was alone and safe from his own kind. He began to feel the calm that always came over him in this place built so lovingly by Old Mo. He could hear Ursula's breathing, now steady and measured, no doubt sleeping the sleep of the exhausted after her long and eventful day.

Slowly he drifted off to sleep.

He awoke with a start to the sound of a long sobbing cry of distress. For a moment he thought it came from some wild creature from outside the cabin, but then he realised it was Ursula. He half sat up wondering if he should go to her, but immediately became aware of his own nakedness.

The sobbing continued, and he realised that Ursula was still in her sleep and being racked by nightmarish dreams the nature of which he could all too readily visualise. After a time, the sounds of distress subsided, and she relaxed into a more peaceful slumber. For a long time afterwards, Matthew remained sitting up staring into the blackness of the night. When he eventually lay back once more, he realised his feelings for Ursula and her plight had undergone a subtle change.

Finally, he slept.

10

Prospects for the Future

The day following Manuel's dramatic announcement of Ursula's death, George felt it safe to leave without arousing suspicion from those who might still be keeping watch for Killcaid. His father on his return would no doubt be angry at the loss of a hand, particularly since a replacement slave with the skills of a lady's maid would be costly. His mother would insist upon the best. He would probably never know of Amelia's intention to have Ursula flogged, and, if he did find out, would doubtless ignore it, since no actual beating had taken place. To George's disgust, his mother had shown no sign of remorse at Ursula's drowning, despite being the alleged cause of her venturing into the perils of the bayou. Her attitude, it seemed, was to be summed up in just those two words he had heard her mutter when she left the yard after Manuel's dramatic disclosure, "Silly girl".

George had but one desire now and that was to see Ursula, to reassure her and to tell her of her new status. At least she would not now be hunted as an escaped slave, but he was none too sure how she would react to being thought to be dead. She still thought that her mother might yet somehow seek to find her or perhaps would hear of her death and be heartbroken. She was, too, still very superstitious despite the education she had received whilst in the service of his grandmother. She might fear she was simply tempting fate. With Samuel's help, he gathered together some few things which he thought she might need during her stay in Old Mo's cabin to soften and divert her from the news he brought.

On his arrival in the bayou, George located the dugout that he and Matthew had made together, it seemed an age ago. He made his way to the landing platform by Old Mo's hut. He gave a shout when he saw Matthew at work in front of the cabin. Matthew's heart lifted at the sight of his friend and he waved a welcome as George strode up to join him. He was about to clasp his friend about his shoulders in brotherly greeting when there was a cry from the cabin and Ursula rushed out. In an instant the two were in an embrace so intense that Matthew felt obliged to turn away.

"Thank God you're safe," murmured George.

"But I mus' look so dreadful," lamented Ursula. "I's so muddied and dirty, not fit to be seen no-how."

The two broke from each other and George surveyed the damaged partner of his embrace. What he saw made him smile as he looked at her for the first time in her modified Nethergate attire. "Never seen a maid's dress better worn in ma' whole life. You looks lovely to me however you are," he declared and both knew in the intimate language of lovers that he referred to other moments of past tenderness between them.

"Truly?" she asked.

"Truly!" he echoed, so relieved was he to see her and to observe the adjustments she had already made to her new circumstances.

"But I can't stay here for long," she lamented, "There's so little room and I shall be robbing poor Matthew of his comfort."

"That's partly what I came to see you about," replied George. "We need to set up the Underground Railroad to take you away, but that often takes a deal of time. Samuel is working on it even now, but he says of late the law has been cracking down hard on all the links. Some folks have forfeited their entire farms when they have been caught sheltering runaways. There are now free rangers who make a living out of capturing those as gets away. With the Yankees spreading ever southwards more each day are making a bid for freedom; some are even joining the Federal Army. But that wouldn't do for you," he added with a laugh.

"Oh George, how long will it take? And how will I see you if ever I gets to Canada?" Canada seemed like another world to her and then an entirely new thought occurred to her who had never in her life had to consider such matters. "How will I live without money and no master to give me food and shelter?" The whole enormity of her new situation once more enveloped her. Then she thought of her own, virtually blind mother, whose closeness she had so vividly felt the evening before. Despite her lack of vision, she still hoped that, somehow, her mother might yet seek her out. All she would know was that her daughter had been sold to the Nethergate Estate. How would she now find her if she had left for Canada? "Oh, George, this is such a tangle. It might have been better if I had taken the whippin."

At this last utterance, all George could do was to take her once more in his arms as if this very act might stifle the thought of what a flogging would do to her and the pain she would have to endure. But he could not escape the picture in his mind of that lovely creamy back torn, flayed, bloodied and bruised and he hugged her yet harder.

"You mustn't say that," he admonished. "I could never stand aside and see that happen to you." He wondered how his mother could have grown into such a tyrant.

All the same there was no answer he could give to the host of questions Ursula had fired at him. He realised he had not really thought much further than avoiding the immediate peril she faced. He had not considered how she might feel, facing an uncertain future. Now he had to tell her of what Manuel had done.

"Ursula. Things could be different for you from now on," he started. "I don't know what inspired him, but Manuel claimed to have seen you perish in the swamp. He was so convincing that for a dreadful moment I almost believed him myself. I'm certain that Silas Killcaid was satisfied, for he hasn't bothered to put up any of the usual notices about runaways. I have let Samuel know how things are here. Once he gets things organised it should make your journey easier, for no-one will be looking for you."

Ursula digested this information, not sure quite what to make of it all. For a moment a cold tentacle of fear seemed to reach out and wrap itself stealthily about her heart. There was a part of her that superstitiously felt that in pretending to be dead she might be tempting the hand of fate. She shuddered at the thought. Then it occurred to her again that as a slave there was always a master or mistress who had a duty to care for you and provide for you. Now there was no-one. She was simply cut adrift. She longed to be back again at Nethergate even with a cruel mistress, with things all in place as they were before. Anything was better than this.

All this time, Matthew had been standing, a neglected witness to the strength of feeling between the two of them and wondering where he featured in all this. He envied the obvious passion the two shared and was beginning to think that his friendship with George counted little besides George's new-found attachment. He began once more to resent this girl who had in a few short hours shattered the equilibrium of his existence and the peace he had found in his new way of life. She had been pushed upon him in such a way that he could not have refused, but it was his life here in the bayou. As Old Mo's successor, the cabin was his and yet George was treating him as a white man always treated his slaves, as someone whose opinions were of no matter, whose concurrence was a foregone conclusion.

George, as if he had been reading his thoughts, suddenly turned to him.

"Thank you, brother, for your forbearance. I have forced your hand, I know, but truly I had no choice. Does all this meet with your approval?"

Matthew could only smile inwardly, perhaps a trifle ruefully at his sudden prescience and nod his assent.

"I have news for you too. I have written to our grand mama telling her of the situation we now face. It will take some time for the letter to reach her, for mail is very uncertain at these times, but we must hope that she can do something to amend matters. I dare not use the telegraph for fear that the contents would be revealed to my parents, or, worse still, to Killcaid."

"Does that mean I shall have to stay here until they return?" suddenly interrupted Ursula.

"No, no," George reassured her. "Your plans will not be affected."

"But what if my mammy come lookin' fo' me?"

George and Matthew exchanged glances for both knew well her story and the futility of her hoping to ever see her mother again. Neither wished to be the one to say it.

"Samuel would be certain to hear of it and I'll make sure he knows to tell me," replied George. It seemed to satisfy her for the moment and the two young men fell to discussing the implications of George's letter and the return of their grandmother and Matthew's mother, together with their plans for the immediate future.

"Will I be able to see them when they return, do you think?" asked Matthew.

"I don't know." replied George. "The posters that were displayed for your arrest will soon be forgotten and pasted over. I don't think Killcaid is still looking for you. Father says he thinks you have perished in the swamps as I so nearly did myself." George was referring to the day when Matthew had rescued him from nearly drowning in the swamp and had ended up facing a flogging from Killcaid for trying to escape. It was the event that had ended up with him as a fugitive in the bayou wanted for a murder that had been committed by Killcaid.

At the mention of George's letter to their grandmother, Matthew had had a sudden thought. "Does my mother know of the charges against me?" he asked. He could not bear the thought that his mother might think he could have done such a thing.

"No," replied George, "I thought it best to explain in person, lest they both be unnecessarily alarmed. My father is convinced though, for it justifies the way he has acted. If you go back to Nethergate at night with extreme care you should be able to get to explain to your mother in person. Killcaid has some of his overseers out after dark, because of what happened when his cabin was burnt down. I don't know if he also patrols the wider areas of the estate. With the war so close soldiers often come sneaking around at night to see if they can find anything worth the picking, but we're such a long way from the nearest town that we're not much troubled. I would need to speak first to Morella for she's sure to know."

The thought of seeing his mother again made Matthew suddenly aware of how much he had missed her in the long lonely evenings he had spent in Old Mo's cabin before the advent of Ursula. What would she think of him the way he now looked? She was always so neat and tidy in her appearance. On his own, with just George for company, it had not seemed to matter. Now he was acutely aware of his unkempt, bearded appearance and the ragged state of his clothes. He wondered whether his mother would even recognise him. Suddenly, like

Ursula, he longed for the ease and comfort of the life he had known at Nethergate House and for the loving presence of his mother with the warmth, comfort and security she always seemed to bring. But these were things of the past now. It was a life to which he could never return.

11

We Happy Band of Three

Matthew had discreetly withdrawn, ostensibly to check his traps, leaving the two young lovers to be alone together. When he returned, they were seated about the fire with coffee brewing. He envied their flushed and feverish air that told him how they had spent their time alone. Whilst he had been away, he had been thinking of his plans once Ursula had been spirited away by the members of the Underground Railroad. There would be little need for him to stay in the bayou. He could make his bid for freedom too. But there was always the risk that once he had joined the Yankees they might check his past and find he was wanted for murder. Then there would be no escaping from the awful consequences, for surely no-one would believe that he was innocent.

When they were seated comfortably with coffee mugs in their hands, Matthew voiced his plans.

"Listen, brother," he said, "Life in the bayou is a kind of freedom in its way. I have enjoyed being my own master for the first time in my life, doing what I want to do when I want to do it. But I fancy as time goes on it could get mighty lonely, here on my own with George my only visitor. Ah bin thinkin' what to do once Ursula is took on the Underground Railroad. There's the war and we have both spoken of this. Ah don' want to miss my chance. I was thinking that I might take the risk in a month or so and try and join the Yankees an' hope they won't ask too many questions. What d 'you think?"

George felt he should have guessed that his friend was bound to consider such a choice in the end. He could hardly sit in judgement, conscious as he was of his own rash desire to take part in the fighting and the consequences for them both. Then the thought occurred to him that Matthew might want to leave before Ursula had been spirited away along the Underground Railroad.

"You don't mean to think of leaving before Ursula leaves?"

"Good Lord no! I said so, didn't I?" rejoined Matthew. George was relieved at Matthew's prompt denial of such a thought. Then another idea occurred to him.

"Look, brother, I know how you long to join in the fight before it is all over. And I s'pose I can't object to the side you chose to fight for, but because of the posters out for your capture you are always going to be at risk if you use your own name. Why not travel as, say, 'David or Jonathan, or any damned name – Styles'? You can then give my name as your owner. Then if you are taken they will notify me and I can cover for you and make the necessary payments for your redemption and Killcaid and my father need be none the wiser."

Matthew thought for a moment. The more he considered the plan, the more it appealed, and his heart lifted at the real prospect of escaping and joining in the struggle before the war was over. Now he could have a definite objective. As soon as Ursula was on her journey north, he would embark upon his own journey to freedom and to fight for the cause of enslaved black people like himself. For Matthew it was the best possible news and made the intrusion of Ursula into his little idyll more than tolerable.

His eyes filled with tears of gratitude at the suggestion of his friend. He grasped George's hands. "Thank you, brother. Thank you," was all he could say. Then laughingly added, "If you join the Rebs too, I'll have to make damn sure you're not in my sights afore I shoots." They both laughed, but George's laughter was hollow for he felt again the guilt of his own secret.

Then George put his arms around both Ursula and his friend in a sudden surge of affection. "You are the two people I care most for in all this world," he said smiling, at each in turn, making Matthew feel immediately guilty for his earlier uncharitable thoughts about Ursula. "Let us enjoy these moments whilst we may. It is in a way, true freedom for us all: for me to be free of all the things expected of me and for you two to be free from slavery. It is indeed true amity, the truest, the best, the most natural state for mankind. And I shall join you here as much as I can whilst we wait for Samuel to make the arrangements for your escape, Ursula. I'll bring things from the Hall to make life as comfortable as I can. I'll make some excuse to visit relatives or go on military training and perhaps stay with you both for days at a time. For this evening, I am not expected back before nightfall so let us make the most of the time we have."

That afternoon Matthew, helped by Ursula, prepared a meal for the three of them, both anxious to show George how well they could live in the inhospitable swamplands. After a surprisingly good meal of game, finished off with fruit, the three relaxed on the veranda of Old Mo's cabin. It wasn't long before Matthew brought out George's flute and both played their favourite melodies. Soon the evening chorus of birds and animals in the bayou was enhanced with their playing and with their voices as Ursula sang to the tunes that Matthew and George both played. When the evening was well advanced, they moved to the warmth of the fire and fell to talking.

Their conversation ranged over the war and the chances that the victory of either side might bring. Then when it looked as if Matthew and George, on opposing sides, might get too heated the topics changed to ideas that were the talk of the moment, then on to more personal things that they all wished the future might bring at this time of change and turmoil.

The evening was a time of pure happiness, when all their cares were put aside, and they simply basked in the warmth of true friendship. Towards the end of the evening Matthew excused himself, saying he must look to his traps once more, leaving George and Ursula to say their farewells in the way that lovers do.

As Matthew left them in the moonlight, he was aware of the familiarity of the bayou and a feeling of being at one with the place which he now looked upon as his home. He envied the extra dimension that George enjoyed in the love of a woman and thought of them entwined in each other's arms and wondered what the true love they clearly shared must be like. He had had experiences with some of the young maids at Nethergate House, but it had been all laughter and giggles with no real emotion involved.

In truth it was too dark to look at traps and dangerous to stir in the wilderness at night, so Matthew just lingered at the edge of the clearing and enjoyed the night enclosing securely about him and all the sounds and rustlings of the creatures going about their nocturnal business, as they had a thousand years before Old Mo had decided to make this his home. It had been a perfect evening.

At length, when the insects became too attentive, Matthew returned to the cabin, making sufficient noise to warn the two lovers of his approach. With a last embrace, they said their final farewells. Then Ursula went back into the cabin and Matthew accompanied George to the dugout. Matthew had to concentrate hard, the familiar bayou looking so different in the

61

moonlight. Both too were absorbed in their own thoughts until they reached the spot where they always met and from whence George would be able to find his way back in the dark.

They embraced on parting, but George lingered a moment before moving off. Matthew waited, sensing that he wished to say something else.

"You'll look after Ursula, brother," he said at last, but it was clear that he meant more than he said.

"Of course," replied Matthew.

"She's... she means a great deal to me. You know that."

Matthew nodded. "I won't pretend that I particularly welcome her here. Things were good with just you and me. I don't think she'll find it easy; she's not used to this sort of living, but I'll take care of her. Trust me."

"I do trust you, Matthew," he said. Both knew what he truly meant.

George basked in the memory of the evening he had just spent as he made his way back to Nethergate Hall, but guilt was now dragging at his spirits. It had brought on his sudden show of affection for the company of his two friends. It was the news that for the moment he dared not reveal. He had that very morning received a letter from the Militia calling him forward for active military service in the Confederate Army. He did not yet see a way to break this news to the two people who would now be most affected. Every day he searched the table on which all letters were placed, for a reply from his grandmother to his carefully penned communication, but no such letter came. For the present, he meant to make the most of the few weeks he had left and to play them out to the full. It would be a taste of perfection to take with him to the chaos of war.

In his youth and simplicity, he was unaware of how his guilty secret might bring with it its own insidious poison and unaware too of the undercurrents of resentment that Ursula's presence brought to Matthew's world. With the knowledge of his own duplicity came the thought of the long hours Matthew and Ursula would be spending together. Matthew resented her now, but how long would that last? And if it were to change, what then? George ground his teeth as his own thoughts tormented him. He found that he had quickened his pace with the riot of his own imaginings and was almost out of breath. He paused a moment. He wondered too about his letter to his grandmother. The post was notoriously unreliable, particularly if it ran into areas where military activity was taking place. It could be months before it reached its destination, but what would she do then? What could she do? Two women travelling through the war zones would be very vulnerable unless they moved as a large escorted party and that would further delay their return. By that time, he might be away and already involved in the fighting.

He forced his thoughts back to the evening he had just spent to savour again its contentment. He wiped the sweat from his eyes and in so doing caught a suggestion of the musky scent of Ursula on his hands. He buried his face in them to recapture the memory of their intimacy. There was no point in worrying about the future, he thought. He must make the most of the few weeks he had left and live the time for the moment. Let the morrow take care of itself.

When George reached home and stole upstairs Manuel was waiting for him with warm water for a bath, and relieved him of his clothes to be cleaned of the mud from the bayou. Manuel also told him that his father had returned. Soon he was ready for bed, exhausted after the eventful day he had just spent. On the mantelpiece was the letter from the military, like a spectre at the feast, reminding him of how transient his present joys were. He had much to think about before sleep claimed him.

The next morning when he went down for breakfast his parents were unusually both at the table. His father was full of concern at his now inevitable departure, for the news was all about the household. His mother seemed largely indifferent, being more concerned about the poor quality of maids she had seen as replacements for Ursula. George had barely two weeks before he would be joining the next draft going for further training before they joined in the fighting. George had already told Samuel who had promised to do all he could to ensure that arrangements for Ursula's departure was within that timeframe, but he was realistically doubtful.

George was determined to spend as much time as he could down in the bayou. It would be a time for all three to remember, to sustain them for the separation that lay ahead for them all. The next day George let it be known that he would be away for the whole day and made his way down to the bayou, full of anticipation.

12

Mary Fights Her Corner

Mary, in New York, now spent a considerable amount of time with her father. He seemed genuinely to enjoy her company and increasingly valued her thoughts and judgement about the future of Nethergate. She understood like no other the undercurrents of interests that dictated life at Nethergate, from the aspirations of Amelia Styles to the malign influence of Silas Killcaid over Anthony, whilst also never denying the overseer's value to the smooth running of the estate. She felt that for the first time she was really being appreciated by her father and a growing mutual respect enhanced their new relationship. With their increasing intimacy and trust she felt able at last to let him know of the existence of Matthew. With some trepidation she broached the real purpose of her visit to see her father in New York.

"Father," she said, "what would you say if I said that I think you might have another great-grandson apart from George?"

"What do you mean?" he asked in surprise.

"Mark had a child outside wedlock before he died. In private I have acknowledged the child as my grandson, but in public I cannot do so."

"Why's that? Who is the mother?" he inquired with growing curiosity.

"The mother was a slave, so her child by law is a slave also."

Henry gave a snort of dismissive laughter. "No doubt she tried to seduce him to improve her lot. Don't think I don't know how such people behave, not that I blame her for all that. But I have no intention of acknowledging a slave bastard as any offspring of mine. I would become a laughing stock."

"It wasn't a bit like that," Mary replied with sudden asperity. "Though Mark was my son I can never condone what he did to that slave girl. It was never with her consent. He beat her brutally so much so that she was unable to work for nigh on a month after."

He shook his head at that. "Even so, boys will be boys. I don't see why you are telling me all this."

Mary remained silent. She had half hoped that he might take a different line, particularly since the Federal States were now at war with the Confederates, partly over the very issue of slavery. She was tempted to let him know the identity of the mother for she knew what a high regard he had already formed for Ruth. That, however, was out of the question for it would reveal that Ruth was nothing more than a mere slave.

That evening when the two Southern ladies met prior to going down to dinner she related her conversation with her father. Ruth was silent for a while and Mary feared she was upset by his reaction.

"I don't blame him," she said at last, then lapsing for a moment into the argot of the slave. "It will be many years before us folks is looked upon as anything different. Even if the Yankees wins this war and we all gets our freedom, Lord knows how some will survive. Who will look out for them when they gets old, if they got no master? Lord knows too how some will survive if all their masters need do is to pay them wages. Where will they live? How will they have enough money to buy food when they can't work no more? They will simply be thrown out to fare as best they might, jus' like white trash do now. If 'tis done in a rush, there's many as will perish or starve. It all needs to be done gradual like, but that will never be once the war fever sets in. It'll be like buffaloes stampeding over a cliff."

Mary could only nod in agreement. But Ruth had not finished.

"You know," she said, "I often look at your father and think that I see some of Matthew there." She paused. Then, after a moment's reflection, she asked, "Could you do something for me?"

"Of course," replied Mary. Ruth then left and returned a moment or so later with a drawing. Almost shyly she showed it to Mary. Ruth had always had a gift at drawing, much encouraged by Mary. She had drawn a portrait of Matthew dressed not as a slave but as a gentleman casually at his ease. In the background was the outline of Nethergate House and the suggestion of the parkland beyond. It was a remarkable drawing and immediately Mary was aware of the striking likeness to Henry Bragg in the stance and posture of the subject. Ruth had caught Matthew's features in a reflective mood, but there was nevertheless just a hint of his great grandfather's resolve and determination in the set of his shoulders and the angle of his chin. It was a truly masterly portrait.

Mary could only cry out in admiration as she continued to study Ruth's work. "Oh, Ruth, when did you do that?" she asked.

"Shortly before we left," she said. "I wanted to have something to remind me of him whilst we were away, but I couldn't draw him as a slave in case others should see it and guess my true status. I hope you don't mind."

"Of course I don't. It's how I see him anyway. "She considered the portrait further. "There is truly so much of my father in the likeness you have drawn," she said at last. Then a sudden thought occurred to her. "May I show it to him?"

"I thought of this drawing as soon as I met your father," said Ruth. "But do you think it wise to let him see it?"

"Of course I do," said Mary emphatically.

"But you must not let him know that he is mine. I have formed a great regard for your father whilst we have been here. There is far more to him than the face he chooses to show the world. I see it in the gentleness and concern he shows for your mother in her afflictions and in the affection he clearly has for you."

"I know," agreed Mary, "but whatever else he is, he is at heart an obstinate old man. Once he has stated an opinion, he would see it as a weakness to adopt another. You never know with my father, but I doubt that he will change his view."

But Mary was wrong. When the next occasion arose, she showed her father the portrait of his great grandson without saying who it was. He was immediately arrested by the quality of the drawing. Then as he looked closer, he recognised in the features the echo of his own. For a while he studied it. Then slowly he looked up at Mary, a mistiness in his eye. "Is this he?" he asked. "The boy of whom you spoke?"

Mary nodded.

"Who is the artist? He has an uncommon skill."

"It was drawn by the boy's mother," she replied.

For a long time, he studied the portrait, saying nothing.

"May I…" he began. "May I keep it for a little while? She has a great talent, this mother of his. Remarkable," he muttered, almost to himself. "Quite, quite remarkable."

The day after Mary had given her father the drawing of Matthew, he again invited her to join him in his study. He asked her to sit down with unusual diffidence. Clearly there was something on his mind.

As usual he came straight to the point. "Mary, my dearest, I am not altogether sure of what your plans are, but it is clear from our conversations that you do not now wield much influence in the happenings back at Nethergate. Poor Anthony is so much under the influence of Killcaid and of Amelia that anything you wish for or any advice you might care to offer will fall on deaf ears. I must confess that in our talks I have been impressed – no, more than impressed – by your knowledge and understanding of what goes on at Nethergate. For one of your gender you have an uncommon grasp of such matters."

Mary forbore to comment at this dismissive reference to her being a mere woman, for she was anxious to hear what was on his mind. Her father, she knew, was typical of his generation who considered that ladies were creatures only of the hearth and bedchamber. "Anthony would have been wise to have taken heed of your counsel," he continued, "but clearly that was not to be. Now I have a proposal for you to consider. General McClellan is marshalling an army such as would be the envy of any European country, the best equipped and trained, the largest army in the history of mankind. Even that wily old fox, Lee, won't be able to withstand a force of such magnitude. I expect the war will be over in a matter of a few months. Why don't you and Ruth both stay here until the war is over and whilst you are here you and I can talk over what is best for Nethergate? A Northern victory will spell the end of slavery and there is no way that Nethergate can continue just as a tobacco plantation without slaves to do the work. It must diversify to survive as a going concern into areas where machines can replace the work done by the nigger. I have bailed it out for long enough. What I want now is someone I can trust to take the estate beyond the end of the war. I don't believe Anthony can do it. I want you to be in control. I will allow you to hold the purse strings. That way Killcaid, Anthony and his wife will have no choice but to dance to your tune. You would be in all but name the Master of Nethergate. What do you think?"

The whole concept of what her father had just revealed to her, appealed enormously. It had grieved her greatly to see the estate failing before her eyes. The ideas that Adrian had, although he would share them with her only in passing because it was not a womanly matter, had long since been forgotten by his sons. The great enterprise that Nethergate had once been was in ruins and in hock to her father and the banks. Now she could put all that right. She would have the power to build it up again as her husband would have wanted. She owed it to his memory. She knew too that it would be a lifeline to Anthony who would in secret be delighted to have the responsibility for Nethergate taken away from him. To the world he would still be the Master of Nethergate, but she would call the shots. His waspish wife would be incensed, but she felt no remorse for that. She felt a flood of happiness at the thought of it all and a longing to get back and be about the business. She had so many ideas coursing through her mind – so many plans to put things right.

But her father had not finished. "There's one other thing," he said. "You wouldn't believe the change there has been in your mother since you came. She accepts your guidance with such tender trust. It's almost at times as if she is back with us again. What do you think to my suggestion that you delay your return until the war is over?"

"You wily old man", she thought. He knew that she would not be able to resist that plea, but what he proposed fell so much in accordance with her own wishes, that she could not deny him. However, on his desk, placed where she could not fail to see it, was an even more cogent reason for her to follow her father's wishes. Among the family portraits and pictures her father had placed Ruth's drawing of Matthew, now in a silver frame.

"I'll think about it, Father," she said. "It makes good sense, but I think I should talk it over with Ruth before I decide. She has a wise head upon her pretty shoulders and will also be affected."

"As you wish," he said as she left and then added, "Oh, by the way, I'm afraid you will be deprived of Colonel Gladstone's company quite soon. His exchange has been accepted for a prisoner of the Confederates. I shall miss him, I don't mind saying so. I've known him years. He's damned good company and I could listen to his playing for ever."

When Mary told Ruth of her decision to stay in New York until the war was over, Ruth was delighted. She was even more pleased to hear that the enigmatic Colonel Gladstone was returning south. He had always seemed a threat. His presence was unsettling, but she knew she would miss his musical virtuosity. In a funny way she realized, she would miss him too, for he was a constant reminder of the South, of her servitude and of the life from which she had escaped. Now that freedom was going to be extended and her heart thrilled at the prospect. But chief among her reasons to be elated was what Mary had told her of how her drawing of Matthew now occupied a place on his desk with other photographs and pictures of the family. She would regret not seeing Matthew, but she was confident that he would be secure in Nethergate House away from the malign influence of Killcaid. She was surprised that there had been no news from Nethergate, but neither Mary nor she had received any letters, but put it down to the uncertain state of communications.

13

The Train Wreckers

On a lonely stretch of railroad track some thirty miles south of Louisville, Simon Turner and a small band of twenty-five Confederate rebels lay in the long grass, on the bank overlooking the track, listening. The rail lines glinted molten silver as they ran along the embankment that took the tracks over the marshy valley bottom until they vanished into the rippling blur of a heat haze. Half-way along the valley they lay twisted upwards like mammoth tusks in what had become known as a Johnstone's necklace. It had been over an hour now since Simon, a miner by trade, had crept down to the railway lines and laid charges under the tracks. The detonation had sounded like Armageddon itself in the peaceful rural setting. Surely someone must have heard, but it was a deliberately chosen lonely stretch with no settlements or cabins. There had been no sign yet of anyone coming to investigate. The soldiers had begun to breathe again, but there was no sign either of the train. It was now over forty minutes late. Simon began to think that the explosion must have warned the occupying Yankee troops and that either no train would come or a trainload of soldiers would come in its stead with every carriage window bristling with rifles.

A lone figure down by the rail tracks suddenly detached himself from where he had been lying with his ear pressed to the railway lines, waiting for the singing of the rails that told of the approach of the locomotive. The figure waved briefly before vanishing from view.

The train was coming! A word of command and the men took up their firing positions, not knowing whether they would be faced with a lamb or a lion. It seemed an age before they could all hear the train's labouring approach. Then the sound changed as the locomotive hit the downhill gradient and gathered speed. They had sited their ambush at a bend in the track where the railroad followed the curve of the valley. If the driver was especially alert and spotted the necklace as he rounded the valley bend, he would just be able to stop in time.

The stillness of the valley was shattered by the blast from the train's whistle to clear livestock from the track. Simon had marked a stunted tree where the lines straightened out. He told himself that if the train had not started to brake when it passed that spot, then it was doomed. Suddenly the train was there rounding the bend. A billowing cloud of white smoke stuttered from its barrelled smoke stack above the single cyclops eye of its head light. It gave the impression of irrepressible, bustling energy as it gained yet more speed on the straight. Then its whistle sounded again filling the valley with its racket. It roared past the stunted tree, gaining yet more speed. Surely, they must see it by now thought Simon. Still the train raced on. At the very last minute the driver spotted the twisted rails ahead. The whistle sounded a single prolonged howl of warning. Sparks streamed from the wheels as all brakes were locked on. Then the engine hit the necklace.

The train appeared to rear up like a breaching whale. It seemed to briefly hang in the air. Then it plunged down the embankment, twisting onto its side as it fell. The front two carriages plunged pell-mell after it. The remaining carriages and wagons ploughed concertina-like into the wreckage. Some reared up vertically, some lurched sideways, some hung precariously over the embankment. The whole valley was filled with the awful roar of the continued impact and the screaming of tortured metal. It seemed as if it would never stop. At last all movement and commotion ceased.

For a moment everything seemed to be held in suspense. The crash area was obscured by dust and smoke. Slowly the breeze brushed the dust away to reveal the engine, a stricken leviathan, the steam still wheezing and hissing from its belly as its vital organs closed down. The first two carriages were nothing but splintered wreckage; the remainder were scattered at random like a child's abandoned toys. Some were already on fire.

A stunned silence seemed to settle over the scene as if nature itself was holding its breath. Even the watching rebels were awed at the mayhem they had caused. Then from the area of the crash came a low subdued moaning as bodies reacted to shock and pain.

Simon snapped out of the paralysis caused by the carnage before them. "Open fire!" he roared. For a moment or so the crackle of rifle fire drowned out all other sounds. There was no response. Then, almost as if ashamed of what they were doing, his men gradually ceased firing into that cauldron of misery. "Cease firing," said Simon into the void.

Simon led the raiding party down to the rear wagon, where all the mail was kept. They were to look for official and military mail and any money that could be looted and then return to base. They would have achieved their mission to have disrupted Yankee rail traffic.

There were only six soldiers in the rear wagon, but none of them was going to put up a fight. Only one was still conscious and he was badly hurt. The soldiers took their weapons and slit open the mail bags before coming across the official mail. This was taken, but there was nothing of obvious value to loot and the soldiers were soon done. They were anxious now to leave the scene of their little military triumph, for now the air was full of the sounds of the injured, the cries of those searching for loved ones and the desperate screams of those still trapped in burning carriages.

Simon rallied his men and they prepared to leave their scene of slaughter. As they passed one of the carriages, they saw a young woman trapped by her legs, trying desperately to reach her child, who was dangling by one arm from what had once been the side of the carriage. It was obviously dead. They freed the woman and reunited her with her dead child. The men looked almost accusingly at Simon as if they blamed him for all the suffering they had caused. A bare few months ago most had been on their farms and homesteads living ordinary lives with their loved ones. Deeds such as this would have been unimaginable. Every man there wanted now to do nothing so much as to escape from the slaughter they had created.

"Come on!" said Simon gruffly. "Let's get the hell out of here." His men followed. Around the track, frightened groups of passengers were gathering, some trying to rescue their baggage, others attending to the injured, but most standing mute, pale and shocked. As the raiders left, a voice cried out. "Bastards! Fucking cowardly, Rebel bastards." Then a man stepped forwards holding a pistol. A shot rang out.

One man turned about instinctively, ready to return the fire.

"Hold your fire!" shouted Simon. "They've suffered enough." Soon they had rejoined their fellows up on the bank and returned to where they had left their horses. They rode off to rejoin their unit, conscious of a military duty well executed. But none of those who had witnessed the havoc they had created could quite bring themselves to feel the satisfaction that should have gone with it.

Back at the train the fire had now caught hold in the mail van. Much of the mail from the split-open bags lay scattered on the rail track. Amongst them was a letter addressed to "Mrs Mary Styles". A current of air created by the fiercely burning carriage caught at its edges and lifted it briefly. Then the full force of the draft took hold and it danced and gambolled almost joyfully towards the flames.

14

New York

Still blissfully unaware of how events were unfolding back at Nethergate, Ruth and Mary were falling into the routine of Henry Bragg's household. In their different ways both women were enjoying the experience. For Mary, although she missed the broad green sweep of the parklands about Nethergate House, it was a holiday from the restrictions of living a life that was a violation of her conscience. She delighted also in the way in which Ruth had blossomed in response to now being a free member of their society, albeit that her flowering might be but the glory of a one-day lily.

For Ruth of course, it was a taste of what she had missed by being born to servitude. The only clouds on her horizon were the sinister presence of Colonel Gladstone, but he would now soon be gone, and also the thought that was always at the back of her mind, that she must eventually return once again to the life of a slave. But even here she could never be totally free, for in New York, if something were to happen to Mary, she would become a piece of property again to be returned to her owner or sold off as no longer required. Sometimes she wondered whether she really would go back when the time came, but then she thought of her son and knew the answer. Such feelings however she kept to herself.

Inevitably, it was the war that seemed to monopolise everyone's attention, always forming the main topic of conversations about the dinner table. Mary had noticed how much more personal talk of the war had become. Raw emotions were apt to spill over, particularly from those who had friends or relations who had been lost to bullet or bomb. There was a rawness about their talk. For the first time, Mary felt the bitterness and hatred that some in the North bore towards their fellow countrymen in the South. Their great nation had endured so much to cast off their servitude to the British crown. Now it was placed in jeopardy by the loss of the lucrative southern trade. Secession was an act of treason and treachery, a stab in the back, an act which had torn their fledgling nation apart and was hard to forgive or forget.

There was a change too in the attitude to the Negro in the struggle. Although the war ostensibly involved the whole issue of slavery, there was as much hidden prejudice against the Negro becoming an equal member of the society of the North as there was open acceptance of their inferiority in the South. With the mounting casualty lists of native-born white Americans, there was a burgeoning awareness of the immense price in blood that was being paid. There was also a growing conviction that the war could only end by the total defeat of one side or the other.

As James Fletcher, one of Henry's fellow manufacturers, put it, "A nigger can stop a bullet good as any white boy can. Don't see why we has to shed white blood alone in this war. Arm the nigger is what I say. Let black blood flow as well as white. Let there be black battalions fighting alongside true American battalions."

As if the Negro was not just as true an American as the native white man, thought Ruth, but said nothing.

People expected Mary and Ruth to defend the institution of

slavery. At times, to retain her creditability, Ruth found herself arguing for the very institutions which had caged her. She even half believed some of the things she was saying, for many of the slave community would truly be hard pressed to survive if given their freedom. But whose fault was this when they were simply the products of a lifetime of being treated as no more intelligent than oxen, fed, housed and watered simply for the worth of their labour?

Almost by the same token there was a general feeling that the North was not best served by its own soldiers. Those from the South were born and bred to saddle and rifle and were taking their toll on those bred to factory and lathe. There was criticism too of the Northern generals, many of whom were political appointees, lacking any military experience, and making up for their lack of martial merit with military fluff and flummery.

Attitudes everywhere were hardening. Rapprochement was a thing of the past. The talk now was of defeat and punishment. There were even rumours that Abraham Lincoln might soon come out with a decree to outlaw slavery in the whole of the sub-continent.

"If they do that," Ruth remembered saying when pressed for the Southern viewpoint, "there will be no turning back, no hope of a negotiated peace, for the whole way of life of the South is based upon the economic necessity of there being a slave culture, whatsoever the moral objection." But many about the table saw no alternative. The South was a cancer that had to be excised, a rebellion that had to be crushed.

They were now, of course, much better informed of the progress of the war from the Yankee outlook than ever they had been at Nethergate. The high hopes in the spring of 1862 that General McClellan would take Richmond and the war would be over in a matter of weeks had begun to fade as the summer months advanced. Some, like Henry Bragg, who had once met General McClellan, still held faith in the Northern generals. There was a real anxiety now that the Confederate Army might take Washington instead and outflank the Federal force entirely. No-one was sure exactly where General Lee and his Confederate Army were in the east, or what surprises Lee might yet pull out of the bag. In Kentucky the Union Forces under General Halleck were almost in complete control but spread out now in relatively small pockets of occupation after their earlier successes. There were no further advances made on that front since all Halleck's reinforcements had been siphoned off to support McClellan, who was to deliver the decisive blow. But, despite Lincoln's champing at the bit, McClellan never moved whilst his great monolith of an army marched, counter-marched and paraded in pomp and splendour. It bled the rest of the Northern armies of recruits, but never actually went to war.

In addition, recruiting for new volunteers for the Federal Army had slowed to a trickle in anticipation of an early victory, but now there was a panic over recruitment. Escaped slaves, quaintly termed "contraband", were being encouraged to enrol not only as general labourers, but some to bear arms as well. There was now a regiment formed entirely of slaves. But under all this ran the shared fear from both sides of the consequences of training the ex-slave to bear arms.

Mary, and to a lesser extent Ruth, had little doubt as to how it would all end, for in New York they had seen evidence of the stirring of the industrial muscle of the Northern states. They had taken a trip once to see the harbour crammed with shipping destined to resupply McClellan's mighty army. The veritable forest of masts contrasted with the wide expanses of empty waters to be seen in the harbours of the South, now beginning to feel the full force of the North's naval blockade.

It seemed impossible that the South could survive for many more months and Mary and Ruth had settled down in the comfort of Mary's father's substantial residence to sit the war out in ease and security, confident that they would not have long to wait. Their easy complacency was however shattered by the belated arrival of George's long-overdue letter, bearing the scorch marks and mud of its adventurous journey. Both women were immediately thrown into a flurry of anxiety as to what might now have happened in the interim, particularly to Matthew. All thoughts that Ruth may have had of staying to enjoy her freedom were overwhelmed by her maternal instincts to do what she could for her son. Mary was no less concerned. There was no question now. They must return as soon as possible.

15

Returning South

Mary Styles's first action on receiving George's letter was to show it to her father. She had thought that he would regard the urgency of her desire to return as a little unnecessary. After all, her main worry was the welfare of a slave connected with her family in a manner that would hardly bear close scrutiny. She was however surprised by his apparent concern on receiving her news. He had glanced across his study at the mention of Matthew's name to where his portrait rested.

Her father questioned her closely about the conditions in the swamplands where Matthew would now be fighting to survive. He seemed relieved that there were parcels of high ground well clear of the swamps where a man might exist in relative ease with sufficient shelter from the elements. He saw at once that arrangements would have to be made for their travel overland, but this would inevitably take time, for passes and travel documents would have to be arranged to allow them safe passage through the warring states.

"Leave it to me, my dear," he said." Your mother and I will be more sad than I can possibly say to see you go, just when we seem to have got to know you once again. And too your delightful companion, who seems to have blossomed during her stay with us. I know that Colonel Gladstone will regret her departure." That last remark of her father's puzzled Mary when she thought about it later, but her main concern now was to hasten their return.

Mary was confident that her father, with his connections, would speed up the process. She left him in a thoughtful mood. In these last few weeks he had become as much friend as father, as her mother paradoxically had become more like a child to her. She was full of sadness at their imminent parting. Yet part of her was looking forward already to returning to Nethergate. George's letter had made her realise where she really belonged. It was a timely reminder. There was something not quite real about her stay in her father's house, with her parent's roles so changed and Ruth now grown into another person, both friend and social equal.

She had noticed of late how her father had taken to questioning her ever closer about Nethergate and its operation, as if testing her out. She noted that he listened to what she said with a new respect. They discussed ideas for how the estate might be run once the war was over. Clearly, he meant to have more of a say in the management, in recognition of the stake he now held in the enterprise. She noticed with an inner smile how often now he would repeat back to her some of her own plans and ideas as though they were his own. Secretly she was elated, for clearly he now valued her judgement in matters which hitherto he had considered to be a male preserve. She knew how hard it was for her father to change his point of view.

Mary knew more about the running of Nethergate than ever he or even her late husband had ever imagined. She had always kept herself informed when Adrian was the Master, mainly because he was so dismissive of her ability to understand such matters. It was almost as if he suspected her of some secret deceit, whilst all she had wanted to do was to surprise him with some useful and incisive comment to see the look of appreciation and amazement on his face. But she had never had the chance to do so with Adrian and Mark was far too headstrong ever to listen to her. As for Anthony, he was too much under the influence of Silas Killcaid to pay heed to her advice. Then there was the hostility of Amelia who would see every suggestion as a ploy to undermine her husband. On this visit she had clearly impressed her father and the thought of how they might expand and broaden the activities on the estate once the war was over had begun to excite her with a real sense of anticipation.

With the certainty of her father's backing she was confident that she could override Silas Killcaid's influence and perhaps even circumvent the torrent of objections that were sure to pour forth from Amelia. She had also started to consider how things might be run without slave labour. She was certain now that the war would not be won by the South against the industrial might she had seen gathering in the North. They would have to abandon their preoccupation with the production of one crop and widen the range of produce from tobacco to other crops that could more suitably be cultivated by such agricultural machinery of the kind her father manufactured. The prospect of all this change with so many thoughts and ideas flying around inside her head excited her. For the first time, she felt the stirrings of the passion which had driven her father over the years. This realisation made her feel yet closer to him.

Mary was full of anxiety about how Ruth would take their change of plans and the alarming news in George's letter concerning her son. Ruth had been so clearly delighted at the prospect of remaining a free woman in the North until the cessation of hostilities. News had also come through of Lincoln's address to Congress and his Emancipation Proclamation, freeing all slaves in Confederate territories occupied by Union forces. Ruth was a free woman now. If she went back with Mary she would be returning to the life of a slave, for the Proclamation explicitly did not apply to Kentucky, which, nominally a neutral state, still retained the right to own slaves. It was a lot to expect of Ruth after enjoying these heady months of freedom. Mary saw at once the necessity for her return to Nethergate, but for Ruth the decision would be immensely more difficult. She gave Ruth George's letter to read without comment as to her decision to return. Ruth read it through twice, then looked up.

"I shall be going back home," Mary said. "I cannot expect you to come back with me and I will fully understand if you decide to stay a free woman in Yankee territory."

Ruth did not hesitate in her reply. "No, Mary," she said, "My duty is to my son. I shall be coming back with you."

The two women embraced. Mary had no words to say, knowing the sacrifice that Ruth was making after tasting the tantalising fruits of freedom. Instead, she spoke of the conversations she had had with her father and told her of the plans she had. She told her of her belief that once the war was over there would be an end to slavery in all the South. It could only be a matter of time.

Ruth was thoughtful. Although her response had been instinctive, the prospect of returning once more to the life of a slave had filled her not merely with dread but with a burning anger at the injustice of her position. She had discovered in herself a new confidence as a new person in a new world. It was a world where she was judged for who she was, a world where she was respected and valued for the quality of her thoughts and what she did, a world where she had a right to be truly herself and a right to her opinions. Above all it was a world where she had a right to choose what should happen to her own body. The temptation to remain had been almost overwhelming. The humiliation of becoming once again no more than a piece of property was an abomination, yet her desire to ensure the safety of Matthew overrode all other considerations. She could not help but wonder at what her mistress was saying about the future after the war was over, when all slaves would be free. What would her position be then? She felt entitled now to ask.

"Mary," she said, "you once promised me my freedom. How would I stand if things fall as you suggest? What would I become to you then? And what would become of me if between then and now some accident befell you? Would I just become a piece of property to be disposed of as your heir thought fit? Amelia has no fondness for me, and I can see her being only too pleased to have the chance of humiliating me, or even disposing of me entirely."

In truth Mary had been mulling these thoughts over in her mind too. She had always valued the friendship and companionship of Ruth as her maid. During the last few months she had come to appreciate her even more. Ruth had grown into her new role, not now as a slave, nor even a lady's maid, but now as a true friend and an equal. In Ruth she had a friend like no other, in whom she could truly place her trust. She could not see things returning to how they had been before they left Nethergate but how these changes might be made she could not quite foresee. But as far as Ruth was concerned she had no such doubts.

"Ruth dear," she said, taking her arm, "truly I don't see how things will be in the future, certainly not for all the hands on Nethergate. As to what would happen should I meet some accident, I shall make it plain that in that event it is my wish that you be given your freedom. The difficulty, as you know, is that your ownership lies legally in the hands of the Master of Nethergate. I valued you greatly as my maid, but now I have grown to treasure you even more as a companion and friend. I would like you to stay on at Nethergate. In what capacity, though, is up to you. I would welcome you in the role you have now, as my companion. It has been lonely since Adrian died and I have found your company in your present capacity more than pleasing. That is how I would wish things to be once this war is over, if that be your wish too."

"Oh yes," cried Ruth, tears springing to her eyes, "and I too. I too," and the two women embraced. Ruth, though, was tormented by the culpability that lay deep in her heart over the death of Mark and wondered how she could ever assuage her guilt or repay the kindness of her mistress.

"Quite how we manage things once we return to Nethergate," continued Mary, unaware of the remorse that consumed her maid, "I have not yet considered. We'll just have to let that complication lie for the moment." But there was one further difficulty that neither had foreseen and that was in the sinister and enigmatic figure of Colonel Gladstone.

16

Complications

A day or so later Mary and Ruth were both in the garden of her father's house, enjoying the cool of the summer evening. It was a favoured spot for Mary's mother. Henry had spared no cost in keeping it neat and full of colour so that she could enjoy it the more. This evening Mary and Ruth had the garden to themselves and were relishing it to the full, enhanced by the knowledge of their imminent departure. Ruth had drawn a picture of Mary's parents. She had captured precisely the look of devotion and love in Henry's features and the tender trusting confusion in those of his wife. She was now completing the setting of the picture in the garden in which they now sat when a maid appeared and bobbed to Mary.

"Beg pardon, ma'am. Your father says he wishes to see you, soon as you can." Another of my father's abrupt summonses, thought Mary as she left Ruth finishing off her drawing.

When Mary entered, her father rose to greet her.

"Mary, my dear," he began without preamble, "I have had to change the plans for your return home. The complications of getting you back to Nethergate overland are likely to be protracted. I have arranged instead that you and Ruth return by sea."

"But the Union blockade?" she queried. "Surely no ships are allowed through."

"I have interests," he explained, with she thought, a touch of guilt, "in a private sail-assisted paddle steamer called *The Lucy May*. She is due to sail on the noon tide tomorrow, bound for Nassau in the Bahamas, where her cargo will be transhipped to smaller, lighter and faster steamboats that will run through the blockade. Believe me, the Union Navy has nothing to touch them for speed and manoeuvrability. The danger is minimal. And I am sending back Colonel Gladstone to be your mentor and your escort. His parole has come through and he is to return to the South, but no longer as a future combatant – much to his regret. He has agreed nevertheless to monitor certain transactions on my behalf."

Mary was not deceived for a moment. She knew precisely what her father was doing. Not content with providing equipment for the Union armies, he was supplying equipment for the Confederates as well. She wondered how he squared all this with his strong religious beliefs, but she had no doubt that he would – in some way.

Mary's face must have betrayed her thoughts, for her father sought to justify himself.

"It's not entirely what you think, my dear," he explained. "There's some profit in it for me I own, but it is working towards a higher purpose, I promise you."

Clearly that was all he intended to say on the matter, but she was certain that the call of Mammon had a stronger resonance for her father than any other cause. All the same, the imminence of her departure was a shock, but she was glad that at least they would have the steadying hand of Colonel Gladstone to guide and protect them on their homeward journey. Whatever else he might be, he would be a competent mentor and guide and above all he was a true gentleman and man of honour in whom they could rest their trust.

As Mary was turning to go, her father rose from his desk and came round to where she was standing. There was a look of earnest sincerity in his eyes.

"Mary, dear," he said, gently grasping her shoulder and turning her to face him. "I cannot tell you what it has meant to me to have you under my roof once again. I don't think I have been a good father to you and certainly not to poor dear Caroline. I think I drove her away from her home here. And I never had the chance to let her know how much she really meant to me. I think she died thinking that I never cared for her. No – no. Don't deny it," he added as Mary shook her head in disagreement. "My mind perhaps has always been too occupied with other things. But I have enjoyed having you close to me. Your mother I know has grown to depend upon you, as once we all depended upon her. I have come to value your judgement as well. I wish I had made that assessment earlier. It might have saved a lot of heartache. This war can't last much longer. Once it is over, things will be a lot different, I promise you. As you well know, I mean to have a much greater say in the running of the Nethergate Estate. Damn it, I darned nearly own it now. And I will trust you as no other to be my eyes and ears on the ground and in every way to act for me. I shall give you letters of intent to give to Anthony and to the estate's lawyers."

At these words, Mary immediately saw the troubled waters ahead, not so much with Anthony as with Killcaid and Amelia. But in her own way she loved Nethergate. It was where her married life had begun, in the old Nethergate House, before the grander creation of Nethergate Hall. She loved the broad leafy acres and the hum and hubbub of life in the slave lines and the wisdom and mystique of Morella. She felt a sudden longing to be back where she belonged.

But her father had not finished. "I am going to entrust you with a very large sum of money in good old Yankee dollars. That's why I have persuaded Colonel Gladstone to accompany you on your journey south. I want you to use the money as you see fit for the benefit of the estate on the lines we have discussed and as you think necessary to put things right with Matthew." He turned to look again at the drawing Ruth had made and muttered almost to himself. "I wish I could meet him. He looks a fine young man."

Immediately upon her father's words a sudden hope had leapt into her mind. "You mean, I could also use it to purchase the freedom of Matthew?"

"Anything you see fit," her father repeated.

"And of his mother?" He nodded and there was a knowing twinkle in his eye, as if they both shared an unspoken secret. Had he guessed the identity of Matthew's mother, she wondered? But he said no more.

When she left her father, she immediately hastened back to tell Ruth the news. Ruth's natural concern over their imminent departure was lightened by the prospect that both she and Matthew might truly be released from bondage when Mary returned to Nethergate. Mary knew that with the threat of losing her father's further financial support for the estate, Anthony would quickly come to heel. He would have no option but to release both Mary and Matthew from bondage. Now at last Mary had the means of fulfilling the promise she had made to Ruth all those years ago.

Ruth however had news for Mary of almost equal significance. When Mary had left the garden to go to her father, Ruth had been joined by Colonel Gladstone who had something to say which was to change everything.

17

The Confession of Colonel Gladstone

When Mary had been summoned to her father, Ruth had lingered on in the garden completing her drawing of Mary's parents in this same tranquil setting. She would have liked to stay here for good where she had discovered so much about herself, yet she could not divorce herself from the love of her child, which now dragged her back into servitude in Kentucky. She had changed, and she knew it. The change was permanent. She even thought differently. Now for the first time in her life her thoughts were truly her own and not in part owned by someone else. So engrossed was she in her drawing that it was some time before she realised that she was not alone.

Slowly she became aware of a shadow cast by the sinking sun. She looked up to see Colonel Gladstone standing some way off. Her spirits sank. He was the one person whom she feared. It was almost, she felt, as if he could read her thoughts. Whenever he was present, she was constantly aware of his vigilance even when she was engaged in conversation and laughter with others. He was always a reminder that she lived a lie.

He bowed slightly when she looked up. "Forgive me, ma'am," he said in his familiar southern drawl. "Ah did not mean to disturb you. In truth I was just enjoying the peace and the beauty of this place, as I see you were too. May I?" he asked, drawing closer and indicating the space on the seat beside her.

"But of course, Colonel," she said, moving up to make room whilst every nerve was alive with caution and alert to whatever trap he might lay before her.

"You know, ma'am, in all the weeks Ah have had the honour of knowing you I have never managed to see you alone."

That came as no surprise. She had always engineered matters so that they were indeed never left alone. Now she felt trapped. There was no escaping. She wondered what would come next. Had he somehow seen through her guise? What would he do about it? Her mouth was dry. She didn't answer. But what he said next took her completely off her guard.

"Ruth… may I call you Ruth?" She nodded mutely. "Ah have been watching you these past weeks and what I have seen has intrigued me, fascinated me even." She waited for him to continue. "You must have realised how I feel about you. You are the most…" Here he paused, searching for words. "The most exciting and perplexing woman I have ever met."

She could not believe what she was hearing. She turned to face him, convinced that he was still trying to entrap her. But she read in his blue eyes only utter sincerity. Slowly the truth dawned. He had not been seeking to trick her. His interest in her was for the most natural reason in the world. She blushed despite herself. She had never remotely considered Colonel Gladstone in that light, for her fear of him had been too acute. But now she thought about it, she wondered if the heightened awareness she had always felt whenever he came near her might not have been for reasons other than her fear of discovery. She was not sure whether this new situation might not now perhaps be more dangerous than the previous one. But all the same she had to admit that his confession excited her in a way that she had never felt before.

Her mind flew back to the billiard room all those years ago, when she was little more than a child, to the brutal humiliation she had endured at the hands of another "gentleman". And yet she had to concede that the moment was often rekindled in her dreams. The anger and degradation was still there and as powerful as ever, but sometimes it had awoken in her other longings to which she dared not put a name. She had to admit that she had been drawn to Mark. His laughing, cavalier attitude to life, his contempt for the opinions of others and yes, his cruelty had drawn and fascinated her despite Mary's warnings. Did she think she could have tamed him? Things might have been so different had he not so roughly seized what he might have won by other means. And now, she allowed, this handsome, impenetrable colonel had awakened in her once again those same dark, stirring emotions. This time she thought, with her new self-awareness, she might better be able to control the situation. The Colonel was undoubtedly a handsome man, who exercised a steely self-control over himself. Yet in his confession of his affection for her, he had deliberately exposed his own weakness. He would not have done that unless his emotions were very powerful indeed. The tables, she realised, were suddenly turned. She felt for the first time that she might have the means of controlling this man who hitherto she had so deeply feared. It excited her in a way that she did not fully understand.

"Colonel Gladstone," was all she could mutter, such was her confusion.

"You must call me Thomas," he said.

"Thomas," she said dutifully, still not fully comprehending how things had changed between them. "You must forgive me. I truly had no idea. I thought… I thought you had something against me."

"Something against you? Dear lady, nothing was further from my mind. But tell me, can I hope that you are not entirely indifferent to me?"

This was yet another of the surprises that her assumed status had sprung upon her and for which she was totally unprepared. Her relief at his explanation of his interest in her was certainly very flattering. It was however a complication which the imminence of his departure would perhaps resolve. She realised suddenly that the Colonel was expectantly waiting for a reply to his last question.

"Colonel Gladstone – Thomas. I did not realise you felt this way." She couldn't think what to say next, then the words just came out. "You see, I am not entirely a free woman."

"You mean there is someone else?" queried the Colonel. But she was saved from replying for just then Mary reappeared hurrying towards them.

Colonel Gladstone rose. "You must forgive me, Ruth. I fancy that Mary has something of some moment to tell you." He bowed slightly to Mary and to Ruth. His eyes lingered on Ruth's face as if trying to read her thoughts and then he hastened on his way.

"Ruth," said Mary. "I have some news for you."

"And I, Mary, have news for you," rejoined Ruth.

18

Secrets Revealed

After Colonel Gladstone's departure from the garden, Mary was about to share with Ruth the information about the imminence of their departure when a maid appeared. Carrying covers and cushions she asked if she could prepare the garden for Mr Bragg's evening walk with his wife. Mary suggested they retire to her room. She couldn't imagine what could possibly have happened to Ruth whilst she had been with her father and wondered what the inscrutable Colonel Gladstone had said to her.

When they had reached the privacy of her room, Mary broke the news of their earlier departure and that it was to be by sea instead of the land route. Ruth's heart froze. This wonderful interlude in her life where she had discovered her true self, was going to be suddenly curtailed. She knew it must end, but surely not now. Surely not so soon. She hardly registered what Mary continued to say. "I think my father has some business interests to pursue, the nature of which I think he would prefer me to remain in ignorance. He has arranged for Colonel Gladstone, who is returning to the Confederate side on parole, to be our escort."

At the mention of Colonel Gladstone Ruth's heart lurched and she inhaled sharply. Why now was that suddenly so important to her and why did it strangely sugar the bitter pill of their imminent departure? She had been looking forward to spending the remainder of the war discovering this fresh world of freedom. Now all that was to be torn away and she would once more sink back into the world of slavery where, despite every kindness and consideration, she could become at any moment simply a piece of property. But the thought now that Colonel Gladstone would be accompanying them on the trip back was an added complication. It would have been so much easier to say farewell upon the start of her journey to Nethergate before she had sorted out how she felt about Colonel Gladstone's sudden and so unexpected declaration. It would then be like a dream that had vanished before the dawn. Yet she could not deny the sudden surge of excitement when Mary had declared that Thomas Gladstone was to be their escort. How would he react should he ever discover that she was a slave? She realised with a sudden clarity that she did not want him ever to know. It mattered to her how he thought of her. She wanted to remain in his memory just as she was now, a free woman. But whether that was vanity or something deeper she was unable to tell.

She became aware that Mary had finished talking and was regarding her with a somewhat puzzled expression. "What is it, Ruth? I do believe you have not heard the half of what I have said." Then another possibility occurred to her. "Is it the thought of returning once more to your true situation that upsets you so? Believe me, I do understand, but there is something further I have to tell you."

"No – no, Missus," replied Ruth, at the mention of Nethergate, unconsciously reverting to the slave's form of address. "It is not the thought of going back." Then she told Mary of what Colonel Gladstone had said to her in the garden. Both women now considered in silence the implications that this news might have on their return journey.

"Do you have any feelings for him, Ruth, after all our fears?" asked Mary.

It was an unexpected question. "Truly I don't know," replied Ruth. "Of course, I find the whole idea very flattering. I had always thought that his constant attention was because somehow he suspected our secret. But when he told me how he felt and knowing of our imminent departure I saw no harm or danger in it, for soon we would be gone, and I would never see him again. But now I don't know. Certainly, it would be a comfort to have an escort, but I fear for what his reaction might be should he ever discover my true position."

"Did you give him any encouragement?" asked Mary.

"No. Quite the contrary," replied Ruth with sudden heat, her mind going back to the billiard room and comparing Mark's violent attack all those years ago with the Colonel's courteous approach. It was as if her mistress was in some way implying that Mark's ravaging assault may not have been due entirely to his unprovoked passions. "I said I was not entirely free."

Mary smiled. "That was clever," she conceded. "But I don't think it will make much difference. You will have to be careful how you handle him. Maybe let him think there is someone else, for I do feel we will have need of his protection in the days ahead. The war grows ever more bitter, and we will need all the safeguarding and support we can muster. It won't be easy."

For a moment, the thought of departure from this happy place preoccupied both women. Mary was thinking of leaving the father whom she had got to know and understand so much better over the past months and who she now knew trusted her almost as an equal. Then there was her mother, who now looked to her as trustingly as she had once depended upon her as a child. Her heart filled with tender sadness and she wondered whether her mother would even notice her absence. Ruth too was full of melancholy now that their leave-taking was so immediate. She realised how much she had felt at home with Mary's parents and how rich her life had become under their protection. Now all that was to revert once more to the narrow confines and uncertainties of life as a slave.

The thought of Mary's parents made her think of the drawing she had made of them both seated together in the garden that brought them so much peace and tranquillity. She had intended to give it to Mary as a memento of these days of happiness. "I have a drawing…" she began, then suddenly remembered that she had left it in the garden in the haste of their departure. "Forgive me," she continued, "I have a drawing I should like you to have, if it pleases you. It is of your parents in the garden they both love so much. In the haste of our departure I have left it there." She got up to leave, but Mary restrained her.

"Ruth, my dear, I haven't finished. There is one other thing I wish to tell you that I think you will find of even greater moment than our sudden departure." Ruth could not imagine what could possibly outweigh that event. Then Mary told her of her father's gift to tide Nethergate over the months until the end of the war, of her absolute control over its disbursement and that they included funds for the purchase of both Matthew's freedom and that of his mother. The fact that the funds were in the greatly more flexible greenback dollars was not lost on Ruth either. Mary continued, "Ruth, my dear, many years ago I made you a promise to right the wrongs my son did to you. To my shame, I found that I was unable to keep it at the time, but now things are different. It is my intention to release my father's funds how and when I choose to Mr Styles, but only on the condition that he grants freedom to you and to Matthew also."

The ground seemed to lurch under Ruth's feet. Suddenly all her dreams seemed to be once again within her grasp. The world she had enjoyed in the past few months like a reflection of reality could become an actuality. The delight showed in her face and for a moment Mary too basked in the radiance of her joy.

But Ruth's euphoria was short-lived, for immediately she thought of her own guilty secret about Mark's death. Her conscience would not allow her to accept this gift from her owner whilst she remained ignorant of what she had done to her son. In any case, the loyalty of the rest of the slave community about her act performed in front of them all would remain solid, but only so long as she was one of their number. Once she ceased to be a slave that loyalty would vanish.

19

Confession and Compassion

Ruth's sudden delight as Mary told her of her coming emancipation slowly faded from her face as she realised that this was the moment that she would have to tell Mary of her hand in the death of her son. Mary's smile too was replaced by a look of utter bewilderment when she saw how Ruth was reacting.

"Ruth, my dear, whatever is the matter? I thought you would be delighted."

"Oh, Missus, I am," she replied. "I am truly grateful, but I don't know that you will want to give me my freedom after you hear what I has to say."

Ruth's mind went back to that hot July afternoon among the ripening leaves in the tobacco fields. The slaves had gathered for a brief midday rest under the shade of the great chestnut oak and Mark was with the slave traders, laughing and prodding the slaves like farmers at a cattle auction. But most of all, she thought of the well-dressed trader with his dirty fingernails probing and testing the pale skin of Matthew and smelling his breath and the raucous, debauched laughter of the other traders at Mark's suggestion of how her son, his own kin, might best be used for the gratification of his new master.

She found herself sobbing as she related to her mistress that noon-time gathering and her fears for the degradation that awaited her son. Then she described how she had walked over to Mark's spirited Arab stallion. How she had placed the sharp stone under its saddle. How she had calmed it. How she had waited for Mark to mount. How all the other slaves had watched what she was doing. How too they had stood, in silent approval; co-conspirators by their silence in the punishment of their master.

"I didn't mean that he should die. I only wanted the traders to go. I thought if he was hurt, hurt bad, he would not be able to go ahead with the sale and Matthew would not be sold to that awful trader. Truly, Missus, I didn't mean that he should die. Can you ever forgive me?"

For Mary this was a shocking revelation. She still mourned her son as any mother would. In her memory he was still the little boy that romped and played with Samuel and his father on the lawns of Nethergate House in happier times. The squeals of excited childish laughter still rang in her ears. She preferred not to remember the man he became. She felt resentment that Ruth should remind her again of how cruel a Master of Nethergate he had turned out to be. Ruth's revelation came as a shock. But in her heart, she knew that Ruth had had little choice. In Ruth's shoes she would have done anything to save her son. But that didn't help. How do you forgive the person who killed your son?

Her reply when it came was cold. "You must have known that Mark would never dare sell Matthew without referring it to me." As soon as she said it, she regretted it, for Ruth's face dropped. In any event she knew that what she said was untrue, for Mark in his last months had become a law unto himself. There was nothing he might not do if the fancy took him. Ruth was now making her face this truth, but, rather than understanding Ruth's motives, it added to her resentment. She wanted Ruth to suffer for the news she had just given her as she was suffering too. She knew that she was being unreasonable but couldn't help herself and hated herself for it.

"Truly, Missus, I did not know that. He was bargaining with the trader for a higher price because of where he intended Matthew should go. This has been on my conscience ever since. I have so many times wanted to confess to you what I did, but I never could. Now I have ruined everything. All the same I am glad, for now there are no secrets between us. Even though the price for it is my very freedom and the friendship of the one person I respect most in all this world."

At these words, Mary's anger melted, to be replaced once more by the tenderness she had always felt for her maid. "No, Ruth. Mark wronged you, wronged you deeply. I am the only one left who can try to put that right and I will be true to my word. Just give me a little time to come to terms with what you have just told me. Will you leave me now?"

Ruth wondered if, after all, it would have been better that her mistress had remained ignorant of her guilt. Surely Mary could not be a friend to the killer of her son. She left Mary, feeling truly that the bottom had dropped out of her world and at the very moment when everything seemed to be coming together.

As Ruth left Mary's room, she remembered again the picture she had drawn of Mary's parents which she had intended to give her as a gift. She hoped suddenly that it might brighten her mistress's melancholy. She turned and retraced her steps to the garden, where she had left her sketch pad. When she reached the garden, she saw that Henry Bragg and his wife were already there. They both smiled a welcome, though it was an unwritten rule that this time was to be theirs alone.

"Forgive me," she said, "I left my sketch pad here." She moved to collect it, but Henry, forever anxious to play the gentleman, forestalled her.

"Allow me," he said and before she could stop him he

strode to where her drawing lay. "May I?" he asked and then he stopped as his eye fell on the drawing of himself and his wife. He stood spellbound for a moment, examining the picture in every detail. As he did so his eyes moistened as he read in the image the message of his own care and compassion for his wife, which Ruth had so deftly captured.

He shook his head in wonderment. "Remarkable. Quite remarkable," he repeated, over and over again. The very same words he had uttered when first he had seen her portrait of Matthew. He seemed reluctant to tear his eyes away from the picture before him. "You have, madam, a truly amazing talent." His eyes returned to the drawing. He seemed to be struggling with his emotions.

"Here," he said, turning to his wife, "What do you think of this, my dear?" His wife took the sketch and seemed to stare at it for an unconscionable length of time as if without recognition. Then she ran her fingers over the two faces as if by so doing she could feel the contours of their features. Her eyes were misted with tears. But in them now was a new understanding. Then she turned to him.

"I've been away so long, haven't I, so very long? Yet you have waited for me. When I'm lost, alone and frightened, I always know that in the end you will find me, and I'll be safe again. I don't say much, I know, but I am always comforted when you are with me." She opened her arms and the two embraced. Both were trembling with emotion. Ruth looked away, not knowing if she should steal quietly from the scene. There was something enormously compelling about seeing a man such as Henry Bragg, so much the master of his world, yet humbled and weakened by the very strength of his devotion to his wife and not afraid to show it. Ruth felt honoured to be a witness to such devotion.

Henry and Rebecca broke from their embrace. One glance at Mrs Bragg and the empty, bland expression in her eyes and the vacuous smile was enough to show that she who had so briefly returned was once again a prisoner in that shadowy world in which she lived out her days. Only the damp about her eyes betrayed that for a moment she had returned. Henry tenderly brushed the tears away with gentle fingers. He was wrestling with emotion, which he made no attempt to hide. "Ruth, my dear, I cannot tell you what it means for me to know that my beloved Rebecca is still there, that somewhere she is still a part of my life, that she knows I still care for her. Sometimes, like this, she comes fleetingly back to me and then is cruelly gone again. It happens less and less. It was your picture that brought her back." Then he looked up at Ruth. "Would you do me the honour of allowing me to keep this drawing?"

She hesitated. She could easily do another for her mistress. "But of course," she said.

Almost reverently he detached the drawing from the pad. As he returned her sketch pad, their eyes met, and she read in his a sudden warmth and understanding. "You see," he said slowly, "I have another drawing which I greatly treasure too, for I know both are by the same hand."

20

Journey Home

The journey home for Ruth and Mary Styles was to be full of incident and far more of an adventure than any had bargained for. Colonel Gladstone was full of purpose and practical advice and had already assumed his role as leader of their small expedition. There seemed little enough time to pack their things together. Mr Braggs had arranged for the bulk of their baggage to be sent on after them but warned of considerable delays.

Then it was time to say goodbye. All the family and household were lined up in the hall to bid them "bon voyage". There was no time for sentiment, but clearly there was a new understanding between Mary and her father. Her mother was there too, smiling sweetly, as she always did, but without understanding. Ruth's maid was there as well, smiling and bobbing as she passed and wearing the bracelet Ruth had given her. "If only you knew," thought Ruth, and she returned the warmth of her smile.

Ruth had related her conversation with Mary's father and his realisation that he had guessed who she was, but that it seemed to have made no difference to him. Quite the contrary, he now treated Ruth as truly one of the family. Mary too had put

Ruth's mind at rest over the death of her son. She had drawn Ruth aside before they left. Placing a hand on Ruth's arm, she had said, "Ruth, my dear, I have not changed my mind about what I intend to do once we are back home. What you said was a shock, but God knows I cannot blame you for protecting your child and my grandson in the way you did. It was very brave of you. Had you not done so I would not have been able to watch my grandson become the fine young man I believe him to be. When I get back, I will have the power to make both of you free and you can both begin a new life."

"Oh, thank you, thank you," was all Ruth could say, her heart was so full.

"In truth, it wasn't the Mark you knew I have been mourning over the years. It was the little boy I once held in my arms and he had ceased to exist long before Mark became Master. Mark chose his course," she said, "but you had no option. What you did saved my grandson who would have been lost to me and lost in a particularly distressing way."

Henry Bragg accompanied them as far as the quayside at New York harbour and embraced Mary and Ruth with equal regret at their final departure. Then both women and their maids negotiated the host of gangplanks that led to their ship. Mary's maid carried the bag containing the money Henry had placed in his daughter's care and stowed it in her mistress's cabin.

Both women had been impressed by the forest of masts lifting and falling on the gentle swell in the harbour, a sobering reminder of the muscular might the Union had mustered to its cause.

The Lucy May was not as big a vessel as some in the trade, but sleek-looking, purposeful and clearly built for speed. Her boilers were already steaming up. The top of her funnel was shrouded and distorted by the heat and smoke coming from her engine room. There was an acrid stench of burning coal that both women could taste in their mouths. Everywhere there was movement and bustle. The cries of labour gangs as they scurried about loading and unloading cargo, and the swinging derricks lifting and lowering along the quayside, gave the appearance of a freshly disturbed anthill. But with all the apparent chaos there breathed a grim underlying sense of purpose.

Colonel Gladstone was already aboard and was there to greet them. The two women shared a cramped cabin. *The Lucy May* was clearly not built for luxury travel. The cries of the seamen and the thud of discarded lines spoke of activity. The two women hastened on deck to witness their departure. The rhythmic thump of the engines of which they had been aware, like a muffled heartbeat, suddenly increased in tempo. The ship shuddered like a living thing. There was a rush as her paddles churned the water at her sides into two boiling mill races. They broke free of the surrounding ships, agitated now by their movement. The tempo of the engines abated as *The Lucy May* eased her way out of New York harbour. The two women continued waving to those on the quayside until they were no longer visible.

Standing at the taffrail Mary and Ruth watched the slowly receding shoreline. Mary was sad at the thought of leaving again the security of her father's home and already missed the presence of her parents. For Ruth it was farewell to a dream world in which she had for a short while become alive as a different person. It was almost like a bereavement. The future was uncertain. Deep in their own thoughts, both women watched the retreating skyline of New York slowly spreading out before them and marvelled at its size until it all became hazy and misty with distance.

The Lucy May butted out into the Atlantic, to the rhythmic thud of her engines and the thrashing of her paddles leaving twin tracks in her wake. When they were clear of the harbour traffic, the bosun shouted an order and the seamen swarmed up the rigging to release the sheets. The engines were cut. In the sudden silence, the wind surged into her sails, groaning, creaking and straining in her rigging. *The Lucy May* heeled over and became a live thing once again as if the very thought of steam, paddles and engines was an insult to nature itself.

The two women were fascinated by the novelty of travelling in a steam-assisted sailing ship. For Ruth sailing was a totally new experience and she tried to hide her excitement and sense of wonder. Even Mary had never travelled on a steam ship before other than the river boats.

Colonel Gladstone joined them when New York was a mere smudge on the horizon. He had been busy arranging for the security of their cargo, about which he seemed very secretive.

"You must be longing for your real homecoming now your journey has started," he remarked. But in truth they were not, for both missed the life they had left in New York and were anxious for what might await them back at Nethergate. It was over two months since George had written his letter. A lot could have happened since then. Mary never enjoyed a confrontation, and she knew that Anthony would not readily grant Matthew and Ruth their freedom, knowing how Killcaid would react. But with her father's money at her command, she felt she could deal with Killcaid and Anthony and with his formidable spouse too.

For both women the novelty of their method of travel was soon forgotten as they began to react to the movement of the ship under the Atlantic swell. It was Ruth who suddenly realised that she did not feel at all well. Colonel Gladstone was quick to realise what was happening as Mary too began to feel ill.

"It's the mal de mare," he announced. "If you permit me, I have a remedy that has always worked for me." He rolled back his sleeve to reveal a leather pad bound with a leather thong about his wrist. "The pad is soaked in cedar wood oil. When you feel unwell just draw in three or four breaths of the oil and it will help. But the real solution is to go below and sleep. With most people the body finds its own solution without the distraction of outside movement. "Here, I fancied you both might need some remedy, so I have prepared bands for you both." With that he offered one to Mary and deftly tied it on to her wrist. With Ruth he took longer, and she looked up to find him staring hard at her. It gave her a curious feeling of pleasure to feel his hands upon her and she smiled. "You have not answered my question," he whispered, but any chance of a reply was forestalled by the proximity of Mary.

"Come, Ruth," she said. "I think I might take the second part of the good Colonel's advice and head below decks." Both women departed only too glad to seek the shelter of their cabin, where the motion seemed somewhat less. Soon both were secure in their bunks lulled by the creaking of the ship's timbers and the slap of the waves against the hull, but both heartily longing for the ship's motion to be stilled. Mary eventually managed to fall asleep, her mind full of Nethergate and its problems. As for Ruth, her mind was full of the gentle touch of Colonel Gladstone's fingers lingering as he fastened the little leather band about her wrist. It had felt for all the world like a caress.

21

Nassau Bound

Mary had been told by her father that *The Lucy May* would meet up at Nassau in the Bahamas with one of the three fast steamers used to make the final dash through the Yankee blockade into the Confederate port of Wilmington. He didn't mention their cargo, but she knew him well enough to suspect that he had more than a passing interest in its safe delivery to the Confederates. It was typical of her father, she thought, to meet the warring needs of both sides. Even at his great age he was still burning the candle at both ends in the relentless pursuit of profit. Yet now, thanks to her last visit, the paramount vision she had of her father was of the gentle tenderness he bore towards her mother bound by the enduring ties of love. She marvelled at the complexity of human nature and of her father's in particular.

The next morning dawned cloudy and cool with a brisk north-westerly wind that sent *The Lucy May* scudding before it with a real sense of purpose. Colonel Gladstone's remedy seemed to have worked, for both ladies awoke with an appetite free from nausea. Breakfast was a simple meal during which they were introduced in the ward room to the two officers they had not yet met. They were both British and on unpaid leave from the Royal Navy awaiting further commissions from the Admiralty.

Colonel Gladstone proved a solicitous travelling companion and both ladies began to see him in a different light now he was no longer beholden to his host. He was clearly looking forward to his homecoming after so long an absence as a prisoner of the Yankees. He urged them to enjoy this leg of their voyage, where there would be no danger except from the sea itself but warned them that their final run into Wilmington through the naval blockade would not be without its hazards. He assured them that they were to travel in British-built fast steamboats which could outrun anything the Yankee navy had. However, he also informed them that their quarters on the final leg would not be as comfortable as those they presently enjoyed. What they thought of their present cramped conditions they wisely kept to themselves.

"To be perfectly honest," he confessed, "I doubt that there will be any accommodation for ladies, and you will just have to make do with a canvas screen for privacy. "There is little real danger," he added. Seeing their looks of anxiety, he added, "The Union ships are unlikely to open fire. They are more interested in seizing the ship intact and securing the cargo. Their captains can make as much as $60,000 on a good cargo and every sailor might get a share of $2,000 or more. With that at stake they will treat the ship as gently as a basket full of eggs."

The manner in which their young captain consulted with Colonel Gladstone made it clear that he was more than just a passenger on this trip. Mary suspected that he had probably been tasked by her father to ensure the safe delivery of their cargo into rebel hands. However, it meant he had some influence with them.

When he was not engaged in such business activities the Colonel sought, at first in vain, an opportunity to catch Ruth on her own to clarify his position following his declaration in Mr

Bragg's garden. Such a pronouncement had not come easily to him, being a man not usually ruled by sentiment or emotion. He fancied he detected a softening in Ruth's demeanour towards him, but that may, he acknowledged, have been a case of the wish being father to the thought. What, he wondered, were the mysterious ties that restrained her? "Not entirely free", she had said.

As for Ruth, when she had time for reflection, she found her mind increasingly turning to thoughts of the Colonel. She remembered the softness of his lingering touch as he placed the leather band about her wrist and the excitement that that simple action had engendered in her. It had awakened all the longings she had supressed for so long following her brutal awakening at the hands of Mark. She wished heartily that she could have left him in New York as an impossible dream, a magical endorsement to go with all the other fantasy memories of herself as a free woman. She could never see the mysterious Colonel denying his background to such a degree as to consort with a slave unless it was as mistress, but she could not see him in that situation either. She knew, as a quadroon, she could pass for a dark-skinned European. Indeed, she had already been accepted as such by Mary's family and friends in New York. But if ever he knew her as a slave, somehow, that would be different. He was a Southerner through and through, but then not all Southern gentlemen were cast in the mould of Mark. She dreaded the reaction the revelation of her status would bring. She could not face his anger and disappointment that he had been misled by a creature so much his social inferior. She wished even more that their parting could have been in New York and that their memories of each other could have remained uncorrupted, just a beautiful fantasy.

Nevertheless, despite these undertones, the Colonel, or Thomas as they now found themselves calling him in private, proved to be an entertaining and knowledgeable companion.

But always there was the assumption that they shared with him the traditional views of the South. He spoke of the war, of being wounded at Mill Springs and his subsequent capture and of his work before the war.

He had been born the third son of Francis Gladstone. His oldest brother had assumed the running of their cotton estate as their father gradually relinquished his hold. His next oldest brother had joined the Navy as a career and was now fighting for the Union. Thomas had remained on their cotton plantation. He had a special interest in mechanising the harvesting process. Hence his connections with Henry Bragg, whose factories before the war, had been engaged in the manufacture of cotton gins and other farm machinery.

He spoke of his vision of how machinery could be developed to supersede the cotton gin and enhance other aspects of harvesting the cotton crop even, perhaps, to the picking of the cotton harvest itself as slaves became more expensive and harder to come by. He envisaged the diversification of tobacco and cotton estates to restore vitality to the soil by growing wheat and maize and using machinery to harvest the crop. Though not a defeatist by nature, he was essentially a realist. Before the war, he had seen the enormous stirring of the powerhouse that drove the Union. Sooner or later the North would prevail, for there was nothing that the Confederates could bring to bear to match their colossal mechanised might. He considered that ,even if the outcome of the conflict was a stalemate, many slaves would migrate north to freedom. If the war was not won, there would be a shortage of labour in the South. Mechanisation was he believed the answer and he meant to be in at the beginning. He was delighted to find in Mary someone who shared these views and was more knowledgeable than any other woman of his acquaintance. But it did seem strange to him to be discussing such matters with a woman, when he would far rather have been discussing other matters with her companion.

This was a side to Colonel Gladstone neither had suspected and they could not but admire his foresight and vision and indeed his enthusiasm for what he termed the "path ahead". For Mary, it was of added interest in the light of her conversations with her father about the running of Nethergate and she was in accord with much of what he said.

In the end, it was Ruth's love of drawing that led to her meeting Thomas alone. Whilst Mary had been content to chatter, Ruth had her sketch pad out and took delight in recording on paper the sailors going about their duties. On the second morning she was awakened early by the cry "Ship ahoy!" and hastened on deck to witness the passing of the two vessels. The stranger was a clipper, magnificent under full sail, and she hastened to capture the dramatic scene for her sketchbook. So engrossed was she in her task that for a time she was unaware that she had an audience. She looked up and Thomas was standing there watching her hands at work. She half rose, but he placed a hand gently on her shoulder.

"No, no, please. Don't let me stop you."

She continued, once more becoming engrossed in her task and almost forgetting his presence by her side. When at last the clipper had passed and Ruth had captured the ship sailing away against the vastness of the Atlantic Ocean, he vouchsafed to comment. "If you will pardon me for saying so, you have a quite remarkable talent."

"Do I?" she asked modestly. Then, sensing that he was about to ask her the question which she did not want to answer, she asked on a whim, "Would you allow me to draw you?"

Looking somewhat confused he assented. Then Ruth took over, arranging him on the rail and turning to speak as if he had been caught in a moment of secret reflection. Whenever he tried to speak, she cautioned him with, "No, no. I cannot draw and speak at the same time," thereby neatly forestalling the subject he was most anxious to broach.

She let her eyes rest upon his features and began to draw revelling in the excuse of being able to look at him and study his face. Every stroke of the charcoal was like a caress. It was she felt one of the best drawings she had done. At least now she would have something tangible to remember him by. She was tempted to let the moment linger but knew instinctively when a piece of work was finished and resisted the temptation to overdraw.

"There," she said at last, laying aside her charcoal.

"May I see?" he asked.

Almost shyly she brought it over to where he stood.

For a long time he seemed to gaze at it without comment, then his eyes seemed to grow misty. "It's beautiful," he said, then realising the implication of what he had said he hastily corrected himself. "No, no, that's not what I mean. Not the subject. Your creation is beautiful. Is that how you truly see me? It's very flattering."

She smiled. She had indeed caught him as if looking up from some deep inner thought, but with a sudden gladness just coming into his eyes. It was how she would like to remember him.

"You cannot stop me talking, now that you have finished. I must know what you thought after our conversation in Mr Bragg's garden? Do you in any small way reciprocate my feelings?" There was a look of such desperate appeal in his eyes, in a face normally so stern and in command of any situation, that she could no longer hold back her feelings.

"Oh, Thomas," she said. "Of course I do."

"Then you have made me truly the happiest man in the world," but a look of perplexity crossed his face and he asked, "What is this difficulty of which you spoke before? Is there someone else in your life?"

"No, no, Thomas. There is no-one else. You must not ask me anymore – please." And her eyes held an appeal more eloquent than her words. "Perhaps in a month or so things may be different. Then perhaps I will be free, free to tell you all. Then maybe it is you who will not wish to know me."

"That, my dear, will never be," said the Colonel emphatically. All the same he could not imagine what her secret could be. He thought perhaps it might be of some family pledge or commitment, a parental promise perhaps. But as far as he knew her parents were both dead or lost to her; certainly she never spoke of them. It made the thought of her even more tantalising.

22

An Idyllic Prospect

Matthew awoke early as the first rays of the morning sun spread across the rising ground on which Old Mo's cabin lay, alerted by the subtle change in the sound of the bird song. For a moment he lingered, listening to Ursula's regular breathing and remembering her distress in the night. It wasn't her fault that she was now his companion and he determined not to let it spoil his delight in the fruits of Old Mo's labours. He felt ashamed of the surly reception he had given her and determined to make amends. Quietly he left his bed, slipped on his clothes and made his way outside to pick fruit, to prepare their breakfast and to await George's promised arrival.

George, when he had arrived home the previous evening, had gone to his room. There the letter on the mantelpiece reminded him all too painfully of the dilemma he now faced. It appointed him to a governor's commission in the rank of lieutenant, with joining instructions to report to the 3rd Kentucky Infantry at Spring Hill in three weeks' time. He heartily regretted the impulse that had led to his application to join in the struggle following his quarrel with his father. It could not have come at a worse time. But there was nothing he could do about it. He had promised to take Manuel with him and now there would be no-one to ferry supplies to Matthew and Ursula unless he involved Samuel, but he needed Samuel above all to arrange for Ursula's escape. He wished his grandmamma were back at Nethergate House, but that would not be for weeks yet, assuming she had decided to return on receipt of his letter. He regretted now not telling her of the full extent to which Matthew was in trouble with the trumped-up charge of murder levelled against him. That surely would have sent her hurrying back.

He decided in the end to send for Samuel. If nothing else it would be a help to talk it over with someone else, someone whom he could trust.

"Please sit down," he said, when Samuel arrived, indicating the chair next to his. Samuel looked shocked at the invitation.

"That would not be proper, sir," he said. "Ah prefers to stand."

"Oh, don't be so stuffy! We are both conspirators now. There's no difference between us."

Samuel relaxed briefly, and a faint smile appeared at the corners of his mouth and lingered in his eyes. "All the same, Massa, Ah feels better standin'."

George regarded him for a moment. "As you wish. I suppose old habits die hard." Then he got down to the topic foremost on his mind. "How soon can you arrange for Ursula to travel safely up the Underground Railroad?" he asked.

"To travel in safety, to be sure of every link, could take upwards of five or six weeks, maybe more," he replied. "But if'n she were to go as an ornery fugitive and take the risk – why she could be whisked away this very day." George saw Ursula dressed as a maid of Nethergate in the swamp about Old Mo's cabin and looking so uncomfortably out of place that every instinct urged him to get her away as soon as possible. But even suitably clad Ursula was not a woman who would pass easily in a crowd, for her beauty would turn any head and stamp her passing on the memory of most men, black or white.

"No, Samuel. We dare not trust to luck. We must plan carefully for her escape. There must be no slip ups."

"Ah thought as much, sir. I have already taken certain steps. It's good there won't be no hue or cry now she assumed to be a goner. We got Manuel to t'ank for dat."

George nodded. "Yes, he's full of surprises."

George then explained to Samuel about the letter on the mantelpiece. "I have the governor's commission in the rank of lieutenant and am to join the 2nd Kentucky Infantry at Spring Hill in less than three weeks."

"I think you'll find it is the 3rd, sir," replied Samuel, with a perfectly straight face. George thought for a moment and then smiled.

"Yes, you are right of course. I should have known you would all know about it. But it does mean time is very short if I am to ensure that Ursula is cared for and set on her way. I will need you to make sure it happens whilst I am absent."

"I will do my best, sir. You can rely upon that. But what of her care whilst you are away?"

George then revealed the full details of how Ursula was being sheltered by Matthew during his absence.

Samuel thought for a moment.

"It won't be so easy for me to get away from here, without folks knowin'," he observed, "but not impossible. There's some Ah can trust and others I'm not so sure." That for the moment was the most George could hope for.

He made excuses with his father and mother that he would be away for the next few days, getting equipment ready for his forthcoming military adventures and saying goodbye to friends from their old life in New Haven. Then, giving Manuel strict instructions for the purchase of military equipment for himself and for suitable additional clothes for himself too, he set off to enjoy the last few days of freedom in his spiritual home among the wetlands of the bayou with the two people he cared for most in all the world.

The memory of these days he knew he would carry with him into the uncertain world of war. They would be the idyll from which he could draw comfort when facing the trials ahead. But, even before he embarked upon these sublime days, he was all too conscious of the worm that lurked in the bud of all his hopes. He was yet to learn the impossibility of living a lie amongst people you love.

23

Living the Lie

Matthew and Ursula were sitting down to a breakfast of fruit and cuts of meat from yesterday's supper. They were enjoying a meal that was as filling as any they had had at Nethergate House or Hall and doubly satisfying for Matthew, as coming from his own endeavours.

Ursula seemed to have recovered her spirits after her night's rest and was chattering animatedly, no doubt buoyed by the thought of George's promise to visit them again, when suddenly Matthew cautioned her to silence.

He had been alerted by the sharp cry of the blue jay. A moment or so later the cry was repeated.

"It's George," he announced. Pursing his lips, he repeated the cry. Immediately there was a response.

Ursula felt a sudden surge of excitement, followed by a frisson of anxiety. Together they made their way to the landing stage, where George would by now be hauling up the dugout. Ursula's main concern was how she looked after her stay in the bayou. But she need not have worried, for when George emerged through the trees he threw his arms about her with a tenderness sharpened by his anxieties. When Matthew, who had tactfully held back, joined them, all three marched, arm in arm up, to the cabin where George joined in their interrupted breakfast.

George told them that he could be with them now for three whole days. He had told his parents he would be visiting friends in New Haven. The thought of three whole days together was an added spice to their sense of freedom from the cares of the world. The conversation and laughter washed and eddied about them as if there were no tomorrow.

George had brought a knapsack of new supplies and some little luxuries from Nethergate Hall and Ursula and Matthew joined in the unpacking and delight as if it were Boxing Day and they were all opening their Christmas presents. George had been saving until last a small rectangular parcel which, unlike all the other items, had been lovingly wrapped in tissue paper.

"A special gift for you, Ursula," said George.

With excitement written large upon her face Ursula carefully unwrapped the present, savouring every second before the moment of revelation. Then she gasped with delight. It was indeed just what she wanted, a small ornamental mirror from one of the guest rooms in the Hall.

"Oh, I looks awful," wailed Ursula, studying her reflection, but in truth knowing that she looked just the opposite, for, even though she had lived in the bayou for only a few days, somehow the sense of freedom from servitude had lifted her features.

"I have never seen you looking better," said George, meaning every word, then a note of seriousness crept into his voice which he could not hide. "Remember, my dearest, whenever you look into that glass, imagine me on the other side staring right back at you. Wherever you are, I shall come and seek you out to the very ends of the earth."

Both looked up sharply at the sudden seriousness of his words, thinking that he referred perhaps to the escape plans for Ursula and her possible journey to far off Canada and freedom, but George was thinking only of the dangers and uncertainties he was about to face once he joined the Confederate cause.

That sombre moment was like a brief cloud and soon they were planning the days ahead and what to do in the bayou, as if it were their own exclusive playground, as indeed it was.

They spent the time exploring in the dugout, watching the wildlife in its infinite variety and fishing for its bounties whenever the need arose. In the evenings, they would linger about the glowing embers of the fire whilst Matthew and George played melodies upon their flutes and Ursula sang in a rich contralto, redolent and deep with hidden passions. They sang the songs of the moment and songs that the slaves often sang, full of longing and sweet melancholy. And they talked. How they talked! They spoke of religion and of the individual, of the rights of man and they too revealed their innermost thoughts to each other. It was a great awakening for them all. It was a time they would always look back upon as near perfection.

For George, though, there always lurked that tiny drop of poison that marred his enjoyment of those memories: the knowledge that he alone bore of his imminent departure into the tumult of war and the guilt he felt for cutting them both adrift from his support from Nethergate Estate. There was also the gnawing doubt of how Ursula and his friend would be, thrown together in such proximity whilst they awaited the fruition of Samuel's arrangements. What would he see if truly he could be a spy behind the mirror that he had just given to Ursula? He did his utmost to supress the thought, but it festered.

As time wore on, both Ursula and Matthew noticed the change in George's behaviour. He seemed consumed by an almost frenetic desire to extract the most from their every activity. When there were pauses, his face would lapse into a pensive cast and a worried preoccupied frown would wash across his features.

It was Matthew who broached the subject with Ursula on the morning of the third day. He had been concerned that she and George might have had a falling-out and when he had caught Ursula on her own had asked her straight out.

"Oh, Matthew," she said, her face clouding over, "I is worried too. I do believe it is something I might have said. He seems at times so deep within his own thoughts, that I dare not ask him."

Things came to a head when Matthew came back unexpectedly having mislaid his skinning knife and blundered in on George and Ursula at a moment when they were more than preoccupied with each other.

George turned on his friend in embarrassment. "Do you have to come creeping about like a damned busybody?" he shouted in annoyed confusion.

Matthew rounded on him and angrily stared him down. Then he spoke in measured tones. "There ain't no-one talks to me like that now. Least of all you, *brother*. I ain't no-one's slave boy now. Not your'n, not no-one's. And this here is mah cabin and mah home and you had best not forget it." With that he turned on his heel and stalked out, seething with anger. It was not the first time that George had glimpsed the man behind the erstwhile slave. His mind flew back to when they had first met in the bayou and Matthew had held him at his mercy, caught helpless in one of Old Mo's traps. He had felt then that Matthew might be capable of anything even though it was he that held the rifle. Matthew was not a man to be crossed.

When he had gone, Ursula turned on George. "You should not have done that, George," she said. It was the first time she had ever had cause to disagree with something George had done. She began to gather her clothes. But George was angry too and humiliated.

"That's right. Take his side against me. Or would you rather it was him instead of me? Is that it? Perhaps I'd better get back to Nethergate." He began to collect up his things from their end of the cabin and stuff them angrily into his knapsack.

This was too much for Ursula, who burst into tears. "Don't leave me George, not like this," she cried. George's anger evaporated. "What is it?" she sobbed. "What ails you? Are you cross with me? Matthew is worried too. You bi'n so strange, he asked me if we quarrelled or somethin' and now we have."

George was overcome with remorse. This was meant to be such a special time for them all, but he realised that the secret he nursed to himself was poisoning these precious moments and that he could no longer keep it hidden. He realised how selfish he had been in trying to keep it all to himself.

He told her how things really were and that there was no escaping his being called up to join in the fighting. He reassured her that it would be some months before he ever came face to face with the Yankees and that there would be a long spell training the raw recruits up to be fit enough to go head to head with the enemy.

Ursula was appalled at the thought that George was going to the war to face danger and death, no matter that it might be months away. The thought of life without George was the end of the world for her. What was the point of fleeing to Canada, if she would never see George again?

"Oh George. If you was to be killt'... I could not go on living," and she threw herself into his arms. "But what about me here? What about me goin' on the Underground Railway?"

"There's no change to that and Samuel has it all under control. He won't let us down. And I'll make sure you have sufficient money for all your needs once you get to Canada." All the same Ursula was filled with a profound sense of unease at this turn of events. The war had been such an abstract thing, like hearing of a storm in a different state. Now it was here, right beside her, threatening the life of the man she loved, the man who was the whole world to her. All over America countless other lovers, wives and families were having to face the self-same nightmare.

When Matthew returned George could see by the set of his shoulders and the force of his stride that he still simmered with resentment. He strode to meet him with his arms outstretched. "Forgive me, brother. I was wrong to speak like that. Am I forgiven?"

Never one to bear a grudge, Matthew's brow lightened and he relaxed. "All forgiven, brother."

Their friendship restored, George then explained the reason why he had tried to keep his secret from them; he related how he and his father had quarrelled over the attempted scourging of Matthew and how in a fit of pique he had declared his intention of joining the Confederate cause. Once he had voiced that intention, there was no turning back. Now his joining instructions had come through, and he would be gone in little more than two weeks.

The outside world had however now shouldered its way into their little utopia. Matthew was envious that George would soon be engaged in the war in which he himself longed to play a part and frustrated that he was now anchored to his job of nursemaid to Ursula until Samuel managed to release her into the arms of the Underground Railroad. He felt angry that George would be fighting for a cause that would perpetuate the scourge of slavery. Then reason told him that he could hardly blame George for his action, when it was protecting him that had been the cause of the quarrel between George and his father. And was it not his dearest wish to do the self-same thing, but under the Yankee flag?

"I wanted this time to be special for us all," continued George. "Had I told you at the outset, it would have clouded the time we have had together. Now I think, in trying to hide it, it has spoilt everything. But it has been special, hasn't it? These last few days?"

The look of appeal was so earnest in his face that the two could only nod their assent. "I shall carry the memory of it with me in all the times ahead," he added.

"Oh, must you go, George?" suddenly wailed Ursula. "Isn't there some way you could delay things?"

George could only shake his head. Then he explained the arrangement he had made with Samuel, and that Samuel would make contact through the links they had already established whilst continuing to work on the plans to spirit Ursula away to Canada.

Then George turned to Matthew. "Brother, I have a special request to make to you." He had been mulling it over in his mind over the last few days. It seemed the obvious solution. "Can you be Ursula's escort along the Underground Railroad to Canada? Knowing that you would be there to care for her would be such a comfort to me and I am sure to Ursula too. Will you? Can you do that for me?"

There was such a depth of longing in George's voice that, despite Matthew's anger at having been misled by his friend, he found it hard to resist. There had been times when despite the delight of the freedom he enjoyed in the bayou he had longed for company. At such times he had seriously considered making a break for freedom and going to join the Yankee Army. But being wanted for murder complicated things. Despite the war, the forces of law and order on both sides still co-operated for the common good. Now any thoughts of joining in the war would have to be held in abeyance whilst he escorted George's woman to freedom. It would be his freedom too once in Canada, but he would run the risk of returning once more to slavery if he were apprehended on the journey. For him capture would mean certain death.

Once in Canada, if he wanted then to return to join the Yankees he ran the risk of being treated as an escaped slave, for there was still money to be made from bounty hunting for runaways and there was always the risk that his identity would be revealed and that would have one result, with Killcaid ready to weight the scales of justice against him.

"Do you think it wise though, brother, me with a price on my head? If we were took, would I not be a liability if Ursula be linked with what they say I did?"

"I meant what I said the other day," rejoined George, "about giving you another identity as my slave. I know a man in New Haven who could draw up papers for a new identity for you. That way no-one will link you with Killcaid's act."

It seemed to Matthew that his mind had been made up for him and he truly wanted to help his friend. This way, once Ursula was safe in Canada, he would be free to return to the cause closest to his heart.

"I will brother. I surely will," he said and with that the die was cast.

George then produced from his money belt a wad of money for each of them.

"It's in good old Yankee greenbacks," he explained. "I'm afraid our 'greybacks' are unlikely to get you anywhere, particularly if you move into Yankee territory. It's nearly all I have. My father gave it to me to ease my passage into the Confederate Army, but your need is greater."

Both were warmed by this act of generosity despite their anxiety at the realisation of the difficulties they would now face living in the bayou without the support from the estate which George had supplied. It might be some weeks, months even, before Samuel would be able to arrange for their departure.

That evening as they lingered after their supper it was a sombre gathering, so different from the merriment of the previous evenings. Their songs and music had a melancholy flavour, but nevertheless they all found solace in the singing.

The next morning it was a solemn gathering at the spot where George had left his dugout three days before. Ursula was tearful and Matthew still pondering their change in plans and the prospect of going to Canada. His friend was now leaving them for an uncertain future, and he wondered too what his position would be were his friend to perish. George's promise to him to grant him his freedom would be valueless and his hopes of joining the Yankees were impossible whilst he was still wanted for murder. Life was full of uncertainties over which he had no control, but that was the lot of the slave.

George embraced Ursula one final time, then turned to Matthew.

"Goodbye, old friend," he said.

All the affection between them welled up once again as they realised that this might be the last time that they would see each other. "God preserve you, brother," whispered Matthew, trying hard to hide the emotion from his voice.

The two broke apart. "I haven't forgotten my promise to you," said George. "I have left a letter to be opened should anything happen to me, saying that if they treasure my memory then you must be given your freedom wherever you are. That will allow you, if you reach Canada, to come back here to live." But George seemed to have forgotten the charges that hung over Matthew's head.

Nevertheless, at these words Matthew felt guilt at his anger the previous night when he had considered George's decision to go to the war and leave Ursula and him in such a state of uncertainty. George turned to face him and laying his hand upon Matthew's arm he looked earnestly into Matthew's eyes. Matthew read in George's face a look of vulnerability as he said, "Take good care of Ursula. She's as dear to me as my very soul. Be true to me, brother. Be true."

Matthew was not altogether sure what George meant by these last words, but he nodded, still brimming with affection and gratitude for George's friendship.

"Of course I'll be true. You know that."

George turned his back on them both, so they could not see his face, and launched off in the dugout. With a final wave, he vanished from their sight amongst the greenery. The water weeds slowly closed back over the track of the dugout. It was as though he had never been. Ursula sobbed softly at his departure and hidden tears for a moment smarted in Matthew's eyes. Despite his resentment, Matthew's heart went out to the distressed creature beside him.

"Come," he said gently, turning towards the cabin, "there's work to be done."

She turned to follow. It seemed the most natural thing in the world to Matthew to put his arm about her to comfort her in her distress. She, in turn, buried her head in his chest, her small frame racked by sobs, seeking only the comfort of another human being. A sudden wave of tenderness for the sad little creature beside him swept over Matthew as he felt her slender figure clinging to him for comfort. It felt good.

24

To Arms

As George turned his back on Matthew and Ursula, he knew that things would never be the same again. In a few months if all went well his friends would be in Canada and free and he would have been sucked into the maelstrom of war and who knows what that might bring?

As he paddled the dugout to its hiding place, he savoured every moment of his passage through the bayou, lands that he had learnt to love and to respect: the call of the birds, the soaring height of the cypress trees, the vines that hung from their branches reaching to their ridged and gnarled roots embedded deep into the swampy ground, the mysterious grunts and cries of the wildlife abounding about him and the splash and suck of his paddles driving him inexorably away from those whom he truly loved.

The remaining days slipped by in a headlong rush until soon it was his last evening at home. He was sad to go. He was fond of his father, doing his best in a world not of his choosing, pulled this way and that by events, pushed by Killcaid and harassed by his wife. He remembered how his father had been when he worked as a solicitor for Forbes and Sons in New Haven. Then he had been a man fulfilled, confident in his worth and master in his own small world. In those days he had often played with George. George recalled the excitement and fear he had felt as his father had pretended to hunt him down in their garden or on damp days when he had been sent off to hide in the house and the sound of his father's approaching footsteps, heavy with menace. He remembered the excited anticipation of capture and the hug that always followed. His father used to sing and hum to himself then. He always went to his father when he was in trouble, never to his mother. That had all changed when his father became Master of Nethergate. He had a sudden premonition that his father was not destined to make old bones, probably because he would not wish it, and his heart went out to him in a sudden surge of affection.

His mother had never been one to show him any warmth. He could not recall ever having been kissed or cuddled as a child or played with for that matter. He was just an extension of her social ambitions. What others thought of her was always more important than anything else. She had positively swelled when she discovered that she was to become Mistress of Nethergate. But how she had grown so cruel and full of spite he could not understand. He would not miss her and felt guilty at the thought. He could not imagine his parents loving in the way that he and Ursula loved, but they must have done so at least once. He imagined it must have been a bit of a surprise to them both. Then he smiled to himself at the thought.

But the resilience of youth coursed through his veins. He could not help but feel a surge of excitement for what lay before him. How would he react to the stresses of war? Then there was fear, the fear that he might not rise above the challenges he was about to face. Above all, there was the fear that in the final analysis he might prove to be a coward.

George, on that last evening at Nethergate Hall, had lingered talking to his father, now both warm and comfortable in each other's company. It was late when he went upstairs, but Manuel was there to greet him. After he had bathed, he looked once again over the equipment that Manuel had purchased for him. The leatherwork felt stiff and hard, but he could not resist the temptation to try it all on and to see himself as the soldier he was soon to become. He posed before the mirror, trying various expressions to see which most suited. The thought passed before his mind of this soldierly figure lying still and heroic upon some distant battlefield after some act of valour, clutching the Confederate standard with a sea of Yankee dead about him and Ursula grieving, tearful but proud, over news of his heroic demise.

It was but a fleeting fantasy and not the way he wanted things to be. Instead he imagined on some distant field of conflict receiving the letter from Matthew and Ursula that told of their successful arrival in Canada. Then after this conflict was over, as surely soon it must be for General Lee was running rings around the Yankee armies, he dreamt of their joyful reunion and perhaps a new life together in Canada. Suddenly he felt tired. It was all illusion. He shed his military accoutrements and Manuel neatly laid them out for the morrow.

He was about to dismiss Manuel, when with a guilty thought he realised that it was Manuel's last night too in the world that had been his entire life. In all his preoccupation with Ursula and Matthew down in the bayou, he had hardly spared a thought for Manuel, the architect of Ursula's escape.

"How're you feeling about going soldiering, Manuel?" he asked.

"I be mighty proud, Massa George," was his enthusiastic reply. "I's ready to give dem Damn Yankees a real bloody nose. Ah surely am." He seemed to be delighted to have been asked.

George suddenly realised how much Manuel knew about what he was doing and his life down in the bayou. Yet not a word had leaked out. Manuel had simply busied himself with procuring all his necessary military equipment through the estate's purchasing agents with faultless efficiency and yet somehow had always been there when he had need of him. As patient as a mule, he didn't expect thanks, but simply got on with the job. George began to suspect that in Manuel there was more than met the eye and that his opinion had perhaps been clouded by his past disloyalty due to his terror of Killcaid.

"Thank you, Manuel, for keeping quiet about what I've been up to these past weeks and for getting things so well prepared for us going off to war. We'll make a good team, you and I, eh?" and he clapped Manuel affectionately on the shoulders.

Manuel swelled with pride. George dismissed him and clambered into bed, wondering when he would next lay his head upon this pillow and what sort of a person he might have become by then, maybe with some hated Yankee blood upon his hands.

Sleep at first eluded him. It wasn't thoughts of military valour that filled his mind, but the image of Ursula and Matthew standing side by side as they bade him farewell. How he wished that it might be him standing where Matthew stood; he who would be spending every waking and sleeping hour close to the woman he loved. The slow poison of jealousy and suspicion seeped into his mind. Could he trust his friend? What shared dangers might they endure together in their flight to Canada? Such proximity must surely lead to other intimacies and to the blossoming of affection and understanding between the two. He knew that she loved him and him alone. George knew how much his friendship meant to Matthew. Would that alone keep the two from the emotional dependence that must assuredly follow from so many shared perils and anxieties? He couldn't stop himself from imagining them entwined in the intimacy that he and Ursula had shared in this very bed and he ground his teeth. His eyes strayed to the mantelshelf, where he had placed the letter he would give to Samuel to be delivered only on his demise, the letter that contained his wishes for Matthew's freedom. It was all he could do to stop himself from rising out of bed and shredding it there and then.

He got as far as actually getting out of bed and taking the letter in his hand. Then he remembered the day he had been trapped in the swamp thinking his end had surely come and the peril Matthew had faced to rescue him. His mind skipped to the time they had first met and their growing friendship: the laughter they shared, the talks they had, the books they discussed and the music they made together. Then he realised the unique relationship he and Matthew shared and that in Matthew he had a true and loyal friend, a brother indeed.

Ashamed at his own unworthy thoughts he made his way back to bed and soon surrendered to sleep to be ready for what his new life would have to offer.

25

Land Ho

The cry "Land ho!" brought Mary and Ruth to the deck, peering in the direction the sailor at the masthead was pointing. It seemed to them a featureless expanse of ocean. They were soon joined by Colonel Gladstone, whose eyes seemed sharper than theirs.

"Can't you see?" he queried, pointing with his chin. "Look hard over in that direction, what looks like a smudge of grey on the horizon. That'll be Nassau." Soon the ladies too could see where he was pointing. Gradually the island became more clearly defined and they could make out tall palms, the shape of buildings and the old fort dominating the harbour from which fluttered the British UnionFlag.

They felt the frisson of excitement that every voyager feels at the sight of dry land. The captain ordered the sails to be furled and the sudden rhythmic thudding of the engines filled the ship with a new sense of purpose. Black smoke spewed out of her funnels. They steamed into the harbour under their own power and dropped anchor in the bay.

It wasn't quite the bustling scene of the harbour in New York, since the bigger ships had to moor in the bay. The quaysides were crowded with smaller craft, scurrying to and fro. The quays were a hive of activity. There were huge wharves where cotton was stored and monstrous piles of bales spilling out into the open, where it seemed some Negro families had taken refuge and set up homes. All the cotton, so Colonel Gladstone informed them, was bound for Liverpool and the ever-ravenous cotton mills of Manchester in England. Huge profits of 700 or 800 per cent could be made by those buying cotton from the Confederate states and then running the Yankee blockade to sell it for onward shipment.

In the distance were sprawling heaps of coal with streams of Negro workers, some carrying great boulders of coal on their heads cushioned with sacking, whilst others trundled barrows loaded with their precious black cargo. All was bustle and movement as the distant cries of the workers floated across the water.

Colonel Gladstone then pointed out three sinister-looking craft that were like no ships they had ever seen. They had almost no superstructure apart from twin smoke stacks and but two masts each. They were side-wheeled iron steamers painted dark grey to make them near invisible against the grey Atlantic sky.

"They are the swiftest craft afloat," Colonel Gladstone informed them, "built in England; the Yankees have got nothing that can touch them. They are owned by Captain Semmes, a former US Navy captain sailing under a letter of marque from President Jefferson Davis himself. They're built for speed and little else. You'll be sailing on one of them. I'm afraid there's nothing by way of cabins and you'll have to make do with a shelter rigged between the lighters on deck, but it's only for about thirty-six hours and then we'll be running in to Wilmington and thence – home."

Both women exchanged glances. Suddenly thoughts of Nethergate filled both their minds with anxiety for what awaited them. Just then a lighter appeared alongside, and they saw some of their luggage being loaded onto it.

"We're going ashore now," Colonel Gladstone advised them. "We'll be staying at the Royal Victoria Hotel. It's a grand place and you'll enjoy the change from being cramped up aboard ship. But it's not a place for a quiet life I'm afraid and there's all sorts staying there, but it does have a certain style. Nassau has really come alive with the war and the whole island is teeming with all kinds of folk that have been drawn to this place with the hopes of striking it rich. And believe me, many have."

The ship's lieutenant approached and indicated that their boat was ready for embarkation. The lighter was bobbing at the ship's side manned by Negro oarsmen, and they descended the rickety rope and wood ladder and were soon ensconced in her bows and scything their way to the rhythm of the rowers across the bay to the quayside. As they clambered up the landing stage steps the smell and warmth of the land assailed their nostrils. They welcomed its solid and familiar feel once more beneath their feet, challenging their sense of balance. A fleet of pony traps awaited the travellers and they and their baggage were soon winding their way up the hill to where the Royal Victoria Hotel dominated the hillside.

On their arrival they could not fail to be impressed. No expense had been spared. It was a truly impressive building with cool verandas stretching around its three stories and a hexagonal cupola sitting like a regal crown upon its head. The grounds with secret pathways and sudden shady bowers spread like a mantel from its walls with statues and sculptures set to surprise and delight the wanderer and invite the lover.

It seemed that a veritable army of white-coated servants was there to greet them. They and their luggage were soon ushered up the stairs to their rooms whilst Colonel Gladstone completed the formalities. The rooms were splendid in their luxury and seemed as spacious as lawns after the cramped quarters on board. The windows that stretched from floor to ceiling were wide open and, in the distance, they could hear the sounds of the band of the Second West Indian Regiment playing its afternoon concert on the parade ground of Fort Charlotte. All in all, they rejoiced in the feeling of well-being with their feet once more on dry land and only another two days travelling before they would be home in Confederate territory.

Both Mary and Ruth had been allotted personal servants, for being British territory, slavery had long been a thing of the past. Ruth's servant was a slip of a girl called Mandy, the daughter of a one-time slave on the island, but bright and cheerful and full of respect for the grand lady she took Ruth to be. If only, thought Ruth, she knew of their true relative positions.

Their baggage had been brought up to their separate rooms. Mandy, full of chatter about her island home, unpacked the baggage and sorted out Ruth's clothes for washing and cleaning. In Ruth's baggage there was one plainer-looking case than the others, which Mandy went to unpack too.

"No, no. Leave that one," she cried out, unexpectedly sharply. Mandy looked up, crestfallen at the implied rebuke.

"I is so sorry, ma'am," she cried. "I did not mean to pry. I meant no offence." Ruth felt a sudden rush of remorse at Mandy's immediate humility and assumption of some form of guilt for an entirely innocent action.

"I'm sorry, Mandy. I did not mean to be so sharp. That is not my case, you see. I have no right to open it. I… I'm taking it for another person." For a moment all the hopeless subservience of being a slave herself engulfed her, causing a sudden surge of bitterness. The case that Mandy had begun to open contained all the clothes she had changed out of at Nashville all those months before when she was making the metamorphosis from slave to lady's companion. It seemed so long ago since she had changed from being a slave into thinking, breathing and feeling like a free woman. In only a few days now she would have to tie up her long hair under a head-cloth and hide those dark tresses.

140

She would have to cease feeling like a real woman and don those clothes that would mark her for all to see what she truly was. How would Colonel Thomas Gladstone see her then? Would Mary succeed in getting her son to grant her freedom when she had failed in the past? Would Mary's younger son, so much under the malevolent influence of Silas Killcaid, dare to go against his wishes, for surely he would have no desire to see her freed from bondage?

She shook herself free from such dark thoughts of the future as Mandy, bobbing all the time to please her after her sudden outburst, informed her that her bath was ready. There she enjoyed the luxury of bathing, washing her hair and ridding herself of the clammy feel of the salt that seemed to get everywhere. Mandy, her spirits now restored, helped her bathe and dried her in thick luxurious towels, whilst resuming once again her animated chatter. Ruth, smiling all the while relaxed once more, determined to enjoy these last few hours of freedom, her thoughts always turning somehow to her inscrutable admirer.

Colonel Gladstone sent word that he would join them for luncheon and Mary and Ruth, when their toilette was finished, descended to the lounge together, where they found him waiting. They were indeed glad of his company for the hotel seemed to house a veritable kaleidoscope of nations. Everywhere they could hear different American accents and a veritable Babel of foreign tongues.

It was clear that Colonel Gladstone was no stranger to the Island and that he intended to take charge of their stay at the Royal Victoria and make it as memorable as possible in the short time they had. He informed them that they were not lunching at the hotel but were bound for what he called the "maroon". He escorted them to where a row of carriages waited with horses patiently bending their hooves in their traces. Soon the remaining carriages were filled, some with noisy parties of men and women who were clearly bent on more than just casual enjoyment, and the cavalcade moved off. They wound their way down the hill to where there were more formal gardens owned by the Royal Victoria. There, carpets and chairs had been set out by the sea shore under a canopy of coloured umbrellas, shaped like huge flowers. Some sat on the carpets and others relaxed into the cushioned luxury of cane chairs, whilst luncheon was served of every variety of sea food imaginable. All about them was such merriment and laughter that it was impossible not to be caught up and carried along on this veritable tidal wave of pleasure. All the while a small group of musicians played local airs to the gentle rhythm of the sea lapping at the shore.

Ruth knew that Colonel Gladstone had eyes only for her and all this entertainment was laid on for her benefit. She felt her heart responding but knowing that it could lead nowhere and yet praying that somehow it might. Perhaps if she were given her freedom once they reached Nethergate and Mary exerted her new-found financial authority? Perhaps if Thomas were prepared to overlook that she came from slave stock. But would any Southern gentleman so demean himself as to marry a slave? But then she knew of some who had, but again they were spoken of with sympathy at best and more generally regarded with contempt as outcasts and betrayers of their class. In New York she had been accepted without question for what she pretended to be. Poor demented Rebecca had been the only one who had challenged her status. She knew though in her heart of hearts that it was all a dream and that reality was a harsher place where dreams had no substance. Yet still she could not help herself and dreamt on.

After their experience at the "maroon", the party moved on again to a place beneath Fort Charlotte where races were held. Today, Colonel Gladstone explained, it was to be a donkey derby. There was something comical about these stubborn little creatures being involved in the sport of kings. But the jockeys were nevertheless dressed in silken colours and took their role with the utmost seriousness. The betting was fast and furious and huge sums of money seemed to be wagered on the most uncertain of outcomes. Thomas Gladstone showed them how the betting was done, and the two women were soon caught up in the excitement of the occasion, although their wagers were for very modest sums indeed.

In the evening there was to be a ball held in the Royal Victoria's sumptuous ballroom, where the famed grand piano stood in which at the turn of a cranking handle the sounds of overture, waltz or quadrille could be produced as though a full orchestra were engaged. It was but another wonder of this island of intrigue and pleasure.

"I do hope," said Thomas Gladstone, "that I may have the pleasure of the company of you two ladies at this evening's entertainment?"

Ruth looked to Mary to see her response. "I have had rather too much entertainment already today," said Mary. "After our travels I think I would rather spend a quiet evening in my room." Then turning to Ruth she added, with an understanding twinkle in her eye, "But you go, Ruth, my dear, and keep the Colonel company."

"The evening will be the less for the lack of your presence," said the Colonel gallantly and then, "Do I take it, Ruth, that you will do me the great honour of accompanying me?"

With a glance at her owner and feeling somehow as shy as a young girl, Ruth replied, "I should be delighted, Thomas."

"Well then, that's settled. Are you sure you won't join us, Mary?"

"No, really," she replied. "I'm getting much too old for such frivolities, but you two enjoy yourselves. I shall dine in my room and rest in a bed of a decent size that does not move under me. And be ready for our next foray onto the high seas in those dangerous and sinister-looking boats," she added with a laugh.

Ruth glanced across at Thomas and their eyes met and for a moment lingered. Ruth felt a sudden almost hedonistic spasm of delight. She was to spend a whole evening in the company of this strange man who had so surprisingly expressed his love for her. As for her own feelings, she had never been in love before. She did not know if she could ever love a man, but Thomas, she owned, roused emotions within her that she had never felt before. There had been fear at first, fear that he had somehow discovered her secret. Then with the realisation that it was not suspicion that drove him, had come relief. Now it seemed that his gentle gaze and courtly respect were never far from her thoughts. Although the future all seemed so hopeless, she knew it would be an evening she would treasure for the rest of her life.

26

To War

George was awake even before Manuel knocked gently on his door. He stepped self-consciously into the room, wearing an ill-fitting Confederate uniform, together with a gleaming, white-teethed grin.

"My, you look grand," chuckled George appreciatively. Manuel's smile, if that were possible, grew yet wider. "Every bit the Confederate soldier," he added, in case Manuel should think he was laughing at him.

"I's mighty proud to wear it, Massa." It was clear from his face and bearing that the Confederates had a willing recruit.

George couldn't help but smile inwardly at Manuel's enthusiasm and indeed it made him feel better too. The introspection and doubts of the night were a thing of the past and he thrilled too at the thought of donning his uniform of Confederate grey and riding out on the greatest adventure of his life.

He had worn his uniform before whilst training with the militia. Now it felt somehow different. He had never before been fully kitted out. Now he was armed, ready and going to war. He took from beside his bed the much-thumbed copy of Hardee's *Tactics and Training*, which had been his Bible. It was the

145

only military manual they had when meeting with the Militia at Bentham Springs, where his father, as Master of Nethergate, held the rank of honorary major. Absentmindedly he brushed the mud smear on the cover and his mind flitted back to those early days in the bayou with Matthew.

Together they had both pored over this manual and tried to understand its meaning. Together they had practised the arms drills with their Kentucky rifles, barking out the words of command as they imagined seasoned soldiers might. From thence his mind turned to Ursula and he felt a sudden twist at his heart that was like a physical pain. Resolutely, he thrust the thought to the back of his mind.

Squaring his shoulders, he strode downstairs into the dining room, his riding boots echoing as they struck the wooden floor. Both his parents were waiting for him. His mother was bursting with pride and no doubt rehearsing what she would say to her acquaintances at Bentham Springs. His father was less ebullient and more thoughtful.

"It's not over the disagreement we had, lad?" he asked, "that you have decided to join in the struggle?"

"No, sir," George assured him untruthfully. "I must do what so many others of my age are doing to keep the Confederacy free of interference from the North. It's a grand cause and one worth fighting for." It was a fine little speech, he thought, and in his present mood he half believed it.

"I would be with you too son," replied his father, his voice breaking a little, "but for my responsibilities here. You know that?"

Both knew of the exemption from military service that came with the ownership of twenty slaves or more and Nethergate's total was many times greater than that. But it did not stop his wife from uttering a contemptuous little snort at this remark, though what precisely she expected him to do was not even clear in her own mind.

It was perhaps the liveliest breakfast he had ever shared with his parents. For once, they seemed interested in what he was about to do and not wrapped up in their own concerns. His father was full of advice he had gleaned from others, some of it hopelessly impracticable, but his real concern for his son was apparent and George expressed his gratitude for the guidance proffered. The appreciation though was more for the sentiment that lay behind it. Perhaps for the first time he realised that his father did really love him in his own way but had never found how to express it. His mother as always was overly concerned with appearances, but somewhere, he suspected, in the depths of the tortured person she had become, a genuine spark of real love might glimmer yet. Not for the first time he wondered how much simpler his life might have been had his uncle not met with his sudden riding accident and his father not inherited Nethergate. However, then he would never have known Ursula.

His parents were going to accompany him in the carriage to Bentham Springs. There was to be a grand send-off for the draft that George was going to take to Fort Coldstream. There they were to complete their training before joining a fighting company in the 10th Infantry Regiment (the Old Waifs and Strays). It had acquired its name because so many of its number came from territory now under the flag of the Stars and Stripes and off limits to the men in grey. George set off, with the proudly uniformed Manuel following behind on the spare horse laden with their equipment.

At Bentham Springs a grand send-off had indeed been prepared for them. Tables had been laid out in the High Street and the town band was playing martial music interspersed with popular Southern songs and tunes. Even the slaves were rejoicing with them and joining in the festivities to wish them all "bon voyage", despite them going to fight to preserve the very servitude under which they laboured. Everywhere there was bustle, music and noise.

George joined his draft, many of whom he already knew.

He had been elected to command them. His election he knew was not through any merit or skill of his, or popularity for that matter, but because of whom his father was. Nevertheless, he meant to exercise his command with fairness and fortitude and to earn the respect of his men. Just now, however, there was a party to be enjoyed and George intended to make the most of it, before riding off to war.

Some of the other planters and large estate owners were there and his parents were soon deep in conversation, his mother no doubt parading the sacrifice she was making for the Confederate cause.

All too soon, however, it seemed the time for departure came if they were to reach Fort Coldstream by nightfall. The men fell in in four ranks and those with weapons shouldered arms for the march. The Corporal reported to George for permission to move out.

George, feeling the glow of public attention, grandly barked out the order, "Right face!" Most managed this manoeuvre though one or two turned in the wrong direction. "For–ward!" he roared, in a suitably martial tone, and the men surged off to war, swinging out of Bentham Springs in fine style, with the band playing and the crowd cheering, waving, whooping and clapping.

All too soon the tumult in Bentham Springs faded into the background and became suddenly a distant memory. They were alone with the steady tramp of their feet, the rattle of their equipment and the dust their movement kicked up on the road. For a moment it seemed the enormity of their collective decision to go to war weighed upon their minds, but suddenly one of the men began to hum the tune of "I'll Place a Knapsack on My Back". Soon all were rolling along to the marching tune and those who didn't know all the words hummed away and joined in the chorus, "We'll march away to the firing line and kill that Yankee soldier." It filled them all with fine patriotic fervour and a grim and determined sense of purpose.

27

Camp Coldstream

The evening was beginning to gather in as George and his troop rounded the corner to see Camp Coldstream spread out before them. There were neat rows of tents, some square, some bell tents from most of which plumes of smoke rose like feathered hats. Soldiers in Confederate grey moved about seemingly, with a sense of purpose. The whole panorama spoke of order and efficiency.

They were challenged by the guard with a rifle levelled at them. "Halt! Who goes there?" he said somewhat self-consciously.

George answered proudly with "New draft of one officer and twenty-five men for the 10th Infantry Regiment."

"Pass, friend," replied the guard, "we been expectin' you. Welcome to the army, boys."

At the Guard room, they were met by the duty sergeant who took them down to where their tents were located. There were four truckle beds in each tent and a brick-built oven just outside. Soon the men were cheerfully offloading their equipment and finding their beds for the night. George sent Manuel off to stable the horses and to find the officers' tents whilst he set about making sure his men were comfortably housed. They had been issued with rations at the guardroom and soon the men had managed to collect wood and start up the chimney ovens, thus adding to the all-pervading smell of wood smoke. There was little he could do, but he felt his responsibility as their officer and the men responded with cheery comments which showed their appreciation that he had stayed with them. He in turn felt the first stirring of the affection that is shared between men at arms. Only when he was sure that the soldiers were well settled did he leave them and make his way to the officers' lines. By the time he arrived, Manuel had stabled the horses in the horse lines and had got all his kit neatly stowed. George thanked him, then asked, "How do you think you'll settle down to life as a soldier, Manuel?"

"I really don't know, Massa George, but I sure is mighty glad to be away from dat Mr Killcaid, an' I praise de Lord for dat."

George laughed. "Well I sure am mighty glad to have you with me, Manuel, and that's the truth," and he placed a hand warmly upon Manuel's shoulder. Manuel's eyes showed his appreciation.

"I won't never let you down, Massa George, never agin' – you know dat."

"I know you won't, Manuel." With these warm words between master and slave, George dismissed Manuel to go and settle himself down in the slave lines.

Neither in this new world of arms knew what the future might have in store for them.

George then prepared to go to the officer's mess, where dinner had been prepared. The mess was for E Company only of the Old Waifs and Strays. There were only two other officers with whom to share his meal. One, called Nathaniel Summers, was, like George, a second lieutenant and new that day. Nathaniel looked incredibly young and fresh-faced even to George's eyes, with only a light fuzz on his upper lip and a collar that seemed several sizes larger than his narrow youthful neck. George now sported a fine beard and moustache of which he was inordinately proud, which made him feel far more the man than his young fellow officer. The other officer was an older man, sporting two worn bars on his shoulder and clearly their mentor. He introduced himself as Captain Paul Knight. He had seen service already in a number of minor skirmishes, though to hear him talk you would have thought they were campaign-winning battles.

There wasn't room in the mess tent for them all to sit at their ease so a table had been spread for them outside where they could sit and relax. In attendance were two Negro slaves, only one of whom was dressed as a soldier.

When they were all seated, Captain Knight brought out his flask and offered it around saying, "This here's good Old Crow Kentucky bourbon straight from the barrel. They don't make it no more now the distillery's closed down. They needed the copper from the stills for munitions, though how they think we can win this war without Old Crow is beyond me. By the end of this war this'll be worth more than gold dust – so make the most of it whilst you can." With that he poured himself a generous measure and a much lesser amount into each of their campaign mugs. George sipped at it with caution and young Nathaniel seemed to shy away at the mere smell of it.

Captain Knight leant back in his chair and regarded them both. "I done a bit of soldierin' in my time a'fore this little squabble," he started, though he didn't enlighten them as to where. "Soldierin' ain't all hurrahs, glory and barrels of fun, you know, and the sooner you forget all that, the quicker you'll be of use to me, to the major and to the 10th. It's fifty per cent jaw-aching boredom, forty-nine percent drillin', marchin' an' training, an' that can be boring too, and one per cent gut-wrenching terror when you ain't got time to be bored and that, I can tell you, sorts the men from the boys."

After that wise little homily, he then explained the routine for the next few weeks. It was to be a regime of drill and weapon cleaning. The drill was particularly important and had to be taken by the officers in order that the soldiers should get used to their words of command, so they would respond instantly in the chaos of battle. The weapon handling and cleaning could safely be left to the sergeant and the corporals. After a time, he warned, the men would get tired of this constant repetition, but it was vital that, untrained as they were, they should learn instinctively to follow orders without question and to be able to handle their weapons as if they were an extension of their own bodies. "They won't like guards and camp duties either," he continued, "and they decidedly won't take to the restrictions of army life and not being able to come and go as they please. Any disobedience or refusal to obey orders is to be harshly dealt with under the Confederate Army Disciplinary Code. And it don't get much harsher 'n that," he added. "If we do our job properly we'll all be joining the Old W. S. inside of ten weeks. Then we can take a crack at them damn Yankees."

28

New Life in the Bayou

For days, scarcely a smile appeared on Ursula's face. She did all that was expected of her and helped in every way she could to assist Matthew in running the cabin in the swamp, but her heart and mind were clearly elsewhere. She imagined that already George was facing shot and cannon. She really did not understand why he had to go and fight. As for Matthew, he was envious of George, for he too longed to join in the struggle but on the other side. Instead his friend had committed him to acting as escort to his girlfriend in the long and hazardous journey to Canada. There would be dangers aplenty, but not the glorious hazards of war. His dangers, by contrast, would have all the glamour of a rat cornered in a barn. Both their thoughts were of George and for both they were tinged with a touch of bitterness.

Every day they would journey together down in the dugout to the rendezvous to see if Samuel had managed to leave any message as George had said he would. Each day they drew a blank and their sense of seclusion and abandonment increased. But a subtle change was taking place in their relationship. Matthew was determined to show that he was more than equal to the task of survival in the wildness. Ursula, for her part, was keen to dispel Matthew's obvious doubts of her ability to cope with such a challenge. Such was their mutual determination to prove each to the other that gradually their seclusion was driven to the back of their thoughts. Ursula's naturally sunny disposition began to return. The realisation dawned upon her that she was, for the first time in her life, no longer a slave. What she did now about the cabin and assisting Matthew in other ways she did of her own will. She found herself humming, sometimes singing with a new lightness of spirit.

It wasn't all work. There was time for themselves: time when they could do the things that they wanted to do, time to follow a whim or pursue a passing fancy. It was a luxury new to them both. Ursula gradually grew accustomed to the new rhythm of her life and her new environment and she stopped fearing that which she didn't understand. Matthew no longer wandered off in the evenings to play his flute, but now remained on the veranda of Old Mo's cabin. He and Ursula sang to some of the tunes and the slave songs they both knew. They talked about their feelings and expectations as human beings and how things might and should be in an ideal world. They talked about the end of slavery, about slaves taking part in their own government. They owed much to the education they had both had under the benevolent eye of Mary Styles. They discussed the formation of a whole free state for slaves. It would be part of a United States of America. It would be just like any other of the states with its own governor and legislature. They talked too about the possibility of travel and of seeing parts of the globe that were just exotic names to them. They talked of impossible things that with their freedom might somehow suddenly become possible. Because there was no emotional entanglement between them, they spoke to each other with a freedom and frankness they had never shared with any other human being. In short, they began to enjoy each other's company in a way that they would not have thought possible a few weeks before.

The days turned to weeks and still there was no sign of Samuel. Their trips to the rendezvous became just a daily routine, a ritual without any sense of anticipation or purpose. To both it seemed as if they were suspended in a golden sphere where time no longer mattered. There was nothing they could do to hurry things up and the prospect of returning to Nethergate to get news, was for the moment far too risky.

Then one morning, as they paddled towards the rendezvous, Matthew noticed a change in the way the birds were calling. He raised a finger of caution to Ursula. Silently they guided their canoe towards the meeting place.

Someone was standing there. It was Samuel. Though both would never have admitted it, even to themselves, both felt a frisson of disappointment, for his presence meant the intrusion of the outside world into what had become their own private domain. As they approached him though, they noticed a marked change. It surely was Samuel, but a changed Samuel; he looked so gaunt and haggard.

Matthew and Samuel formally shook hands. It seemed the right thing to do.

"Whatever's the matter?" asked Matthew as he beached the dugout. "You look so unwell."

"Ah's been back out workin' the 'baccy fields," replied Samuel with great dignity, displaying the cracked and pink surfaces of the palms of his hands, now slowly healing. "Mistress sought to teach me a lesson for ma 'high an' mighty ways'. But dem critters in de house started acted up so ornery dat every darn t'ing went all awry. Nutting got done." Samuel permitted himself a deep-throated chuckle at the recollection of it. "In the end she orders me back to de house ag'in wid a 'let that be a lesson to you, Samuel'. But dat Mr Killcaid made de most of de time Ah was in de fields. He give me all de hardest jobs. Ah s'pose Ah's not as young as I was an' not used to sich work. When I was back in de house agin, Ah fell sick. Morella, she was God's blessing to me, so she was. Without her I think de' blessed Lord would ha' called me to his bosom. She was de only one dat Ah could truss', but she bin far too old now to venture down here. Ah couldn't truss no-one to get a message to you as I promise, Massa George ah would."

It was a long speech and Samuel paused to regain his breath and regarded them both as they thanked him for coming.

Both had their own burning questions to ask.

"Any news of the old Mistress Styles and my mammy?" asked Matthew.

"Any news of when Ah can go North?" asked Ursula at the same time.

Samuel raised his hands as if to ward off their barrage of questions and slowly shook his head. "No firm news on both scores, but Ah do hear as your mammy and de old Mrs. Styles have left New York and should be back here any day soon. T'ings is lookin' hopeful wid de railroad," he said. Then his face broke into an amused grin. "And thars no ways any o' you's a-goin' anywhere the way you is."

For the first time the two fugitives looked at each other, Matthew wearing the tattered remains of his trousers, his hair grown long and sporting a magnificent beard, and Ursula dressed in a parody of the Nethergate servant's uniform, but with bare arms and legs. Both broke into smiles, aware for the first time how they must appear to Samuel.

"Things were delayed whilst I was worked in de fields and because we had to include one more fugitive in de arrangements now that Massa George say he want you to go too, Matthew. But in de next few days Ah is seein' the porter and maybe, jus' maybe, yous'll both soon be on de train to freedom."

The two young people looked at each other with hope bright in their eyes.

"Next time Ah come, I'll bring you both sometin' more suitable for you to wear," and he began to chuckle deep in his chest. Ursula and Matthew smiled too, for it was good to hear old Samuel laugh that way again.

Slowly their smiles froze. Samuel's laughter had changed to coughing and the colour, as they looked, was draining from his face. He was fighting for breath his hands clawed at his throat. Then a spasm wracked his body. He clutched his chest, his face contorted with pain. He went rigid. His body sagged. Before they could reach him, his knees buckled and he fell to the ground.

29

Samuel

Matthew and Ursula stared in horror at the crumpled form of Samuel lying still at their feet. At first, they thought he was dead, but he was still breathing. They propped him up by a tree and loosened his shirt, both feeling helpless. It seemed impossible that such a dignified and authoritative figure as Samuel should be laid so low.

"What shall we do?" asked Ursula in desperation. "We can't leave him here."

"Give him a few more minutes. Then we'll decide." But truthfully Matthew did not have a plan either. However, their dilemma was saved by a low moan from their patient and Samuel opened his eyes. At first, he seemed to gaze about in confusion, but then understanding returned. He struggled to rise but fell back into Matthew's anxious arms.

"I'll be right in a moment or two," muttered Samuel, but his voice was slurred, and it was clear to both that he was in no condition to walk. They stayed with him for some time until Samuel again tried to get to his feet, but it was no use.

"You'd best leave me," said Samuel. "Happen in an hour or so I'll maybe git ma strength back agin. We can't have either of you goin' back for help. That'd give de whole game away."

But Matthew would not hear of it. "No, Samuel. I'll go back now to the cabin and fetch some water and a blanket to keep you warm. Ursula will stay with you. Then when it gets dark, I will go back to Nethergate and see if I can contact Morella. Sure as anythin' she'll know what to do."

Before Samuel could raise any further objections, Matthew turned away and made his way to the dugout, leaving Ursula in charge of their patient.

After what seemed to Ursula an age, he returned carrying a blanket, a water bottle and some food. It was beginning to get dark as they fed Samuel a few drops of water, which was about all he could manage. Matthew had changed into his best pair of pants and the remnants of a shirt, but even so he still looked like a wild man.

During his trip back to the cabin, he had formed the beginnings of a plan. "Ursula, you must stay with Samuel. I've brought some food for you, and a little fruit for Samuel, but I doubt he'll want any. I will go back and find Morella. She is the only one I can truly trust."

"Have a care," mumbled Samuel when it became clear that Matthew planned to return to Nethergate House. "Killcaid sometimes has watchers placed at the House."

"But she's too old to come," protested Ursula at the mention of her beloved Morella.

"I know, but she will know who she can rely on to come and collect Samuel and take him to Nethergate House, where she can take care of him until he is well again. She will be able to spin a convincing tale as to how he came to be found, for they will have missed him at Nethergate Hall." He thought for a moment and then added, "As soon as you hear us approaching you must hide, for no-one must know you are still alive. I'll call out Samuel's name so as you'll know it's us."

159

For Ursula this was a sudden moment of crisis. Matthew and Samuel were the props for her journey to freedom. Now both were placed in jeopardy, for Killcaid still had people out at night since the uprising that led to the destruction of his cabin and to give warning of marauding gangs of Yankee soldiers bent on looting. The thought suddenly rushed in upon her that if Matthew were captured then he would certainly face a trial, a trial that could have but one outcome. Suddenly the thought of losing her sometimes gruff and taciturn but so competent companion filled her with more than dread. How would she live alone in the cabin? She realised, with a sudden rush, that it was not only the thought of being stranded that filled her mind with fear. The awful truth suddenly rushed in upon her. She might never see Matthew again.

On an impulse she leapt to her feet. "Oh, Matthew, take care," she cried. "You bin so good to me, and I is so grateful," and she threw her arms about him and kissed him. Then, before he could react, she abruptly broke away again, whispering, "Take right good care."

For a moment Matthew stood still, experiencing a rush of emotions. All he could think to say was, "I'll take good care. Surely will." With that he turned and was lost to them in the undergrowth. His mind was in turmoil. That kiss had awakened in him desires and longings that he had hitherto refused to acknowledge.

He had every young man's natural yearnings. Living so close to a young woman, and a beautiful young woman at that, he had been prey to his own imagination. His loyalty to George had stifled any overt indication of the sometime direction of his thoughts, but not so the direction his mind took at night. Unfettered by conscious restraints he would awaken hard with the warm flow of his stifled desires, leaving him unsettled for the remainder of that day. Then in secret glances he would savour the occasional glimpses he might see of her young body as she moved about engrossed in her daily tasks. He admired too the fall of her hair when she let it down in the evenings. His pledge to George and his understanding of his own natural urges had held him in check, but now what he was feeling was more than just a youthful craving. He had to acknowledge a much deeper affection for the once forlorn and lost little creature who now shared his life in the bayou, whom he had got to know, like and admire as they had grown ever closer in their isolation. As she coped with the complete change in her life, her confidence had grown too. She was finding a new strength. She had been tested and not found wanting.

She was another triumph of the old Mrs Styles's illegal desire to educate her household slaves. She had joined in with insight and understanding the discussions that he and George had had, sometimes over the books from Mrs Styles's library and then over wider subjects and the new ideas they engendered. He owned now how much he had looked forward to those magical hours at the end of each day when he and Ursula had sat on the veranda of the cabin and talked, sung and made music. The thought that his present venture might mark an end to this way of life was almost like a physical pain. He had to admit to himself that, far from being an intrusion, it had been a tonic to share his life in the bayou and doubly so with one as attractive and lively as Ursula.

Abruptly he forced away such speculation. Assuredly it would all be over if he did not now concentrate on the task ahead. He had a long way to travel if he were to alert Morella in time for her to be able to launch a rescue mission for Samuel under cover of darkness.

Swiftly he moved through the familiar leafy foliage of the bayou until he reached the track that led up to the tobacco fields. Then he broke into a run, secure in the knowledge that he could quickly hide amongst the tobacco plants at the least hint of danger. His mind leapt back to the last time he had run along these tracks, pursued by the Nethergate hounds, and he allowed himself a grim smile at Killcaid's discomfiture.

At last he broke through into the parklands that lay at the heart of Nethergate in which the twin Houses of Nethergate stood. He paused to listen with a keen, practised ear and allowed the night sounds that had been drowned by the rush of his own movement to wash about him. He would not allow the urgency of the situation to outweigh his natural caution. Experience and Old Mo's teaching had shown him time and again that such moments of watching and listening were rarely wasted.

A soft breeze gently stirred the undergrowth and trees. Through the leaves of the oaks about the grounds of Nethergate Hall he caught occasional flickering glimpses of lights from the grand house, but the surrounds of old Nethergate House seemed to be bathed in a darkness more suited to his purpose. When he was satisfied, he moved stealthily forward. It had seemed an age since he lived there, but he felt the tug of nostalgia for the way things used to be, the warmth and love of his mother and the benign presence of the grand lady he knew to be his grandmother by blood.

He avoided the main gate. There were plenty of other, more secret ways into the grounds. Some sixth sense however made him pause. Suddenly a commotion broke out some way off. There was the noise of distant shouting. Two figures immediately detached themselves from the darkness by the gate, hesitated a moment and moved off towards the sound of the disturbance. They had with them a large dog. As soon as they drew level with where Matthew lay, the dog growled. Matthew froze. With surprise on his side he might overcome one of them, but hardly both and then there was the dog.

The dog growled again and dug in its paws. The man swore and stopped too, his curiosity aroused, but his companion called impatiently and with a harsh tug at the lead they were gone. But it taught Matthew an important lesson. Even if his mother were not there, Killcaid was still alert to what was going on at the house.

Matthew wormed his way through a familiar gap in the hedge and made his way to the slave quarters at the back of the house. Morella, he knew, had a room on the ground floor. He crept to her window and knocked stealthily with his knuckles. Putting his ear to the window pane, he could hear the old lady's steady breathing. He remembered then how deaf she had become. He picked up a small pebble and rapped on the window. There was still no change in the steady rhythm of her breathing. Thanking the good fortune that had diverted the attention of the two watchers he rapped again even louder. Morella slept on.

Matthew realised then that he would have to enter the building to rouse Morella. He had done so many times before when he used to roam the estate at night, despite the nightly curfew on all slaves. He tested the creeper outside his old bedroom window. Faithfully it held firm. It was the work of a few moments to shin up its familiar limbs, prise open his window and slip silently inside. It felt good to be back home. He paused at his mother's room, half hoping she might have returned and been there, but he knew Samuel would have said so. He opened the door and paused a moment. It smelt of his mother and he wondered if he would ever see her again. Then he hastened on down through the slumbering stillness to Morella on the ground floor.

Although Matthew's rapping on Morella's window had failed to awaken her, it had however alerted another member of that household. Though she could not positively identify the shadowy figure in the darkness, she had a fair idea as to who it might be. When Ruth and Mrs Styles had left for New York, Killcaid had inserted Laticia into the staff of Nethergate House to be his eyes and ears. It had been her reward for informing him of Matthew's movements after their departure. Killcaid had plans, approved by Anthony, that Laticia should eventually take over Ruth's job as maid to old Mrs Styles. He knew that Ruth would forever poison the mind of her mistress against him. She would now be doubly enraged at his treatment of her son. How he would get rid of Ruth was a matter that would tax even his ingenuity, but he meant to achieve it and he rarely failed. He knew that once Ruth returned to find her son wanted for murder, she would do anything to save him.

Ever hopeful of once again gaining Silas Killcaid's approval, Laticia had taken to her new duties with enthusiasm and reported to him in detail everything she saw. She had reason to believe that this time he would be really pleased at her news. She hastened down to tell the slaves Killcaid stationed nightly at the gate to Nethergate House.

30

Samuel's Rescue

Matthew paused to knock on Morella's door, but, realising that that would be futile, he eased his way silently in. The old lady was still noisily asleep. Gently he shook her. Her snuffling ceased. He realised she was awake and probably alarmed as to who had woken her.

"Morella, don't be frightened, it's me – Matthew. I must talk with you."

It was typical that the old lady's immediate thought was for his safety. Her first words were, "Matthew! Child, have a care. Killcaid has watchers at the gate."

"I know, Morella. There was some sort of a disturbance and they went away to investigate. I came in unseen."

"Now just you wait a moment and I will light a candle so I can look at you. You best make sure the curtains are drawn."

Obediently, Matthew drew the blinds tight across the windows and Morella lit her candle. She let out a gasp when she saw him.

"My, but, Matthew, I'd never have recognised you with that beard had I not first heard you speak. I don' know what your mammy would say could she see you. What have you been doing with yoursel'? Now, let me look at yo' proper."

After a brief inspection, she declared herself satisfied. "Well, living in dem swamps seem to have done you no harm. You's as healthy looking a young pup as I ever did see, though you look like the wild man of the woods hisself."

She would have gone on, but Matthew cut her short and hastily explained the situation now facing Samuel. At the mention of his name, Morella became all concern.

"Dat Samuel. He's a good man, a very good man." With that she threw on a robe to cover her night clothes. "We mus' fetch help fo' the poor man." Then, placing her finger to her lips in caution, she added, "Now yo' mus' be quiet as a mouse for there's folks here now as would sell their very soul to that Mr Killcaid."

Motioning for him to follow she led the way to the men's quarters, where she roused Jacob, who fulfilled Samuel's role at Nethergate House. When Jacob realised who Matthew was he greeted him with warmth, then hastily left to rouse three of the men of whose loyalty he was certain.

Soon all five men were gathered, shivering partly in the night-time chill and partly for the risks that lay ahead. Matthew had been surprised and moved by the warmth of their welcome when they recognised the wild figure confronting them. He quickly briefed them. "We will need a stretcher or a carrying frame for Samuel: he can't walk," he added, finally.

"We'll take one from the stables on the way out," said Jacob.

"Are you coming too, Jacob?" Matthew asked.

"Samuel, he's my friend," replied Jacob, simply.

"I'll be waitin' when yo' come back," assured Morella. With that the five shadowy figures detached themselves from the darkness about the slave quarters and crept silently to the stables. The horses stirred restlessly as the party sought out one of the carrying frames that were kept there. Keeping to the shadows, the rescue party moved to the hole in the hedge. Laticia, now back in her room having found no-one at the gate, watched in frustration. She was in a ferment of excitement. When the party came out of the stables she was sure she had recognised Matthew. She was certain that Killcaid would be more than interested. But with no-one at the gate she had no way of passing on the news.

The rescue party made good time under Matthew's surefooted guidance. There was still the sound of some sort of disturbance in the distance, but it was not unusual in these restless times. Once out in the fields they were able to relax. Brief whispered conversation and words of encouragement passed between them as they all hurried on. All of them were intrigued as to how Matthew had escaped the dreaded Nethergate coonhounds.

Soon they reached the area where the track vanished in the vastness of the swamplands and Matthew led them on in single file. As he neared where he knew Samuel and Ursula to be, he paused and gave the agreed signal to give Ursula time to hide.

When they reached Samuel, he again struggled to get to his feet. This time he succeeded. Clearly, he would need the carrying frame. With hasty greetings and willing hands, he was soon readied for travel and the party left with Matthew guiding them back onto the track that led to Nethergate. There they paused, and Samuel beckoned Matthew over to him.

"I'll be back," he whispered, "but give me a day or two to get back on ma feet."

"You be sure to get yoursel' good and well," replied Matthew. "We can wait."

With whispered farewells, Matthew watched the party making its way back down the track. With a pang of regret, he realised how much he pined for the company of others and the life back at Nethergate House. It had been good to be back with the familiar smells and feel of the house he still called "home". Good to sense the comforting assurance of Morella's presence and the warmth and welcome from the others. He realised how much he had missed it all, but then his thoughts turned to Ursula, who would be anxiously waiting for him. A feeling of more than warmth surged suddenly through him. He remembered again her farewell embrace and the feel of her young body pressed so fleetingly close to his.

31

The Ball

After Ruth had bathed and started to dress, Mary came in to talk as her maid prepared her for the evening ahead. Ruth was wearing her favourite red ball gown, which she and Mary had chosen in New York for one of her father's entertainments. It set off her dark complexion and raven hair to best advantage. As she donned it, she could not help wondering when and if she might wear it again. This was the last evening on which she would truly feel like a free woman. This evening alone was a certainty. The future was unknown, whatever Mary might have promised.

Mary gazed at her in frank admiration. She had always somehow thought of Ruth more as a daughter than her lady's maid. She knew that Ruth had grown very fond of the enigmatic Colonel and had been won over by his confession of love for her. What woman would not be flattered and impressed. Yet she knew the nature of the times in which she lived and the inbred prejudice of Southerners against those who came from slave stock. Colonel Gladstone was in all respects a man true to his times. She doubted that even his confessed love could survive such an exposure. She looked again at Ruth, seeming so radiant and beautiful in her ball gown, her eyes alight with anticipation of the evening ahead. Her heart moved for her.

Once the maid had been dismissed, she spoke to her frankly, "Ruth, dear, you will have a care tonight. I have seen how you look at the Colonel. I should hate you to be hurt."

"I know," she replied, "but this may be the last chance I have to feel like a free woman, indeed to feel like a woman at all, for I don't know how long. Even if your plan comes to fruition and the Master grants me my freedom, nothing about me will have changed. Nethergate will always be my home. It is where my son is, as well as my mother. Being your maid is the only work I have ever wanted to do. If at midnight tonight the clock chimes and I am revealed for what I truly am, then at least I will have had this evening to remember."

Mary felt the sting of tears in her eyes at these words. She had always hated the slavery which gave her wealth and comfort, but there was little she could do about it. "Ruth, dear, I want you to have this to wear this evening and to keep, to remind you of this moment in your life." With that she produced a sparkling blue lapis lazuli choker, which she fastened about Ruth's neck.

Ruth stared at her reflection in the mirror. She liked what she saw. "They look beautiful on you, my dear," said Mary. "In fact, you look truly beautiful too. I hope this will be an evening that in every way lives up to your expectations."

With tears of gratitude shining in her eyes she thanked her mistress. Just then they were both arrested by the distant sound of a solo violin playing outside their open window, not unusual in this place given over to the senses and to pleasure. They both continued their conversation, but there was something about the quality and urgency of the playing that arrested their attention and their conversation died away as they were drawn to the balcony to better hear the music.

On the lawn was Thomas playing his heart out, as he always did when a violin was under his chin. He looked up briefly when the two women appeared and inclined his head in acknowledgement of their presence. It was a strangely quixotic gesture for a man of Colonel Gladstone's natural reserve. Mary recognised the music immediately as a piece from Vivaldi. It was a tune that had a joyous lightness of touch and yet a sense of urgency too. It was wholly appropriate for the evening ahead.

At last Thomas finished and bowed at the two ladies looking down. There was a ripple of unexpected applause from other balconies which people had been drawn to by the sounds of his melody. Clearly embarrassed by this unforeseen acclaim, Colonel Gladstone again bowed formally in acknowledgement and then left hastily for inside the hotel.

Mary looked at Ruth, who was flushed at this public display of his regard for her. "Well," she said, "that was a very pretty compliment. Not, I think, a very easy gesture for him to make. He must care greatly for you my dear."

At that moment there was a discreet knock at the door and a uniformed servant respectfully informed Ruth that Colonel Gladstone was expecting her. With a heart brimming with expectation she made her way downstairs, to where Colonel Thomas Gladstone was waiting.

The Colonel stood at the foot of the stairs, where they ended in a broad and graceful sweep. He could not recall having ever seen a sight so captivating as that of Ruth as she gracefully descended the stairs towards him, with her eyes shining and a shy smile playing about her lips. As for Ruth, she could hardly believe that a man as grave and distinguished as the Colonel could possibly find her interesting and attractive enough to make such a public gesture of his regard.

"Thank you, Thomas," she said, laying a hand on his arm. "That was a lovely gesture and such a beautiful way to start our evening together."

He smiled, still slightly embarrassed at his own temerity in such a public declaration, and greeted her with a formal kiss to the cheek, saying, "My dear, you look absolutely wonderful. I will surely be the envy of every man here tonight. Let me look at you." Ruth smiled up at him. She felt she had never been so happy. From the ballroom came strains of familiar music and gales of male laughter. Colonel Gladstone offered her his arm and together they were embraced by the beguiling, hedonistic atmosphere of an occasion where everyone was hell bent on enjoying themselves.

It was an evening such as Ruth had never experienced, even in the household of Henry Bragg at his most expansive. They danced; they engaged in conversation with some of the people there whom the Colonel seemed to know. They visited the gaming tables and somehow Ruth always seemed to win. There were performers from all over the world; Indian snake charmers, Chinese dancers, Egyptian conjurers and Asian acrobats.

Then they entered the cloistered balcony for dinner and were at last able to talk above the bustle and clatter of the gaming tables and the sweeping rhythms of the ballroom. They found it easy to talk to each other and their conversation ranged far and wide. After dinner Thomas took her arm and led her outside into the famed gardens of the Royal Victoria Hotel. They walked together, arm in arm. The sound of the music and laughter was soon muted by the enfolding tropical greenery and they moved into one of the small bowers that were discreetly scattered about the grounds. There they felt truly alone at last. Then, witnessed by a statue of the naked four graces, Thomas turned her face gently up to his and their lips met in a kiss that Ruth wished would go on forever.

Her mind could not help but return to the last time she had been kissed. Then it had been Mark, raw and ugly in lustful hunger, now it was the gentleness of love and respect, but no less passionate for that. However, the magic of the moment was rudely shattered by a sudden eruption of giggling laughter from a young woman and the deep pleading of a male voice as a young couple burst in on their privacy.

"Oh, occupé! Pardon monsieur, madam," said a French voice and the couple left as abruptly as they had arrived in a wave of fresh squeals and male exhortations. Colonel Gladstone released Ruth with a wry smile for the magic of their special moment had been shattered by the naked desires of the Frenchman. He ushered her to a bench. "I have a small memento of this evening which I hope you will accept," he said. "May I?" he added taking her hand. Ruth felt something cold being wrapped about her wrist and heard a soft click as Thomas fastened a bracelet. Even in the dim light it seemed to burn with its own inner fire. For a moment she was overcome. No man had ever given her a gift such as this and in this way. She held it up to the light. The jewels seemed to gather to themselves all the light there was in their shaded grotto and throw it back again.

"Do you like it?" he asked anxiously.

"Oh! It's lovely," she said, overcome with the delight of the moment. She threw her arms about him. Again, their lips met and this time they were not interrupted.

Never had Ruth experienced such an evening, but she knew it had all to come to an end and the real world must be acknowledged. Tomorrow they were due to sail again on the last leg of their journey home, back to Nethergate and back to her life as a slave. Her face must have betrayed her thoughts for she suddenly realised that Thomas was staring at her with concern.

"What is it, my dear? What's the matter?" and he placed his hand reassuringly over hers.

"Oh, Thomas, dear Thomas, it is the thought of the morrow and my return to the life I know back at Nethergate."

"What is it that hampers you so? What is it that you cannot

tell me? We talk of so many things, but never the thing that I burn to talk of. Won't you truly let me into your life? You know that I love you and it is not easy for me to say that. Indeed, I have never said it before, because I have never met anyone like you. Won't you let me in?"

Ruth found it hard to resist his appeal. She was on the point of confessing all and facing the consequences, but she could not bear to break the spell that bound them.

"Please, Thomas, I must go now," she said and when he was about to protest she pressed a finger gently to his lips.

"At least let me take you to your room?" he asked. Together they mounted the spiral stairs of the Royal Victoria Hotel. When they reached the first floor and the sound of the ball below was muted, he took her hand and pressed the palm to his lips. At her door he halted. Her heart beat faster. She knew what he wanted, what she wanted. He let go of her hand and turned her face up to his. Then their lips met in a final, lingering kiss. She felt the tightening and hardening of his body against hers and a longing she could hardly resist.

Then he relaxed and, smiling down at her, gently caressed her cheek.

"Goodnight, my dear mystery lady. Don't think for one moment that this is the end. Someday I will discover your secret and then I assure you I will not be denied."

All she could do was to smile up at him as he bowed and left.

She opened the door to her room, still feeling the touch of his hand upon her cheek and placed her own hand over the place where his had been.

For a long time, she stood still, conscious only of the wild beating of her heart and her own passionate yearnings.

She caught sight of her reflection in the mirror. Her face was flushed. She looked the same as all the other women she had seen that night. Yet she wasn't. She alone of that number was a slave. A wave of bitterness swept over her and she clenched her fists. Then the memories of the evening came flooding back and she relaxed and basked once more in the recollection of being so close to the man she now knew she truly loved. She knew in her heart of hearts it was a hopeless love, and yet?

Donning her night attire, she clambered at last into bed feeling the cool caress of the sheets and ran her hands over her body, wishing that her hands were his. She still wore the bracelet he had given her. Its feel was a reminder of the gentleness of his touch as he had placed it on her wrist. When she did sleep, she dreamt of him with a sweetness that was past understanding.

32

Running the Blockade

Ruth was awakened next morning by her maid. She had warmed immediately to Mandy's cheerful nature and sometimes quite shocking revelations about the goings on in the hotel. She empathised with her, conscious all the time that the maid occupied a higher place in society than did her mistress. Mandy treated her as a grand lady whom it was her privilege to serve.

"Beg pardon, ma'am," said Mandy, bobbing neatly, "but I is to tell you that you sails today on the noon tide. I is to pack one case only fo' you, the rest to come later."

The maid helped her dress and she instructed her as to what should go into the single suitcase. She knew that she would have to unpack most of the things once Mandy had gone. She would take instead those clothes which she had discarded at Nashville all those months ago into that plain and battered suitcase that was a constant reminder of her true status.

For the moment she put such thoughts aside. It was the first time she had seen the bracelet Thomas had given her in daylight. It was a linked gold chain set with a mixture of rubies and diamonds. In the morning light it glistened with secret fires of its own. The choker Mary had given her was exquisite too, but she thought the bracelet the most beautiful thing she had ever seen. The memories of their evening came flooding back upon her so that she found it hard to concentrate on the tasks ahead. Whatever else she took with her, she could never be parted from Thomas's gift and she brought it to her lips and kissed it tenderly, shutting her eyes and seeing the man who had given it to her screened in the intimacy of the garden bower.

Colonel Gladstone had breakfast with them. During the meal she caught his eye and there passed between them looks that conveyed more than words. She could not believe that the feelings she now felt could possibly end in emptiness and in never seeing him again. How they might come together was an enigma. She could not in reality conceive of anything that would overcome their differences in background. Yet, still she hoped. Now she meant to live for the present and to savour and store in her mind every fleeting moment that they might be together in the busy two days of danger and hazard which lay ahead.

The Colonel left early, saying he had much to do in preparing for the voyage and for their passage on one of the blockade breakers. He warned again that it would not be a comfortable voyage and that they should dress for heavy weather and comfort. Conditions below decks were spartan and he explained that the fumes from the boilers would be intolerable, but that he had rigged a shelter for them on the afterdeck, where they would be shielded from the worst of the weather and from most of the fumes from the twin smoke stacks.

Mary was not blind to what was going on and only grieved for the disappointment and sadness that could be the only outcome. She could have put a stop to it all by revealing Ruth's status to the Colonel, but she had not the heart to do so, knowing now how emotionally involved Ruth was. She knew that Ruth must realise there could be no future for them as a couple. She would not deny Ruth her memories and her dreams. She could but hope that, when the time came, her natural concerns for her son would not allow her time to dwell too deeply upon her personal loss.

The morning dragged by. They both missed the company of the Colonel. After breakfast they briefly retired to their rooms where Ruth had repacked the case containing her slave clothes. The last few months seemed surreal, like something that had happened to someone else. The two ladies had agreed to meet to enjoy a last stroll about the pleasure gardens of the hotel, before the final leg of their journey. The flowerbeds and lawns had all been meticulously tended and cared for and were vibrant with colour and the scent of flowers. The air was full of the cheerful clamour of birds, the gentle murmur of bees and the clatter and chatter of crickets and other insects. Yet, somehow, they had ceased to be a part of it all, as if the imminence of their departure on the noon tide had already divorced them from this world of business, intrigue and pleasure. As the pony and trap finally carried them away from the hotel hill, Ruth turned about for a last look at the place where she had acknowledged to herself her real feelings for the Colonel.

The Colonel was on the quay, supervising the loading of what looked like gun carriages. Mary recognised immediately the mark of her father's factory upon them. There was no name that she could see, but the style and quality of the product and its protection for the journey she recognised as bearing the stamp of her father's manufacture. It explained the Colonel's interest in their travels and came as no surprise. Her father was the strongest of patriots for the Yankee cause, but that did not stop him making money from the Confederates too. He would see no conflict of interests in providing war materials for the enemy if there was a profit to be made. "If I don't do it you can be damned sure there's someone else as will," she could hear him saying. If a Yankee should die as a result of what he had supplied, well, they would have perished just as finally were it to be provided by someone else. His worship of profit and enterprise gave him a sort of innocence as to its consequences.

The Colonel came over to greet them and smiled warmly at Ruth. He was accompanied by another young man, whom he introduced as Captain Moffitt of the Confederate Navy who would be skippering their craft, the SS *Adventure*. For the first time they had a chance to look closely at the ship in which they were to run the Yankee blockade. It was a sleek-looking craft specially built in England for the purpose, narrow of beam, plainly a greyhound of the seas. It had twin paddles and fore and aft masts, that would carry no great weight of canvas. Apart from their twin funnels there was no superstructure, just a few cabins on the foredeck for the captain and his officers. Beside the two flat-bottomed lighters a temporary superstructure, no bigger than a small hut, had been erected. The Colonel pointed to it with an air of apology.

"I am afraid, ladies, that is to be your accommodation for the next day and a bit. The funnels are high enough to keep the smoke clear from where you are. There is a small table for you to take your meals and two beds, secured to the deck."

"What is that in the middle?" asked Ruth, pointing at a stall made from stout planks in the middle of the craft.

"Oh, that," said the Colonel, a hint of disapproval creeping into his voice. "That is a special gift for President Jefferson Davis all the way from Arabia. God knows what it must have cost getting it here, let alone the purchase price. It is a gift from a group of state senators no doubt wishing for some preferment or other."

"But what is it?" pressed Ruth, consumed with curiosity.

"Unless I am very much mistaken, it is coming now," he answered. She turned and being led down the quayside was a fine Arab stallion. Every movement of his body, every toss of his head, spoke of class and pedigree. He seemed entirely at his ease, despite that his feet were wrapped in cloth so that his approach was entirely silent. The groom looped thick leather bands about his underside and at a signal he was hoisted off the ground. He struggled at first then relaxed and surveyed the world passing under his belly. Gently he was lowered into the pen on the deck. With a couple of savage but muffled kicks he tested the walls of the pen then, deciding nothing further was to be gained, settled down to eating the hay which had been provided.

"An extraordinary animal," commented the Colonel. "He's been travelling now for nearly nine months on and off and seems to have got used to all the comings and goings. He's rested for months at a time at each stopping off point in order to cope with the next leg of the journey. He seems to take it all in his stride, even having his hooves wrapped like that to give him a bit more of a grip on the deck and now of course to stop him making a noise when we run the blockade."

The two ladies now boarded, stopping to say hallo to the stallion, which came over to greet them with a little whinny of interest and accepted their attention as of right. Ruth had always understood horses and soon had the stallion's special interest, whilst the Colonel looked on with smiling approval at the revelation of yet another talent in the woman upon whom he doted.

"I see you have a special way with horses," he remarked approvingly, and Ruth smiled at the implied compliment.

It didn't take the ladies long to settle into their cabin and they soon came out on deck, conscious now of the gentle movement under their feet. They took stock of their surroundings. They could feel the rhythmic throb of the engine from somewhere deep within the *Adventure*, like a heartbeat. Both funnel tops were distorted by the heat of the boilers below, leaking wisps of black smoke into the clear blue of the tropical sky.

Words of command were barked, and it suddenly seemed that seamen were scurrying everywhere. The ship cast off and the sails were run up. The SS *Adventure* heeled over and grasped the wind with its little stubs of canvas and became a living thing. She slowly made her way out from the shelter of the harbour, caressing the gentle swell as the helmsman set a course westward.

The Colonel was standing beside them. "I hope you have those bracelets I gave you on the way out from New York. I don't know how they work, but they seem to do the trick with me and the SS *Adventure* does roll a bit. I expect the skipper will test the engines before long."

Almost on cue, the noise from below increased in tempo. Great gouts of black smoke belched forth from the funnels. The canvas was run down from both mastheads. Slowly the paddles began to turn with a sound like a slow millrace. The sails were stowed, and the *Adventure* righted itself. The paddles turned faster and faster yet, leaving a frothy wake either side of the ship. Suddenly it seemed the ship was in the grip of something stronger than the wind. She began to surge through the water at speed that seemed impossible. The paddles were engulfed in a fine spray. The sea seemed to be flying past under them. It was so exciting that Ruth began to laugh and shout at the sheer delight of the experience. Then almost as suddenly as it had started the engine slowed down and became muted once again. The paddles turned now with their own momentum through the water. The sails were run up and the ship once again became a slave to the wind.

By then the sun was beginning to set and both women stared out as its great red orb settled further below the horizon. They had only the blockade to pass and they would be home.

"We go as far as we can under sail," explained the Colonel, "to save fuel and costs. We will hope to reach the area of the blockade within about thirty hours and then we'll run through it under cover of darkness."

33

A Kind of Betrayal

When the party carrying the stricken Samuel back to Nethergate House had been swallowed into the night, Matthew's thoughts turned once more to Ursula. Her embrace on their parting had quite changed the way he now thought of her. As he sped back to where he had left her his mind returned again and again to that farewell embrace. The heady memory of her body pressed against his, the firmness of her breasts and the sudden molten warmth of her body flooding through his scant clothing had filled him with hope and expectations that he dared not acknowledge, even to himself. He thought of George and was overcome with a sense of guilt and betrayal. George was the only true friend he had ever known. Each had been prepared to sacrifice their lives for the other. That was the measure of their friendship. George had entrusted him with the care of the woman he loved and now, in his thoughts, he had already betrayed that trust. In the face of such monumental duplicity how would he ever be able to look him in the eye again? Then another thought occurred to him. How then would George feel about granting him his freedom? He resolved finally to be firm and to resist the passions that threatened to engulf him.

He reached the spot where he had left Samuel. There was no sign of Ursula. A sudden wild alarm seized him. Then there was a rustle of foliage and Ursula emerged framed against the grey light of the early dawn. Before he could think, she was in his arms again.

"Oh, Matthew. I bin so worried 'bout you. In case you got catched," she sobbed. And indeed, she was sobbing with relief at his safe return. Matthew's resolutions vanished as though they had never been. He felt his hands caressing the soft tresses of her hair. Ursula shuddered at his touch and seemed to melt into his arms. For what seemed an age they both clung to each other conscious only of the unspoken change in their relationship. Neither wanted to break the magic of this moment, or to face the reality that it must bring.

It was Matthew who spoke first. "Oh, Ursula," he murmured, his face buried in her hair, "I love you. I think I always have."

"And I love you too, Matthew," she said. She turned her face up to his and their lips met in a long, passionate kiss in which their bodies seemed for a moment to become one.

It was Matthew again who broke away and voiced the thought that was uppermost in both their minds. "What about George?" he asked. She looked away.

"George bin so good to me. Without his help I don't know what I would have done 'bout his mother. And he save me fro' the whippin'. I don't know, Matthew. I still love him for all he's been to me. Is that possible, do you think? Can one love two people at the same time?"

Matthew for his part too had to examine his conscience. He still loved George like a brother, and he felt keenly the betrayal of that trust and friendship. The memory came back to him of the last time he had seen George when George had paddled away from the cabin's little jetty. The mystery of those final words of George haunted him now, "Be true to me, brother", and his reply said with such certainty, "O' course I'll be true. You know that."

"Come on," he said, turning with sudden resolution. "This ain't no place and time to talk over sich matters. Let's get back to the cabin. For one thing I'm beat and for another I'm starving."

Glad to postpone what was in both their minds they made their way back through the freshly awakening swampland to the cabin they both thought of as "home". There they satisfied their hunger from left-overs and exhausted by the night's anxieties and activities sought the comfort of their beds. Soon, as day was breaking over Old Mo's cabin, they both slept.

Matthew was first to waken and lay for a time considering the night's events. There had been no news of George since he had joined the Confederates. Now Samuel was laid low it might be weeks before he was fit enough to make his way into the bayou. They were truly on their own. The burden of responsibility for Ursula weighed heavily upon him. She was so vulnerable. He could hear her soft, regular breathing and his heart was filled with yearning. He imagined her breasts rising and falling to that gentle rhythm. He tried to match his breathing to hers as if in some way that brought them closer together, but he found that his breath was coming in shivering gasps.

She had said that she loved him. The thought made him light-headed. He just had to see her sleeping. He crept over to the sacking screen that concealed her bed. The day was well advanced, and he thought of awakening her.

She had no night clothes, he knew that. Like him now, she slept naked. In the gathering warmth of the day she had carelessly shrugged aside the blanket in her sleep. One smooth brown shoulder only partly hid one bare breast. His eyes caressed the entire length of her body exposed to view. He seemed to breathe in the gentle swell of her belly and the start of her mound of Venus. He was filled not with passion but a sudden overwhelming realisation of her innocent childlike vulnerability. He felt only a desire to protect her and a sweeping emotion of tenderness and compassion. With infinite care he moved the blanket back to hide her nakedness, though he could have gazed on it for ever. He leant gently over her and allowed his lips to brush as soft as gossamer over the perfect roundness of her bare shoulder.

She moved. Her arm came up and wrapped about his neck in a sleepy embrace, drawing him down to her.

"You been lookin' at me," she said, her voice still drowsy with sleep. "I knows you were."

"I jus' covered you up. What I saw was…" He fought for words, "just beautiful."

"I don' mind, Matthew. I want you to see me. All of me." Her arm now gently pulled his face to her lips. In one heady rush he was lying beside her, feeling her nakedness against his. Her drowsiness was forgotten as both eagerly sought the other in one long, breathless torrent of pent up passion.

At last, their desires spent, they lay side by side, basking in the wonder at what they had found in each other. They stayed thus full of content for what seemed like hours. At last Ursula stirred and slowly followed a trail of gentle kisses from his chest down to his stomach. Then with a sudden playful laugh she nipped his stomach with her teeth and jumped to her feet with a "Come on, lazybones. We can't stay like this forever."

With a yelp of surprise Matthew aimed a lively slap at her bare backside and joined her.

"Race you to the pool," she cried, pushing him so that he lost his balance and tumbled in a heap. Then she was gone, naked as she was, down to the pool with running water where usually they bathed alone, observing the strictest privacy. Now, naked as they were, they gave themselves up to a day in which they played and made love, deliriously happy in the newness of the birth of their relationship and in their discovery of each other. It was an undeclared holiday after the stress and anxiety of the preceding day.

In the evening Matthew prepared a special meal for them both, whilst Ursula was busy in the cabin telling him to keep away. After they had eaten Matthew played on his flute and Ursula sang until the light began to fade. Then hand in hand they made their way once more into the cabin, where Ursula revealed what she had been up to whilst he prepared their evening meal. She had decorated it with wild flowers, their fragrance heavy in the stillness of the evening. Matthew noticed at once that his bed was missing. Laughingly Ursula pulled him into the curtained area of her domain where the two beds were side by side as one. That night they lay in each other's arms, content to let the morrow take care of itself, both blissfully happy in the discovery of their love for each other, the more intense for having been so long denied.

34

Under Fire

During the night the wind had changed, and the captain had to restart the engine once again to keep on course. Mary and Ruth were awakened by the thump of the seamen's bare feet on the deck as they rushed to bring down the sails. It was followed by the rising pulse of the engine coming to life. Warm in their bunks they felt the sudden surge of movement as once again the SS *Adventure* came under power and surged forward, its paddles thrashing the water, defying wind and tide. By dawn they were again under sail and all was calm and peaceful.

The two women were glad of their thick coats as they came out on deck after a very plain breakfast. They immediately noticed a changed atmosphere about the crew, an air of alert anticipation. They noticed now a man in the crow's nest at the top of the foremast scanning the grey horizon with a telescope for any sign of Yankee ships, although they were not expected this far east. It was clear that despite his youth their captain was not taking any unnecessary risks.

Colonel Gladstone kept their company for most of the day but there was no chance of him and Ruth meeting alone. The thought of their imminent separation at the end of their journey hung heavily between them. The voyage was like a prolonged farewell where everything meaningful seemed somehow suspended.

Eventually the light began to fade. Both women had been warned to stay alert during the night and to be packed and ready for any emergency. They were again now under power and the sparks that flew from the ship's funnels and the black smoke that trailed in their wake seemed to advertise their presence, like the dragging of a bullfighter's cape. But they had confidence in their young captain and his record of successful runs.

As darkness closed in around them all lights were doused, and the ship forged its relentless passage through the waves. The Colonel joined them and in the darkness secretly grasped Ruth's hand. She found the contact enormously comforting and looked up at him, smiling in the gloom. He informed them that he would be staying with them during the run through the blockade. Little smoke was now coming from the funnels. The *Adventure* would now be burning anthracite, Colonel Gladstone informed them, to give her more power and avoid the tell-tale smoke trail and sparks which could be spotted from miles away, especially at night.

A sudden shout from the crow's nest turned all eyes upward to where the lookout was silhouetted against the night sky. He was pointing to starboard. At first there was nothing to be seen.

"Light. Nor' nor' east," cried the sailor. Then, "She's signalling."

Straight away the *Adventure* changed course, heading diagonally away from the distant light. An atmosphere of tension and excitement spread like wildfire among the crew.

"I don't think we've been spotted for sure. I don't see how they could have seen us at this distance, but sometimes a stray spark can betray you. But we've got the legs on anything they can muster," reassured the Colonel. "Clearly though we're taking evasive action, just to be on the safe side. He knows his stuff, our captain," he added confidently.

The *Adventure* slowed her pace to avoid the risk of more sparks. The wind had dropped, and the sea was running a gentle swell. As long as they were under power, they had the advantage.

"This lull won't help the Yankees. They're mostly under sail," remarked the Colonel reassuringly.

"Light on the port bow," suddenly yelled the lookout. They all saw it then. A steamship was making towards them at a smart pace and would intercept their present course in a matter of minutes. Just their luck, thought Ruth, to encounter one of the few steamships the Yankees had, and her grip tightened on the Colonel's hand.

"Full steam ahead! Starboard ten!" yelled the captain. Instantly the *Adventure* responded. The tempo from her engines increased and the ship shuddered under the sudden surge of power. Soon they were racing along at a fine rate, but still the blockader seemed likely to converge on their present setting. The captain changed course again. The *Adventure* was beginning to show her class and the gap between the two craft began to widen.

Mary and Ruth clung together, not so much from apprehension as from excitement. A sudden flash appeared from the pursuing craft. At the same instant something roared with a banshee wail over their heads. Its pressure waves made their ears pop and seemed briefly to suck the air from their lungs.

"Get down!" shouted Thomas Gladstone. "They've opened fire!" At that moment the thunderous roar of the gun's discharge reached them. Almost at the same instant there was another flash from the enemy warship as a second round was fired. A huge spout of water reared up some hundred yards to their front. They all felt the sudden rush of spray as the *Adventure* powered through the point of impact. Both women fell to the deck. Thomas spread his body protectively over Ruth as the booming discharge of the second round reached them from the Yankee ship.

The SS *Adventure* changed course yet again and the pitch of her engines increased to a frantic level. She seemed to be flying through the water, ever faster, with renewed energy. Every moment widened the distance between them and their pursuers. The two women had not had time to be frightened. Everything had happened so quickly. But, now they were waiting for the sound of a third round, they had time to contemplate their predicament. Mary, not so agile as Ruth, had bruised her knee as she had fallen to the ground. As for Ruth she felt no fear at all. She was conscious only of the man whose arms were spread protectively about her and the heat of his body as it gradually percolated through her clothing. She had never felt so safe or so secure. She wished this moment might go on for ever. But Mary was already sitting up rubbing her knee.

Thomas rose too, looking in the direction of the enemy ship, which was fast vanishing from sight.

"What's that smell?" asked Mary suddenly, "Have we been hit?"

"I reckon we must be out of range of her guns by now," said Thomas, extending his hand to help Ruth to her feet. "Please forgive the liberty, Ruth."

Ruth looked into his eyes and smiled. "Thank you, Thomas," she murmured, but both knew that the thanks were for more than his gallantry.

Thomas then helped Mary to her feet. "Are you alright?" he asked.

"Just a bruised knee, I fancy," she replied. "No harm's done. Well, that was an experience. But what am I smelling?"

"Well we've certainly not been hit," said Colonel Gladstone sniffing at the air too, "I'm told that sometimes these craft will burn cotton soaked in kerosene. It burns very hot and adds even more speed in an emergency. I guess that's what we're smelling, but they only dare use it for short spells."

The pace of the engines had now dropped to a more measured

rate. It seemed as if the ship itself was relaxing after its sudden sprint for safety and regaining its breath and composure. The Yankee ship was out of sight but for the occasional dull flicker in the distance when the sparks escaped from her funnels. Soon too even that was lost below the horizon and they were once more alone on the sea. The darkness was their friend, but about its edges they all felt the menace of the blockading fleet.

A sudden impossibly long, whinnying sigh reminded them of their other fellow passenger. Ruth instinctively rushed to where the stallion was imprisoned in its stall, full of guilt that in her own alarm she had forgotten entirely about it. The stallion tossed its head at her approach and moved about restlessly on its swathed hooves, trembling more in indignation than alarm. She patted, stroked and whispered to it. Her presence soon calmed its agitation and restiveness until its shuddering ceased and it was at ease once more and ready again to accept the world with its own remarkable aplomb, like the seasoned traveller it was. The Colonel smiled his approval.

"I sure wish I had your talent with horses," he remarked as Ruth rejoined them in the shelter of the cabin. She warmed to his praise as they all settled down to await what further adventures the night might bring.

35

Running the Gauntlet

Colonel Gladstone, Ruth and Mary remained huddled in the lee of the cabin, the only shelter they could find on the *Adventure*'s cramped deck. There had been no further signs of Yankee ships, but Colonel Gladstone warned that the earlier gunfire would have alerted others to their presence. They were proceeding with the utmost caution as they neared the coast. This was where enemy ships were likely to lie in wait of silhouette approaching shipping against the skyline. "The *Adventure* has a very low profile," explained the Colonel, "and we still have a fair chance of escaping detection." He again reminded them of the competence and successful record of their young captain. Thus, marginally reassured, the two women awaited events huddled together in the darkness.

The *Adventure*'s engines slowed still further. They could all smell land now. A crew member came to them from the captain and cautioned them to silence and not to show any light. The penalty for silence was a loss of speed. With hardly any sound from her engines the *Adventure* crept yet closer to the darker mass of the shoreline, much of which might be in Yankee hands.

"We can't be far from Wilmington," whispered Thomas.

The wind had dropped now that they were in the lee of the land. It seemed impossible that even the muted throbbing of their engines and the wash of the water against their bows could not be heard.

Suddenly their attention shifted to Jefferson's horse. It was stamping and moving about in the confines of its pen, showing every sign of an agitated restlessness. It began to nicker, shaking its head. It was a penetrating sound that would travel for miles. Ruth and the Colonel rushed to the animal to try to calm it down, before it betrayed them all. But even Ruth failed to lessen its agitation. Its lips were drawn back, its nostrils flared, sampling the night air, its tension growing every moment. Then unmistakably from across the water came the sound of an answering whinny. The stallion's head went up and it emitted a full-throated neigh. It began to kick against the planks that restrained it. Each booming impact would travel for miles.

Almost immediately lights appeared where Yankee ships were waiting in ambush.

Colonel Gladstone was wrestling with the gate to the pen. "It's some damned mare in season," he muttered. "There'll be no silencing him now." He managed at last to open the gate. With one final defiant kick at his prison wall, the stallion leapt over the side and landed in a fluorescent flurry of spray. Immediately it began to swim, its ears back, frantic to make the distant shore.

"The president will have to forgo his horse now," muttered the Colonel wryly, "Let's hope it's not done for us too. Come, let's get back to the side of the cabin and get what shelter we can."

Their cover now blown, the tempo of the engines increased. Below decks the stokers worked frantically to get up a full head of steam. Caution was thrown to the wind. There was now no need for silence. The captain roared out orders. They were hell-bent now on one mad dash for the shelter of Wilmington harbour.

As the ship gathered speed the three passengers all clustered to the lee of the cabin, away from where they expected the Yankee ships to be. Once again Thomas sheltered Ruth with his body, and she felt his warmth creep through to her.

They didn't have to wait long. With a shrieking whoomph that popped their ears a round flew over the *Adventure* and struck the water some half a mile distant. The sound of its discharge reached them almost immediately. "They're close," observed the Colonel, "but they've not got our range yet. It's damned difficult in this light. Happen we'll run the gauntlet without mishap yet."

The *Adventure* was now almost fully up to speed and was surging through the water at a fine rate. A few more shots were fired, but none was a cause for anxiety. The booming detonation of the discharge from the Yankee ships was more alarming than the distant fall of shot. The two women began really to believe they might yet reach the defences of Wilmington unscathed.

"Enemy, starboard bow!" suddenly came a cry from the crow's nest. All eyes turned to the starboard. With sparks flying from her funnel another Yankee steamship was bearing down on them on a course that would intercept them in a matter of a few thousand yards. No-one had seen her approach so preoccupied had they all been with being rid of the stallion and then the subsequent gunfire.

Immediately the captain turned away and ran yet closer to the shoreline. A huge spout of water just across their bows drenched them all. The two women huddled even lower into the flimsy shelter of their cabin. Suddenly Mary grasped Ruth's wrist.

"If anything happens to me, Ruth, dear, there's a black bag in the cabin. Be sure to get it to Anthony."

"Yes, ma'am," replied Ruth, reverting to her slave form of address. "I'll sure do that. Yes I will," and she pressed her hand against that of Mary's to reassure her.

Colonel Gladstone had heard their urgent whispering and sought to comfort them.

"She's firing across our bows. She wants us to heave to. We've nothing to fear. They'll want to capture the *Adventure* intact and press her into service with the blockade. She's a prize well worth having. But our skipper's not beat yet."

The *Adventure* was leaping like a greyhound through the waves and drawing away from her pursuer, but she was perilously close to the shore. They could see the darker mass of trees and clearly the breaks between them. Ruth now clung to Mary, sensing her distress.

Ahead was the bulk of a small island in the middle of the channel.

"We're mighty close to Wilmington now. I recognise Smiths Island," said the Colonel. "If we can squeeze between that and the land, we'll be in the Cape Fear River and clean away. The Yankee's screw-driven and has a deeper draft. She'll not dare to follow."

Another shot screamed over their heads. All three instinctively ducked.

"She still wants us as a prize," the Colonel reassured them.

The pursuing ship was clearly dropping behind. Suddenly the *Adventure* struck something. They were all thrown forward. No-one was left standing. All the sailors were on their knees. The ship was not moving. Her port side was solidly grounded and the whole ship heeled over to starboard. In the gathering light they could see that their pursuer had hove to, clearly taking their fate as a warning.

Their captain appeared as they were brushing themselves down. He seemed strangely buoyed by their grounding, as if it were all a fine adventure.

Seeing the Colonel he remarked. "We're all secure below. Say what you will about the English, they build damned solid ships. We're not scuppered yet." He then peered over the side to get a better look at the sandbank on which they were lodged. Then, shouting orders, he returned to his station. Straight away they heard the sound of the engine increasing its power. Suddenly the starboard paddle began to revolve, slowly at first, dredging up mud, branches and detritus from the river bed, turning the water dark with its agitation. With a scream of tortured metal, the *Adventure* began to swing to port, then with another juddering impact, movement ceased. Immediately the captain put the starboard paddle into reverse. The paddle again began to thrash the water. They were all drenched in the spray. Nothing happened. Then at last with another scream of protesting metal she began to swing her bows to starboard. All at once she righted herself. They were afloat. Cautiously the captain ordered the port paddle to turn. The paddle squealed metal against metal in protest. It was badly damaged, but it turned. Once more they were under way.

The pursuing Yankee ship had launched two boats full of sailors, bent on seizing their stricken victim. Now seeing their quarry once more on the move they turned about. The Yankees could see their prey escaping and were suddenly no longer interested in her as a prize. The Northern Navy was still equipped largely with the old smooth-bore cannon with the ability to skip solid shot across the water and strike at the hulls of enemy ships. The *Adventure* was now to fall victim to this old-fashioned weapon. A flash from their cannon and those on the *Adventure* saw a plume of spray rising. It was followed with impossible swiftness by another spout almost upon them. Then the projectile roared over their funnel with a sound like a steam train. A sudden white scar appeared, as if by magic, in the wooded slopes beyond. A great cloud of dust and debris was thrown up by its final impact. It was an awesome display of destructive power.

"She only has one forward cannon," reassured Colonel Gladstone. "It'll take her time to reload. By then we'll be round the bend and out of sight. She dare not follow us."

But the *Adventure* was not as sprightly as once she had been and was limping ahead at half her accustomed pace. Nevertheless, she was still increasing her distance from her Yankee pursuer. At every turn of her paddles their chances of escape increased. But it was not to be.

The Yankee gunners must have been better trained than Colonel Gladstone had credited. Another flash appeared from the bows of the Yankee ship, another plume of water and then one more. Now they could see the projectile swooping towards them with a swiftness that paralysed movement. Their cabin vanished in a roar of destruction. One funnel disintegrated. They were engulfed in smoke and sparks from the engine room.

Ruth was the first to recover. She groped about her amidst the smoke and touched something soft, something which emitted a low groan. It was Mary.

"Oh, Mary, ma'am. Is you alright?"

Suddenly it hit her. Where was the Colonel? Wildly she sought about her amongst the debris and confusion of smoke. Of the Colonel there was no trace.

With smoke pouring from her shattered smokestack, the crippled *Adventure* limped around the corner of Smiths Island and vanished, safe at last from the menace of the Yankee guns.

"Thomas! Thomas! Oh, Thomas!" screamed Ruth in despair. There was no reply. There was only the thump of the engines, overpoweringly magnified by the lack of a funnel and the shrieking protest from the damaged paddle to mirror her own anguish.

36

Remorse

As the *Adventure* changed course, the smoke cleared, revealing the full extent of the damage. With it went the last hopes that Colonel Gladstone might somehow have survived. Ruth felt as if part of her heart had been torn away too. All hope was gone. She stared with despair into the dark swirling waters as they rushed by. The splintered remnants of their cabin were fast vanishing astern, and with it all her dreams.

A low moan brought her suddenly back to reality. Her mistress was lying awkwardly where the Yankee shell had thrown her. Ruth's immediate concern now had to be for Mary. She rushed over to her. Her face was cut and bleeding, and she was clearly in shock.

"Mrs Styles. Oh, Mary, are you alright?" She helped her into a sitting position, propping her against the ruined side of their cabin. Her clothes were in disarray and covered with dust and debris. Life couldn't be this cruel ,she thought, in one fell stroke to deprive her of two of the people she loved most. Then she thought of the further consequences. There would be no place for her at Nethergate without Mary. Hope of emancipation would be gone. She would be sold again and parted for ever from Matthew and unable to help him.

With renewed concern she knelt beside her mistress and made her comfortable. Mary clasped her head. She mumbled incoherently, clearly still confused. Gradually she seemed to come to grips with the situation and Ruth could see that she was not seriously injured. Then Mary noticed the destruction of their cabin and a look of alarm leapt into her eyes.

"My bag!" she cried, "Where is my bag? Tell me it's still there," and she tried to get to her feet, but was in no state to stand. Ruth pressed her gently back.

"I'll go and look for you," she said, but all the time her heart was crying out, "Thomas! Thomas! Oh, where are you? Pray God you may yet be safe." Her mind was only half on what she was doing. She made her way back to where their cabin had been. Both their cases were still there, though Mary's bag had been ripped open and some of the contents had spilled out. Mechanically she started to replace them, barely noticing that she was handling bundles of Yankee dollars. Mary had told her that the bag held money, but she had no idea how much. Then she looked about for something to use as bandages to stem the bleeding from Mary's head. She found some remnants of sheeting and tore it into strips, making a pad with the remainder. Returning, she pressed the pad to Mary's head and fixed it with the makeshift bandage. Only then did Mary notice the absence of their escort.

"Where's the Colonel?" she asked.

With a barely stifled sob, "Gone," was all Ruth could manage to say. When she saw the stricken look in Ruth's face, Mary was overcome with compassion, her own injuries forgotten.

"Ruth, my poor child. My poor, poor child."

"Gone". In that one bleak word, Mary read the utter desolation of Ruth's world and of her hidden hopes. Mary's arms went out to her maid. Faced with this sudden sympathy, Ruth's self-control snapped. She found herself wracked with great shuddering sobs. It was at that moment that the captain came upon them.

"I am so sorry about Colonel Gladstone," he said. "Normally we would have turned about, but in the circumstances, that was out of the question." Then, seeing Mary's bandaged head. "I trust you are not too badly hurt, ma'am?"

Mary shook her head. "No, no," she assured him. "It's more shock than anything else."

"Is there anything I can do?" he asked, clearly anxious to be about his business.

"Thank you, no," she replied, "there's nothing."

The captain inclined his head formally with a slight bow. His youth gave him boldness in action, but he had not yet the years to deal with raw emotion in others. "If the Colonel did survive you can be assured the Yankee ship will have sent a boat out to pick him up, if for no other reason than to gather information." With that he left them to their grief.

Mary's mind was already turning on more pressing matters. "Ruth. Is my bag safe? All our futures depend on that."

"Yes, Missus, and the money." Mary looked at Ruth quizzically, for a note of bitterness had crept into her voice.

"Don't you care, Ruth? That money will force Anthony to do as I say. Even Mr Killcaid will not be able to influence him otherwise and it will also purchase Matthew and you your freedom. Don't you want that too?"

But Ruth was still too stunned by her loss.

"What good will freedom do me now?" she muttered, half under her breath.

Mary had not heard what she had said but responded to the despair in her maid's voice and embraced her once again.

"Ruth, my dear. There's still hope. As the captain said, the Yankees are sure to send a boat to investigate and, if Colonel Gladstone is alive, they will surely pick him up." The words sounded hollow even to her ears. Mary's arms about her released once more the dammed-up restraints on her grief and she gave way again to the full torrent of her despair.

A sudden cheer from the sailors distracted both women and brought them back to the present. The sailors were waving to distant figures on the shoreline, where a Confederate flag was being waved to and fro. They had reached the safety of Wilmington's defences and their cargo would soon be safely in Confederate hands. Henry Bragg would have delivered his goods, honourably earned his profit and cheaply too in these times of war. But one life had been lost.

Mary had meant to spend a few days resting in Wilmington with friends to recover from the ordeal of the last few days. Out of deference to Ruth's state of mind, however, she thought it best to keep her occupied and therefore decided to continue with their travels. Her inclination to linger, she acknowledged, was also due in part to her desire to postpone the inevitable confrontation that she must have with her son and with the formidable Mr Silas Killcaid. Although George's letter had said that Matthew had taken to living in the bayou, she was confident that he had sufficient resources to survive in such an environment, particularly with George to support him. It delighted her that her two grandsons had been united in such amity after the discord of their father's lives together at Nethergate Hall. With the power that her father's money gave her she was confident that she could dictate her terms. Although, with Killcaid, one could never be sure.

Ruth had fallen seamlessly into her role as slave once the two finally embarked from the battered SS *Adventure*. The captain had assured them repeatedly that if the Colonel had survived the Yankees would be sure to have picked him up. But his optimism fooled no-one.

Ruth and Mary had little by way of baggage and were soon ensconced in the Railroad Hotel in rooms that seemed amazingly spacious after the cramped quarters on the *Adventure*, but nothing like the grandiose splendour of the Royal Victoria. Mary had been treated like a heroine, for the story of the bold little *Adventure*'s escape from the Yankee gunships was soon on everyone's lips in Wilmington. Mary and Ruth changed and dined, and then returned exhausted to the room they shared.

Mary soon clamoured wearily into bed, her head still aching and her ears still ringing from the strike of the Yankee shell. As for Ruth, she eventually got into her bed, where she gave herself up to her grief. It seemed impossible to think that at the start of this day the Colonel had been with them, their mentor and guide, strong and indestructible, but now no more. Towards dawn she at last fell into an exhausted sleep.

37

Homecoming

The railroad journey for Mary and Ruth took three weary days, such was the chaos to civilian travel caused by the needs of the military. They sent a message home by telegraph. A carriage was waiting for them at Louisville. They slept most of the last leg until at last they passed through the imposing gates to the Nethergate Estate. The workers in the tobacco fields paused for a moment to watch their progress; some waved, but there was a listlessness about the place that was hard to define but was immediately apparent to the two women as they returned from their long absence. Soon they were clattering up the old, familiar avenue to the welcoming arms of the old house that both women in their different ways regarded as home.

The entire staff at Nethergate House had turned out with broad smiles and all burst into a welcome song as the pair alighted. Anthony was there and even Amelia had turned up to honour the occasion, a formal smile pasted across her face. A table had been prepared in the yard and the entire staff sat down to a feast organised by Jacob and Morella to mark the homecoming. Samuel was there, looking frail and ill. Mary and Ruth were both shocked at the change in him. The household were so obviously delighted to see Mary's safe return that soon her face was aching with smiles. Even Ruth, her features still pale in grief, was forced to smile too at the genuine happiness brought by the return of her mistress.

At last the singing and entertainment over, Mary was able to retire to the inside, motioning to Anthony, Amelia and Ruth to follow her. Finally, she was able to ask of Anthony the question that all along had been uppermost in her mind.

"I hear that George has joined the Confederates, but where is Matthew?" Although Anthony had been expecting this question, its directness made him pause.

"We are so proud of our boy," gushed Amelia. "You should have seen him, Mary, looking every inch the soldier in his uniform and sword. I thought my heart would burst with pride. And entirely his own decision. That not so, dear?" she asked, turning to Anthony.

Glad of the diversion, Anthony agreed. "Quite so. I discussed it with him, of course, but his mind was set and there was no dissuading him. I only wish you could have been here to see him."

Mary continued relentlessly, "And Matthew?" she asked.

"That worthless little toe rag," interrupted Amelia. "I really wonder what good you ever saw in the lad, Mary, the way he's turned out."

"Let me be the judge of that, if you please," replied Mary icily, then, pointedly turning to Anthony, she continued, "Where is Matthew?"

"Mater dear, I am afraid that without your steadying hand to guide him he has revealed his true colours. He struck up a friendship with George and lured him in to the bayou, where he became trapped. By God we nearly lost the boy! Had it not been for the quick thinking of Mr Killcaid, I dread to think what might have happened." He then recounted Killcaid's version of events, ending with a highly dramatised account of the supposed murder of the preacher. "The boy's a vagabond and a murderer and has a price now upon his head. Fortunately, Mr Killcaid had the measure of the varmint and put the coonhounds onto him but with the luck of the Devil he escaped somehow into the bayou, where we all assumed he had perished and justly so," he concluded with feeling. "And if ever he does turn up here again I swear to you I shall have him arrested and hung, for he damned near killed your only grandson."

At these words there was a gasp from Ruth who could not believe what she was hearing. "Matthew is never a murderer!" she exploded.

Amelia rounded upon her. "I'll thank you to hold your tongue, missy, and keep your opinions to yourself. I know he's your son and I'll forgive you this once, but no more." Ruth was about to respond when she caught a warning look from her mistress, bit her lip and held her tongue. The contrast to the way she had grown used to being treated over the last few months and her treatment now was almost more than she could bear. She couldn't believe what she was hearing and was full of anxiety for what had really happened to Matthew. She knew only too well that any slave accused of such a crime would find "justice", swift and savage. It was a white man's justice and rarely smiled on a black face.

Mary was not finished yet and was determined to find out what had really happened to Matthew.

"You said 'assumed', as if you now think he has not died. Tell me, what is known of his whereabouts now?" she asked. "You must have some ideas."

Anthony hesitated. "We thought that he had succumbed in the bayou, it's a pretty hazardous place. That, or fled the district making for Canada. It seems though that one of the girls here thought she saw him coming one night to this house. But I don't see how that could be and Killcaid does not believe it either."

Mary realised she would get no more information from Anthony and changed the subject. "You must forgive me Anthony. I am tired after our long journey and my head still aches from that Yankee shell, but tomorrow I should like to talk to you about the estate. I have some interesting views from your grandfather which you and I alone must discuss." Then, because she knew Amelia was all ears, she added, "There is a considerable sum he wishes to invest." Glad of the diversion, Anthony immediately adopted a rather condescending tone of voice, for he still could not believe that his mother could grasp the complexities of an enterprise such as the Nethergate Estate.

"I'll not try to deceive you, Mater, things now are not good. The blockade prevents us reaching our markets and there is little income to be had. Grandpapa's money will certainly come in handy for the banks are forever pressing. I can take charge of that now, if you wish, or perhaps tomorrow would do after you have rested. The big estates are all having to sell off hands. Fortunately, there is still a good market for them in the Southern rice fields. They at least are doing well with the need to feed our armies and I have a vested interest in that, now that George is serving the Confederate cause," he ended proudly.

But Amelia's mind was not so easily diverted by such patriotic considerations and had been following an entirely different trail. "How much did you say your father had entrusted to your care?" she inquired with a disinterested air, through which the claws of avarice were barely concealed. "We have had to close down half the Hall and the rest is badly in need of refurbishment."

"I didn't," Mary said shortly, then, turning to Anthony, she continued. "I had many conversations with your grandfather whilst I was away. He has certain ideas for the profitability of the estate which I think you would be well advised to heed."

"Mater dear, grandfather may be very good at running a factory, but he has no idea how to run a tobacco plantation.

However, I will gladly look over what he suggests if you will be good enough to give me his letter, but I cannot guarantee that I or Mr Killcaid will agree with what he says."

"It is no letter that I have, only a document which says that I am to act on his behalf and to speak with his authority. The funds he has entrusted to me are to be disbursed entirely at my discretion."

Anthony looked at his mother in amazement and then a look of barely concealed greed came into his eyes at the notion that his mother was the sole arbiter for the use of the funds. His mother, he fancied, knew little of finances and would easily be parted from the funds she apparently controlled. The estate had barely recovered from the debts incurred by his brother before the war struck a further body blow to its viability. He was badly in need of money. In common with many such enterprises, much of his assets had been placed with the banks. The bulk of what income there was was in greyback dollars, which had little value outside the Confederacy. Whatever funds his mother controlled, he doubted that they would anything like cover what was needed. Even Amelia had at last come to realise the nature of the estate's plight and in common with so many of her neighbours had been forced to cut down on the extravagancies of her lifestyle. She had realised finally that Nethergate was not immune from ruin and had persuaded Anthony to open a separate account in their joint name, to preserve their own assets from those of the estate's. It was into this account that he would divert his mother's money, or at least as much as he dared. He glanced over in Amelia's direction and saw by the look in her eyes that she was thinking along the same lines. She gave a barely perceptible nod and he knew he had pleased his wife. He was badly in need of her approval.

"You?" he said at last after he had digested what his mother had just said. "He has entrusted you with money and to act on his behalf? No doubt you will show me his letter, so that we can all see what his real intentions are." He found it hard to believe that his grandfather, whom he knew to be a hard-headed businessman, would entrust such authority to a woman, even if that woman was his own daughter.

Mary nodded. She was about to rebuke the presumption of poor Anthony, but at that moment she had not the stomach for an argument. "I think we should talk this all over tomorrow when I am rested from my journey," she said.

"Very well, Mater. Tomorrow then."

But Amelia could not let it go. "May we know just how much your father has vouchsafed to your care? I doubt that living in the North he has any idea of the difficulties under which the great Southern estates labour because of the Northern blockade. It would take a great sum indeed to make any difference to such a large enterprise as Nethergate."

"You must rest assured, Amelia, dear, that it is what I consider to be a considerable sum indeed," was all Mary was prepared to reveal, knowing how such an ambiguous reply would gnaw at Amelia's curiosity and keep her tossing and turning through the coming night, "And in good Yankee greenbacks," she added to feed her expectations the more. Anthony was delighted. If he had access to additional liquid funds from his grandfather, that would relieve him of many of the burdens which the estate now faced. But it all depended on how much money his mother held. He was sure that he could easily persuade her to place the money in his care without too much inconvenience. He left then with Amelia, feeling more optimistic than he had felt for months, leaving his mother to settle back after her long absence.

Once they had left, Ruth turned to Mary, full of anxiety. "We must find out from Jacob or Morella how things really stand with Matthew. They're sure to know something." The thought that she might lose Matthew so soon after the loss of Thomas was almost more than she could bear.

However, before they could do anything further, there was a discreet knock at the door and Morella came in.

"Forgive the intrusion, ma'am, but I have news for you of Matthew." Both women were immediately alert.

"Where is he?" asked Ruth eagerly.

"He is alive and well, but somewhat changed in appearance. Samuel, he see him only ten days ago. But Samuel he been very sick an' staying here till he be better."

Then Morella related the true version of what had happened whilst they had been away in New York. Mary was furious at the way Matthew had been treated, but both women were delighted that at least Matthew was safe and well. The situation was complicated now by Matthew being a fugitive from justice. That would not be so easy to circumvent. The case would have been prepared against him, with witnesses unlikely to dare to change their evidence. Morella finished by saying, "Ah can get a message to him if you wish?" Both women said they would like that very much and that they would write to him.

Morella was dismissed with thanks. Shortly afterwards the two retired to bed, Mary to run over her plans for the morrow and Ruth to mourn afresh the death of her Thomas, but glad at least that her son was safe for the moment, albeit with a price on his head. It had been a long day.

38

A Third Party

Matthew and Ursula were so wrapped up in each other that for a time they allowed all other considerations to fade into the background. He truly hoped that Samuel would make a full recovery, but not quite yet. Each day Matthew would religiously make his way to the meeting place he had agreed with Samuel, but secretly hoping that nobody and no message would be there, and nothing would come to disrupt their happiness. Each time that he came away with no indication that anyone had visited the spot, he determined that he must make another visit to Nethergate, but perhaps another day.

Then, one afternoon, he found a note placed in a leather bag in the hollow tree that they had reserved for such communications. It brought him up with a shock. It was a reminder that he could not go on for ever living in such a paradise. Carefully he opened the bag. It was a brief and affectionate note from his mother informing him that she and Mrs Styles had returned and hoping that he would be able to come to her as soon as possible. It also advised him of the need for extreme caution, since he had a price on his head. There was also a warm and kindly note from Mrs Styles saying much the same thing.

His first reaction was of delight that his mother and Mrs Styles were back safely from their travels. Then there was a feeling of guilt that his mother should hear that he was a wanted criminal. Above all else he felt the need to assure her of his innocence. And it was important too that his grandmother should receive the same assurances. He was surprised at how that mattered to him. But a wave of sadness swept over him, for he realised that the outside world had now reached out to burst the little bubble of perfection that he and Ursula had created. He hastened back to impart the news to Ursula. She was delighted for his sake that his mother had returned safely, but at the same time he could see that she too mourned the passing of this little oasis of perfection in their lives. They both knew this time was sure to come.

"You must go and see her, of course," she said immediately, but Matthew could see that she was deeply troubled at the thought.

"Have no fear on that score," he reassured her. "I can move as quiet as a ghost and, believe me, I'll not take any risks. Ah've too much at stake now," and he gave her a gentle squeeze. She smiled, but there was a pensive look that came into her eyes. There had been no lessening of her desire for him, but he had noticed of late that same faraway look of troubled thoughtfulness that settled upon her face in repose. He was sure that her love for him was not the cause for she clung to him in their moments of passion with an almost frantic intensity. "What is it, my love? There is something else that is troubling you? Is it the thought of leaving here and travelling north?"

She shook her head. "You must first concentrate on safely seeing your mother and to see what Mrs Styles can do." She had a child-like faith in the ability of Mrs Styles to move mountains. But in her reply there was a tacit admission that something else was indeed bothering her. Matthew could not now let it go.

"Ursula, you mus' tell me. There should be no secrets between us. How will I concentrate on going to see my mother when I am worried about you?"

Ursula shook her head and turned her eyes away from him. But Matthew was not to be denied. Gently he took her face in both his hands and drew his own close to hers so that she had to look him in the eye. "What is it, my love? You must tell me." Then, with a sob, it all came pouring out.

"Oh, Matthew, promise me you won't be angry. I don't know how to say this, but I think... I think I am with child."

The news burst like a bombshell into Matthew's world. Suddenly everything was changed. "Is it mine?" he half-muttered with incredulity, not being altogether sure how such things worked.

"No, Matthew dearest," replied Ursula with a soft smile and a little chuckle, despite her distress, "not even you with all your ardour could be that potent." A few weeks ago, at the very start of their relationship they could never have spoken of such matters, but now they had come to understand each other with a much deeper intimacy.

"George's," murmured Matthew. "Did he know?"

"Of course not. How could he? I only just realise it myself. I think at first maybe things stopped because of the shock of coming here and George's going. Then I think it was 'cos of how things change when I came to live out here. But now I think I is sure," and her hands crept of their own accord to cradle the unborn child in her belly.

Matthew truly did not know how he felt. It was as if in some way George was making his prior claim to the right of Ursula from the distant Confederate battlefield.

He felt a pang of jealousy, but at the same time he had to acknowledge George's prior claim to the love of Ursula and his own sense of guilt at betraying the trust of his only friend. George would surely never now grant him his freedom, if ever he learnt of his relationship with Ursula. But what use was freedom with a price upon his head?

Once George returned, then Ursula would have to face an awful decision. He could offer her nothing, whereas George could offer her the prospect of becoming the Mistress of Nethergate. What a glittering prize that would be for a one-time slave. But would George marry a slave? He would earn the contempt of every white man in the state and become the laughing stock of all his peers. His father would never permit such a humiliation to the family name. He would sell the estate rather than let a slave become the future Mistress of Nethergate. All these thoughts rushed around in his head and then crystallised into one certainty. They would have to leave the bayou as soon as possible. They could no longer wait for the fruition of Samuel's delayed plans for a safe journey to Canada. They would have to trust to luck and the random workings of the Underground Railroad to spirit them step by step to safety with all the risks and dangers that that entailed. It was now essential that they reached Canada and security as quickly as possible before Ursula's condition created additional risks for travel. This way he would be carrying out George's wishes too.

There was also another reason why Matthew did not wish to delay. He wanted to do what George had done and join in the struggle between North and South. He wanted to be part of the battle for freedom from slavery so that he could say to his children that he had played his part to rise above the humiliation of his birth. He wanted to be a man and to earn the right to look every man he met in the eye as a true equal. The more he thought about it the more certain he became. He had, no matter what, to join in the struggle before it was too late. Then Ursula broke in on his thoughts again.

"Matthew, dear Matthew. There is another reason why we must go north as soon as possible. I cannot let my baby be born

213

here in the South. I must reach Canada, so my child is not born a slave same as I was an' you was too."

"My baby", "my child", the words cut into him like a knife. He realised with a shock that his thoughts had been only for Ursula, but hers had been for the unborn child she carried. If only it could have been, "our baby" and "our child". George had somehow claimed Ursula for his own in a way more powerful than being there in person. Things were different now between him and Ursula and always would be. But what she said was true. They could no longer delay their departure, but they had at least an advantage over many in their situation. They had George's money to ease their way from station to station. Ursula at least would not be the subject of wanted notices and the object of some enraged owner seeking her capture, but against that was the criminal charge hanging over Matthew's head. For a long time neither spoke, each deep in their own thoughts.

"You are right," said Matthew with sudden resolution. "We must make our move as soon as we can, but first you must let me see my mother and see what help we can get from her and from Samuel and maybe from Mrs Styles."

"Of course you must," said Ursula. "Oh, Matthew, thank you. Thank you for understanding." With that she threw herself into his arms and clasped him close. But both were aware that someone else had entered in to their relationship and was demanding a say in how they should feel about each other and what they should do. It was a small, tiny voice that neither could ignore and in many ways was more powerful than them both.

39

Matters Put Right

Matthew assembled the most presentable set of clothes he had. All the same he was aware of how disreputable he must look and was ashamed that his mother must see him so. Ursula cut his hair and trimmed his beard so that the two looked reasonably under control. They had lain together on their bed so that Matthew could rest up before the busy night ahead and something of their old warmth and spontaneity had returned. But sleep was impossible, and both ate their evening meal before the sun left Old Mo's cabin. The spare dugout was moored at their jetty. Matthew gave strict instructions that no matter what the emergency she would wait at least twenty-four hours for his return. In the gathering gloom, Matthew waved farewell. Ursula found it hard to hide her anxiety. The very cabin seemed to protest at his absence. She knew she would count every moment to his return.

Matthew, for his part, tried to shut his mind to thoughts of Ursula and to concentrate upon the task ahead. He went as far as he could by water and moored the dugout close by the place he had first met up with Old Mo. Memories of Old Mo flooded back, as they often did when he revisited places first shown to him by that indomitable old man. Now they were particularly poignant with the knowledge that soon he would be leaving this place for ever. It was here too that he and George had first met. His mind filled with memories of the laughter and the spontaneous merriment of those early days. With these recollections now came the guilt of his betrayal. Ursula's confession that she was carrying George's child would be a constant reminder of his treachery. He shook himself free from such thoughts. He must concentrate or risk losing all.

Soon he was on the familiar path which led up to the plantation. He caught glimpses of lights coming from Nethergate Hall through the trees. He kept as far as possible to where the tobacco fields were still being cultivated, where he could hide at a moment's notice. There was little sound coming from the slave lines. No doubt they were sleeping the sleep of exhaustion. All was quiet too as he skirted Nethergate Hall and made his way towards Nethergate House. He felt excited and warmed with the anticipation of seeing his mother again and hearing all her news.

He reached the house and noted straight away that there were no longer slaves keeping watch at the gate. Mrs Styles would not have tolerated such an intrusion. Nevertheless, he approached the house with caution, keeping to the shadows. He shinned up the creeper that led to his old bedroom window and was soon inside. Once again, he felt the old walls embracing him with the familiar warmth and comfort of childhood memories. Hastily he changed into fresh clothing, then gently knocked on his mother's door. Inside someone stirred. There was a sudden flair of light from under the door as his mother lit a candle. The door was cautiously opened. For a moment she hesitated, then with a delighted cry she embraced him and ushered him in.

Once inside she scrutinised him more closely. "Matthew dearest, I am so glad to see you! You've changed a great deal. I don't know about the beard. But perhaps that's just a mother's reluctance to see her boy changed into a man."

In his turn Matthew searched his mother's face. He found her much changed too, somehow more assured, but there was an aura of sadness about her and he believed he saw dampness about her eyes as if she had recently been crying.

"What is it, Mother?" he asked, full of concern. "There is something troubling you. Is it about the things I am supposed to have done?"

Ruth was surprised at his anxiety. He would never have noticed such things before. It was another sign that he was no longer a boy. "No. No, my dearest. I do not believe for a moment what they say. I know my own son."

"There was a man killed mother, but not by my hand. He was a slave like me, a giant of a man on loan from another plantation. I believe he was a preacher. I was exhausted, without hope of escaping from Killcaid and the hounds. Without a word he carried me and broke my trail from the hounds. Truly I owe him my life. I fear, though, he may have paid for it with his own. He was a worthy servant of his Lord. I am no murderer. I can only see the hand of Killcaid in all of this."

"I believe you, son, of course I do, and I know the Mistress will too. She will not believe for one moment you have turned killer."

"But what then troubles you?" insisted Matthew, still unsure of the cause of his mother's sadness.

"A lot has happened to me since I left for New York," she said at last. "Some day when there is time I will tell you. All I will say now is that I met a man who I loved."

"Did he betray you?" demanded Matthew, suddenly all fire for his mother's sake.

"No, no, dear. Nothing like that. He was killed escorting us back here to safety. There are so many things I should have said to him. And now he is gone," and her voice broke. Matthew had never seen his mother like this, and he moved to place an arm about her. Then he felt her stiffen with resolve. "But, Matthew, I cannot bear the thought that I may now lose you as well. We must see what is to be done. I must speak with the Mistress."

"But, Mother, is it wise to bring in Mrs Styles to this?"

"Believe me Matthew, she will want to be involved."

So it was that mother and son made their way through the darkened corridors of Nethergate House to where Mrs Styles slept. Gently Ruth awakened her mistress and told her of the situation. Mary Styles quickly grasped how things stood as Ruth helped her on with her dressing robe. Matthew was ushered into the room, more than ever aware of his disreputable appearance. Then he was asked to relate the things that had happened since both had been away, but he kept Ursula's name out of it for fear that Mrs Styles would frown on George's love for a slave girl. They heard him out without interruption.

"I will get my lawyers to look into the facts of the case against you," said Mary Styles. "That must be our priority, but it won't be easy for there is a lot of prejudice in the judiciary against slaves, particularly now with the war. But at least we will understand what we face, what the evidence is against you and who your accusers are." She looked questioningly at Matthew. "I must admit, Matthew, as you appear at this moment I could believe the very worst of you."

Matthew smiled for there was a twinkle in Mrs Styles' eye when she made that observation. Mary now assumed control.

"You must stay here concealed whilst we see how things stand and so that we can make you look less like the wild man from the swamps. This house is big enough for you to lie up where no-one has any cause to go." Matthew's immediate thought was now for Ursula and what she would do should he not return. "No. Please, I cannot let you take the risk of protecting a wanted man. I must go back to the bayou."

Mrs Styles looked at him thoughtfully and Matthew realised that his alarm at the suggestion of staying the night had betrayed him. He knew that he would have to reveal all. He then told them of Amelia's cruelty to Ursula and how George had tried to protect her and how George and she came to fall in love and then of her supposed death in the bayou. He told them of the half-formed plans to use the Underground Railroad and of Samuel's treatment and the delay due to his sickness. He did not however say anything about his own relationship with Ursula.

At the end of it all Mrs Styles was silent for a while. Then she said, "It certainly adds a complication to the situation. Ursula is a lovely child and I feel a special responsibility for her. It was my suggestion that she went to work for the Mistress. I will do all I can for her. I had no idea the new Mistress would turn out the way she has." There was another silence between them, but it was clear that Mrs Styles had not finished. Mrs Styles looked at Ruth and then turned to Matthew. "Matthew," she said, searching for words, "you must know the circumstances of your birth. Nevertheless, you are my first-born grandchild. I want you to know that I regard you with just the same affection as I have for George, though one be slave and the other freeborn. You and George have an equal claim upon my affections. In other circumstances you would now be Master of Nethergate. There is so much in you of Mark when he was a boy. He was the joy of my heart, before he took to his waywardness. It has given me untold pleasure to watch you growing up, particularly when you have been under my roof. It gives me great joy to know that, unlike my two sons, my two grandsons feel such kinship for each other."

Matthew realised what an effort it had been for this grand old lady to make this confession. With a spontaneous gesture he grasped his grandmother's hand in both of his. "Thank you," was all he could say. But he could not help wondering at how far that amity might now go should George learn of his perfidy.

"Bless you," replied his grandmother, but there was a mistiness in her eye. "Now we must see what help we can give to get you and Ursula away to Canada, for until this war is over I am sure that is the best thing. If it were in my hands, I would ensure that both you and your mother were given their freedom. Whilst I have high hopes of achieving that for your mother," and she looked at Ruth as she said this as if to declare the sincerity of her purpose, "with you it will be more difficult until the criminal charges against you can be cleared. And now you must make haste if you are to get back to the bayou before the plantation wakes up. Come back in three days with Ursula to give me a little time to see what is to be done. And take great care you are not seen, for Killcaid, I fancy, has his spies even, I suspect, in my own household." Then for the first time she seemed to see his dishevelled appearance. "I think too it will give your mother time to find some more suitable clothes for you both to wear."

Matthew left Nethergate House with much to ponder. He had been overwhelmed by Mrs Styles's confession of their kinship and thoughts of freedom in Canada. He felt now that at last things were moving and that now he had powerful friends. Yet at the same time he didn't want things to change, for now he had but three days left of the simple, natural life that Ursula and he had so enjoyed.

Mindful of his grandmother's final warning note, he took particular care in exiting Nethergate House. But when he was in the cover of the garden he turned once more to look back at the house which had been home for so much of his life. It was a mistake he knew to stay too long on such dangerous ground, but he thought it safe, just for a moment or two, to let his mind linger and savour the memories of the safety and security he had enjoyed whilst he was living there under the protection of his grandmother and the mantle of his mother's love. Then, with sudden determination, he turned to go. As he did so he thought he caught sight of the outline of a figure in one of the windows in the slave lines. He peered into the gloom and the figure suddenly vanished. Killcaid had his spies in every part of Nethergate, but surely not in his grandmother's house, where her gentle benevolence had won over all in her service. All the same it made him uneasy.

40

Last Days in the Bayou

Ursula was waiting as Matthew moored the dugout by their little jetty. As soon as he set foot on dry land, she wrapped him in a wordless embrace that revealed more cogently than anything, her anxieties at their separation. She had prepared their breakfast. As they ate, Matthew recounted the events of the previous night and his grandmother's suggestion that they hide in Nethergate House and make their way north with what help she might be able to give them. Both were filled with a sense of comfort that they now seemed to have such powerful friends, although Ursula was perhaps more wary. However, the thought of being in the shelter of a proper house, where she could wash and do her hair and wear dresses again, filled her with eager anticipation.

A lassitude seemed to have crept over them both after they had finished eating. Perhaps it was due to tiredness with a night in which neither had slept, for Ursula had been kept awake through anxiety as to how Matthew might fare and because of the strangeness of a night totally alone in the bayou. Now too there was the thought that they would be leaving forever this little oasis of happiness, so cut off from the real world. It was their fantasy world, where they could dream dreams and where they could believe in a bright future, free from overseers and bondage and perhaps free from reality too. As they looked about the little world that Old Mo had created and never been able to enjoy, a world where they had discovered each other and a happiness that seemed so perfect that it was unreal, they were filled with sadness that it was shortly to be abandoned. The garden would soon become overgrown, the fences broken, and the wildlife would enjoy all the fruits of their labours. Old Mo's cabin would stand for a time and then slowly become derelict and eventually crumble back into the landscape, as insubstantial as the very nature of dreams themselves.

Matthew visited his traps and collected more than enough game to last their two remaining days. He then disarmed all the others. It was a reminder of the finality of their departure. After visiting the traps, it was usually Matthew's habit to join Ursula in tending the produce growing in their garden, but there seemed little point in so doing. Nevertheless, it was a ritual that neither wished to abandon for there was something very satisfying in work done together.

In the evening they again made music and sang together and rekindled the magic of all the previous times they had done the self-same thing, sometimes when George too was there. They were both fatigued and retired early to bed, lying naked beside each other without making love, simply enjoying the proximity and intimacy of just being together. Soon both were sleeping.

Matthew had been right to be suspicious of the figure he had glimpsed at the window as he left Nethergate House. Laticia, ever vigilant for Killcaid, had seen the light go on in Ruth's bedroom and suspected the cause. She was even more convinced when candles were kindled in Mrs Styles's bedroom. There was nothing she could do at that moment since the watchers from the gate had been withdrawn on Mrs Styles's orders. Instead she made sure she remained awake through the night. Her patience was rewarded when as dawn approached she observed a shadowy figure departing from the house and moving cautiously through the shrubberies. The figure paused for a moment to turn back and gaze up at Nethergate House, before vanishing into the grey of early dawn. In that moment she recognised without any shadow of doubt the shape and the set of shoulders of the fugitive Matthew. She rejoiced in anticipation of Mr Killcaid's pleasure at the information she would bring.

Shortly afterwards the lights were extinguished in her mistress's room and finally in Ruth's. Late the next day, when she could leave the house without raising suspicion, she hastened to report to Mr Killcaid. He showed his pleasure at her vigilance with an affectionate squeeze of her buttocks. It seemed he may have been wrong about the fate of Matthew after all. Once again rage smouldered within him at the thought of that arrogant young man whom still it seemed he had not entirely humbled and he wondered who might have been sheltering him. But Killcaid had weightier matters on his mind. Anthony had told him of the meeting with Mrs Styles in the morning and that he intended to insist that Killcaid too be present. He wondered how strong that determination might be should Mrs Styles stick to her guns and what might happen were he not in attendance.

41

George and the Confederate Cause

All George's letters were waiting for Mary when she returned to Nethergate. He told his grandmother much about his life as a young officer in the Confederate Army. She learnt of his growing pride in the 10th Kentucky Infantry Regiment, "the Old Waifs and Strays", and he told her with pride the origin of that epithet. Nethergate was also nominally part of the territory under the Yankee heel and she readily understood the feelings of her fellow Kentuckians. Out on the plantation, though, they had seen little evidence of the occupying forces. On rare occasions they had been troubled by groups of drunken soldiers out rampaging and causing mayhem. But Nethergate was so far away from any other habitation as to make it hardly worth their while. Only once had there been any real menace and that was when a group of deserters had set up camp on the edge of the estate, but they had been ruthlessly hunted down by troops from their own side and by all reports savagely despatched.

George's letters told of his growing friendship with Nathaniel Summers, who had joined the Regiment at the same time, of the bombastic Captain Paul Knight, who enjoyed playing the veteran, and of the occasional visits from their commander,

Major Blunsden-Butts, referred to by the soldiers and anyone else out of his hearing as "Old Blood 'n Guts". He was a complex character who had his favourites but was experienced in the ways of war having cut his military teeth in the Mexican wars. He was the consummate soldier. His men trusted his experience and military wisdom whatever other oddities of character went with them. He was frequently at odds with his superiors, many of whom owed their rank to their political savvy rather than military skill.

But there was much that George could not tell his grandmother. At first, he had been shocked by the coarseness of the soldier's language, by their easy familiarity with their own sexual natures, needs and gratification. Fresh from the discovery of the unique wonders of the love he shared with Ursula, it went against his nature to cheapen its mystique to the humping, rutting animal processes the soldiers joked about. He was though wise enough to realise that this was soldier-talk the world over.

George told of the one active engagement they had with the enemy and related their courage and success in glowing terms. He also told of the loss of John Beddows, one of the recruits who had marched out with them from Bentham Springs with such high hopes all those months ago. He had died like a hero, sudden and quick, and his parents could always draw comfort from that. There was thus one of their number who would never see his homeland again. Implicit in that thought was the unspoken question of how many more, and may God forbid that he should be among that number.

He told her of Manuel, who had taken to wearing the Confederate uniform with more pride than most of the soldiers. He strutted and stamped about like a circus clown and grinned and saluted like an automaton, but George could not fault his devotion or his efficiency. He really seemed to revel in the military life. He was always there when needed and no discomfort seemed to daunt him. He was a treasure. All in all it was a glowing account and Mary could not but feel her heart surge with pride in what George was doing for what he believed in, even though it was a cause she could not embrace.

Of course, George in his letters had hidden from his grandmamma much of what life was really like as a soldier. The sheltered nature of the latter part of his upbringing on the Nethergate Estate had not prepared him for the close contact with men of his own age, some of whom he would have categorised as, "poor white trash" and thus almost below slaves in the social pecking order. He was not prepared for their cruelty to each other and for their casual acceptance of pain and discomfort for their fellows, or the sheer physicality of their lives. But amidst all of this he became aware too of the strange love that bound these men together. They would torment one of their number to the edge of suicide but, were a soldier from another unit to strike him, push him around or just insult him, they would fall to his defence with the frenzy of a pack of ratting terriers. He experienced this strange loyalty on the field of conflict too. Soldiers who were at each other's throats in camp would give their lives for their comrade on the field of battle without a moment's thought as if it were the most natural thing in all the world.

So much of his life as a young officer he was unable to express or share with his grandmother, but he and Nathaniel talked and wondered at the things that now directed their lives. They had joined the 10th Regiment some eight weeks after arriving in Camp Coldstream. They had marched most of the way and that in itself had helped them all to bond together as a fighting unit. They had come swinging in to join the 3rd Company of the 10th Regiment after some two weeks on the road, striding in to camp with arms swinging and singing the marching song of the 10th. They expected their Company Commander, "Old blood 'n guts" to at least commend their fine spirit, but he didn't. He lined them up and inspected them and found fault with every one of them, including the young officers. He lingered particularly over Nathaniel and adjusted his uniform, then peered closely into his face whilst the young officer stood, blushing and rigidly to attention. Then he snorted and passed on, but, as they were to learn, that was the way of Major Blunsden-Butts. He never did what you expected him to do. Thus, he kept everyone on their toes. He was severe, nothing seemed to please him, and his punishments were swift and harsh. In the end the soldiers came to fear him more than they feared the enemy. About their camp fires they took a perverse pride in recounting his eccentricities, cruelties and whimsical injustices, but they knew they could trust in his military judgement. They knew he would not ask them to do anything he was not prepared to do himself and that he would be as penny-pinching with their lives as any miser on this earth. In short, though they hated him, they would follow him anywhere. This was proved on their first contact with the enemy.

They knew that they were part of some larger outflanking movement. As far as they were concerned it had been a case of moving, then halting, then moving again. Never really time to snatch a meal, to take stock of what they were doing or where they were going. But they were new to war. Each man was full of bravado and bombast, yet each was aware of that nervous flutter at the very heart of all their bragging. In each man's thoughts was not the dread of injury or death but the thought of how they would react to their first taste of battle. Would they be found wanting? Above all, would they turn coward?

Soon, they began to hear the distant rumble of war, the rumble and thump of artillery and the sharp crackle of rifle fire, some way off, but getting forever closer. They advanced across open farmland towards a homestead that was still burning. It had been the site of a recent small engagement. Here they caught their first sight of the enemy, a group of three dead Yankee soldiers. Two had the grace to lie down with faces pressed to the earth as they had fallen, but the third was lying with his leg impossibly twisted under him. Half his jaw had been shot away, but the upper half of his face revealed a man of extraordinary good looks with a cascade of curling brown hair and grey eyes wide open, staring in shocked disbelief. All gazed as they passed. There wasn't one of them that didn't feel the urge to straighten his leg into a more comfortable position. All wondered whether they too might not become just such an object of morbid curiosity to other passing soldiers.

Suddenly the din of war erupted all about them. A shot crackled over their heads followed by a brief fusillade. Every man took cover. George peered up. A group of Yankee soldiers was running to the cover of the nearby wood. Suddenly his blood was up. He leapt to his feet.

"Up, boys!" he shouted. With a yell, the famed "rebel yell", sounding so contrived in training but now gifted with a sudden spine-chilling savagery, they rose as a man to their feet. Blood up, they set off in pursuit, the fever of battle coursing through their veins. Two of the enemy turned, knelt and fired. The forward men replied, but none of the shots was aimed. The two Yankees turned again, running and dodging for the shelter of the trees. George's men, all screaming like madmen, were in for the kill.

They could still see the fleeing Yankees, but once in the trees the undergrowth and brushwood checked the impetus of their headlong charge. Soon they were struggling against fallen branches and the uneven terrain. Their shouts died on their lips. Every man now was fighting his own battle struggling for breath. Then suddenly a volley of musket fire rang out. The woods in front of them were clouded in powder and smoke from the discharge. All about their ears was the crackle and snap of rifle and shot and a rain of twigs and branches severed by the hail of lead showered down upon them. It was a trap. The men turned, blood-lust suddenly chilled. They started to run.

"Take cover! Stand your ground!" bellowed George. But their passions had been turned, in a moment, to fear and confusion. Every man thought only of saving himself from that murderous fire. Then, with a roar like an avalanche, something crashed over their heads, snapping trees in half as if they had been matchwood and erupted in a huge explosive impact to their rear. They were under artillery fire! Another round followed and another. The men hit the ground and then staggered to their feet, then down again. Floundering back one moment, then scrabbling into the soil for safety the next. The whole area was now shrouded in smoke. Then as abruptly as the gun fire started, it ceased.

As the smoke cleared there was Major Blunsden-Butts, "Old Blood 'n Guts" in person.

"Stand your ground!" he thundered. "I'll shoot the next man as turns to run. By God I will!" There wasn't a man that doubted him. They hesitated. In a thrice he was telling them where to lie, to take cover and to return the enemies fire. Then he spotted George. "Get this rabble and disgrace to the 10th into some order and return the fire. I'll be moving to outflank them. Keep the enemy occupied here. Understand?"

"Yes, sir!" yelled George. Suddenly the fear was gone. The men were soldiers once again and fighting as they had been trained to do. Soon a sharp rattle of return fire was thumping purposefully out at the enemy, now obscured by the smoke of their own discharges. George crouched and ran between his men, directing some to better positions and encouraging them to make up for their initial loss of nerve. He felt a curious elation. He could feel that the men had suddenly gained confidence in him as their leader. They wanted him to notice them. He felt invincible. That was when they discovered that John Beddows was missing.

42

The Death of John Beddows

John Beddows did not have the comfortable death that had been related to his parents and those at home. It had been like one of those moments in a crowded room when for a second no-one speaks and silence falls. So it was in the discharge of the shot. There was a brief respite when everyone seemed to be reloading. Out of the depths of this silence leapt a long, piercing cry. Hitherto it must have been drowned by the din of war. The scream seemed to go on and on beyond the capacity of human lungs, shattering the sudden stillness. It was a cry more animal than human. It made the hairs rise on the back of each man's neck. Both sides paused, not knowing its source, whether it was friend or foe, animal or human that had released that endless peon of pain.

"Keep firing!" roared George, recovering first and mindful of Blunsden-Butts's last orders. "Keep firing!" The men responded, glad to do anything to drown out the memory of that agonised howl. The rattle and snap of fire returned, and smoke once again obscured the battle field. Mercifully the artillery fire had now been directed elsewhere, but they could still hear the distant roar of discharge and thanked God that someone else was on the receiving end.

Then it came again. Startlingly shrill, like a stricken hare. This time, the men's ears were attuned to the cry as if each man were unconsciously dreading its repetition. Not so long as before. It ended in a series of sobbing whimpers that were unmistakeably human. Both sides searched for its source. There was no sign of movement in the forest undergrowth. Each side was appalled by the sound. Firing ceased.

It was possible that their Yankee opponents were new to war too. This might also be their baptism of fire. Both sides were horror-struck by this lone despairing cry of a soul in torment.

Then came a voice. "Oh God, Oh God, let it stop. Mother of God, Mother. Dear Mamma ah – ah-ah." The voice lapsed once more into a long, moaning howl of pain. Then there was movement. An arm appeared briefly above the level of the undergrowth in a random purposeless gesture. It was an arm clad in Rebel grey. Next to George, one of his men said, "It's John, John Beddows. I saw him go down." George shouted his name, but there was no response. It made it worse now, knowing for sure who was lying out there alone, so close to the Yankee lines. There was nothing they could do.

Both sides now were somehow unwittingly united in a common bond of humanity: a soldier's feeling for a fellow soldier in distress. Above all else both sides wanted those cries to stop. Veteran soldiers would never have behaved in such a way, but it seemed that, by the random coincidence of conflict, the soldiers on both sides of this skirmish were more civilians than soldiers. John's cries once again rent the conflict, a child now pleading for his mother.

There was a sudden movement from the Yankee side. A white cloth was tentatively waving close to where John Beddows lay. Cautiously a large soldier with a shock of blond hair and a huge blond moustache rose above their earthworks. One hand held a piece of white cloth, the other empty of weapons, was extended, palm towards the Confederate lines as if hoping to ward off their bullets. No-one fired. He made his way to where John Beddows lay. Kneeling, he cradled John's head upon his lap. John's screaming ceased as when a mother lifts her fretting child.

"Oh Mother. Oh Mother, make it stop," he sobbed.

Then the Yankee soldier tried to lift the injured man. Immediately agonised screams shattered the air. Gently the giant lowered John to the ground. The screams changed to low tormented moans. The Yankee turned to face the hidden Confederates and shook his head. Then he drew from his side a large Bowie hunting knife. Everyone at once knew what he was going to do.

The blade caught the reflection of the sun as the knife moved in one swift motion. The cries ended abruptly in a gagging gasp. John's arm flew up and then gently subsided as if in a last farewell. The Yankee soldier stood up, saluted the corpse, then turned to face his enemies and saluted once more. George was so moved by this courageous act of mercy that he too rose from behind his cover and returned the Yankee salute. For a moment both men faced each other in an instant of shared humanity. Then with a swift bound the Yankee soldier was gone, but each side was aware that they had been the witness of an act that somehow transcended the cruelty and crudity of war.

The firing started again with renewed fury. Once again friend and enemy alike were concealed by the smoke and confusion of conflict. George spotted movement to the left of the Yankee position. Grey figures were streaming fleetingly through the trees with the silent purpose of hunting wolves. Nathaniel was leading. Then with the shouting maniacal screams of the rebel yell they fell upon their enemy. Blue and grey became inextricably mixed in hand-to-hand fighting.

"Cease firing!" roared George. The smoke cleared, and the men could see what was happening. As of one, without any order being given, they rose to join in the fray and whooping and hollering rushed through the undergrowth to close with the enemy, passing without a glance to where John Beddows lay, his eyes staring into eternity.

The blue line broke and was gone, leaving only their dead upon the ground to bear witness. A wild cheering broke from each mouth as Nathaniel and George's men mingled in the euphoria of victory. Each man was aware that they had faced the ultimate challenge and had not been found wanting, their initial reaction to coming under fire, now conveniently forgotten. Above all they had won. Each man would have his own tale to tell of his part in the conflict that would doubtless grow with the telling. Some of the more opportunistic were already looting the bodies of the dead, looking for Yankee dollars and anything else of value. Some were even pulling off the boots of the better equipped-dead Yankees, for even if they didn't fit they could be used for barter.

Among the dead George's eye fell upon a shock of blond hair and a blond moustache streaked with blood. His death had been mercifully swift. His boots were already gone, his feet cold, naked and white. Two men were squabbling over the contents of his breeches pockets and in their struggles had exposed his nakedness to the world. Both men paused in their squabbling to laugh at what they had exposed.

"'E won't need that no more," guffawed one.

George felt sickened at his men behaving like vultures over carrion. He recognised the man who a few moments before, he had been proud to salute as a fellow human being across the divide of war. Scattered about his body were letters and other documents of no value to the looters. Hastily George picked them up before the wind scattered them forever. He had some vague notion that he might write to the soldier's loved ones to tell them of his courage and humanity.

At that moment Major Blunsden-Butts burst upon the scene, having followed Nathaniel's assaulting troops with the Company reserve.

"In the name of Jesus Christ what the Devil do you think you are playing at!" he roared, mixing the two extremes in his fury. "Mr Styles! Mr Summers! Be so good as to get a grip of your men at once. You've no sentries out, I'll be bound. Take up firing positions at once. You can expect a counter-attack at any moment. The Yankees are no way as foolish as you are. And, when you are satisfied, both of you report back to me."

Thus military order was restored and when George and Nathaniel did eventually report back to "Old Blood 'n Guts" it was to receive not a word of congratulations for their victory but the harshest dressing down of their young lives.

43

Confrontation in the Estate Office

The day following her return Mary made her way towards the Estate Office. She was dreading what she knew would be a confrontation. Armed with her father's money and his letter of authority she felt certain that she would emerge the victor. Her victory would be her son's defeat and she didn't want that either. If he would listen to her, they might yet work together. But she had no doubt that Killcaid would be there, despite her instructions to the contrary. With Killcaid advising and steering him, she doubted that words alone could persuade her son. Then there was the matter of freedom for Ruth and Matthew and she felt she had a mountain to climb.

Anthony had prepared himself for the meeting with his mother. He was seated at the huge office desk, designed to intimidate, determined that he would assert his position and authority as Master of Nethergate. Mr Killcaid stood at his right hand to guide and support him. He was comfortably of the opinion that he could soon extract from his mother the necessary funds to put the estate on to a firm footing once again and more besides, depending on the size of his grandfather's new investment. However his grandfather might posture, his pride and his affection for his only child would never allow him to permit the estate to go under. Much would depend upon what was in his grandfather's letter, but with his lawyer's training he was certain he could manipulate that to his advantage. Then of course there was Amelia and her expectations. He longed to bask in her approval for what he might divert to their own private accounts.

There was a knock at the door to the office and Mrs Styles was ushered in. The door was discreetly closed behind her. Anthony descended from his Olympian desk to welcome his mother to her chair at the foot of that mighty edifice.

"Mamma dear. Do take a seat," he effused, before returning to his seat of power. Mary however remained standing, staring at Killcaid. She had no intention of arguing with the redoubtable overseer as well.

"This meeting, Mr Killcaid, is between my son and I only." Killcaid did not move but licked his lips before preparing to speak.

"With respect, ma'am, I knows the workin' o' the estate better than any other, as you is well aware. My knowledge will help us all in resolving the present problems. I am here at your disposal," he added with an uncharacteristic and obsequious little bow and he looked to Anthony for support. Anthony nodded his head. Mary sat down. Ignoring Killcaid, she began to take out some of the papers she had brought with her. Then she sat still and looked up expectantly at her son.

"Surely, mamma, our business will be better conducted with Mr Killcaid here present. He knows the business so well."

Mrs Styles said nothing. She sat still, patiently waiting.

"Ah have worked, as you know, Mrs Styles, with your revered husband, with Mr Mark and with Mr Anthony here. These are unusual times and we must all adjust to them. I offer you my understanding of the estate, which is, I venture to maintain, unequalled."

Still Mrs Styles did not venture a reply. The silence

lengthened until Anthony felt compelled to break it. "Perhaps, Mamma, if Mr Killcaid were to remain, but not to speak, so that he will have a better understanding of what Grandpapa has in mind." With slow deliberation Mary began to retrieve the papers she had spread out before her and replaced them in her bag. Seeing the determined set of his mother's mouth, Anthony capitulated.

"I will hear alone what my mother has to say Mr Killcaid. I am sure we will call you in if we feel it is necessary." With that crumb of comfort Killcaid had no alternative but to leave. With a frosty little bow, he did so, inwardly seething against the weakness of the Master and fearing that he might make promises that would not meet with his approval, for he knew that in the old Mrs Styles he had both an implacable enemy and a formidable opponent. Thus, without saying a word, Mrs Styles had gained the upper hand.

As the door closed on Killcaid, Mary handed Anthony her father's letter, giving her authority to disburse the funds entrusted to her care as she saw fit. There was also a gentle reminder from Henry Bragg that, in view of the estate's indebtedness to him, he was now the de facto owner of Nethergate. As such he had plans for the estate's future which he had discussed with his daughter, which plans Anthony would be well advised to heed. In such matters she was now empowered to speak for him and to act as his representative. Anthony read the letter without comment. After his initial defeat over Killcaid's attendance, he was determined to haul back the initiative. Like his father before him, he refused to believe that a mere woman could understand the complexities of the Nethergate enterprise and least of all his own mother.

"How much does Grandpapa intend to invest in the business?" he inquired.

"As much as I decide is necessary. The rest I shall hold in reserve," replied his mother evenly, "after I have seen the books." Anthony had the accounts laid out in piles of intimidating, leather-bound volumes, hoping thereby to overwhelm his mother by the sheer complexity of the business.

"I am afraid," he started condescendingly, "that you will not be able to make head or tail of what you see before you, but I will do my best to simplify things into what is essential for your understanding."

"I will do my simple best, unaided," she rejoined coldly. "But, if I need your help, I will ask for it."

The hours she had spent when first she came to Nethergate and had so wanted to help her husband by understanding the intricacies of the estate's management were now to be repaid. She quickly revealed that she had perhaps an even firmer grasp of the business than did her son. Soon he found himself stumbling over the replies to some of his mother's more penetrating questions.

It rapidly became clear just how much the estate was indebted to Henry Bragg. Anthony had been forced in common with many other great estates to take credit from banks at crippling rates of interest. Some of the banks themselves had gone into liquidation and their creditors were demanding repayment of sums owed. In some cases, Anthony had been forced to take out further loans to meet these commitments. The income from the sales of tobacco since the start of the blockade had been minimal. Investment from his grandfather had been too attractive to be resisted, leading to the latter's dominant position.

Mrs Styles knew that she was in for a long tussle with the estate's creditors, but she had enough funds from her father to more than cover the loans. She had room to negotiate with the creditors too, since she would be offering payment in greenback dollars from the North. This was the only American currency fully acceptable on the international markets. Possession of the greenback was a substantial bonus to any negotiator in the Southern states which was the reason her father had risked allowing her to take such a large sum in cash.

At last Mary looked up from her study of the books. "You

must give me a list of all our creditors, and I will arrange for the closure of all the estate's debts, at least all those I consider legitimate. Those which I consider of be more of a personal nature and not proper creditors to the estate, I am afraid, you must make whatever arrangements you see fit."

Anthony's face fell. He knew that his mother was referring to the many of Amelia's extravagances to which he had succumbed. At the same time, he could not see how his mother could possibly master all the detail on her own. Now that he had an inkling of the sort of sums his mother was holding, he knew that life with Amelia would not be worth living unless some of it was diverted to their own accounts.

"Mamma, this is good news indeed and will be the saving of Nethergate. I don't know how you are holding this money, but as it seems a significant sum, it should be transferred as soon as possible in these uncertain times into the estate's accounts and then I will gladly monitor the termination of all our debts. You can leave it all to me." Poor Anthony, even as a child could never hide anything from his mother. She had seen that look in his eye when as a small boy he had lusted for some toy or treat. It was like a beacon now. She felt a wave of affection for her son and for all his weaknesses. How much better it would have been for him had he not had to shoulder the burden of Nethergate and had continued working as a lawyer, where right and wrong were clearly defined. But she knew that once the money was in the estate's hands her power over its disbursement would be lost.

"Anthony, I must tell you that there were certain other conditions that Grandpapa laid down for your consideration. He was much taken with Ruth when she was with him. It is his desire that she should be granted her freedom immediately. I know that you hold all the necessary documents and I would like you to put this in train straight away."

Alarm bells started ringing in view of the decision that he

and Killcaid had already taken concerning Ruth's future and her eventual replacement at Nethergate Hall by Laticia.

"What would you intend that she might do once she gains her freedom?" he asked cautiously, playing for time.

"Why that would be entirely up to her, but I rather think she wants to stay on doing what she does now, but as a paid employee of course."

"I think that would be unwise, Mamma. It would be most unsettling for the remainder of the hands, particularly at this time, and it would send all the wrong signals. It would be as if we were condoning the acts of a murderer in view of what her son has done. She should be sold off now. Laticia, in your absence, has been taken into your household to take over Ruth's duties. We felt that once you knew what her son had done you would not wish to remain so closely connected with such a person. I have already arranged to have her placed in the next sales at New Haven. I felt sure you would agree." He could almost see Killcaid's head nodding in agreement on the other side of the door at this determined stand. He was after all the Master of Nethergate and the sole owner of all the hands employed by the estate.

44

Nemesis

Mary felt her anger rising at her son's high-handed assumption that she would wish to dismiss her maid because of what Matthew had supposedly done. Determined not to lose her temper, she waited several moments before replying. The delay was such that Anthony began to think that she was going to raise no objections or perhaps had not heard him.

"Mother?" he queried.

"I heard you," replied Mary. She continued in measured tones. "Surely who I trust to employ in my personal service is my concern and mine only. I certainly would not wish her to leave Nethergate just because of what her son is alleged to have done. Unless of course she wants to do so."

Anthony sensed that he had his mother on the run. "Mater dear," he said patiently, "you can see what hard times we face. We all need to make sacrifices and you know full well that the disposal of all hands on the estate rests with me as Master of Nethergate. I really cannot condone the presence of the mother of a murderer in a position so close to the matriarch of the family. You do see that?"

Very deliberately Mary began to tidy up her things and to

prepare to leave once more. She had reached the door when Anthony asked with some alarm, "Where are you going?"

She turned. "Why, back to Nethergate House of course."

"But what about Grandpa's money?"

"On his instructions I can use it as I wish. I intend to use it to purchase Ruth when she comes up for sale. I guarantee no-one will be prepared to offer the price that I can pay. Then I shall give her the freedom to do and go where she wishes." She opened the door abruptly to reveal the figure of Killcaid hastily backing away. She nodded to him politely, continuing on her way without a pause.

"Mamma, wait!" cried Anthony, hurrying after his mother's rapidly retreating figure. "Perhaps I was hasty. These plans can be changed. We have much more to discuss."

Mary hesitated, allowing Anthony to catch up with her, then turning to Killcaid she remarked, "I am sure Mr Killcaid must have much more urgent things to do rather than to loiter about this office." Anthony nodded to Killcaid, who looked for a moment as if he would dispute the issue, then with ill grace, he turned and left.

"Perhaps now we can continue in private," she said to her son, returning to his office. "First I must have a manumission document for Ruth duly signed."

"That will take some time to draw up, Mamma," he said, settling once more into his chair and trying to resume an air of authority. "Perhaps after we have discussed the financial matters we can get our lawyers to draw up such a document." Mary was having no such excuses.

"With your own legal experience from the years you spent with Forbes and Sons, are you telling me that you are not capable of drawing up such a simple document?" retorted his mother acidly. Anthony acknowledged defeat.

"Of course, Mamma," and he set to do as he was asked. As he set to his task, Anthony was conscious briefly of the pleasure he had always experienced in the role of lawyer in doing something he understood and could do well.

When he had finished, he gave her the document, not without a certain pride. It was beautifully worded, precise and accurate.

Mary read the document through carefully, then said, "Now, Anthony, I would like you to prepare another such document, but this time in the name of Matthew Styles."

This was too much for Anthony. "Mamma! You cannot be serious!" he exploded.

"Indeed, Anthony, I am, deadly serious."

"But the man's an out and out rogue, a criminal and a murderer."

"Nevertheless, I require him to be given his freedom."

"This is ridiculous, Mamma. It can't make any difference to him. He committed his crime as a slave, and he will be tried and executed as such. That's the law. Manumission cannot save him."

"So, it won't hurt then to grant him his freedom."

With ill-concealed reluctance Anthony again had to acknowledge defeat and sat down to draw up a second declaration of manumission.

"Both need to be witnessed, Mamma, before they are legally binding," he said, as if this were another insuperable barrier to completion.

"Then who better than myself and Mr Killcaid?"

Anthony was aghast at this suggestion. "But Mr Killcaid will never agree to do that," he spluttered.

"He's not being asked to agree to it," reminded his mother, "only to bear witness to your signature. I dare say you will still find him lingering outside the office anxious to speak with you."

And so it proved. Ruth's and Matthew's manumission was signed by Anthony Styles and witnessed by Mary and, with very ill grace, by Silas Killcaid, looking all the time as if he had swallowed a barrel full of lemons.

After promising Anthony that they would discuss again a rescue package for the Nethergate Estate once she had digested the information she had gathered from her first reading of the accounts and after he had produced a full list of all their creditors, Mary left her son. She could not help but feel sorry for him facing the tasks of managing the estate and harnessing such a powerful beast as Silas Killcaid, when nature had so singularly denied him the means to do so. The price she had agreed for the freedom of the two slaves was a generous one. In addition, she had agreed a further sum to be paid into his personal account. She knew this would appease, somewhat, the avaricious Amelia, and give Anthony some small crumb of comfort when he confronted his wife. She did not want to make his life any harder than it already was.

As she neared Nethergate House she felt her pace quickening. She could hardly wait to present the documents of manumission to Ruth, to bring some happiness to her sad and heartbroken friend and to put right wrongs that had been allowed to linger without redress for far too long.

After that there was the challenge of what to do about Matthew and Ursula and how to help them on their journey north. She had much to think about.

Mary had already read much of the most urgent correspondence which had awaited her on her return, including, of course, letters from George. It had been from these that she had learnt the true nature of the relationship between her grandson and Ursula and of his avowed intention to marry her. Her first reaction had been of shock that someone in his position as the future Master of Nethergate should intend to embark upon such a socially disastrous marriage. She could quite understand the implacable opposition of his parents should they get to know of this relationship, indeed she felt strongly averse to the union herself. Then she realised with sudden guilt that her reaction was the opposite to that which she privately endorsed for others. But it was different somehow when it was your own kith and kin that were involved. She wondered too whether the mere suspicion of such a liaison might not be at the root of Amelia's overt cruelty to Ursula. She blamed herself in a way for not thinking things through. George as a young teenager led such a restricted and lonely life up at Nethergate Hall that it was almost inevitable that he should fall for a young girl with such obviously good looks and with such a lively temperament and personality as Ursula. She was a bright girl and had benefited from the illegal education that Mary had encouraged in all her own household slaves. She would be a challenge to George and would excite him intellectually as well as physically. That they should fall in love, now she thought of it, had been almost inevitable. Add to this the uncertainties of war and the possibilities of death and parting forever; it became a yet more volatile combination. She should never have suggested Ursula for service as Amelia's maid, but that had been because of her desire to bring Ruth back into her service and to save her grandson from Silas Killcaid. It was also, she had to admit, so that she could watch him mature under her roof. She could live again through him the time when Mark, his father, was a young boy and truly the darling of her eye before he had turned so wilful and defiant. Perhaps too, she imagined, she might have been able to avert any signs of Matthew becoming like his father.

As she neared her beloved Nethergate House she put all these thoughts aside in anticipation of the pleasure with which she knew Ruth would receive news at last of her personal freedom from the shackles of slavery with that of her son as well.

45

A Surprise in the Bayou

Matthew and Ursula awoke late on the eve of what they both knew was to be their last full day and night in the only real home either had ever known. Here they felt snug and secure. They felt that they would be safe enough in Nethergate House, but it could only be the platform from which they would launch their long and hazardous journey to Canada and to freedom. The heat of the day had not yet reached them and, as lovers do, they lingered in bed, delighting in the joys that each brought to the other. Then, with passion spent, lying in each other's arms but with fingers still gently and lovingly exploring, they let their minds dwell upon the ordeal ahead and the fruits of freedom in far-off Canada. Neither dared to look too far into the future for dread of the awful decision that Ursula must one day make.

They bathed in the stream, savouring each moment of their routine in their own little bubble of freedom, as if by this means they could sear it forever into their memories. After breakfast they tended their garden. It was a pointless gesture, but it seemed right that they should leave it all as they would wish to remember it. In the afternoon Ursula tidied the cabin and placed wild flowers to please the eye and add fragrance to their home. Matthew checked through his domain, remembering the time when he and Old Mo had first passed this way and the things the old trapper had taught him. He wondered what had happened to him and wished heartily that his end might have been swift and sudden.

As the shades lengthened, they gathered together finally to sing, play the flute and make music. They talked of George, without embarrassment or jealousy on Matthew's part, for both in their own way loved him. He would be with them in spirit on their journey north, for there was no doubt that the money he had given Ursula would greatly ease their travels. It gave them more chances than most embarking upon such a journey.

The darkness was soon upon them and they sought the shelter of the cabin. Since there was no need to preserve their resources, they lit candles and their home took on a festive air. However, the room quickly became so full of flying insects and beetles that they blew out the candles and settled down on their bed for the last time. Soon both were asleep.

It was still dark when Matthew awoke with a start. He was instantly alert. Something had woken him. He was unsure what. He lay still breathing shallowly, listening hard. He was used to the sound of the occasional curious animal that visited them at night. This noise he was sure had been no curious possum. It was entirely different.

His mind raced back to his recent visits to Nethergate House. Because of the need to rescue Samuel more people now knew that he was living in the bayou. He could vouch for most, but there was always temptation for some to ease their lot by currying favour from those with power; none was more powerful than Silas Killcaid. Then he remembered when he had lingered outside Nethergate House, allowing himself a self-indulgent moment to savour happy memories, mingled with thoughts of his mother. He remembered the figure he thought he had seen at the window in the slave lines. He cursed his carelessness now for what it might now cost him and above all Ursula.

Rigid and alert, he searched his mind, trying to remember what it was that had woken him. The sound came again. It was the creaking of a floorboard. There was someone outside. He was aware that Ursula had stopped breathing. She was awake, roused by the sudden tension in his body.

"What is it?" she whispered.

"There's someone outside," he replied. "Get to the floor!" he ordered. "I'm getting the rifle. There may be some shooting."

Quietly he crept across the floor to where his Kentucky rifle was kept. It felt cold, but comfortable and familiar to his hands. They would not expect him to be armed.

Now he could hear someone fumbling at the catch on the door. They always placed a stout branch across to stop any animal coming in. The door was being gently rocked to and fro as if someone was testing the lock prior to bursting in upon them.

Very quietly Matthew cocked the rifle. Even so there was a slight metallic sound. Immediately the testing of the door ceased.

Matthew now had formulated a plan where at least Ursula might be saved. As far as he knew no-one suspected her presence here. He moved swiftly to where she lay upon the floor.

"Listen," he whispered urgently, as he shrugged on shirt and hose. "They won't expect me to be armed. In a moment I shall fire off a round. That'll set them scurrying off. They'll seek cover. I'll make a break for it with the advantage that I know the ground. They will be very cautious going into the swamp after me. As soon as the coast is clear, make a break for it. They don't know you are here. Try to get to Nethergate House. They'll help you even if I can't reach there."

For a moment he held her close to him once more. Then he kissed her. "Thank you, Ursula, my love," he murmured.

"Thank you for everything." He crept to the door. Cautiously he moved aside the branch. Gently he released the latch and grasped the door handle. With one wrench he tore it open, prepared to leap at his attacker and then to discharge his rifle. What he saw silhouetted against the moonlight was a sight that made him reel back in astonishment.

46

The Return

Standing in the doorway of the cabin silhouetted against the light from the moon was the unmistakeable figure of Old Mo himself, or his veritable ghost. Even as he stood there the figure lurched to the side and reached out to the doorjamb for support. It was clear that he was either injured or in the last stages of exhaustion.

"Mo! Mo! Is it really you?" was all Matthew could say as he rushed forward to embrace him. He felt incredibly thin and frail to Matthew's eager hold and he reeked of days on the road, but it was unmistakeably Old Mo.

"Matthew. Matthew," muttered the old man, "be that truly you too?"

"It is, Mo. As true as ever an' takin' good care o' your cabin fo' you," he added as he helped his old mentor to a chair.

By this time Ursula had been able to struggle into her clothes and shyly came forward.

"You must be starving," she said, by way of introduction.

"Who's this?" asked Old Mo, starting at her sudden appearance.

"This is Ursula," replied Matthew. "She's my…" and he paused, wondering suddenly what to say.

"Welcome, Mr Mo," said Ursula, stepping into Matthew's moment of hesitation, "an' welcome back to your home. Matthew has told me all 'bout you, an' how you learn him to hunt and to live out here. Ah cannot tell you truly how many time we ha' blessed your name for building this here cabin. Now let me get you sometin' to eat?"

Old Mo smiled in the darkness at this effusive greeting.

"God's truth," he said, "Ah'm starving. I cannot think de las' time I ate."

Matthew lit a candle from the embers of the fire and placed it on the table, whilst Ursula busied herself in gathering in some food from their store outside. From the light of the candle both men studied each other. Old Mo stared in astonishment at the bearded figure before him.

"Truly, Matthew, you have become a man now," he said. "I'd have pass you on de road an' never have know'd you."

"An' you, Mo, have not changed one jot," but Matthew lied, for whatever had happened to Old Mo since he had been taken away to be sold had taken a terrible toll upon him. His frame was gaunt and thin and his face under the shadow of his emblem hat bore witness to the privations of his journey. But the one thing that Matthew could read that gave joy to his heart lay in the eyes of Old Mo. Those eyes, though clouded with exhaustion, still sparkled with the indomitable defiance of the spirit that dwelt within.

Matthew started to tell his old mentor of what had happened since his departure, but Ursula's production of food and drink drove out the old man's ability to concentrate.

"Ah knew someone was in ma' cabin. I could smell the woodsmoke. Guessed it could only be you," he mumbled between mouthfuls. He ate ravenously, but in a surprisingly short time professed himself satisfied. Meanwhile Ursula had split up their co-joined beds into their original single state and prepared one for Old Mo. With his hunger satisfied, it was clear that his body now cried out for sleep. They led him to his bed and almost before they had drawn the blanket over him he was asleep.

Matthew and Ursula returned to their single bed, not minding one bit the enforced contact with each other. The candle extinguished, they both had too much to think of now to return to their interrupted slumbers. Instead they whispered to each other of what this new happening might have upon their plans for the morrow. Much would depend upon how the old man recovered after a night's sleep and a full stomach. If he was sick as well as exhausted, they could hardly leave him alone in the wilderness.

All too soon it seemed daylight began to filter through the shuttered windows and the gaps in the outer wall, casting shafts of sunlight across the floor, setting the dust dancing in their beams. The two went about their breakfast as quietly as possible, mindful of the slumbering figure inside, but it soon became clear that no amount of noise was going to rouse their visitor. The two resumed their normal pattern of behaviour as if no-one else was there.

They returned to tending the garden, now with a renewed sense of purpose. Occasionally they would peer in at Old Mo, but he slumbered on, oblivious to whatever was going on about him. Matthew removed the blankets from him as the warmth of the day percolated into the cabin. The stench of the old man's body was overpowering, but for Matthew it was somehow a badge of pride for the old man's fortitude and determination. He could not imagine what privations he had suffered. His body was emaciated, but he did not seem to be suffering from anything other than exhaustion.

Ursula had got together her little canvas bag containing the treasures of her life which she had brought with her into the bayou. The Sunday dresses had long since been sacrificed to the needs of modesty. Her eye fell upon the mirror George had given her when first she had fled into the bayou. She remembered his words that he would be there looking right back at her. Matthew noticed her hesitation.

"You must take that too when we finally leave. It was a special gift from George." She thanked him with her eyes. Otherwise the only things she had to show for her short life were simply her memories. As for Matthew, the total of his belongings consisted of his flute, his music, his Kentucky rifle and a Bowie hunting knife Old Mo had given him. They both stared down at their little pile of possessions by the cabin door. It was a reminder of the end of their time in their little world together: a closing of the book, a time of sadness.

"Strange," remarked Matthew, "how the most precious things in both our lives should come from George."

All they could do now was to wait until the old man emerged to see if he was well enough to survive on his own. Ursula, now aware of her own body-clock ticking away, was anxious to be away, but she acknowledged all they owed to their slumbering visitor and did not press Matthew for a decision. Later in the afternoon, Ursula prepared a meal, hoping it would be their last in the bayou. Perhaps drawn by the smell of Ursula's preparations, Old Mo finally emerged from his slumbers. Sleep had restored his vigour and he was alive with curiosity as to why Matthew and Ursula were sharing his cabin. Like a child with a new toy, he was delighted to see how everything had been both used and improved. He was also full of appreciation for the care they had taken over his garden of herbs and vegetables and the store of seeds Matthew showed him, collected for the future. With renewed hope that the two might yet depart that night, Ursula busied herself with the preparation of their final meal in the bayou whilst Old Mo washed away the stains of travel.

Later, Matthew showed Old Mo round the traps closest to the cabin and basked in his old mentor's praise at their skill and execution. Some of them Old Mo set again, for once more they had a purpose. Matthew could only marvel at the old man's recovery after his rest in the cabin. Again and again, though, it was Old Mo who expressed his gratitude as to how his cabin and garden had been cared for and how much the thought of it all had sustained him whilst he had been away.

Matthew explained where the other traps were sited and was amazed at the old man's memory of the terrain. Now confident that Old Mo would be well able to look after himself, he also told of his and Ursula's experiences whilst he had been away and of their new plans for an imminent departure.

There was almost a festive air when all was ready for Ursula's meal. Old Mo had given them snippets of how he had fared since being sold but it was only when everything was cleared away that Old Mo embarked upon the story of his adventures since leaving Nethergate. It would be some time before it would be safe to move and the two listened spellbound to the old man's tale.

47

A Traveller's Tale

Old Mo began his story at the point when Matthew had fallen seriously ill and was no longer able to help him with the supply of game for the cabins. He had meant at that point to put his plan into action and to disappear to live his life out in the freedom of the bayou, but he delayed. It had been his intention to tell only Matthew of his plans, so that he had at least one link with the outside world, should the need arise. He had delayed his move out of concern for Matthew. That lingering had been fateful. Killcaid had become convinced that because of the sudden cessation of the flow of game from the bayou Old Mo was becoming a liability. On the chance visit of a passing trader he had been sold leaving only time to give Morella, for Matthew, the coded map to his secret cabin in the bayou.

Old Mo related how, in all the months of privation that followed, this little oasis of cultivation with its cabin had been like a beacon of light for him. It was the determination to return that had kept him alive when otherwise he might have given way to despair. Now he was back and had found his dream once more, but in far better shape than he had left it, thanks to them, and now he meant to make the most of it. Both Ursula and

Matthew smiled at the old man's gratitude, secretly relieved that it would not after all affect their plans.

Then Old Mo continued with his tale. When he had arrived at New Haven with the trader, it was to find that the slave sale, which normally attracted a modest amount of interest, had now erupted into something of a bonanza. Two of the tobacco estates in the district had gone bankrupt and were offering their entire stock of slaves for sale. There were some four hundred in all and the telegraph wires had been buzzing for days with news of potential bargains to be had. There was particular interest from the deep South where the rice fields were forever in need of new hands, such was the mortality rate of stock working in those unhealthy conditions. The need to feed the Confederate Army provided a ready market for rice so there was no shortage of cash.

At first Old Mo had seen the potential advantage of this situation. If he could exaggerate his disabilities, he might not attract a buyer with so many to choose from, in which case he would be returned to Nethergate. Then he could select his moment and vanish into the bayou, where none would find him, to live out his days as a free man at last.

There was a large carriage barn in New Haven, which doubled up on sales days as a holding pen into which slaves were herded and held where they could be prepared for the sales. Food was good and there were facilities for slaves to make the best of themselves. There was much competition to create the best impression possible, perhaps to appeal to a kindly or more considerate buyer. On this occasion, however, the numbers far exceeded the capacity of the holding barn and other accommodation was called into use. In some cases, there was so little security that slaves had to be shackled together to prevent the more desperate from escaping. It was a time of unbridled anxiety for the merchandise, the greatest of which was the splitting of families. "At least," Old Mo said, "Ah was spared that anxiety."

As the day for the sales drew near the more forward-looking of the slaves would rehearse what they intended to say when they were standing with their family on the sales block and run each member of the family through their lines, even down to the youngest child, who might claim to be able to run errands and prepare vegetables in the kitchen. There was a rumour that they would all be wanted on the cotton estates, so all were preparing little speeches, claiming that they could sort through the cotton like no other and that they had every variety of skill their new work might demand.

As for Old Mo, he cultivated a limp and bore the agony of exposing to the sunlight the scar tissue on his head from where he had been scalped so that no-one might consider buying him. If they did, he reasoned, his price would be so low that over the coming months he might be able to earn or steal enough money to purchase his own freedom.

As the day for the sales drew near the entire slave stock were moved up to the race course so all could be accommodated in one place to allow prospective buyers the opportunity of inspecting the stock. "By then," Old Mo remarked with a wry laugh, "Ah was sich an ornery looking critter thet no-one come to look at me. Only some weasel-faced-lookin' men seemed remotely curious an I made damn sure they could see me limpin' about an' shakin' like I was wid de palsy. But Ah should hab been mo' wary, for dese men were buyin' in job lots at de end of de auction for de Army. But Ah did'n find that out till afterwards."

Streams of buyers came through to assess and evaluate the display of humanity and judge the quality of each lot. As a show of compassion families were given consecutive lot numbers, but no regard could be taken for lifelong companions and friendships. Future bidders required the men to strip to the waist to judge the strength of their backs and the bulk of their muscle and sinew. That way they could evaluate the work output from each creature and perhaps judge from the marks of flogging whether they were likely to be a docile purchase. They prodded, poked, felt, squeezed and peered in mouths whilst the slaves, anxious to please, endured all as meek as cattle. With the women, the young ones in particular, they often required them to strip to the waist so they could truly see the quality of what they might be purchasing.

On the day of the sale many of the slaves were given new garments to wear so that they would look their best. Some kept their own if it was a cut above what the auctioneers provided. Those being sold in bulk lots, like Old Mo, were left as they were, not being considered worth the extra window dressing.

The sale began with slaves with special skills, for which the bidding was brisk. Then came the family groups. The group that Old Mo had seen earlier was still convinced that their buyers were from the cotton plantations. The father put on a fine show for the man he thought had shown an interest in his family. He had seen in his gentle features a kindly disposition.

"Look at me, massa; Ah'm prime cotton planter an' tend dem plants better'n a mother tend her chile. Sure, you won't find a better cotton carer than me in de whole worl'. Ah does carpenter work too an' Ah's fus' rate wid de mules. You sure won' find a better sarvant than me, massa. An' Sarah here she fus' rate cotton picker an' cotton carer, 'mos nearly as good as me. Come show the gen'leman how strong you is, Sarah." And Old Mo told how the lady turned about on the sales block and rolled up her sleeves to show her short, muscular arms.

"Plenty work left in dem arms. And plenty work left in me too, eh, massa." Then he called forward his daughter.

"Come Molly, come here an sho' your new massa what he gettin' fo' his money. She work in de house ob de ol' massa. She plenty good any job in de house, she wash, iron, serve at de table." Molly stepped forward shyly and turned round with a bashful glance at her prospective owner. She had a natural grace of movement that was immediately apparent. It was clear to Old Mo that her new master, despite his benign appearance, was more interested in the daughter than the work he might get from her parents. The whole family shouted and hugged themselves when the "kindly" gentleman's bid was successful. Old Mo could only wonder what disappointments might lie ahead for that family.

Old Mo told how the sale was conducted, not by a white man but by a mulatto slave, who seemed to think the whole business of selling off his brothers and sisters was a capital joke. He ushered each individual or fearful group up onto the stand, all the time giving a running commentary of what was on offer. A thin old man with greying hair, walking with the aid of a cane, came onto the stand.

"Dis here fine young buck," began the auctioneer to a mirthful response from his audience. "Dis here, reckon to clear an acre and a half o' thick scrub in under half an hour." More laughter. "An' after dat, ready to sire more'n a dozen tar-babies a night." Guffaws. "Been employed as a bookkeeper by Mr Andrews at the hotel here and good at it. What a waste of all those other talents. Ehh! What am I bid?"

Most individuals themselves were too anxious to take any offence or note of what he said. Even if they had it would scarcely matter, but it kept the bidding going and the audience entertained. The sale moved on at a brisk pace. At each fall of the hammer lives and destinies were changed.

Old Mo watched the sales, but it was at the tail end of the day that his job lot came to the stand. By then, most of the interest had died away and the more discerning buyers had left. The only buyer who remained was a man in Confederate grey from the Army.

"It seemed," continued Old Mo, "that we was jus' wanted for de Army to repair de railway lines and to dig de canals an' sich like work. Any task in fact where many hands is required an' where yo' could break your back workin' 'till you drop. You can guess how we all felt when we saw what was a-happenin'. There was a whole lot of grumblin' an' moanin', but dey appointed the biggest and strongest to be our overseers an' promise them more rations and an easy time. So we was all driven together to be march down to Richmond to build defences 'gainst Yankee cannon. Sich was the mood of the slaves that we was all manacled together, each man coupled to de neck of de man in fron'. Marchin' like that yo' got mighty sore. By evenin' time we was all ready to drop."

"I was lucky," continued Old Mo, "after de second day, 'cos I was old they let me go wid de women. I think that save me. It was on the third day that the firs' man fall sick. After dat they was goin' down like skittles. Soon there were so many ill dat we had to stop. I don't know how many died. There was no way we could go on. We was rested up. I were sen' wid a small group to a local farmer and we all hole up in his barn. He was a poor, man dat farmer, almos' as old as me, wid a hackin cough, like he were not long for dis world. He had to feed us all. Mos' people there were so sick they die off like flies. Ah don' know how many ah bury. De farmer he had jus a few cattle an' pigs. I slaughter de pigs, fo' food, but not so many, 'cos there weren't many as had much hunger. Clem, de farmer, he don' mind 'cos the army pay him well. Ah jus' digs de holes for dem's as died an' all de while me wonderin' when ma time 'ud come too."

48

A Turn of Fortune

Clearly, Old Mo had more yet to tell. Whilst Matthew stoked up the fire in the gathering twilight, Ursula fetched them all a drink. Once they were settled again, the traveller continued his tale.

"But de Good Lord he don' wan' me yet, so ah use de time he give me to mend de roof of de barn where we was livin'. Den de farmer he ask me to repair another barn. Soon I was helpin' him in other ways 'bout de farm an' dis farmer he give me extra food. We got on well an' I grew to like the old man.

"One day when de Army man come to see how many was lef' Ah sees dem talkin' an' de Army man writin'. Then the army man come over an tell me to move ma body an' that Ah's been sold to dis farmer. By evenin' dey was all gone, 'cept those as was a-rottin an' a-mould'rin under de soil. Ah was now Mo Atkinson, de property of Mr Clem Atkinson, farmer of Little Meadow Farm, Tennessee, what had never owned a slave afore."

Old Mo explained how his new master treated him more like a helpful friend than a slave. He lived in the house in a room that had once belonged to one of Clem's sons and shared meals with the farmer much as he had done in his days when he was a trapper out West, before he had got scalped by Indians and left for dead. His new master had been a good farmer in his day, but now he got very short of breath at the least exertion and clearly could not have carried on much longer without help. He made good use of Old Mo's skill with his hands and before long the two of them had the farm looking in better shape than it had for years. The Army had paid well for the accommodation and for the feeding and burying of the slaves. Clem and Old Mo built new stockades and took in more pigs, for which there was an ever-ready market through the military. Within a few months the farm was in profit.

Old Mo leant back in his chair and remarked reflectively, "He were a good Massa, were dat Mr Atkinson, de bes' Ah ever had. I grew to like him mo' dan any white man I know'd. Ah really think 'dis time de Good Lord he smile on me an' Ah foun' marsel' a new home." Old Mo's eyes grew misty at the recollection, which told of the true affection he felt for his new owner. "It was like we was good friends, workin' out our lives together. He never treat me like a slave. He allus ask me to do summat, never tell me so. An' he'd do things fo' me in a thousand little kindnesses. Truly I grew to love dat man as I love no man, black or white, afore."

As the months passed, even his longing for his cabin in the bayou began to fade, so contented was he with his new home. Old Mo learnt more about his master. His wife had died when his children were still quite young. He had brought up his two sons, whom he had hoped would take over the farm from him. He had tried to get them interested in the farm, by getting them to help when they were still quite young. He blamed himself for what happened in the end, thinking that perhaps he had forced farming onto them. Other farmers' children seemed willing to help their parents, so why not his? But his sons were not cast in that mould. They were always contrary, seeming deliberately to misunderstand and then treating each disaster as if it were a joke. As they got older and stronger, they joined forces and simply refused to help. Eventually, he concluded that they never would take to farming. He began to wonder, with his wife gone, why he worked so hard to keep the farm going. When he died, he knew his sons would sell it off, without a thought for all the work he and his beloved Sarah had put into it.

His sons had both left home as soon as they could. He had given them as much money as he could raise, taking out loans from the bank. One had gone to study law and then it seemed both had taken up a life of gambling and gaming on the Mississippi river boats. Being a man of strong religious beliefs, their choice a living was particularly repugnant to their father. They had only once returned to see him and that was to borrow more money. When he had refused to finance their wayward way of life, they had got drunk and tried to kick open the metal strong box where they knew he kept his cash. But he had taken the precaution of securing it firmly to the floor. Eventually they left home vowing never to return until he was dead, when they would take it all anyway. Since then there had been no communication.

Keeping the farm going had proved ever harder as his health worsened. He began to fear that its residual value might not even cover his debt to the bank. He was determined to pay off what he owed so that he could die debt-free. He had been forced through physical weakness to watch his life's work disintegrate about him. There wasn't a thing he could do about it. It went against the whole grain of his beliefs. Then, like a gift from the Lord, Old Mo had come upon the scene and infused life back into the farm.

Having Mo to help had given his owner a new lease of life, but all the same it was clear that he was still a very sick man. The least exertion was liable to bring on fits of coughing that left him weak and gasping for breath.

Old Mo told of one evening when he had stayed out late looking after one of their sows that was having a difficult birth.

Mr Atkinson had been away all day in Newchurch, the market town.

"Ah come in dog tired," related Old Mo, "to find dat Mr Atkinson he had cook me a meal his sel' an was waitin' fo' me afore startin' to eat. We say grace an' eat together same as always. Ah was too beat to say much. When we finish, he say to me, 'Mo,' he say, 'you work fo' me like you was twenty men an' ah is real grateful.'

'Ain't nothin', Boss', Ah say. 'That jus' the way de Good Lord made me.' He allus like mention of de Good Lord.

Then he say, 'Mo,' he say, 'Ah wants yo' to know that when I dies, an' Ah don' think it be long now, Ah wants yo' to know as I is goin' to give yo' your freedom. I don't think it be right for anyone to own another, body an' soul. Dat is fo' de Good Lord and Him alone. Without you dis farm would long ago have failed. Ah don' want ma sons to have de farm, 'cos they jus' sell up and use de money gamblin' an riotous livin'. Ain't no way I want to be party to that. So here's what I gonna' do.' He produced a document. 'This here yo freedom, Mo,' he say, 'an no man more deservin' than you. When de Good Lord in his mercy come callin' fo' me, den yo' be a free man. An' this other documen', this paper say that yo' be de rightful owner of dis here farm, dis house and all dats in it to do as yo' wish. Dat's where I bin all day. Now 'tis all sign and witness.'

He git up then and go to the strong box and locks de papers in where he keep his money an' pats the key he allus wears on a chain 'bout his neck.

Ah is speechless, Ah never know'd such kindness an' trus' from a white man afore. All Ah can do is grip his han' wid tears in ma eyes.

Dat night Ah goes to bed wid such joy in ma heart an' thank de Good Lord fo' directin my way to become de willing slave of such a good masssa. Now I had sometin' to look forward to. Ah had real hope."

49

Treachery

Old Mo halted for a moment in relating his experiences to his young listeners, as if gathering his thoughts and emotions together. Continuing his tale, he told of his joy at Clem Atkinson's revelation for his future. Not long after this, since he was no longer able to manage the stairs, he was forced to move his master's bed downstairs into what had been the family room when his wife was alive. Old Mo always ensured a good fire was blazing in the hearth and that his master had his favourite things about him ready to hand. The kitchen still remained their meeting point, where they lingered and talked until finally his master took permanently to his bed. Then Old Mo had his meals in with his master and related the day's events.

When Mr Atkinson took a turn for the worse Old Mo rode into Newchurch and fetched the doctor, who left shaking his head. He instructed Old Mo as to how to make his master comfortable and gave him some medicine to ease the pain of coughing.

Mr Atkinson's condition stabilised for a bit but his mind remained as sharp as ever. Old Mo did everything now. When he conducted sales, he placed the money in the strong box

266

using the key which his master always wore about his neck and showed him the money that was accumulating. Although Old Mo could not read, he had a memory for figures and kept a running total of the contents of the box.

One evening he returned from work to hear the sounds of raised voices. He ran into the farmhouse, thinking his master was being assaulted. There were two men there as he burst in to where his master lay. The old man was trying to say something to them but was overcome by coughing. Old Mo soothed him and as his breathing gradually calmed, he managed to gasp, "Meet my sons."

The two young men had some arrangement with Clem's doctor to be notified when their father was nearing the end of his life. Both had come hastening, concerned that the one might steal a march on the other. When he had recovered from his coughing, Clem motioned for Old Mo to come close. He told him that he wanted his sons to be made aware of his plans for the property after his death. He gave Old Mo his key and Old Mo collected his will. Then Mr Atkinson read the documents to his sons whereby on his death Old Mo was to be granted his freedom and the ownership of Little Meadow Farm and told his two errant sons the reason why. Their faces fell as the full realisation of what their father had done dawned upon them, to be replaced by rage, rage made twice as fierce by the fact that their expected inheritance was to be made over to a slave, albeit one that would be a free man when their father died. At first, they pleaded with him, then they swore at him in their fury and frustration. Finally, when they realised there was no changing their father's mind, they both stormed from the house, eyeing Old Mo with malevolent loathing.

As the sons left the older of the two, poking Old Mo repeatedly in the chest muttered savagely, "Listen good nigger-boy. If you think the likes o' you can worm your way into our father's affections and rob us o' what is rightfully ours, then think again. When de old man dies, it ain't gonna be long afore yo' follows him. Understand! This here place is ours by rights an' that's the way it gonna be."

Old Mo prepared a broth for his master, but the appearance and anger of his sons had taken away his appetite. He stayed with him, soothing him until he slept, and then prepared some food for himself. He had barely started to eat before he heard the clatter of hooves in the yard. He went to the window and saw the two sons returning.

One of them was bawling out, "Nigger boy! Hey nigger boy!"

Old Mo came cautiously out to the yard. A thin drizzle was falling, shining on the cobbles. Both men had acquired casks of liquor which they clasped in their arms for Mr Atkinson never kept any liquor of any sort in his house.

"Look to the horses, boy." He did as he was asked and secured the horses in the stable, rubbed them down and fed and watered them. Cautiously he returned to find the two brothers noisily installed in the kitchen. They had finished off what was left of his meal, washed down with the liquor they had purchased.

"We both fancy some good old home cooked grub, Boy. Right away, eh? We're mighty hungry, boy, jump to it." Though bone weary after his day's work Old Mo had no wish for a confrontation with the two drink-fuelled and angry young men and did as they requested.

When he had finished, he went in to say goodnight to his master, who was sleeping fitfully. He made him comfortable and left.

Returning to the kitchen he announced his intention of going to bed and made his way to the stairs.

"Where yo' goin', boy?" asked the older of the two.

"To bed," Old Mo replied evenly, keeping the resentment from his voice.

"Oh no yo's not, boy. You is sleepin' out in de barn with the pigs. That's war you belong, boy. We's not having no niggers a' sleepin' in our house. That not right, brother?"

"Sure is," replied his brother, cracking his knuckles as he spoke and uttering a nervous, high-pitched giggle as if in anticipation of some further devilment. By this time Old Mo was so dog tired that he didn't much care where he laid his head. He made his way to the barn where he had slept on his first night at Little Meadow Farm. That night, he made a comfortable enough bed in the hay and slept the sleep of the exhausted.

The next morning, he awoke early and doused his head under the pump in the yard. The rain had washed the clouds away and the sun shone from a clear blue sky. The pigs rushed snorting and snuffling to greet him, squealing in anticipation. He fed them, taking pleasure at their delight as he always did. Outside he paused a moment to savour the sense of order, before turning his steps towards the house.

The kitchen was a scene of disarray. A chair lay upturned on the floor, plates and crockery lay broken on the ground with the congealed remains of some of last night's meal. Old Mo stole softly through to where his master lay and peered in through the door. He seemed to be sleeping, snug and peaceful under a pile of bedding, but the room was chill and the fire but a glowing ember. He rekindled it as quietly as possible until it was soon crackling and blazing in the grate. He glanced at his master, but he had not moved, and he thought to delay waking him until the room was warmer and he had prepared his morning broth.

Old Mo returned to restore some sort of order to the chaos of the kitchen and prepare his master's breakfast. He was glad that his master could sleep for he usually slept only fitfully. Perhaps the tension and noise generated by his sons had exhausted him. It would do him good, he thought, to slumber on before facing the inevitable stresses the new day would bring.

269

The brothers had consumed the broth he had reserved for their father and he began to prepare some more. By the time he had done so and restored order to the kitchen, it would be time to rouse his master.

There were sounds of movement from upstairs. One of the men was hacking and coughing and clearing his throat. Then suddenly a thought struck him. There had been something missing. With a sudden cold shock for its implications he realised that he had not once heard his master's habitual dry coughing. He rushed into the room where his master lay. As he entered, he was aware of a smell previously cloaked by the room's chill. During the night, his master had fouled himself. Gently he eased back the bedclothes, knowing how shamed his master would be at this manifestation of his growing frailty.

His master's face stared up at him, his features twisted in the pain of his dying. A thin trickle of vomit and blood ran from the corner of his mouth, running into his beard and staining the pillow. He had been dead for some hours. As he gazed upon his features, Old Mo was overcome by a deep sense of loss. Gently he drew his hand down his master's face, closing the eyes and mouth. Here was the only white man that he had ever truly loved and trusted. With some difficulty he rearranged his limbs into a more reposed attitude, for already rigor mortis was setting in. The resistance he felt was as if his master had something else yet to say and did not want rest until it was said and done. It was then that he noticed something missing. It was the chain about his neck that held the key to his strong box.

With a gasp Old Mo stood up. Only then was he aware of the older brother standing at the door leaning against the door jamb. He was still a little drunk. "Him dead, ain't he?" he said, his voice slurred. Behind him Old Mo heard the falsetto giggle of the younger brother. "This what yo' lookin' fo'?" he continued. In his hand he held the old man's key and chain, which he began playfully to swing about. "Or then again maybe 'tis this." In his other hand he held the document giving Old Mo the ownership of the farm. "For all he may ha' been a good farmer," resumed the older son, "he was pig-ignorant 'bout the law was ma dad. This here ain't worth the paper it's writ' on. My Pa don't know that no slave, especially not a jus' freed one, can own property in the State of Tennessee, or any other state I knows of." With a casual, almost contemptuous gesture he ripped the will in two and threw it into the fire, where it curled and in a moment was consumed. With it died Old Mo's hopes for his future.

"Now we comes to this," resumed the older Atkinson brother. In his hand he held the document that the old Mr Atkinson had told Mo would make him a free man. At the sight of it Old Mo went cold. All his hopes were wrapped up in that document. Owning a farm had never seemed a reality, but his freedom was another matter. It was his life's aspiration. It was held now in the hands of a man to whom it meant nothing. He took a half step towards his tormentor. He hesitated, realising that he would be no match for the younger man with his brother behind him.

"That's ma property," he muttered through clenched teeth.

"You read, boy? No 'course yo' don't, you a nigger. This ain't what yo' think it is, boy. This document…" and he began to scan it as if reading its contents. "This document, written by ma pa, say that any slave he may own should on his death be sold immediately and the proceeds given to my beloved sons." He looked up, daring his victim to challenge him. He continued, adopting a tone of reasoned understanding, "Now, I knows what yo' done here, and me an ma brother, we want that you stay on an look after the farm, that is 'till we sell it. Then you can be sold with the farm. That not so, brother?" There was a grunt from behind the door. "You like that, or maybe we sell you right now? You want we do that, eh?"

Old Mo made no move but stared back in sullen defiance at his tormentor, not for a moment believing what the oldest son had read.

"That settled then," said the older brother with an air of finality. With that he casually threw the document onto the fire. Old Mo lunged forward, but the white man barred his way, still swaying unsteadily, but his menace was undeniable.

"You wouldn't be 'bout to attack your new master, would you, boy? 'Cos you is mine now, mine and my brother's, an' attacking your master's, well, that's worth a floggin' or a hangin' any day. That's the law."

Mo stood still. Waves of bitterness and despair washed over him. For the first time in his life he felt utterly defeated. The hopelessness of being a slave and dying in servitude was overwhelming. There was no way out.

"That," said Old Mo to his listeners in the bayou, "that was 'bout the lowest point I got in all ma life."

50

Retribution

The light was beginning to fade in the bayou. Matthew was starting to get anxious about his departure with Ursula for Nethergate House, but at the same time he wanted to hear the end of his friend's tale. The traveller was given another drink and they all settled down to hear the end of his story.

Old Mo took a gulp from his drink and continued. He had been so preoccupied with his own despair at the end of his hopes for freedom that he failed to register that the two brothers were once again engaged in a heated disagreement. It seemed that the older had suggested that the younger should go and fetch the doctor to certify their father's death. But the younger brother did not trust his sibling not to stash away any valuables that he might find during his absence. In the end both decided to go together, leaving their slave with a final instruction to clean up their father before the doctor arrived.

It was the last service Old Mo could perform for the master he loved and esteemed. He did it with reverence so that his old master could leave this world with his dignity intact.

He cleaned the face and beard of blood and vomit and the rest of his body as best he could for now his master was as rigid as a board. He replaced the lower sheet with the one that covered his body and turned the pillow case so that the blood and vomit were concealed.

Then he made a discovery which was to change everything. He found that there was as much blood and vomit on the underside of the pillow as there was on the top. The old man had been too weak to reverse the pillow himself and it was unlikely that the brothers would have rendered such a compassionate service to their father. The pattern of the stains was different too. It was smeared and central. Slowly the truth dawned. With it came an ice-cold rage. The blood and vomit on the underside must have been deposited when the old man was fighting to breathe, fighting for his very life. His master's callous sons had suffocated their own father. That was why they wanted him out of the house. It was the only explanation.

"Suddenly," said Old Mo, turning to his listeners in the bayou, "I had a vision of all what is 'bout you now. Ah thought 'bout this here cabin, 'bout the things I planted, 'bout where ah could set ma traps an' I vow to myself that, come what may, Ah would come back an' end ma days here. This would be ma answer to thems as had enslave me an' cheated me down the years. Here I would be as free a man as God had made me. Wid dat thought came back hope and resolve." He looked about him and there were tears in his eyes. "Ah never dream that you two would be livin' here an' lookin' after what I already planted and makin' it better than I ever thought was possible. Don't reckon no-one can live without hope. Now Ah had mine back agin'. Hope and a desire to avenge that kindly old man who had been my massa."

At the mention of revenge, a hard and steely look had crept into the old man's eyes as he related the rest of his adventures. He told how the two brothers had returned with the doctor, who had taken one look at Mr Atkinson and after expressing his condolences to the old man's sorrowing sons had certified his death and departed.

The two mourners, after ordering Old Mo to prepare another

meal, set to with a vengeance to drowning their grief with a fresh supply of liquor they had bought before collecting the doctor. Soon they became noisy and full of coarse laughter as they assessed the value of their share in their father's estate, paying not a thought to the rigid corpse that lay next door in an ever-chilling room.

As for Old Mo he went out to the animals and fed and watered them with his accustomed care. Then he gathered supplies for a long journey. When he had carefully gone through all the things he might need, he settled down to wait. It was getting dark before he judged the time was ripe. He returned to the farmhouse kitchen. Mr Atkinson's sons had drunk themselves into a stupor and were sprawled over the kitchen table amidst the debris of their debauchery.

Old Mo rekindled the fire in the room where his master lay so that it was soon roaring away in the chimney. Then he allowed the blazing logs to spill out from the grate. Soon the room was full of smoke as the fire took hold. He opened the window to give the fire plenty of air. When he was satisfied that the room was well and truly ablaze, he said a silent farewell to his master and quietly closed the door.

In the kitchen the two men slumbered on, oblivious to the growing roar of the inferno next door. As he watched, thin tendrils of smoke began to seep through the door. He opened the outside door and the chill night air rushed in drawn by the greed of the flames. The two men stirred but otherwise did not move. Old Mo then closed the outer door and wedged a branch he had left there for the purpose across the door so that it could not be opened from the inside. There was no other way in or out except by the windows and he doubted that in their befuddled state they would be able to manage that or even think of it. Instead they would simply struggle to open the door until they were overcome. He felt no emotion, only a cold sense of purpose.

The flames were clearly visible now from the room where Mr Atkinson lay and licking acquisitively up the side of the house. Still there was no sound from within. Old Mo busied himself in going to the animals, which were growing restless at the sounds and smell of burning, and in making sure that the sparks did not set fire to the other farm buildings. It would be a good half an hour before anyone could arrive, drawn by the sight of the flames. He aimed to be well on his way by then. There was a sudden explosion from the house. Old Mo turned. He imagined the kitchen door had burnt through. Now the fire had found fresh sustenance. It seemed but a moment before the whole house was a writhing sea of flames and smoke, roaring and crackling like a living entity. He thought he heard a cry, but in the thunderous uproar of the conflagration he could not be sure. Nothing could live in that inferno, sending its sparks streaming into the night sky. Mo felt nothing for the two men who by now would have perished. Only a calm sense of satisfaction.

He slung the saddlebags over the horse he had selected for his journey and swung himself up into the saddle. For a long time, the night sky flickered behind him from the light of the fire. Eventually it faded to a dull angry glow. Whoever was drawn by the flames would take care of the animals. That was the only thing which concerned him.

In the bayou the shades were lengthening. The birds were singing their evening songs with a touch of drowsiness as they gathered to roost in the cypress trees, high above the clearing around the cabin. These were the sounds that God had ordained for his ordered world. What they had just been hearing was somehow an affront to nature. Old Mo's listeners shivered, not with the cold but with the realisation of the awesome nature of the events they had just heard. To kill another human being was the most dreadful thing a man could do, but to kill a white man in their tutored minds was beyond sin itself. Both stared at Old Mo. Yet he seemed just the same as before, a tired and weary old man who had suffered much and now was grateful to be home at last.

51

Journey for Freedom

The rest of Old Mo's tale was mundane in comparison with the drama of his escape. He considered it would be some days before anyone realized that there were only three bodies in the house. And when the flames had done their work, he reckoned that a black body looked much the same as a white one. "When you's burnt to a crisp don't reckon thar's much to choose twixt a cooked nigger and a fried white man," he remarked with a throaty chuckle. It might be assumed that he had perished with his master and that one of the two irresponsible brothers had absconded with their father's money. Whatever was eventually decided it would be some days before anyone came looking for him and, even then, they would tend to look north rather than in the direction of Nethergate.

The horse had enabled him to break the back of his journey back home. He had eventually abandoned it, leaving it in the fields of a poor-looking farm, assuming the farmer would keep quiet about his sudden good fortune. His experience out in the trackless West with his fur-trapping master had honed his ability to find his direction of travel. As he drew ever nearer, his excitement mounted. Even so, the journey was not a comfortable one for a man of his years.

But his delight now in finding his cabin so well cared for and his garden so well tended was clear to see.

The old man assured them both that he was well able to care for himself. "Don't reckon the Good Lord will want to call me jus' yet," he said with his soft chuckle. "An' when he does, I shall be ready to answer for what I done. Now God be with you both." With that he turned and took possession of his cabin at last. They could dimly see his shape in the doorway as he watched them go down to where the dugout was moored.

It had been a strange parting. For Matthew the joy of finding his old guide and mentor still alive was tinged by the sadness of yet another leave-taking. It was hard to imagine that they would ever meet again. For Ursula it was the sadness of leaving this secret place, her first home, where she had felt secure and free, but where she had endured the excitement and confusion of being in love with two men at the same time.

They waved farewell to Old Mo, though he could no longer see them, and then paddled through the gloom to where the track up to Nethergate began. Skirting all places of habitation, they made their way without incident to Nethergate House. The house slept, but Ruth had been anxiously awaiting their arrival and ushered them upstairs away from the prying eyes of the rest of the household to where she had prepared rooms for them in the attic. There she took total control with an assertiveness they had not seen before. The two fugitives shed their tattered garments and then luxuriated in the indulgence of a proper bath and washed off the grime of their previous way of life to emerge as fresh as sun-dried butterflies. Ursula was wearing a simple blue dress of a quality no slave would ever wear, with her hair let down and flowing free. She looked so different that Matthew could hardly tear his eyes from her. Matthew had been given a set of casual clothes fit for a member of the gentry. They had been clothes worn by his father, but Ruth did not tell him so. They both stared at each other hardly believing the transformation that their new attire wrought. They had met up again in Ruth's room. It was there that she at last told them the news which she had been longing to impart to Matthew ever since his arrival. They all rejoiced in her new status as a free woman with something like awe.

Now they knew of her good fortune, it was as if she was a different person, as if freedom could somehow change the way one looked. She seemed to move with a new purpose and speak with an assurance they had never seen before. Yet in all this Matthew detected again that heaviness of spirit he had felt on his last visit. It seemed yet more out of place when there was so much to celebrate. He wondered again whether it was his fault. It made him more conscious than ever of his contrasting position as both a slave and a fugitive from "justice" and aware of the risks his mother and his grandmother were both taking in giving him shelter. Ruth then explained that they would meet with her mistress in the morning and cautioned them from revealing any overt indication of their presence in the house.

By this time both youngsters were tired and eagerly thinking of the luxury of proper beds to sleep in, but Matthew was still troubled by his mother's heavy countenance, lest he should be the cause.

"Mammy dear," he said, using the way he had addressed her as a child, "What is it that troubles you so? Is it still the man you lost, or is it me that is causing you so much sorrow?"

Ruth looked at her son with a new compassion. He had changed and matured so much whilst she had been away. "No. Dearest Matthew, bless you, no. It was… it's because of the man I told you of, who became so very dear to me and…" she stifled a sob in her voice, "and is no more."

Then suddenly the memory of Thomas Gladstone flooded back: the moment when he had declared his love for her when all the time she had feared that he was trying to ferret out her secret; the moment he had given her the bracelet in the dark arbour in the garden of the Royal Victorian Hotel on Nassau, and the weight and warmth of his body protecting her from the fire from the Yankee ship. Then she recalled that devastating moment when he had vanished after the Yankee shell had hit their little craft and her own desperate cries still ringing in her ears, "Thomas! Thomas! Oh, Thomas!"

Suddenly all restraint left her, and she found herself weeping uncontrollably and her son with his arms about her and Ursula kneeling beside her. Before this, she had been grieving alone. Now her grief was declared and shared. It did not take the sorrow and sadness away, but in some small way at least it made it more bearable.

"I'm sorry. I'm sorry," she sobbed.

Matthew's strong young arms were about her as he murmured, "I understand, Mammy, I do understand." She knew suddenly that he truly did and that her child was now a man and must have loved too to comprehend her loss. She drew comfort from his compassion and her distress abated as she regained control of herself and brushed the tears away.

"Now off you go, both of you. You must be tired. And thank you," she said, her eyes still glistening in the candlelight with the last of her tears as she ushered them away. The aching void that seemed to crush the very beating of her heart had for a moment been lifted by the concern and affection of her son. Life, she realised bleakly, must go on. Nevertheless, she felt more at peace than she had for days.

52

The Triumph of Killcaid

The next morning Ursula awoke as the sun streamed in through the attic window. For her it was the most luxurious room she had ever slept in. A room on her own. She lay in bed relishing the novelty of the experience, the feeling of lying between sheets and not having to endure the itch of bare blankets. There was a soft knock at her door and Ruth entered. They were to breakfast in her mistress's rooms, where they would not be disturbed. Mrs Styles had let it be known to the household that she had two private guests staying with her to do with the war and they were all to resort to the utmost secrecy. They all knew that the subterfuge might work for a day or so, but that word would soon get out. It made it vitally important that their plans for moving on should be swiftly executed and that no-one should have the chance of recognising them.

Matthew and Ursula met up and went down together to his grandmother's apartment, both acutely conscious of their rich attire. Matthew knocked gently on the door. Ruth ushered them in. Mrs Styles welcomed Matthew with a hug and Matthew, despite his awe of his grandmother, felt himself responding to her warmth. Ursula gave a formal bob. Then Mrs Styles surveyed them both critically in their new clothing and said, "Yes, that will do. That will do very nicely. You both look the part. It is amazing what clothes alone can do." Then she added almost to herself, "It is now only a question of posture and how you speak." Neither of the two youngsters were quite sure what she meant by these last remarks but did not question her.

Mrs Styles did her utmost to make Matthew and Ursula feel at ease, despite their acute awareness of the impropriety of being seated at the same table as their mistress. It was different perhaps for Ruth, who was now a free woman. But such was the warmth of Mrs Styles's welcome that slowly the two fugitives began to relax as they all settled down to a fine breakfast. The two young people were both intensely mindful of their table manners, particularly after the freedom of the etiquette back in the bayou.

After breakfast Mrs Styles heard the two relate their experience of living in the bayou and expressed her admiration as to how they had coped. Both expressed their admiration for what Old Mo had done, for without the shelter of his "freedom cabin" they would undoubtedly have perished. By mutual agreement, neither mentioned the return of the prodigal. After that they settled down to discuss the paths that lay ahead. They talked of the simplest route to safety for them both and that was to reach the nearest Union Camp, which would be only about four days travelling. Once there they could offer their services to the Union cause and Matthew could enrol in a Contraband Unit and there would be plenty of work that Ursula could do. But here there was a problem. The links between North and South were still firmly established where fugitives from justice were concerned. This was clearly in the interests of both sides. In view of the price on Matthew's head, trying to join the Yankees as a recruit would have to be ruled out.

"Have you considered making separate bids for freedom?" suggested Ruth.

"We must go together," exclaimed Matthew and Ursula in unison, with such vehemence that both looked at each other in embarrassment in case they had revealed more than they had intended. The inference however had not been lost on the two older women, who exchanged meaningful glances. Talk then turned to the option of entrusting themselves both to the Underground Railroad. It was at this point that Ruth intervened.

"There are a great many risks attached to taking the route of the Railroad," she declared. "Apart from the added hazard of sheltering a wanted man it can take months to travel from safe house to safe house. Sometimes runaways have to endure the greatest of hardships and privation." Then, looking pointedly at Ursula, she added, "In your condition, Ursula, can you take that risk?"

Ursula blushed. She has no idea that her "condition" was at all evident, but then she recalled that Ruth had helped her with bathing the night before and must have drawn her own conclusions.

Mrs Styles was clearly aware of the situation too for she then took over the discussion. She fixed Ursula with a penetrating gaze that made Ursula drop her head in shame. "I have no intention of passing judgement. What is to be will be. I am assuming that one of my grandsons is responsible. I need know no more." Ursula meekly nodded her head. "It is I think doubly important now that you complete the journey to Canada as quickly as possible and in as much ease as can be contrived. That rules out the Underground Railroad and your plans to join the Union Army are too risky for Matthew with a price on his head and for you both if you still wish to attempt this together."

Matthew and Ursula exchanged glances. For the first time they had been made to confront the true nature of their prospects of escaping safely to Canada or to freedom by joining the Union cause. It looked bleak. However, Mrs Styles had not finished.

"I have however another notion for you to consider," she said. "I had a sister once called Caroline whom I dearly loved. She ran away with a struggling young journalist. They got married and she had a child by him. The child died after living only a few weeks. My dear sister never recovered from the birth and died within the month. Her husband was stricken with grief and took his own life shortly afterwards. All her belongings were eventually passed to me by her lawyers, since my parents had disowned her after her elopement. The point of all this is that I have the birth certificate of Caroline's child in the name of Henry Bradstone. Had he lived, he would now be the same sort of age as you are, Matthew. It is of course a genuine document and you could use it as proof of identity. You have dark colouring, but you have European features and could easily pass as a European with a swarthy complexion."

Mrs Styles paused to let this information sink in.

"You mean," said Matthew, "that I should pretend to be a white man. Ain't that a crime for a slave?"

Mrs Styles looked at him with an amused little smile playing about her lips. "Don't tell me you don't think you could do it. I've seen you aping your betters on many occasions in the past." This time it was Matthew's turn to blush. He knew he had a talent for mimicry, but as to whether he would be able to keep the act going, to play the part of a white man among other white men, he had no idea.

"I think you could do it, Matthew, particularly if your life depended on it and it probably will," assured Mrs Styles. "As to the crime you speak of, that will not technically be so."

Matthew looked puzzled. Then Mary explained to him that he was no longer a slave and gave him the document that Anthony had signed and Killcaid had witnessed with such ill grace. "The trouble is," she continued, "that we can none of us make this document public without bringing down upon you the charge of murder by revealing your true identity. Both

Killcaid and his fellow overseer from the Spielberg Estate have sworn affidavits as to how they found the preacher's body. It won't matter how many slaves swear to the contrary I am afraid, the courts will accept the word of the white men and assume that the slaves are simply trying to protect their own.

Matthew had so often imagined this moment when he finally shook free the shackles of slavery and gained his freedom. His whole life had been moving towards this monumental event. Now here it was. He felt none of the elation he had imagined. Instead he experienced only a sinking of his spirits. Somehow, even at this supreme pinnacle of his expectations, the malign influence of Silas Killcaid had spread its poison to taint his triumph. His enmity and hatred had corrupted what should have been the high point of his life's ambition. Killcaid and his crony from the Spielberg Estate would never retract their evidence. That would reveal Killcaid himself as the murderer and incriminate the other overseer for aiding and abetting him. A dozen slaves must have seen Killcaid strike the preacher down, yet their word counted for nothing. No wonder that the slaves from Spielberg had taken justice into their own hands and tried to murder Killcaid in his cabin. Matthew wished with all his soul that they had been successful. Freedom was his and yet he dared not take it. He looked again at the document of manumission he held in his hand. Killcaid had won. Slowly he screwed and crumpled the document into a ball. He was about to hurl it on the fire that blazed so cheerfully in his grandmother's room when Ruth intervened.

"No, don't!" she cried, "Let me at least keep it. It will mean something to me." She took the document from him and smoothed it out on her knee.

"I knew this would be a bitter moment for you," continued Mary. "I wanted you to have that document in your hand and to know that you are no longer a slave in your heart, even if you cannot declare it to the world. But there is another way in which you can take your freedom."

Matthew, lost in his own bitter thoughts, hardly heard what his grandmother was saying, but at her last words he began to pay closer attention.

"How do you mean?" he asked.

"As I suggested, you can take on the identity of my sister's dead child. You can become Henry Bradstone."

On the strength of that birth certificate, continued Mrs Styles, "I have already obtained for you a travel pass in the name of Henry Bradstone Esquire, gentleman, journeying with your young wife to visit a sick relative in New York. Once in the northern territories you will not need travel passes. Eventually crossing into Canada is likely to be simplicity itself, for the borders are as porous as chalk."

Matthew and Ursula looked at each other. This was the beginning of a plan that had real substance. It was a scheme upon which they could really pin their hopes of taking them all the way to Canada. They both had European blood in their veins and Eurasian features and could pass themselves off as of Spanish descent or from the Eastern Mediterranean. The difficulty was in shrugging off the bearing and attitude of mind of the slave. A slave would never look a white man in the eye, never openly challenge an opinion. He would always phrase any disagreement with due deference, in a manner such that offence could never be taken. Any change of view must seem to be at the white man's behest and never, never at the initiative of the slave.

"From this moment on," continued Mrs Styles, "I want you both to behave as if you were guests in this house. This is the only rehearsal you will get before you embark upon the adventure of a lifetime."

With a slight inclination of his head and a partially raised eyebrow as if acknowledging a compliment, Matthew intoned formally, "On behalf of my wife and I, may I express our deep gratitude," without a trace in his voice of the intonation of the slave.

Mrs Styles's face relaxed into a broad grin and she gave a delighted little cry of surprise and approval. "My God, Henry, I really think you'll do it. I really do." Then adopting a more business-like tone, she got down to practicalities. "Now, the first thing we must do to both of you is to improve your appearance to fit your new roles in life. We must trim your hair and that beard of yours, Matthew, and, Ursula, we must give you a hairstyle more suited to you new position. There are one or two here Matthew, who have seen you, when you brought in Samuel. I am sure I can trust them. As for the rest, you have changed so much. With your beard suitably trimmed and dressed as a gentleman, there's none will recognise you, indeed I hardly did so myself and that was just with the beard."

Ruth and Ursula set to with a will. Ruth gave Ursula some of the clothes that Mrs Styles had bought her for her trip to New York. As for Mrs Styles she had collected together more of the clothes of Matthew's real father, her wayward son Mark. It seemed somehow fitting that they should now be used for this purpose. Ruth, assisted by Ursula, set to making the necessary alterations to clothing for them both and even Mrs Styles joined in. Soon a quiet sense of purpose in their tasks absorbed them all, lending everyone a sense of single-minded resolution and determination.

Perhaps they might not have been so confident had they observed the figure of Laticia steeling away from Nethergate House at dusk and making her way to the house of Silas Killcaid. There she told him about Mrs Styles's mystery guests, the identity of whom was to be kept a secret, but they were allegedly to do with the war. Silas Killcaid was not however to be fooled. He suspected that one of the so-called guests might be Matthew; the other remained a mystery.

"Now, Laticia, my dear," crooned Killcaid as he casually caressed her with familiar hands, "you knows what you has to do. Get a close look at these 'guests' and let me know if one of 'em should be Matthew." Then, dismissing his ever-faithful Allison, who was looking on with jealous eyes, he allowed Laticia to enjoy the warmth of his gratitude before being sent back again to report on the "guests" at Nethergate House.

53

Breakout

The day was spent in rehearsing both Ursula and Matthew in their new roles and status. Ursula was none too easy but learnt to play her part well enough. With Matthew it was the reverse and Ruth and Mrs Styles both had to remind him to refrain from overplaying his hand. Mrs Styles had to smile, for his exuberance reminded her so much of his father when he was younger and still her darling boy. The rest of the time was taken in preparing the two for all they would need on their travels.

They would take only the essentials to support their status. Both were consumed with a sense of anticipation. They would travel in the Nethergate carriage as far as Lexington, having changed the horses en route, and then pick up the Railroad and travel to New York. From there they would make their way using the railroad to the Canadian border. There Matthew would have to hire local transport to spirit them both across the border and to freedom. Mrs Styles gave Matthew the necessary funds to ease their travels in good greenback dollars and promissory notes to enable them to set themselves up in some comfort once across the border.

It seemed impossible to believe that now, perhaps in a little more than a week, they could cross into Canada and be free. They were to use the railroad telegraph to let Mrs Styles and Ruth know of their safe arrival. It all seemed so tantalisingly close.

In the early hours of the morning the carriage clattered up to the front door of Nethergate House. Laticia, ever alert, heard the crunch of the wheels on the gravel. Shivering in the early morning chill she crept like a wraith to a position where she could observe the front of the house unseen. As she watched a Southern gentleman, impeccably dressed for travel, paused to usher his lady companion courteously towards the open door of the brougham. Her heart sank. No way could this elegant grandee be Matthew. Two other figures emerged into the grey early light; the Mistress and Ruth. The gentleman formally embraced the Mistress, then turning he enfolded Ruth in his arms. Only then did Laticia guess the truth, for the hug was unmistakably in the manner of a son bidding his mother farewell. The identity of the lady, however, remained a mystery.

The man stood back. Again, doubts assailed her. This fine figure could not possibly be Matthew, but then he moved. The set of his shoulders, the way he walked. Now she was certain. The two figures swiftly boarded and then with hardly a pause the carriage drew away, sped down the drive and was gone. Laticia could not wait to report to Killcaid. He would be pleased with her.

Mr Henry Bradstone and his young bride, Mrs Ursula Bradstone, relaxed back into the comfort of the Nethergate carriage. Both were acutely aware that this was the first time either had travelled in such a grand manner. They looked at each other with new eyes. Matthew appeared quite the country gentleman, his beard trimmed and disciplined, hiding much of the swarthiness of his complexion. There was just the hint of a swagger about his every gesture. His clothes, enhanced by the confidence of his bearing, spoke louder than words of his new status. Ursula looked as pretty as a posy and her "husband" told her so. She gave a wan little smile. She did not carry the change with quite the assurance of her spouse. They had however passed their first test with flying colours, as Matthew explained.

"Did you see what happened when I asked the coachman his name?" he asked.

Ursula looked puzzled. "No," she said.

"He said, 'Benjamin massa."

"What's so strange about that?" she queried.

"Ben and I worked together down at the stables fo' near a year when I was lookin' after Mrs Styles's horses. If he didn't know me, no-one will."

Ursula was silent. The more she thought of this the more confident she became and the more her spirits lightened. Somehow, before this they had all been playing a game in which they all knew the rules. Now it was for real and they had passed their first hurdle. They were on their way at last, on the boldest adventure of their young lives with the whole of their future at stake. Matthew squeezed Ursula's hand and she responded. What he didn't say however was the frisson of superiority that seeped like a poison into his mind when he was addressed as "Massa". He recognised it for what it was and felt ashamed.

In the late afternoon, after two changes of horses, they reached Lexington. There had been some delay at their first stop due to a shortage of horses because of the demands of the military. They had had a meal there, which did much for Ursula's confidence, finding that everyone treated her as befitted her new status. It restored her natural high spirits. She began now to view the whole experience in much the same spirit as Matthew, though for him, of course, there was much more at stake.

At the Stourbridge Inn in Lexington Matthew demanded their most expensive rooms, which he booked for three days. This had been on the advice of Mrs Styles to avoid any suspicion of the desperate nature of their flight. When they were settled in they dismissed the Nethergate carriage. Matthew pressed a dollar bill into Benjamin's hands and thanked him.

"Bless you, Massa," he said at this unexpected bonus. Again, there had not been a flicker of recognition in his eyes. Matthew watched the departing coach with a sudden pang of remorse, severing as it did his last links with all that was familiar to him and ashamed again of his feelings of superiority over his old workmate.

After that the young couple sauntered down to the railroad station, Ursula delicately picking her way with raised skirt over the mud of the sidewalk. There they inquired after trains to New York. There was a train the next day leaving at eleven o' clock, but such were the priorities for the military that the timing could by no means be guaranteed. Nevertheless, they determined to be on it, reflecting with a sense of wonder how different was their flight from what it might have been had they been using the Underground Railroad.

They spent a little time just looking about the town, strolling casually together, all the time observing closely how other couples behaved. Matthew enjoyed the occasion, but the grip Ursula maintained upon his arm betrayed her unease, despite her apparent high spirits. It was hard to get used to the way the slaves they met on the streets would always stand aside and how even poor whites would give them right of passage.

Back at the Inn Ursula's sense of unease increased once again. She felt that all eyes were upon them and that everyone was watching them. Only when they were alone in their room did she feel able fully to relax.

"Can't we jus' stay here till the mornin'?" she begged. But Matthew was adamant.

"No, my love. We must get used to moving among other people. That way we won't feel any different from anyone else and we won't draw attention to ourselves."

That evening they joined the other guests for dinner in the small dining room. Matthew took over the business of ordering the meal. They occupied a table in the corner of the room where they could watch other people. They ate their meal in a cautious silence, but despite their misgivings no-one seemed to give them a second glance.

An elderly couple was seated next to them and the gentleman pulled out a cigar once they had finished their meal. His wife was clearly of a sociable turn of mind and tried to engage them in conversation.

"Travellin' far?" she asked, leaning over to address her question to Ursula. Ursula started at being addressed so suddenly and was about to reply when her nerve deserted her and she looked appealingly at Matthew.

"Only so far as New York," he informed her.

"Well now ain't that just a coincidence, why, George and I," she said, indicating her husband, "why, we're bound there too. My sister, she's lived there with her husband these past ten years – no, I tell a lie – must be more'n twelve years now. How time just seems to skate along."

George, the husband, nodded his head, as obedient as a clockwork automaton. Clearly, she was a lady who loved discourse. She eased her chair in their direction and settled herself down for a marathon session of light chatter. "Where 'bouts in New York you be bound?" she asked.

Matthew in his turn felt trapped. He had no wish to talk to this lady for fear he might give himself away, but he could not think of any way to stop her garrulous flow.

"Don't reckon as we has decided yet," he hedged.

Matthew was however spared from further questioning by the sound of raised voices from outside. The door to the dining room burst open and a voice he recognised only too well declared to the assembled company, "I'm seeking a fugitive from justice and a murderer to boot who I believe has entered these premises."

Standing in the doorway, still stained with the dust of travel, flanked by two other white overseers, was Silas Killcaid. His eyes swept the room and alighted upon Matthew and Ursula. "And by God I think I have just found him."

He strode towards them, pushing tables aside in his haste.

Ursula gave a little cry of despair and buried her face in Matthew's shoulder.

54

The Devil's Cauldron

After their skirmish with the Yankees, George had not been in action again until Fredericksburg. They seemed to have done nothing but march and countermarch in a seemingly endless pursuit of an elusive enemy. They had once or twice heard the distant boom of artillery, but other than that they had seen nothing of action. It might have dispirited many, but Major Blunsden-Butts was a master of his calling and explained that their marches were all part of the bigger plan to force the Yankees into areas where they could be bottled up and destroyed. After that the men felt better about the endless marching, marching, marching.

Then the orders came to move to Fredericksburg. There, General Lee was concentrating his forces on the ground of his choosing, preparing for an assault by General Burnside's Army of the Potomac, said to outnumber Lee by nearly three to one. Such was the Confederates' respect and confidence in their leader that there wasn't a man who didn't think that Lee would lick them. The Kentucky Boys were to be part of Lee's reserve, but that did not blunt their enthusiasm, for every man felt certain that they would be needed to play a vital part at some point in the coming battle. Blunsden-Butts had every man filing his bayonet as sharp as a needle. Those with hunting knives were honing them so sharp they could shave a man's beard. There was a general air of excited anticipation for the test to come. "Old Blood 'n Guts" rode up and down the lines of deployment, familiarising himself with their every feature so as to be ready in the fog of war to recognise wherever he might be ordered to go.

Then came devastating news. An ammunition wagon train was winding its way to the front from the railhead. An infantry escort was deemed necessary to protect it against the chance of meeting marauding Yankee cavalry. The Major could be seen arguing with the Colonel. Every inch of him betrayed a near mutinous disagreement. The Colonel and the Major had never hit it off. The Colonel was the scion of a third-generation cotton family. What little military knowledge he had was gleaned from books. He owed his position to his political clout. "Old Blood 'n Guts" made little attempt to hide his contempt for the Colonel's lack of experience. To make matters worse, the Colonel was too Southern-proud to seek the advice of those who might know. The two men could hardly bear to be in the presence of each other. Now the Colonel was sending the Major away, with the possibility that he would miss the coming conflict precisely because he knew "Old Blood 'n Guts" yearned more than anything else to be in the thick of the conflict.

In a foul temper the Major led his company away from the hill and towards their distant rendezvous with the wagon train. It was a day's march away.

With the briefest of overnight stops, where the men slept the sleep of the exhausted almost where they fell from the line of march, they were roused again before dawn to continue their march. "Old Blood 'n Guts" urged them on with all the urgency of a drover late for market.

They met up with the wagon train at dawn the next day. The wagoneers wanted to rest up, but Blunsden-Butts was having none of it. After a brief rest, the company fell in beside the wagons and they moved off. It was at that moment that the grey morning sky was lit by distant flashes like far off summer lightning. A stream of profanities escaped the Major's lips. The battle at Fredericksburg had started, and he wasn't there. The distant thunder from the guns rumbled on, borne in on the morning breeze to mock him yet further.

The Major urged the wagon train on like a man possessed, but even he in the end had to let the animals and the men rest. He boiled with rage at the thought of all that drama being played out just over the horizon to the bass chant of the cannon and the sharp chorus of rifle fire. Men were dying in huge numbers, pitting soft bodies against the hail of shot and lead. In everyone's mind was the dread that the endless ranks of Yankee soldiers must in the end prevail against the Confederates' ability to put down yet more fire and shot. What then? Would they see a stream of disheartened soldiers pouring down the slopes towards them in panic-stricken rout? What would they do then?

At last by late afternoon they were able to see the heights above the town where the fighting was taking place. The hill was shrouded in smoke. Some wagons were coming down from the battle bearing the wounded. The drivers, still alight with battle euphoria, threw those toiling up the slopes little tit bits of news.

"We got 'em licked. Sure as fire, got 'em licked. They jus' don't know it yet."

"You should ha' seen 'em come. On and on. Then down they goes, like skittles. Mountains of dead Yankees. Unbelievable."

"Never seen nothin' like it. Them Yankee Irish, they jes' kep' coming. So damn stupid they don't know they's dead till their bleedin' head's blowed clean off."

And so it went on. Soon they could see the explosions on the hilltop. The acrid smell of gunpowder was heavy on the breeze. "Old Blood 'n Guts" was in a fever of excitement. It was as if the mere smell and sound of battle was an intoxicant. They handed over their charges to the ammunition park and set about to march to the battle with the Major barking at their heels. Soon though, the line of march became yet more extended. The men had been on the move without respite for over twelve hours. They were as keen as their leader to be in at the kill, but a human body can only be driven so far, no matter how willing. Men simply collapsed by the wayside. Even the Major could see that in their present exhausted condition his men would be more of a liability on the battlefield than an asset and had to order a rest.

They stopped by a group of cottages where they came across a cluster of terrified women huddled together in one room. They shrank back when the soldiers entered, but as soon as they realised how exhausted the men were they set to with a will to boil water so the men could brew what passed for coffee.

George, despite his own fatigue, moved among his men, heartening those who looked as if they would fall out and encouraging them not to give way to their weariness. But the prospect of coffee and the sight of the women now moving among them gave them all fresh heart and soon the men were exchanging banter with the ladies and reassuring them of a Confederate victory. Only Blunsden-Butts remained aloof and fretful at the delay.

Manuel brought George a steaming mug of coffee. He sipped it appreciatively and then looked up in surprise.

"Manuel," he said, "you got me real coffee. How the Devil…?" He stared at the grinning Manuel. "Best I don't ask, eh?" Manuel nodded, tapping his finger knowingly against his nose, but clearly delighted that his efforts were appreciated.

Not for the first time George wondered at the jewel Manuel had turned out to be. He never seemed to tire. He was always there when needed and somehow always came up with the unexpected at moments when it brought the greatest comfort. The thought suddenly struck him that soon he might be involved in the battle raging a short distance away. He wanted Manuel to know how much he appreciated all he had done for him over the past months in case something should happen in the next few hours. It suddenly seemed very important. He grasped Manuel warmly by the shoulder. "You're a gem to me, Manuel, a real gem. Guess I don't know how you does it. I want you to know how much I have appreciated all you've done for me over the pas' few months."

Manuel's eyes filled with tears. His smile seemed to stretch from ear to ear. He knew he would do anything for his young master. His own heart swelled with content that he had been able as a soldier to atone for the fears and betrayals of the past. He also knew with certainty that were Killcaid to appear at this moment he would spit in his face. His fear of the overseer was a thing of the past. With sudden concern, though, he wondered if this outburst of appreciation by his young master might not be because of a premonition that something might happen to him in the ensuing battle. His heart filled with anxiety at the thought. In his turn he realised how fond he too had grown of his young master and how being his servant had become his whole existence. If his master were killed, he would be returned to Nethergate to face Killcaid. He knew he could face Killcaid now like a man, but he also knew that now he would never return to being a slave to any other.

There was a sudden snort of derision. Major Blunsden-Butts had been watching this tender little scene being played out between master and slave. There was a curiously knowing look in his eye which George could not fathom.

"Don't do to get too friendly with nigger boys," he intoned as if he were quoting from some military manual. "Won't do at all."

Before George could think of a reply, "Old Blood 'n Guts" had turned and stalked away, impatient once more for the battle ahead. He left George, not for the first time, at a loss to understand his inscrutable leader.

The shades were beginning to lengthen for dark came early at this time of year. George realised with a sudden shock that in less than a fortnight it would be Christmas Day. The titanic struggle on the hill above them still ebbed and flowed in intensity but showed no sign of abating.

Refreshed the men clamoured to their feet, waved farewell to the women who all turned out to wave them on. One or two ran forward to embrace the men with the compassion of their kind. Perhaps in their minds the thought that one of them might remember the brief warmth of a woman's embrace before facing the unknown of eternity. Heartened and feeling like heroes, the men swung with renewed enthusiasm towards the sounds of battle, "Old Blood 'n Guts", as ever, in a lather of haste.

Soon they were up in the throng of the fighting. The air was thick with smoke from shell and discharge and too from a blazing house to the right of the road leading up onto the heights. They passed a long row of batteries of Napoleon 12 Pounders. The gunners were resting, letting the barrels cool and lounging about, some leaning on their ramrods. All were blackened by gunpowder and red-eyed from the acrid fumes. Ammunition lay stacked in ordered piles behind each gun.

They could see where the fighting was taking place now, the serried waves of darker blue mustering rank upon rank down the hill to advance and break upon the rocks of the Confederate line. Despite their fatigue the men now were anxious to play their part. They could plainly see the shells bursting over the Confederate front line. They passed corpses, some twisted and mangled, the flotsam of war, and stared in fascination as they passed. All about was the mayhem of the battlefield; the sharp rattle of small arms, the angry sizzle of fire overhead, the boom, boom of the cannon, and the roaring detonation of artillery rounds. Sometimes the occasional spent cannon shot would career past, bouncing and leaping on some mad errand of its own. This, together with the chorus of shouts, cries and yells, all make up one great symphony of chaos.

Major Blunsden-Butts, despite the turmoil, strutted erect and fearless, his eyes alight with battle fever, lusting to find an enemy. He reported to Regimental Headquarters as if he were on a parade ground, scorning the men crouching, weaving and ducking around him.

The Regiment was still in reserve. They were told to take cover by the smouldering ruins of a house and to await further orders. George posted his men in positions ready to repel an attack should the enemy break through and instructed every man to check his weapon was ready to fire. He received a cool nod of approval from "Old Blood 'n Guts" when he strode round to inspect their positions. Despite his aversion towards his company commander, he nevertheless felt a warm glow of satisfaction at this acknowledgement of his military proficiency. What an enigma the wretched man was! And why was it so important to him that he gained his approval?

They waited by the ruined house as darkness spread a healing blanket over all the suffering. The gunfire slowly abated. A strange stillness, like a benediction, fell over the battlefield.

They then received orders to move forward to relieve one of the regiments manning the wall at the very front of the Confederate position. The men were glad to have the excuse to chaff their frozen limbs for a starlit chill had descended. With shielded lights they stumbled over the cratered land, passing many a staring corpse, grotesquely locked in rigor mortis. Then they reached the front. The men who had fought all day filed past them, their shocked faces caught suddenly in the lantern light. These now were men set apart. They had stared into the mouth of hell and had lived to tell the tale. When their parting stumblings had died away, the Kentucky men stared out onto the moonlit battlefield, acutely aware that nothing now lay between them and the enemy.

It was a scene none would ever forget. In front of them was another wall, in some cases higher than their own defensive barrier. It was a wall made from the bodies of Yankee dead. Hearts aflame with battle fever, they had stormed through fire and shot only to be stilled for ever, frozen into a wave that would never break. As the watching eyes grew used to the starlight, they could detect movement too. Many there did not rest in blessed oblivion but hung in anguish between life and death. An arm or leg might twitch, or a body suddenly arch in torment. Occasionally a figure would wrench itself free from the sea of dead to stagger like a drunken reveller down the hill once ascended with such bright valour.

The sounds, too, seared the memories of the silent watchers. Voices, American voices, rose from all over that stricken field, begging for water and pleading with God for pity to end their misery. Some cried out the names of loved ones; some sobbed for their mothers. But worse than all this was the muted moan that seemed to come from everywhere and from nowhere, from a thousand clenched lips too brave to cry out their despair.

As the night lengthened the sounds slowly faded, but the moaning half heard, half imagined, remained to haunt the memory. Then came the strangest happening of all. The northern night sky was lit by a green luminescence that flickered across the heavens, extinguishing the stars with its brightness; an unusually southern display of the aurora borealis. It was as if the souls of the slain could be seen streaming in their thousands into the arms of their Maker. The eerie green and purple lights wavered about that dreadful scene, lighting up one tableau of butchery after another. It was a night none of those raw, young country folks from faraway Kentucky would ever forget.

55

Winter Quarters

After two days of stalemate where the Yankees seemed to have lost heart to launch further assaults they began to withdraw, leaving the Confederate Army in possession of the field. When the Rebs eventually returned down the hill to the town of Fredericksburg they were appalled at the way the town had been looted, fouled and desecrated by the Yankees in an orgy of wanton destruction. It was as if by smashing the property of the Confederates and defecating in their houses, they could somehow avenge the death and suffering of so many of their number and thus wipe out the memory of their defeat.

Most men were laden with riches from looted Yankee bodies. The days were occupied in the grizzly task of burying the dead and the evenings in gambling away the booty from the bodies and in drinking every imagined sort of fermented liquor they could find. "Knock-em-Stiff" was the flavour of the moment. It served to blunt men's sensibilities. All were delighted when they were told they were to move into winter quarters.

George toyed with the idea of returning to Nethergate for Christmas, but there was nothing to draw him there. Ursula and Matthew would he hoped by now be on the road to Canada by way of the Underground Railroad; his grandmother he thought was still in the North or maybe travelling back. There was little appeal in the frosty atmosphere of life in Nethergate Hall itself.

The Regiment took over a camp that had been prepared for them by an army of co-opted plantation slaves. There were rows of wooded shacks with brick-chimney stoves. It seemed like luxury living after what the men had been used to. The lanes between the rows of huts had been laid over with timber to ease the passage of wagons and to keep feet dry. The countryside for miles about was now void of trees.

The men settled down with a will to create their own little home from home in the spaces about the huts. They were kept busy with drill and weapon handling and in deployment exercises to retain their military edge. The only downside was the spread of camp fevers and other more serious illnesses which circulated with alarming rapidity in the cramped camp conditions. The country-born soldiers were the most susceptible, having never been exposed to the ailments that their town-bred cousins had lived with all their lives. Country men were generally the better soldiers and their loss, when campaigning commenced, would be keenly felt. In their regiment, mostly from Kentucky, the deaths from disease soon outstripped the whole of their battle casualties in the campaign so far.

Everybody seemed to be coughing. Indeed, it was claimed that the music from the regimental bands which came to play for them most evenings was largely drowned out by the sound of coughing men. It was good to hear the music of home and to sing the songs of the moment. Even some of the Yankee songs made good singing and were lustily rendered. The men felt calm and mellow after singing. Old enmities were soothed, and all felt at ease one with the other after such entertainment.

The townsfolk of Wilderness Edge were hospitable and friendly enough and invited the officers over, but it was a good hour's hard riding and in the winter the roads were much damaged by military traffic, so officers and men alike tended to make their own entertainment.

Three huts had been allocated to the officers of their Company. One had been taken over by the Major, one for the officers to sleep in and one as the company officer's mess. Here "Old Blood 'n Guts" held sway and told tales of the Mexican wars and of other campaigns as old soldiers will. Occasionally they were invited to the regimental mess, but these occasions were rare for the Colonel and Major Blunsden-Butts could scarcely be civil to each other.

George's friendship with Nathaniel had deepened, during the months of campaigning, but Nathaniel had not been happy as a soldier. It seemed that no matter what he did he could never please the Major. Somehow, he was always in the wrong. His boyish features would often be creased almost in tears after yet another verbal scourging from the caustic tongue of "Old Blood 'n Guts".

Once in camp however, things began to change. Nathaniel seemed to come into his own and received praises now for the smartness of his men and their proficiency on manoeuvres. Slowly his smile returned and the haunted look he had acquired became a thing of the past. George was delighted, for he had come to treasure Nathaniel's gentle nature and to share in his love for all living things. The soldiers liked him and respected his compassion and the way he would champion their concerns. They had resented the way the Major used to pick on him and in a thousand different ways had let him know that they were on his side. Now that he was in favour, they rejoiced in his success and put it down to their efforts on his behalf.

On occasions now the Major would even send for Nathaniel to share in his supply of good Kentucky whiskey, of which he seemed to have an inexhaustible supply. It was a rare privilege and captain and lieutenant alike regarded it as an honour to be asked to share in the Major's bounty. Increasingly, though it seemed that Nathaniel was the one singled out for this distinction. George was pleased at this privilege meted out to his friend, but after a time, despite now being in favour, it seemed to George that his compassionate and sensitive friend was again beginning to be troubled. But despite his gentle probing Nathaniel appeared reluctant to discuss the nature of his problems and George began to think it might be something back home. Both his parents he knew were Puritans and intensely religious.

Early one fateful morning George was woken to the sound of coughing. It seemed strange that he should have been woken by such a familiar occurrence. Then he realised that it wasn't coughing but the sound of stifled sobs. For a moment or two he listened. That night the other two officers were away. Nathaniel and he were alone in the cabin.

"What's up, Nathaniel?" he asked, full of concern. Nathaniel appeared to be confused.

"Nothing, nothing," he replied with obvious embarrassment. "I must have been asleep."

"Asleep or not, something's troubling you, Nathaniel. Has been for weeks."

There was a long pause. George thought his friend might have gone back to sleep, but his breathing told otherwise.

"Come on, Nathaniel," he urged into the darkness. "You'll feel better talking about it."

"It's the Major," Nathaniel replied at last.

"But I thought things were so much better between you two now," queried George.

"They are. Oh, they are in that way," replied his friend.

"So what's the trouble, then?" asked George. There was a long silence and George once more had to repeat the question.

At last Nathaniel whispered barely audibly, "Old Blood 'n Guts" is a molly-houser."

"Never!", exploded George. "How d'ye know?" Then regretted asking the question.

"How do you think I know?" exclaimed Nathaniel bitterly. "I know that's what he wants me for, why he keeps asking me to his cabin to share his damned Old Kentucky. At first, he seemed just to get over friendly as if it was the drink taking over and he'd put his hand on my thigh, then he'd run his hand up and down as if to emphasise the point of his conversation. Then last night I was left in no doubt as to what he wanted me to do. It sickens me, George, to my very soul. It is an abominable sin, hateful in the sight of God. But what can I do? If I do as he wants, I shall be contaminated, damned for ever. If I complain who will take my word against his? And even if I was believed what would become of us all then, for he is the only officer in the regiment who has any real experience and knows what he is doing? He is the only one who dares stand up to the Colonel when he flies off on some crack-brained plan that could be the death of us all."

All of what he said was undoubtedly true and George's heart ached for his friend, but truly he could see no way out. It seemed so out of character for "Old Blood 'n Guts". He could hardly credit what Nathaniel was saying. And if he found it hard to believe, how much harder would it be for others?

"Can't you just refuse his invitations?"

"Then it would be back to how it was before, when he would single me out, but a hundred times worse for what I now know about him. I don't think I could stand that."

For a time, they were both silent as the night closed in about them whilst both wrestled with Nathaniel's dilemma.

"Surely you could say that you admire and respect him as a man and as a soldier and that to do what he wants would be to dishonour the regard you hold him in and that you will never reveal what you know about him."

"It wouldn't do any good."

"How do you know until you've tried it?"

"Because I did, or something very like it," retorted Nathaniel with some spirit. "Do you know what he did?"

"No."

"He went down on his knees and pleaded with me. Can you imagine that? Old 'Blood 'n Guts' on his knees pleading and blubbering like a child. Said he loved me, he always had. He'd struggled against it. That was why he had always had a down on me, trying to fight the way he felt. Said he knew I felt the same way too. Said he could see it in my eyes. Said it takes one to know one. Then he seized my hand and thrust it into his groin, hard as iron. It was disgusting. That's when I fled."

Nathaniel was sobbing with the recollection of his ordeal. George did not know what to say and could only mumble platitudes. One half of him even doubted what he was hearing. He could not see "Old Blood 'n Guts" as Nathaniel had described. All he could suggest was the one solution that could offer release. "You could simply return home. Desert. Thousands do, as you well know."

"Don't think that I haven't considered that, but where would I go? I couldn't go home. My father would throw me out and anyway I owe my mother and father too much ever to dishonour them in such a way. But I would dishonour them the more were I to give in."

There was nothing more to be said and the two friends lapsed into silence aware of the sawing and coughing from of so many men sleeping about them. George at last slept. Towards dawn he was dimly aware of Nathaniel getting up.

"Are you awake, George?" he asked.

"Mmm," mumbled George.

Nathaniel said something that seemed to make no sense and left their cabin. The door creaked shut behind him and the latch was carefully lowered to secure it.

A moment later, he was wide awake. A shot rang out. He

knew instantly that Nathaniel had found his own way out of his dilemma. Then he remembered exactly what Nathaniel had said to him as he left.

"Thank you, George, for being my friend. 'Old Blood 'n Guts' was right, you know – about what he saw in my eyes."

It had been his only possible way out.

56

Facing Down Killcaid

When Killcaid burst into the dining room of the Stourbridge Inn, Matthew had been overcome by a wave of panic and despair. Was their bid for freedom, started only that morning with such high expectations to end so soon, drowned by the bitter hatred of this one man? However, that simple act of anguish when Ursula had buried her head in his chest had hardened his resolve and tempered his courage.

The manager, over-awed by Killcaid's air of authority and bluster, had followed him and his party into the room. Matthew ignored Killcaid and turned instead to the manager. "What," he demanded, "is the meaning of this outrage? Who are these people?"

"I – I don't know, sir," spluttered the manager. "They forced their way in before I could stop them."

"Don't give me that codswallop!" interjected Killcaid, addressing Matthew again. "I know who you are despite your fine clothes and your dandy airs. You're Matthew, Ruth's boy. You're a runaway slave as is wanted for the murder of a nigger priest."

"Absolute bunkum!" roared Matthew, the sudden reminder

of that fine Christian man adding power to his sense of indignation. Turning again to the manager, he addressed him in measured tones, "Tell this drunken ruffian who I am and then kick him and his crew out of here. Or better still call the militia and have him arrested." He turned to glare in fury at Killcaid. At this spirited riposte there was a rumble of approval from the male diners, equally outraged at this unseemly disruption to their evening meal.

Killcaid took a step towards him as if to grasp Matthew by his lapels, but Matthew held his gaze, staring him down. A flicker of doubt crept for a moment into his mind and he held back. He looked like Matthew, but the beard? He was dressed and held himself like a Southern gentleman. His eyes were the same, but they did not hold that droll, superior, half-amused look that never failed to infuriate him. Instead these eyes blazed with indignant fury. But the woman, dressed like a lady, who was clinging in alarm to him, her face half-hidden by the beautiful mass of dark curling hair, looked familiar as well. He glanced round the room to see if he had made an error, to see if Matthew and his companion were there in another guise at another table. All eyes were upon him. The men at the tables had half risen from their seats, all glaring with outraged hostility at this intrusion. Had he made a terrible blunder? Yet his informant had been certain that the Nethergate carriage had stopped at the Stourbridge Inn and this undoubtedly was the Stourbridge Inn.

Matthew saw the look of uncertainty flicker in Killcaid's eyes and knew he had won.

"Well?" demanded Matthew, addressing the manager.

"This here is Mr Bradstone and his wife. I'm afraid you have made a dreadful mistake," said the manager, then with growing certainty continued, "I demand you leave immediately, or I shall call the militia."

A growl of approval again rose from the other diners and

now the ladies joined in too. Killcaid knew he had lost. With mumbled excuses, he and his party bowed their way out of the room, castigated all the way by the now voluble manager. Matthew regarded their departure with outraged dignity. It had been a rout.

Whilst he rejoiced at this rare victory over Killcaid, Matthew could feel Ursula trembling beside him. She could not shrug it off so easily. The manager returned profuse with apologies. Matthew used this as an excuse to leave the table and return Ursula to the security of their room. Muttering excuses about the shock to his wife he rose from the table. The woman from the elderly couple at the next table rose to her feet at their departure and began to clap. Matthew heartedly wished a hole would open up beneath her feet. The rest somewhat self-consciously joined in. They had become what they least wanted, the centre of attention. Now no-one trying to follow them could fail to register their stay at Stourbridge Inn.

Outside, Killcaid was nursing his wounded pride and his humiliation. He thought that perhaps Matthew and his companion might have lodged at some other hostelry. Then he asked himself the question as to why Matthew should head in this direction anyway. Clearly, he was not using the Underground Railroad. He had been surprised to see the gentleman he had thought was Matthew sitting bold as brass dining with the white diners. Then realisation dawned. If it was Matthew in the coach and not some secret envoy connected with the war, then it must be that Matthew and his secret companion were travelling openly, pretending to be whites.

"Sure did look mighty like Matthew," muttered one of his companions. "Reckon they must be as alike as two peas in a pod. It was the beard as throwed me. But you could tell it weren't him by the way he stood and the way he spoke."

"Fool!" roared Killcaid suddenly, smiting his forehead with the heel of his hand. "It were him all along! The woman who was with him, I know I see'd her afore. It was the long hair as fooled me. It was Angela, as was Ursula, the Mistress's maid, the one as that sneaky devil Manuel swore as was dead, drowned in the bayou. Wait till I get my hands on that lying toad, by Gar I'll whip him till an inch o' his worthless life." Killcaid raged on until, choking with his own bile, he had to cease. The vision of Matthew, now no doubt with that superior, little smirk remained to torment him. How he must be laughing!

"Shall we go back?" ventured one of his companions half-heartedly.

Killcaid turned and then stopped.

"No," he said. "They'd never allow us in after what happened. An' if'n we tried to force our way in we'd find ourselves fighting every man jack in there. No, we'll wait. He's pretending to be a white. They're here for one purpose and that's to escape north. They'll be heading for the railroad. Thar's only one train out at eleven every morn'n, regular as clockwork. That's way we'll catch 'em for sure."

Anticipating the triumph waiting for them in the morning, the trio, nursing their fury, sought shelter for the night in quarters far less grand than those being enjoyed by their quarry.

Back in the luxury of their hotel the objects of their wrath were locked in each other's arms. Far from enjoying the luxury of their surroundings, Matthew was trying by the sheer force of his embrace to still the tremors that again and again were shaking Ursula's frame.

"Oh, Matthew, I is so a'feared. I is sure he knows who we are."

"I don' think so. He'd never have left if he thought it was us. Anyway, we're safe where we are. He'll never dare to try to come in here again. Not after what happened downstairs."

"Oh, Matthew, do you think so? Are you sure? We must

get on that train tomorrow. He won't be able to follow us after that."

Matthew agreed, though his instinct was to follow a different course. That night there was an air of desperation as they sought comfort and assurance in each other's arms.

57

Held to Account

At the sound of the shot, George was on his feet. He rushed outside, dreading what he might find. A cold early-morning fog shrouded the encampment.

"Nathaniel! Nathaniel!" he shouted, hoping against hope that he might hear an answering cry. His voice was swallowed in the mist. He moved up the slope, away from the tents and huts, and called out again. No reply. He moved on and with dwindling hope tried once more. He sensed the encampment stirring, awakened by the discharge, but hoping that it would not be repeated, that they could cling to the warmth of their beds. Then he almost stumbled upon him.

Nathaniel's body lay curled in a foetal position crumpled at his feet, looking as diminished and vulnerable as a child. A dark stain spread from the side of his head. With a stifled sob, George sank down beside his friend. He turned his shoulders and the bloodied head flopped over. He had seen too much of death in recent months to harbour any hope. Nathaniel stared up at him through unseeing eyes. His lids were half closed as if still heavy with sleep. He looked so young, so incredibly boyish, so defenceless.

"No. No. No," he found himself muttering, over and over again.

Tenderly he drew a finger over each eye, closing the lid to spare Nathaniel any further sight of the world that had given him so much pain. At that moment he became aware that he was no longer alone. He looked up. Standing outlined against the mist was the figure of Major Blunsden-Butts. He was staring down at Nathaniel's body. In his eyes, a look of unspeakable anguish.

At the sight of Nathaniel's seducer, George's grief turned to rage. Through his unnatural appetites, bloody Blunsden-Butts was the cause of Nathaniel's torment that had led to this. Slowly rising to his feet, his face contorted with fury, he found himself mouthing, "Bastard! Bastard! Bastard!"

For a moment the Major looked stunned, still locked in his own personal grief. George realised suddenly that "Old Blood 'n Guts" was genuinely distraught at the sight of Nathaniel's body. Perhaps it was true what Nathaniel had said, that he loved him. That did nothing to diminish his own sense of outrage. "This is your doing. You and your filthy, unnatural habits," he muttered, through clenched teeth.

Major Blunsden-Butts's features suddenly changed. The vulnerability and the grief vanished. Now he faced danger. The battle fever was upon him. Once again, he was fully in control, his face an angry mask at George's words.

"Be very careful what you say, boy. Be very careful indeed. You're upset, still not used to the sight of a little blood. I'll forgive you this once. But from now on just you remember who you are talking to." Then, in a voice loaded with menace, he added, "and think of the consequences to you – personally." George was not quite sure what he meant by this, but clearly it was a threat.

But George by now was too full of his own anger to step back. "I know all about you. What you were doing. Nathaniel told me everything."

"Did he now?" rejoined the Major, with a look of calm contemplation. "And who is going to believe you? Eh! My word against yours. 'Old Blood 'n Guts' a molly-houser? They'd laugh you out of court."

What he said was true and George knew it. He had found it hard enough to believe himself. "And think," continued the Major, "think how his parents would feel about their brave son indulging in such practices. It would be worse than news of his death. Besides, what proof do you have? Just your word against mine. And whose will carry more conviction? Eh?"

"What's goin' on here?" The camp guard, guided by their voices, had arrived. "Who's been shooting?" Then, suddenly recognising the Major, he sprung to attention and saluted. "Sorry, sir. Didn't know it was you, Sir."

"That's alright, Corporal. I'm afraid there has been a tragic accident. Young officer cleaning his weapon, without checking it was unloaded. These things happen. That not so, Mr Styles?" Major Blunsden-Butts turned to face George.

For what seemed like ages the question hung in the air whilst George wrestled with his conscience. But the Major was right. Who would believe him without proof? Then there was the question of Nathaniel's parents. He had not thought about them. It would break their hearts to hear that his death was suicide and for such a reason.

Slowly he nodded his head.

"We'll take care of the body, sir." said the Corporal, anxious to show his efficiency to the two officers.

"I'll take his pistol," said the Major, kneeling and retrieving the weapon from Nathaniel's limp hand. The two officers left and made their way wordlessly back to the officer's lines. At the hut shared by George and Nathaniel, they paused.

"Now, you just think carefully what you say from now on. These things happen. Let his parents treasure his memory. I shall be writing to them and telling them what a fine, brave

317

young officer he was, what good care he took of his men and how we all loved him." George looked up sharply at these last words, but the Major's face was inscrutable. "Don't you go now tainting his memory." With that he turned and left.

George entered the hut which was so full of reminders of Nathaniel's presence. Slowly he began to gather together his friend's effects and pack them carefully away to be sent back to his parents. He folded up Nathaniel's bedding, still warm from where he had lain. Under his pillow he found a letter. It was addressed to him. He put it aside until he had completed his task. All the time he thought about the letter. It might be the proof that he needed to condemn "Old Blood 'n Guts" for what he was. But what then? What if he were removed in disgrace? Who would shield them from the blunderings of the Colonel? The Major was the only officer with courage enough to stand up to the folly of his senior officer. There was no doubt that Major Blunsden-Butts had preserved all their lives many times over. The soldiers loathed him for his temper, unfairness and unpredictable ways, but they trusted his military judgement and would follow him wherever he chose to lead.

For a long time after he had completed his task, he sat in the hut with Nathaniel's letter unopened on the table in front of him, wondering whether he wanted the proof of "Old Blood 'n Guts's" guilt. Finally, he put it away unopened and prepared to face the days ahead.

The explanation of Nathaniel's death was readily accepted. Such accidents were all too common with people not bred to the use of arms. It looked after a few days as if the whole matter would be closed. But no-one had predicted the Colonel's antipathy towards his querulous major. He saw in this a chance of discrediting him and ordered a full regimental inquiry. A board of officers was duly formed. Major Thomas, a political crony of the Colonel, was appointed president. Major Blunsden-Butts had no doubt that he had been well briefed by the Colonel. Both he and George were to be called as witnesses.

In George's mind his hatred for the Major and his grief for the loss of his friend were all mixed into one confused cauldron of emotions. Since Nathaniel's death, George and the Major had barely spoken. When they met, George had stared out his contempt and the Major eventually would look away, but with an inner look of amused understanding. The day before the inquiry, George retrieved Nathaniel's letter from his locker. He didn't want to be reminded of that fateful morning, but knew he must open it now, before the inquiry was held. For a long time, he held it in his hand, staring at his name written in Nathaniel's boyish, copybook handwriting. Then he carefully broke the seal and read:

"Dear George, by the time you read this I shall be no more. My only regret is leaving you, my dear friend, with all the loose ends. You don't know what your friendship has meant to me since first we met so full of hope all those months ago, or how often your counsel has rescued me from taking the step I am taking now.

"'Old Blood 'n Guts' has been such a dominant force in my life. At first, as a soldier when I was trying so hard to please him and always, always failing. My nights were spent in tears of remorse for being unable to reach the standards he set. I was so often in despair. Now, suddenly there is that other capacity in my relationship with the Major which I revealed to you. At first, I felt reviled for what I know to be a terrible and unnatural sin, but now, God forgive me, I am revelling in the thought of it. At last I have the power truly to please him, to make him happy, to make him care for me and above all to escape his displeasure.

"God has created me the way I am. This is a test, I

319

know, to see if I am strong enough to resist. Now that I know that I will succumb, it is time to end it all so that I bring no disgrace upon you my friend, my parents or my own immortal soul. I can present myself to the Lord knowing that despite the way He made me, I have overcome my weakness in the only way I know how.

"Remember me to my parents and speak kindly of me, for I know they will treasure your words and it will help them in their grief.

"Once you have read this letter, please destroy it for I should hate it to fall into hands other than yours, which alone I know I can trust.

"God bless and preserve you safely through this conflict. Thank you again for the blessing of your friendship.

"Your devoted friend,

"Nathaniel."

George felt the tears stinging his eyes when he had finished reading. If only he had known how deeply troubled Nathaniel had been, he could have been of greater service. Now it was all too late. All that was left were regrets. With this letter, however, he knew that he had sufficient evidence to avenge his friend's suffering, to bring Major Blunsden-Butts to his knees and to destroy him. He wanted the Major to know of the evidence he now had so that he might reflect upon it before the inquiry sat. He wanted him to know what was coming. He waited until the bugle call announcing the closure of the camp for the night. The light was still burning in the Major's hut. There was a rasping sound as if the Major was snoring. He called out his name. After a pause, the Major, said, "Who is it?"

"Mr Styles, sir."

"Come in, boy, come in."

George entered, blinking in the sudden light. The Major's

full dress uniform complete with sword was hanging in readiness for the morrow. On the table in front of him was a pistol, stripped and ready to be cleaned and a glass, no doubt of his favourite Old Kentucky. The Major eyed him with curiosity. "What can I do for you?" he asked.

George came straight to the point. "You said to me that no-one would believe me, that I had not a shred of evidence. Well now I have." With that he held out Nathaniel's letter. "This is a letter from Nathaniel to me shortly before he took his own life. It explains why he did it and the part you played." With that he stared out his hatred. This time, however, the Major did not look away. His chin went up, his nostrils flared and he gave the usual little snort of contempt he always gave when facing the enemy. It was just this look that had steadied so many faint hearts when facing the Yankees. Despite himself, George felt a wave of respect wash over him for the courage of the Major as he faced his own ruin.

"You must do your duty as you think fit," he said. "Now, Mr Styles, I think it best you leave me. You have some hard decisions to make tomorrow. It's best you do so with a clear head."

It had been a curiously unsatisfactory confrontation from George's point of view. George saluted and turned to leave. As he closed the door, the Major spoke again.

"You have the makings, George, of a fine officer. I have watched you grow in stature over these past months. What I have seen has pleased me greatly. You have dash and a fine fighting spirit. At times, though, you are apt to act without thinking things through. Remember, a good officer always has a plan in case things should go awry. I hope you have a plan."

George left, pondering the Major's final remarks. For a time he lingered outside the Major's hut. Curiously he felt strangely gratified that the Major considered he had done well as an officer. But what did he mean by those other remarks? As always the Major had the capacity to leave him and the enemy guessing. Shortly the sound of snoring came again from the Major's hut. He couldn't believe that the Major could sleep so soon after such a confrontation, but it seemed he had.

The inquiry began taking evidence the next day. The president, dressed in his best uniform, ensured that everything had the stamp of officialdom about it. His presence, though, was totally eclipsed when Major Blunsden-Butts appeared. He stood erect, dressed in full dress uniform complete with gold sash and gold epaulettes with his sword at his side. He looked every inch the professional soldier he undoubtedly was.

The inquiry went through the preliminaries and heard evidence from the soldier who had removed Nathanniel's body and the doctor who had certified the cause of death. Then George's turn came to give evidence. He was duly sworn in and recounted the events of that morning, omitting only his conversation with Nathaniel during the night. His eyes were fixed upon where Major Blunden-Butts was watching. He was staring directly ahead as if on parade. In his pocket George could feel Nathaniel's letter. It gave him courage for what he was about to do.

When George had completed his evidence, the president asked him directly, "Do you think that Mr Summers had any other motive to be out at that hour with a loaded pistol? It seems a curiously early hour to consider cleaning his weapon."

George paused before answering. The silence gathered. Nobody stirred. "It was, I believe, because of Mr Summers's feelings about Major Blunsden-Butts."

The members of the inquiry exchanged looks. "What exactly do you mean?" asked the president, sensing that something discreditable was about to be revealed. He looked across to where the Colonel was seated, nodding his head in approval at the way things were going.

"Well, sir," explained George. "Mr Summers had such a high regard for the Major here that he would do anything to please him." Major Blunsden-Butts was staring rigidly to the front; the inference in George's words was not lost on him. "He knew that the Major expected every man to clean their own weapon, including the officers, so that each man was as familiar as possible with the weapon he took with him into battle. I think that was the reason he was up so early, to clean his revolver, his anxiety to rise to his company commander's expectations. Perhaps it was because of the early hour that he failed to realise the weapon was loaded, with the terrible consequences we all know."

George glanced across at where Major Blunsden-Butts was sitting. He was tight-lipped and still, but from the set of his shoulders his relief was clear. George had done what he intended to do. There was no way he could let Nathaniel's death be recorded as a suicide; it would devastate his parents. There was no way he could destroy the Major for fear of what would happen to them all if the Colonel were to have a free hand. Besides, Nathaniel would never have wished harm to come to the man whom he loved, particularly if it had been through any action of his.

It was left to Major Blunsden-Butts to steal the show and finally to frustrate his Colonel. When he was called to give evidence, he strutted to the witness stand. He knew he wore his uniform well and that he eclipsed all the other officers, many of whom did not possess a full dress uniform. He produced the pistol which he had taken from Nathaniel's body.

"Here is the guilty party," he announced with a theatrical flourish. He called to one of the clerks to hand him his pen. Dramatically he held up Nathaniel's pistol and cocked it. Then he began to tap lightly with the pen on the trigger. At the third tap the pistol fired. The entire court fell back at the discharge and a hole appeared in the canvas of the marquee tent.

Without batting an eye, the Major cocked the pistol and repeated the process, causing another hole to appear in the canvas. Thus, dramatically, the Major proved without any shadow of a doubt that an accidental discharge due to a faulty pistol mechanism was how his young subaltern had lost his life. The Colonel left before the inquiry formally announced its findings.

That night, as he lay pondering the happenings of the day, George realised what Major Blunsden-Butts had meant about always having a plan. He thought he understood why he had come into the court with live rounds in Nathaniel's pistol and why he had symbolically dressed himself in his finest military uniform as if for one final heroic act of departure. He understood now the cause of the curious rasping sounds he heard in the Major's tent with Nathaniel's pistol stripped in front of him. What he could not fully come to terms with was why there were two live rounds in Nathaniel's revolver. Clearly the second round was intended for himself. But who was to be the recipient of the first? He thought it might have been him, but on balance he thought perhaps the Colonel might have had a lucky escape.

58

Burgeoning Hope

The next morning as sunlight crept into their room things felt different for Ursula. It was the first time Matthew and she had slept together in a real bed with sheets and blankets and they both revelled in the feeling of undreamt-of luxury it evoked. If only they could stay there until all dangers had passed, thought Matthew.

It was Ursula who was first to rise, for in the stillness of the night she had found a new courage and a new determination. She jumped out of bed and stretched herself luxuriantly so that Matthew could see every curve of her body. Matthew was aware suddenly of the change in her. She seemed to radiate a new resolve.

She was indeed changed. That night, as she lay in Matthew's arms, she had felt the first strange movements of the child within her. It had come once like the involuntary twitch of a muscle where no muscle had ever been before. When it came again, she realised what it must be. A rush of tenderness for a moment overwhelmed her. Now she shared her life with another. Her hands sought the swell of her belly and lovingly she cupped the new little being and whispered words of encouragement to him, for she was sure she carried a boy.

Matthew stirred beside her. She had wanted to wake him and tell him, but then she remembered it was not his child she carried. She thought of George and was racked with guilt as she imagined the dangers he was facing. She longed to share her secret with someone and yet at the same time she wanted it to remain hers alone. Then she thought, it wasn't just her secret, and she imagined the tiny boy within her, perfectly formed, just waiting to grow big enough to survive in this world. She promised him that he would never be a slave, that he would be born free in Canada, that he would have every good thing that life could possibly offer and that she would love him as no child had ever been loved before. In the stillness of the night she was filled with a new resolve: no Killcaid or any other living thing would hazard this life she carried within her.

Matthew watched her as she got out of bed, wondering at the sudden change in her.

"What is it, Ursula?" he asked.

Ursula had thought about this moment during the night. She still loved George, the father of her child, and she loved Matthew. She dreaded the moment when she would have to choose between them. George could offer her comfort, but would he ever marry her? Would his mother condone such an unsuitable union? She had no doubts there. But he was the father of her child. Matthew was much the stronger of the two and he would marry her, but how uncertain would life with him be? He was masquerading as someone else. The real Matthew was a slave like herself, moreover a slave with a price upon his head for a murder he had not committed. If he were discovered, he would undoubtedly hang. Matthew, she knew, still loved his cousin and was stricken with guilt at his own betrayal. But could treachery be a firm foundation for a life together? It was impossible to resolve. What was important was the here and now. So, she told him what had suddenly given her this inner strength and resolve.

She was right about Matthew's reaction. He could not help the pang of jealousy that pierced him anew at her news. If only the child she carried might be his. Nevertheless, he resolved that he would treasure the child as if it had been his own for the sake of the love he bore its mother.

"There!" she cried suddenly. "He did it again," and she sat down beside him and placed his hand upon the round smoothness of her naked belly. "Did you feel him?" she asked earnestly, as if it were the most important thing in the world. Despite himself he could not resist her simple delight. He thought he had indeed felt some movement. He could not help himself when he asked, "Would you rather that it was Massa George sittin' here now?"

She looked up sharply at the question, then her eyes softened with understanding and she let her hand rest gently on his knee. "When I am with you, Matthew, dear, all of me is with you, but George?" She stopped with the question hanging in the air, then after a moment's thought continued, "George, he was the first man I ever loved, and he is the father of this child. I s'pose I love you both, but in different ways. I don't want ever to have to choose between you, but I know that ain't possible."

It wasn't really the answer Matthew wanted, but then he was not sure what answer he did want. If she had declared for him alone his sense of betrayal to his only real friend would have been complete. Like her, perhaps he didn't want to think about it. Instead he allowed himself to be carried along on the wave of her sudden new discovery and the confidence it brought with it.

Slowly he got out of bed, as naked as she was, and stretched. Suddenly she ran across to him and clasped her body close to his. He felt his desire harden as she knew it would.

"Can't you see, my dearest, this is an omen?" she said, "It means all will be well. We'll escape from Killcaid and all his like, to real freedom." Then she drew him back again onto the bed. Both were aware that there was something desperate about their lovemaking. Afterwards they lay still, each alone with their own thoughts.

Abruptly, Ursula threw aside the covers and jumped to her feet. "Come on, Matthew," she said, realising with a sudden wave of guilt that she had nearly said "George", because he was in her thoughts. "It's another day, but now a day of real hope."

"Amen," to that said Matthew, leaping to his feet as well, catching her new mood and only too glad to go along with it.

★

Both would have been even more delighted had they been able to share in the burgeoning of another new hope, this time within the walls of Nethergate House. Mary had just received a letter from her friend in Wilmington, where she and Ruth had stayed after the loss of Colonel Thomas Gladstone. Two young men out riding that morning had watched the entire engagement. They reported that the Yankee ship had sent out a longboat to collect the body of the Confederate sailor who had been blown overboard when the steamship was struck.

She had sent for Ruth immediately. Both the witnesses had said that they were certain that by the way the Confederate sailor had been handled, he must still have been alive. He had been rushed below as soon as he was on board. A corpse would have simply been left on deck to be covered by sailcloth and later buried at sea.

Now, there could be hope at Nethergate House as well.

List of Characters Thus Far

Silas Killcaid is the chief overseer of Nethergate tobacco plantation. He has been at Nethergate for over thirty years and seeks to dominate owner and slaves alike. He wields power through his coveted network of black overseers. He knows all that is going on within the Nethergate community, from the slave cabins to Nethergate Hall itself. He is by nature cruel and cunning, with a penchant for young slave women. Yet in a way he is a prisoner of what he has created, for he is intensely loyal to the world of Nethergate.

Adrian Styles was the third Master of Nethergate following his father and his grandfather, who emigrated from England to establish the Nethergate Estate. Married to **Mary Styles**, he was a man consumed with political ambitions. He despaired of his profligate son **Mark**, who will inherit the estate on his death. **Adrian** dies prematurely.

Mary Styles is the daughter of **Henry Bragg** and married to **Adrian Styles**. As a new bride she tries to take an interest in the running of the estate, but **Adrian** does not think this appropriate for a woman. Like many Northerners she is also opposed to the concept of slavery, naively thinking that she might change things from the inside. She treats her house slaves kindly and, though it is against the law, tries to teach them to read and write so they might better themselves. Her marriage is a genuine love match but constrained by the mores of the period and the tensions caused by her oldest son's wild behaviour. She alone acknowledges **Matthew** as her grandson.

Mark Styles is the wayward son of **Adrian** and **Mary**. He inherits the estate when his father dies and takes it to the edge of ruin but is himself killed through an accident engineered by **Ruth** when he threatens to sell off her son, **Matthew**.

Ruth Styles is a beautiful young mulatto slave, lady's maid to **Mary Styles**. She is raped by **Mark** and gives birth to his child, **Matthew**. She has a very close relationship with **Mary**, who promises her freedom as recompense for her son's actions but is unable to do so. **Ruth** is educated by **Mary** and has a prodigious talent as an artist.

Matthew Styles is a quadroon, the illegitimate son of **Ruth** fathered by **Mark**. He is a talented mimic. During **Mark's** tenure as Master he and **Ruth** work as field hands. To the amusement of the other slaves, **Matthew** lampoons **Killcaid**, thus starting an enmity which threatens the whole of Nethergate. On **Mark's** death, **Mary** takes **Ruth** and **Matthew** into her household and educates him. **Matthew** forms a powerful friendship with **George Styles** when they discover their kinship and that they share the same grandmother.

Anthony Styles is younger brother to **Mark** and has always walked in his shadow. He leaves Nethergate to become a lawyer and finds his niche in life. On **Mark's** death he reluctantly takes over as Master of Nethergate. He is dominated by **Killcaid** and by **Amelia**, his wife.

Amelia Styles is **Anthony Styles's** wife. She is over-conscious of her new status as Mistress of Nethergate and sees slights and insults where none exist. She becomes bitter and vengeful and eventually a tyrant to her husband and her slave household.

George Styles is the son of **Anthony** and **Amelia**. He falls in love with his mother's personal slave, **Ursula** and forms a strong bond of brotherhood with **Matthew**.

Ursula Styles is **Amelia's** personal slave who is cruelly misused by her mistress and becomes the lover of **George**, her son.

Old Mo is an ex-trapper's slave who survives a scalping by Indians. He provides game from the bayou and becomes a father figure to **Matthew**, to whom he passes on much of his skills as a backwoodsman.

Acknowledgements

I would like to thank the following people who have all had a part to play in the production of *The Breaking Storm*:

As ever, to Roger Elgood, who has painstakingly read through the MS and has wisely and thoughtfully voiced his comments, not always to my liking. Irritatingly he is all too often right. I value them and his encouragement greatly.

To Nicola Swanson, who has read the proofs with a meticulous attention to detail that defies belief. I am deeply in her debt.

To Ted Crellin, for the loan of his Civil War material and for his sustained interest.

To James and Alexandra Lloyd for their IT support.

To my children Robin, Sue, Emma and Sally Ann, and my grandchildren Sian, Alexandra, James, Hamish Gemma and Verity, for convincing me that they are really interested.

To my wife, Jacky, who has endured much.

Finally to that wonderful band of enthusiasts and friends, the Cotswold Writers Circle, for their unfailing support and wise counsel.